The  & the Storm

a novel by

Kelsey Kingsley

COPYRIGHT

Copyright © 2024 by Kelsey Kingsley
All rights reserved.

Visit my website at http://kelseykingsley.com
Cover Designer: Murphy Rae Designs
Editor: Jovana Shirley, Unforeseen Editing,
www.unforeseenediting.com

No part of this book may be reproduced or transmitted in any form or by any means, electronic or mechanical, including photocopying, recording, or by any information storage and retrieval system without the written permission of the author, except for the use of brief quotations in a book review.

This book is a work of fiction. Names, characters, places, and incidents either are products of the author's imagination or are used fictitiously. Any resemblance to actual persons, living or dead, events, or locales is entirely coincidental.

A LETTER FROM THE AUTHOR

Dear Reader,

Okay ... *takes a deep breath* ... buckle up.

I guess that's the fairest warning I can give for this one.

See, the thing is, I think something in me changed when I wrote Saving Rain. Don't get me wrong—I love every single book I've ever written—but there was something about that book. It put my heart through the blender and left me bleeding out. Warrior Blue had done it to me years ago, but I had thought it was an anomaly. Saving Rain proved that theory wrong, and I decided then that I only want to write the books that leave me different than I was before they came to me. I want to be shaken. I want to experience a book hangover from my own stories.

And that's how Charlie Corbin was born.

God, Charlie Corbin ...

My spooky spider …

So misunderstood. So damaged by the tragedies and trauma life threw at him over and over again. I think there's a little piece of Charlie in all of us, but there's a bigger part of me in him, and he shattered my heart into a thousand pieces. His happily ever after patched me up, but I think I'll always be a little broken after this one.

And there it is. That's your warning.

Like I said, buckle up.

—Kelsey

PROLOGUE

MASSACHUSETTS, PRESENT DAY

I'd once read somewhere that a spider couldn't get trapped inside its own web.

It had something to do with their familiarity with their own work and knowing where they'd laid the sticky shit down to trap its prey. Apparently—and contrary to popular belief—the whole web wasn't sticky, only some of the strands, and a spider had this crazy ability to remember where they'd put it down.

I know. It had blown my mind too.

Still, even knowing that, I watched this thing—a black widow—skitter along one fine silvery line, glistening in a shred of light cast from a nearby lamppost, and I wondered how many spiders just … *forgot* where they'd laid that sticky stuff. Like, how often did they get sidetracked? How often did they have too much on their mind, walk down one of those fine threads of silk, and—*fuck!*—glue themselves right onto their own trap and become a feast for someone else, maybe even one of their own kind?

A cool gust of wind blew through the cemetery, rustling the remaining leaves overhead, still clinging to the branches of night-darkened trees. The black widow's asymmetrical, tangled web—low to the ground and stretched between the legs of a memorial bench in a family plot—swayed in time with the breeze. She held tight, not allowing herself to move an inch until the interruption to her work had passed.

A solitary creature, the black widow. Feared and often misunderstood for her venom, yet her only true desire wasn't to terrorize, but to simply be left alone to live her life and do her work.

I knew the feeling well.

I'd known it for years.

But soon, with the passing of autumn, after her mating season ended, she would find herself a place to hide indoors. Maybe even inside the cottage on the hill, the one I'd been calling home for the past several years. I'd welcome the quiet company. She'd respect my decision to keep to myself, and for her, I'd do the same. We could spend the winter together until the arrival of spring—if either of us survived for that long—and our time shared would come to an end without so much as a word spoken between us in our departure. Peaceful and perfect. My ideal roommate.

Fuck. There was that chilling wind again, and this time, it brought with it the familiar sense of being watched.

I turned without an inkling of fear from the arachnid's art show to survey the grounds, immaculately kept, thanks to yours truly. From where I sat on the cold stone bench, I could make out the shadowed structures of a row of mausoleums in the near distance, a handful of trees and their outstretched limbs, and a group of headstones sitting alongside the dirt path, beneath the iron lamppost. Nothing was out of place, and the specters I knew well weren't there, hiding between the gravestones.

But there was that old feeling—some would call it intuition—lifting the hairs at the back of my neck. Telling me there was something—maybe even some*one*—out there, watching me watch the spider when I should've been in my bed, asleep.

Seven a.m. would come quickly, as it always did, and my day of working among the dead would begin again.

"Well, ma'am," I said to the black widow while continuing to fix my stare on the row of towering stone structures in the distance, "I guess I'll be heading back home now. You have a good night."

I grabbed my sketchbook, pen, and phone—not that anyone was likely to call, but I guessed you never did know—from the bench beside me and stood. Home was only a short walk down the path and up the hill, and most nights, I looked forward to it. But tonight, I wasn't so sure as an uncomfortable foreboding curled inside my gut and made itself at home. The sensation was familiar but old, like remembering the feel and scent of a worn blanket you hadn't seen since childhood, realizing you would never see it again while also knowing you'd recognize it if you ever had the chance.

The last time I had known this feeling was the last time I was in Connecticut.

Home.

God, could I even call it that anymore when I hadn't lived there in so long? But at what point did the place you had been born and raised in stop being home?

I held tight to my things as I quickened my pace down the path, winding between the markers of marble and limestone, and toward the light shining bright from the lantern hanging beside my front door. A welcome calm wrapped around my thundering heart, and I breathed out my relief as I turned up the flagstone path to head up the hill and to my door when the wind came blowing at my back. Lifting the hair off my shoulders and ripping through the flesh of my neck to the bone beneath.

And with it came a message, one I knew all too well from years before.

A message that said something was about to happen. Something monumental and soul-shaking, maybe even tragic.

And whether I liked it or not, I would have to weather the storm.

CHAPTER ONE

CONNECTICUT, AGE EIGHT

"Charles Corbin?"

I glanced up quickly from my book to see the lady stepping into the boring waiting room, a clipboard in her hand, and then I looked at Mom. She was already starting to stand from the chair beside mine as she nodded reassuringly.

"That's you, Charlie. Come on."

My tummy felt worse now than it had when she picked me up early from school. She had said that it was butterflies from being nervous, but butterflies fluttered and danced through the sky like ballerinas. The feeling in my tummy didn't remind me of dancing at all. This feeling hurt. It felt angry and reminded me of the wasps that had made a home under the porch roof last summer.

My legs felt heavy, like they were full of rocks, as I slid from my seat, reaching down to the floor to grab my backpack and slide my book back inside. I knew why we were here. I knew it had to do with the things Mom and Dad whispered about at night.

"We have to do something about him, Sue. We can't just ... let him be like this."

"I know."

"They're tormenting him."

"I know, Paul. All right? I know."

They thought something was wrong with me; everyone did. I could tell by the way my teachers looked at me, like I was gonna break at any second. I could tell by the way the other kids in school wouldn't look at me at all—unless they were picking on me. But I didn't really care about what they thought as much as I cared about Mom and Dad, and I'd thought everything was fine until the principal called and their whispers began.

Now, I *knew* something was wrong. My brain was messed up, just like the other kids in school said. I was a *freak*. And now, Mom had brought me to this stupid doctor to fix it.

Together, we walked across the waiting room to where that lady with the clipboard stood, Mom's hand on my shoulder and my sneakers scuff-scuff-scuffing against the gray carpet. We tried to walk past her into the hallway, but the lady stopped us.

"The doctor would like to first speak to Charles alone, if that's all right, Mrs. Corbin."

Mom's hand squeezed my shoulder, and she didn't let go. "Alone? Why alone?"

"It's just so we can get an accurate evaluation of the child's condition without the possibility of—"

"Of what? What do you think my presence is going to do?" Mom's voice sounded angrier than before.

"Other than to make him feel a little more secure in an environment he's already nervous about."

The lady swallowed and hugged her clipboard to her chest. "If you aren't comfortable—"

"With my son being forced to speak, alone, to a bunch of strangers? No, I'm not comfortable with that."

The lady puckered her lips like one of my teachers always did whenever she ate one of her green apples. Then, she nodded her head only once. "Fine. Well, if you'll just follow me …"

***

They asked me lots of questions—first that lady and then an old man who looked a lot like my grandpa, except with a mustache.

They asked lots of questions but didn't say much back.

Things like, "What makes you feel afraid?" And, "Is it only at home, or do you also feel scared at school and other places?" And, "What do you mean when you say you get *feelings*?" And, "What happens when you get those *feelings*, Charlie? Do you see people or hear voices? Or do you just … *feel*?"

They asked me questions like they didn't believe me about anything, like my teachers and the other kids in school. And they asked those questions for a long time until I couldn't sit still, and I didn't know the right answers, and I wanted to cry. That was when Mom told them it was enough, that I'd had enough … and she was right.

I had had enough, and I wanted to go home, where my big brother, Luke, might play with me—if his dumb friend Ritchie wasn't around.

Then, the old man said some things to Mom while I looked at my new sneakers.

"Mrs. Corbin, I would strongly urge you to consider antianxiety medication and maybe even antipsychotics if you want your son to have any chance of reaching his full potential, mentally and socially."

"Wait a minute." Mom held up a hand like she was telling the doctor to stop right there. "I understand the anxiety, although I'm not sure I want to immediately jump to medication before trying other coping mechanisms. But are you saying you believe that *my son* is psychotic?"

"That's not what I'm saying at all. But he is clearly having delusions—"

"Delusions? No offense, Doctor, but I don't think having a bad feeling about a Category 3 hurricane makes him *delusional*."

"With all due respect, Mrs. Corbin, your son said he had a feeling that the hurricane would do something bad to your home, did he not? Which would imply that he was imagining—"

"He's an eight-year-old boy!" Mom shouted, making me jump. She sounded even angrier now, all squealy, like the way she had that time Luke forgot to take out the garbage three days in a row. "He was terrified of what was going to happen, and his fear allowed for his imagination to go wild, and that, in turn, triggered his anxiety. Which, I'll remind you, is why I *thought* we were here. Not to discuss whether or not he's *psychotic*."

I slumped deeper into my seat as I thought about the hurricane. The one that had taken our house away.

The bad feeling in my tummy had started when Dad turned on the weather channel one day in the summer when I was seven. The man on TV said we were in for a bad hurricane season, and that word—*hurricane*—wouldn't stop repeating over and over and over again in my head. It made the little hairs on my arms stand up, and it made me scared. When I asked about it, Dad told me not to worry and that we would be just fine. But I didn't believe him, not one bit, because that feeling in my tummy sort of told me not to. That feeling made me think that something really, really, really bad was going to happen.

And I couldn't stop thinking about it for *months*, and that was a really, really long time. I just kept remembering what that guy on the TV had said—that we were in for a bad hurricane season—and I kept on feeling like I needed to do something to make Luke and Mom and Dad listen because what if that bad feeling was right?

So, I talked about it all the time until I cried and yelled and slammed my bedroom door. Finally, that guy on the weather channel talked about *the* hurricane. He said it was coming and that it would be bad, and Mom and Dad looked at each other, their eyes big and afraid. Then, they packed our bags and took us to Pennsylvania to stay with our aunt.

The hurricane had taken our house, but the hurricane hadn't taken us. *We* were okay. I had done good, telling my family about my bad feeling, but the old man doctor looked like I had been wrong. He looked at me the way my teachers did. The way Ritchie and the other kids at school did.

Like I was *crazy*.

"I'm only trying to help, Mrs. Corbin," he said, sounding tired. "I only want what's best for your son."

Mom didn't say anything right away, and I looked up from my sneakers to see her face. Oh yeah, she was mad all right. I could tell by the way her cheeks were splotched red and her lips were all pruney, kinda like she had eaten too many sour candies. Her eyes went from the doctor to the lady with the clipboard, and her mouth opened like she was about to say something. But before she said a word, she looked at me, and the mad look went away.

Then, she smiled, even though she also seemed kinda sad. About what, I wasn't sure, but I did know those angry wasps in my tummy settled down a little bit.

"You know what?" she said, keeping her dark brown eyes on mine for a moment before looking back at the doctor and continuing, "I don't think you know what's best for my son. I don't think any of you—not the teachers, not this office, not *any* of you—know what's best for my son at all. Now"—she hurried to stand, snatched her purse from the chair beside her, and reached out to take my hand—"we are leaving, and you can take your antipsychotics and shove them up your ass."

***

"She did *not* say ass," Luke groaned, rolling his eyes away from the TV long enough to glare at me.

"Oh, yes, she did," I argued before grinning again.

Mom hardly ever cursed. She always yelled at Dad whenever he cursed around Luke and me and told him he was being a bad influence. So, hearing her curse at that doctor was pretty much the coolest thing I thought she'd ever done in her life.

"So, what's the plan now, Sue? I thought you were going to take him down to that doctor the school recommended, get him looked at, and do what you had to do to get this sorted out."

Sorted out. Dad said things like that about the leak in the bathroom and that one time the lights wouldn't turn on. *Sorted out* meant something was a *problem*. *I* was a problem.

The hardened glare in Luke's eyes disappeared as he clamped his lips shut at the sound of Dad's voice in the kitchen. Now, he just looked sad.

Sad for me.

"They wanted to put him on antipsychotics," Mom said.

"Yeah, and?"

Mom made a noise like she couldn't believe Dad would say something like that. "Are you serious? You think he's *psychotic*?"

"Sue, I'm not saying—"

"What *exactly* would you have me do, Paul? Huh? You want me to take him back to that place and let them treat him like he's some … some lab rat and pump him full of pills? You want them to treat him like a freak? Jesus Christ. He's our *son*, Paul. You didn't hear the things they were saying. You didn't see the way they looked at him. You didn't—" Her voice broke, and I knew she was crying.

I didn't like it when Mom cried.

I didn't like that *I* had made her cry.

"Sweetheart," Dad said quietly, and a chair was pulled out from the table.

"He's not crazy, Paul." She sniffled.

"I never said he was. I just …" He groaned loudly. "I want him to have a good life. I want him to be happy. I don't want him to be *alone*. And that school … you know they're going to ruin him if he doesn't—if *we* don't—"

"So … he won't go back."

Luke's eyes got really big then. *What?* he asked silently, his lips moving.

But I didn't know what to say. My heart was beating so hard, so fast.

"I'll keep him home," Mom said. "I'll teach him myself."

Dad didn't say anything right away. I wondered if he was angry. I wondered if he was going to yell at Mom.

But then, "What about Luke?"

"He's fine in school. He gets decent grades, and he has some good friends," she replied, sounding sure and determined. "But if we're going to give Charlie the best chance of making it in this world, I think the best thing is to get him the hell out of there. I'll find some books on helping him to manage his anxiety. If that doesn't work, maybe we'll find a better doctor, one who doesn't immediately jump to medication. But for now, we'll take him out of school."

"Okay," Dad said without a moment of hesitation. "He won't go back to school."

Luke shook his head, one corner of his mouth curling into a smirk as he whispered, "You're such a lucky butthead."

***

The next day, Luke went to school, but I didn't. Instead, Mom said we had to run a few errands and told me to get dressed. Then, we got into the car, and we went to McDonald's for breakfast. That was where she asked if I'd heard what she and Dad talked about, and since I never liked to lie, I told her I had.

"So, you know why you didn't go to school today?"

I nodded, keeping my eyes on my hash browns and hot cakes.

"Are you okay with that? Because, Charlie, if you would rather go back to school, then that's okay. We'll figure it out. But if you want to—"

"I hate that school," I admitted.

But she knew that already. She had to. Hadn't I cried enough times before getting on the bus? Hadn't I begged her enough to keep me home and tell my teacher I was sick?

Mom took a deep breath and said, "Okay. Okay, so after we eat, we're going to the teacher supply store, and there, we'll find some workbooks, and ... we'll figure this out, Charlie. Okay? You and me, we'll figure this out together."

I thought about what Luke had said as I finished my breakfast and then went on a trip to the store. I thought about how he'd called me a lucky butthead as I picked out a math workbook, some cool stickers, and a book about the solar system. I *was* lucky. I was lucky to not be in school, where Ritchie would corner me in the cafeteria and squeeze my juice box onto the floor or eat my sandwich before I got the chance. I was lucky to not hear the other kids laugh at me when I stuttered after the teacher called on me to answer a question—I always knew the answers, but I hated saying them out loud. I was lucky to be with Mom, to go home and watch TV instead of play alone during recess.

I was the luckiest kid alive.

But then Luke came home, and I was happy, until Ritchie followed him inside. It wasn't weird or anything—he lived just two doors down with his younger brother, Tommy, and their mom—but I hated him. I hated Ritchie Wheeler more than I hated school, and I hated school a lot.

"Hey, Ritchie!" Mom said, smiling from the couch. "I bet you're still so happy we moved into this house, huh?"

Ritchie's eyes landed on me first before looking at Mom. "Yeah, it's pretty cool."

"It's nice you guys live so close together now." She reached out to tug at Luke's arm. "Right, Luke?"

Luke rolled his eyes and sighed. He used to like when Mom talked to him after school, but now, he just acted like she annoyed him. "Yeah, sure, Mom. Can we have something to eat?"

She nudged her head in the direction of the kitchen. "You know where the food is."

"Cool."

My big brother looked at his best friend and grinned, both of them ignoring me entirely as they ran toward the kitchen, and I started to feel lucky again.

But then Mom went to the basement to do some laundry, and Luke announced that he had to take a piss and ran into the bathroom. That was when Ritchie wandered into the living room from the kitchen, a peanut butter and jelly sandwich in his hand. He walked slowly toward me, taking a bite and chewing. Those wasps woke up in my belly again, and I shifted on the couch, moving farther away until there was nowhere else to go.

"I was worried about you today, Charlie boy," Ritchie said, taking another bite. "I thought maybe you got sick."

I swallowed and shook my head. "N-no, I'm o-okay."

"Yeah." He nodded and sat beside me, his thigh touching mine. "Luke said you weren't gonna come back. He said your mommy thinks you're too crazy to leave the house now."

"I-I'm not crazy," I muttered weakly.

"Maybe you're just running away from me," he said, like he was thinking out loud as he finished his sandwich. A glop of jelly was left on his fingers and he studied the red blob as he continued, "But you can't run away from me, Charlie boy. I know where you live."

Then, his hand snapped toward me, and those sticky, cold fingers dragged their way down my cheek, leaving the jelly behind on my skin. Tears burned at the back of my eyes, my bottom lip quivered, and I knew I would cry. I always cried, and Ritchie loved it.

"I'll see you soon, okay?" He wiped his fingers the rest of the way on my shirt. "Better go wipe your face off, you little baby. Don't let your mommy see the mess you made."

Then, as he went back to the kitchen and I felt the first of my tears begin to slide down my cheeks, I started to wonder if I could ever truly be lucky at all.

CHAPTER TWO

MASSACHUSETTS, PRESENT DAY

A crisp but silent breeze rustled my T-shirt as the leaf blower removed the dead leaves from the plot. Ellen H. Mills might have died in 1971 at the baffling age of one hundred three, but I liked to think she appreciated my diligence in keeping her burial site tidy.

A gaggle of teenagers meandered down the path I'd just cleared of debris from last night's gale, the remnants of twigs and dried leaves still in the blower's bag. They were all dressed in a uniform of typical so-called mall goth attire. Black tops and black jeans, worn tight and hanging low on the hips of two girls and the singular boy. The other two girls wore skirts to reveal the torn fishnet tights and pasty-white legs underneath. Their faces were all caked in white while their eyes were lined with deep black, and their hair was choppy and dyed a flat black any self-respecting hairstylist would've turned their nose up at.

I only knew this because I had dated one once years ago, long before I had no choice but to run away from the only home I'd ever known.

The group of kids strolled past me, carrying with them an air of arrogance I found nearly infuriating. I might've been well into my thirties now, but that didn't mean I couldn't remember being a teenager myself. Not unlike them in my choice of clothing, but lacking the ambition to dye my hair or lips a color to match. But what had really set me apart was the lack of companionship. Other kids—Luke's friends or others in our neighborhood—saw me as the freak, the weirdo, the outcast too messed up to fit in.

Sure, I guessed having the occasional panic attack over nothing and everything hadn't helped my case much, but neither had my choice in favorite color or my fascination with the macabre.

But anyway, my point was, these kids *tried* to be this weird. And other people—their peers—*liked* them for it. Which, in turn, didn't make them all that weird at all. They didn't know what it was like to be cast aside, to be teased and tormented for being truly strange and unusual, and I didn't like them for it.

Then, somewhere beneath my distaste, I found my envy. Oh *God*, how nice it must be to easily find acceptance. How truly wonderful to have friends without needing to change who you are.

One of the teenagers—the girl in the shortest skirt—caught my eye for one second longer than the others. Not for any reason. It was simply a stutter of the eyes, but in that second, she held my gaze, and she sneered in response, curling her black lips.

"What the hell are you looking at, you fuckin' perv?" she asked, accusation heavy in her tone.

I quickly looked away and maintained my usual silence, focusing on making sure Ellen's plot of neatly trimmed grass was clear of weeds or anything else one might find unsightly.

"Freak," another girl said to my back.

A rush of heat rose from my collar. A frown tugged at my lips.

The fact that a girl who modeled herself after the freaks of the world could turn around and use the word as an insult nearly made me chuckle. The irony nearly made me shake my head. I was tempted to scold her. To tell her to respect her elders—I must've been at least twenty years her senior. But I never did well in situations of confrontation, so I kept my mouth shut and my eyes on the headstone before me while wishing they would just walk away, as I usually did in times of being bullied and tormented.

All but one.

But alas, they didn't.

It could never be so easy. It never was.

I heard the boy say, "Watch this."

I listened as he walked with determination from the path and onto the grass, coming to stand beside me. He was inches shorter, the top of his head barely reaching my nose, but confidence emanated from beneath his black trench coat. More than I possessed in my pinkie finger.

I kept my eyes down, aimed at Ellen H. Mills's name, and used all my brainpower to will this little shit to get back to his stroll.

But of course, he remained beside me.

He pulled a tissue from his pocket and blew his nose loudly, the snot emptying from his nostrils in two strong huffs. Then, he threw it on the ground, right beneath Ellen's etched epitaph.

My eyes slowly lifted from the crumpled wad of white to pin him with my withered glare.

"Keep your goddamn eyes off my girlfriend," he warned, the big, grown-up words passing through his painted boy lips. "Now, clean that shit up, creep."

"You gotta say something, Charlie," I could hear Luke telling me as the nasty little fuck walked away with his arm around the girl in the short skirt, boasting and laughing. *"What the hell are you gonna do if I'm not around to fight for you?"*

"Nothing," I replied in a mutter, turning from the path to stare once again at the decades-old stone marker. "Apparently, nothing."

Then, I bent over and snatched the used tissue off the ground.

***

The mosaic rays of sunlight peeked through the branches of the white oak, its trunk to my back. The sketch pad in my lap stared back at me, the white paper still crisp and blank, untouched by my marker. I had thought the statue of a snarling gargoyle would spark some creativity, but I couldn't convince the Sharpie to lay anything down on the clean sheet before me.

I was a creature of habit. Life was predictable that way. It was *safe*. Living every day exactly the same as the last with few surprises. Time moved quicker; the days passed more efficiently. But today felt different. Something had shifted in me; a piece had somehow fallen out of place.

I considered that maybe the brief run-in with the teenagers had shaken me up. I had kept my head down and existed only in the shadows for so long; it felt disturbing and foreign to be suddenly acknowledged, like a ghost finally seen after an eternity of being invisible. It reminded me of a time before Salem—back when tragedy and trauma had instilled the drive in me to leave everything behind, and it had left me desperate for cover. No longer did my little bubble feel as safe as it had before, and now, there was a brand-new sense of restlessness, scratching beneath the surface of my skin.

I'd been content to sit in this cemetery for years, seldom venturing out and only when absolutely necessary—often in either the early morning hours or late, late at night, when the only people emerging from their caves were others likely to also keep to themselves. But today, I was no longer satisfied to sit behind the safety of my wrought iron fence and eight foot-tall stone pillars. Today—though I knew I might live to regret it—I craved a little more than the hallowed ground could provide.

So, with that unusual desire fueling a flame beside an unsettling sense of foreboding in my gut, I stood from my seat beneath the tree and headed back to my house on the hill. I dropped my sketch pad and pen in their rightful home on the small table between the armchairs in the living room, then grabbed my keys from off the hook beside the front door.

Maybe a quick ride will make me feel better.

After locking the door and double-checking that it was secure, I went around back to where Luke's motorcycle was always parked.

Man, he had loved that bike. It was his pride and joy at a point when he otherwise had none, and when he could no longer use it, he'd insisted I take it for myself. But since I'd left Connecticut years ago, the black Harley rarely left the cemetery grounds. Maybe once a month, when I dared to stop at a nearby grocery store for provisions, but apart from that, the bike was used only to zip around the cemetery.

I doubted it was what Luke had intended when he gave me the keys, but could he have honestly expected anything else from his reclusive little brother? Or maybe he'd thought the damn thing possessed some kind of power to pump confidence and sufficient social skills back into a person—as if I'd had any to begin with.

I huffed a gentle chuckle through my nose as I pulled the helmet on and mounted the bike, remembering Luke and how he had never needed the Harley to make friends or pick up women—but it certainly never hurt.

Me though? All it gave me was the rush of having the quiet wind sifting through my hair, and usually, that was enough.

The cemetery closed at sundown every night. With a quick glance at my watch, I saw that I had about three hours before I had to lock the gate. But that was fine. I wouldn't need that much time to get whatever had awaken beneath my skin out of my system. A quick ride around the city, maybe a stop somewhere for something to eat, and I'd be good for the next several years.

Or I hoped so at least.

***

In the time that I'd been living in Salem, I hadn't gotten any food from any of the local restaurants apart from an occasional stop at McDonald's. The desperation to remain elusive and alone had kept any possible curiosity thwarted. But there must've been something in the air tonight, something sweeter and unexplained because I found myself heading down the sidewalk toward Village Tavern.

It'd come on suddenly, the hunger and intrigue, while I was taking my first impromptu walk through Salem's Derby Square.

It was easy to understand how I'd never found myself strolling through the city's small plaza, crowded by a street market's varied booths full of oddities and curiosities, though I'd heard the tales and seen the pictures on social media. Several years of solidarity might've sounded like a lot to most people, but to me, it was nothing outside of normal. Hell, for a good deal of my life, I'd made it a point to keep myself locked away—whether at work or at home—like a hunchback guarding his sacred tower. Only Luke could ever talk me into doing something outside of my norm with never-ending promises of fun and good times.

What would he think of me now? I'd thought, wearing a melancholy smile as I walked down the wide brick steps toward the street below.

I was imagining his incredulous laugh and shaking head and rolling eyes when my stomach growled, reminding me that I hadn't eaten since that afternoon. After a quick glance at my watch, I was startled by having allowed two hours to pass so easily. My precious and treasured routine had been set so off-kilter, and I nearly tripped on that last step, right into a booth of incense and burners.

It would be time to lock the gates soon, and I needed to eat.

So, I pulled out my phone and looked up restaurants in the area, feeling absurdly embarrassed that I didn't already know. I was no better than these tourists surrounding me, consulting the internet for recommendations instead of knowing from the experience of having had lived in the city for nearly half a decade.

Pathetic, Charlie. That's what you are. A pathetic loser. A fucking creep. A—

Stop.

I shook my head, sending the voice away, as a list of the best restaurants in Salem came up in the search results. Number one was Village Tavern, so that was who I called to put in a takeout order. Because Lord knew there was no way I was going to sit down in a restaurant and eat. But nothing said I couldn't grab my food and get the hell out before anyone had much of a chance to notice me.

And that was exactly what I'd done.

I parked Luke's bike and hurried down the street to the restaurant, where I walked inside, muttered my name, and grabbed my food. The staff was quick and efficient, and I was out of there before I could commit the foolish act of making eye contact with anyone. But I was moving too fast as I neared the corner, ready to cross the street. I was too focused on putting my wallet in my back pocket and taking the keys from my jacket while juggling the bag of food and a highly anticipated soda. I was so distracted, so in my fucking head and thinking too much about a life I could no longer have, that I didn't notice the woman coming around the corner or the people she was with.

The impact was jarring. Her body crushed against mine with the force of a battering ram, knocking the drink from my hand. I took a hasty step back, putting distance between us before I dared to allow my eyes a quick look at her face.

Holy shit.

If the force of her body bumping into mine had been jarring, witnessing how indisputably beautiful she was could only be described as catastrophic. A pile of raven-black hair crowned her head, her face framed by strands kept loose. Her ghostly-white skin was adorned with more piercings than I could count in the brief glance, but those eyes … green and otherworldly …

I'd never seen a green quite so deep, never known eyes could take on such a hue, and just like that, in that instant, it was my favorite. I knew I'd remember it for the rest of my life. I'd hunger for another glance, and I'd have no choice but to starve.

You're a fuckin' creep, Charlie. Look away before she has the chance to see you staring.

Loser.

Pervert.

I hung my head lower and dodged my eyes toward the drink pooling at my feet, but not before I noticed the watching, scrutinizing glare of the tall man standing beside her.

Boyfriend?

Husband?

I wished I could wither away and take back ever wanting to venture outside my wrought iron fence and stone pillars.

"Oh!" the woman exclaimed in a husky, sultry voice. "I'm so sorry!"

I couldn't speak. I couldn't will my mouth to form words or my lips to let them spill, too afraid I'd say something stupid and foolish in the presence of a woman more stunning than the full moon above, shining brighter than the streetlamps and taunting with a watchful, imagined grin. I tightened my grip around the bag in my hand and dropped my gaze to the drink.

"I'm sorry," the woman repeated, digging into the satchel at her hip. "Here, let me pay for it. I can—"

"Don't worry about it," I hurried to say, pushing the words past my lips in a forced, exasperated, and agitated tone.

I held the bag firmer, the food growing colder by the second, and before she or any one of her party members could say something else in reply, I rushed past them all, full of regret and an endless string of nitpicking thoughts barreling through my head, along with a very sudden loss of appetite.

Loser.

Freak.

As my unrelenting brain continued to berate me, I threw the bag in a nearby garbage can and walked with clenched fists back to Luke's bike.

CHAPTER THREE

CONNECTICUT, AGE THIRTEEN

My back was against the wall just outside my parents' room. Luke was inside with Mom and Dad. The door was closed, but they were all talking loud enough that I could hear.

"You can go, sure," Dad said. "But you're taking Charlie with you."

Luke groaned, and my chest ached at the sound of his disappointment.

He was my best friend; he always would be. But his best friend was Ritchie.

If I was being honest, I wasn't sure I was Luke's friend at all.

"Dad, you gotta be kidding, right? He's ..." He huffed out a loud breath, like he couldn't believe our father could be such an unfair tyrant. "He's a *kid*."

Mom sighed, defeated. "I mean, he's not wrong ..."

"He's thirteen; he's not a *child*," Dad corrected, sounding serious. I could picture the twin lines forming between his brows. "And if you're doing anything at that party that you can't do around him, then you shouldn't be doing it at all."

I swallowed, my stomach tied up in a thousand knots.

They were talking about Luke's friend's birthday party. Rob only lived a couple of blocks away, and he had just turned sixteen. Luke had been on the phone all week, talking to his other buddies about the party with so much excitement and mischief in his tone. I knew the things he liked to do when I wasn't around, and I knew he didn't like to have me around because I prevented him from doing them.

Smoking cigarettes. Drinking beer. Kissing girls.

The knots in my stomach tightened at the idea that he might do more than just all of that, but my mind fought to push those things away.

It was bad enough that he had snuck into the house last weekend, more drunk than I'd ever seen someone—even Dad that one time he'd gone to his friend's wedding years back. Luke had tripped up the stairs and fallen into my room, giggling like a girl and leaning all his weight against me. Telling me about this girl at his school and how she'd let him feel her boob or something before he threw up all over my T-shirt—*twice*.

I had never kissed a girl.

I had never felt a boob.

It was weird that Luke had done those things—and probably so much more—and it was weirder how the difference in our experiences somehow put more distance between us.

Maybe I am a kid.

Anyway, I didn't want to go to that party.

I didn't like Luke's friends. They were horrible and cruel, just as they'd always been. But they were older now, meaner, and they made him mean, too, when he was with them.

Luke was quiet now, and I wondered what he was thinking. What did his face look like? Was he mad? I wished Dad would listen to him and Mom. They knew better. They knew I was different. I thought Dad probably knew, too, but he didn't like it. He wanted me to be normal, more like Luke and more into sports, girls, and cars and less into spiders, bones, and books.

"They don't like him," Luke muttered, quieter now than before.

"Who's they?" Dad asked.

"Rob, Pat," Luke replied, like he was counting them off on his fingers. "Tommy … Ritchie …"

"Ritchie?" Mom sounded surprised, like she was clueless about how Luke's best friend picked on me whenever I was around. "Since when?"

"God, seriously?" Luke huffed a disbelieving laugh. "Mom, come on. *Nobody* likes Charlie."

"But Ritchie and Tommy—"

"They don't like him," he pressed harder, enunciating every word with purpose.

He said it like he didn't like me either, and that made my throat feel tight, and my bottom lip began to wiggle like a baby. Like a *kid*.

"He's your brother, Luke," Dad argued. He was *definitely* angry now. "And if you're going to that party, you're taking him with you."

"Dad—"

"End of discussion," Dad cut him off. I pictured him holding up his hand, halting my brother's protests.

"Come. On!"

"Enough, Lucas! In a second, I'm telling you that you can't go at all, all right? Now, make your decision and live with it!"

Luke growled angrily as footsteps approached the door. I raced down the hallway, my bare feet stamping against the carpet, and I turned into my room, jumping onto my bed and grabbing the book I'd been reading.

My parents' bedroom door opened, and Luke's footsteps came plodding toward my open door. He appeared, his face angry as he pinned me with his glare.

"Get dressed," he ordered. "Now."

"Why?" I asked, feigning cluelessness and urging my voice to sound normal and not as breathless as I felt.

He put his entire body into his eye roll. He knew I'd been listening. "Shut the hell up, Charlie. Get ready. We're leaving in two minutes."

***

"Rob's parents are out for the night," Ritchie said in a voice that implied this was the greatest thing to ever happen to them in their lives since they had discovered beer and boobs.

I rolled my eyes the moment the gigantic football player wrapped his arm around Luke's neck.

"You can't tell my mom," he added, giggling like a little girl. "She'd be *pissed*."

"Okay, but you can't tell mine either," Luke replied, laughing along with him.

They almost turned into the house when Ritchie spotted me standing behind my brother. "What the hell is he doing here?" he asked, sneering.

"My asshole dad wouldn't let me come without him," Luke grumbled, already walking through Rob's front door.

My skin prickled at the sound of my brother calling our father an asshole, knowing Luke didn't believe it. He was showing off for his mean friend, and I didn't like it.

Ritchie blocked the doorway with his body after Luke passed. He narrowed his eyes and crossed his arms, pinning me to the stoop with a menacing look. "Are you gonna be a little baby if I let you in?"

I diverted my gaze to the concrete at my feet.

"You're not gonna go running back to Mommy and Daddy like you did last time, are you?"

My cheeks burned with the evidence of my shame at the reminder of that time Luke had taken me to the movies a couple of months ago. We met up with Ritchie, Tommy, and a few girls from their school. Luke smoked a cigarette and kissed one of those girls—with his tongue and everything—when we were supposed to be watching the movie. I told Mom what had happened after we got home, and Luke didn't speak to me for a week.

I hadn't felt bad for saying anything. Cigarettes were bad, and that girl didn't seem very nice. But I hadn't realized Ritchie knew I'd tattled. I guessed Luke had told him, and I tried to glance around Ritchie's big, stupid body into the house to sear Luke with my angry glare.

Ritchie grabbed my arm, squeezing and hurting and probably bruising, and yanked me toward him. He scared me now, just like he always had, and my eyes teared up as my gaze met his.

"Because if you say a fucking thing, I'm gonna make sure you regret it," he threatened, his voice low and intimidating.

"Let me go!" I tried to yank my arm away, but he only tightened his grip until the bone ached. "Ow! Stop!"

"Pinkie promise, little baby. Pinkie promise, and I'll let you go."

A tear slipped from my eye. "Stop it!"

His fingers curled, digging his blunt nails into my flesh. "Say the magic words, Charlie boy."

"Luke!" I cried out, squeezing my eyes shut and wishing I were at home in my room with my book.

"Come on," Ritchie coaxed, his sweet voice playing a stark contrast to the pain he was inflicting on my arm. "Pinkie promise, and I'll let you go. Easy-peasy."

I yelped, sounding like a hurt dog. "Fine! I pinkie promise!"

And just like that, he released me, giving instant relief to my arm, and held up his little finger. "Seal the deal, Charlie boy."

I reluctantly offered the little finger of my left hand, and instead of holding up his end of the bargain, Ritchie grabbed my finger in his big hand and bent it back, nearly to its breaking point. I cried again, wondering where my brother was and why he didn't care—why *nobody* cared—as Ritchie stepped forward and bent down to press his mouth to my ear.

"I will break this fucking finger if you tell anyone anything, I swear to God. Got it?"

"I got it!"

"Good." He let my hand go, then quickly wrapped his arm around my shoulders. "Now, come on. Let's get you a drink."

***

That night, I learned I didn't like beer. It tasted gross, burned my throat, and felt heavy in my stomach. I struggled with every swallow and gagged a little every time, but still, I drank because Ritchie had told me to. With the memory of his threats so fresh in my mind, the last thing I wanted was to make him unhappy.

It didn't help that he never left me alone for long, almost as if he'd assigned himself the job of being my babysitter or something. Like I needed one. And what made everything worse was, I didn't know where Luke had gone. I hadn't seen him since we'd arrived, and between choked swallows of beer, I worried about what he was doing.

Mom and Dad will be so mad, I caught myself thinking more than once, staring into the half-empty cup of beer in my hand. But then I scowled, remembering that I couldn't say anything to them at all … unless I wanted Ritchie to break my pinkie—which I didn't.

What am I gonna do?

I looked up from the nasty beer and hesitantly surveyed the room, looking for my brother once again in the sea of teenagers. Most of them I didn't recognize. I hadn't been to school in almost five years, and besides, these kids were all at least two or three years older than me. Even if I had known any of them at some point, they all looked so much different—*older*—than they would've when I'd known them.

A wave of nerves barreled over me, and my stomach began to hurt, churning with the feeling that something was very wrong. I glanced at a clock on the wall, hanging above an entertainment center, and saw that it was past nine o'clock at night. I'd been there for almost two hours, standing against the wall of the living room with a warm, half-empty cup of beer in my hand.

God, where the hell is Luke?

My hands started to shake and grew clammy. My heart began to flutter wildly when I remembered that Dad had told us to be home no later than ten.

I didn't even want to come at all.

"Hey."

I turned abruptly at the sound of a girl's voice to find a pretty face I didn't recognize looking right at me. She was smiling, and she was holding a cup identical to mine.

"H-hi."

Ugh. I sounded so stupid, like a little boy.

I had no business talking to a girl as pretty as her, easily three years older than me. But she didn't seem to notice my stutter as her smile grew wider.

"Are you having fun? You've been standing over here for a long time."

She noticed? I felt my cheeks growing hot as I swallowed, trying to not feel so embarrassed.

"Um .... y-yeah, kinda." I cleared my throat. "I-I mean, I'm kinda having fun ... I guess."

"Are we in class together?"

She leaned against the wall beside me, and I couldn't believe she'd want to stand there instead of hang out with someone else. Like Ritchie or Tommy or Luke. Someone way cooler and older. Someone who wasn't me.

I shook my head. "I-I don't, um ... I d-don't go to school."

"You don't go to school?" Her eyes widened like it was the most awesome thing she'd ever heard in her life. "I'm so jealous. I wish *I* didn't have to go to school."

"W-well, I mean ... I still ha-have homework and stuff," I answered stupidly even though she hadn't asked. "My m-mom teaches me."

Her mouth opened in a wide O as she nodded. "Ohhh, so wait. You're homeschooled?"

"Yeah." *Good. I didn't stutter this time.*

She didn't look as impressed now, but she didn't stop smiling either. "That's still pretty cool. Do you get to sleep late?"

I lifted one shoulder in a half-hearted shrug. "I-I guess. I—"

"Ooh, what's going on over here?" Ritchie sauntered over, his lips curled into a smile I immediately didn't trust. His eyes twinkled with mischief as they bounced from me to the girl leaning against the wall beside me. "Melanie, I see you've met Charlie boy."

The girl—apparently named Melanie—sighed, like the last person on the face of the planet she wanted to talk to was Ritchie Wheeler. I quickly glanced at her in time to watch her eyes roll.

"Go away, Rich."

I stiffened and held my breath, scared of what Ritchie might do to her. Nobody talked to him like that. Everyone knew better. My eyes moved cautiously to watch as anger darkened Ritchie's gaze for a split second, but the smile never left his lips. He slung his arm around her shoulders and pulled her toward his side.

"Ah, come on. I'm just teasing," he said, allowing his fingers to fiddle with the ends of her shoulder-length strawberry-blonde hair. "I'm just glad someone's keeping my little buddy company. Did you know we grew up together? His brother's my best bud."

"Oh, that's cool. I didn't know Luke had a brother." Melanie's eyes met mine as the smile returned to her face. "But, uh, yeah, we were just talking about how he's homeschooled."

Ritchie nodded. "It's pretty cool, right?" He almost sounded sincere.

Something didn't feel right. Ritchie never thought anything I did was cool, and I couldn't figure out why he'd be saying that now. Unless he was trying to impress this girl, and I didn't like that either. She seemed nice, and Ritchie was anything but.

"I mean, yeah," Melanie replied, giggling and hugging the cup to her chest. "I'd love to stay at home all day."

She grinned at me, and I smiled back despite that sick feeling in my belly. Ritchie noticed, his eyes looking from her to me and back to her.

Then, he gave her a little push in my direction.

"You know what, Mel? I think Charlie boy likes you."

My mouth fell open as I shook my head rapidly. "W-what? No, I—"

"Yeah, I think he *really* likes you," he said, nodding and ignoring my protests. "Why don't you give her a little kiss, Charlie, huh? You want to, right? You think she's hot?"

Melanie's throat bobbed with a forced swallow as her eyes locked with mine. She wasn't smiling anymore, and neither was I.

"Rich, stop it," she said, crossing her arms over her chest in an attempt to stand her ground.

"Aww, come on," he coaxed, giving her back another nudge. "Don't you think he's kinda cute, in a weird, fucked-up sorta way? 'Cause, you know, he *is* weird and fucked up. Right, Charlie boy? Especially when you"—he wrapped his arms around himself and began to shake—"get *bad feelings* and f-f-f-freak the f-f-f-fuck out," he said in a whiny, mocking tone.

That feeling I'd had earlier, standing in the hallway outside my parents' door—the one that made my chest ache and my bottom lip wiggle—it came back with an unrelenting force at the words coming out of Ritchie's mouth. And I didn't even know *why*. I didn't like him, and I knew he didn't like me. Why did I even care what he thought?

Or was it just that he was saying it in front of her?
Why did I care what *she* thought?
God, where is Luke?!

"Sh-shut up," I muttered, weak and warbled.

"Oh no, are you gonna cry, Charlie boy? Poor baby. Melanie, you'd better kiss him and make it—"

"Rich, what the hell are you doing?"

The tension in my shoulders was released the second Luke appeared at his best friend's side. I looked at my older brother, gratitude pulsing heavily in my heart, and I was relieved to find his eyes narrowed with rage.

I just hoped it wasn't directed at me.

"Hey, man." Ritchie's demeanor changed the second he noticed Luke beside him. "I was just keeping Charlie company while you were—"

"The fuck were you doing with my brother, man?"

Before Ritchie could reply, Luke reached out and grabbed the cup from my hand and peered inside.

"Dude, you gave him *beer*?"

Ritchie just laughed and shrugged it off. "I was trying to help him have a good time."

Luke shook his head and shoved the half-empty cup against Ritchie's chest. "Are you *trying* to get me killed?"

"Nah, man. Just trying to help you get laid." Ritchie clipped his knuckles against Luke's shoulder, and I glanced at my big brother, wondering if that was what he'd been doing this whole time.

Had he been *getting laid* while his mean friend kept a watchful eye over me?

The betrayal hurt more than Ritchie's words, and the guy I'd thought was my hero just a few seconds ago was suddenly no better than the jerk he called a best friend.

I looked at Melanie, still standing in front of me, as if she was too scared to walk away. Her eyes met mine, and she gave me a small, weak smile, like she felt bad for me.

I didn't want her pity.

I just wanted to go home.

"Oh, don't you worry about *me* getting laid," Luke said in the voice he used when he was showing off. "Becky's not gonna be able to walk tomorrow."

Ritchie snorted and slapped him on the back. "Hell yeah!"

Luke gave him a big smile, then looked back at me. I was afraid he'd still look mad, but he didn't. Instead, there was something else. Something I didn't understand or really recognize. But the smile dropped from his face, and he clamped his lips together before his eyes bounced to Melanie. Then, another look—another one I didn't understand—was on his face as his chin lifted and his teeth bit his bottom lip.

"Uh, you know, I should probably get this loser home," he said to Ritchie. "My dad gave me a freakin' curfew."

Ritchie threw his entire body into his eye roll. "Lame."

"Right? So stupid. But, uh, whatever. I'll see you Monday, all right?"

Ritchie nodded, seeming to forget all about Melanie and me. "Yeah, all right. Later, man. I'll give you a call."

Luke slapped his hand against Ritchie's back and lifted his chin. "Later."

I stepped away from the wall, anxious to get out of there. But Luke didn't make a move to leave until Ritchie walked away, distracted by a girl with big boobs in the adjacent kitchen.

Then, Luke looked at me and whispered, "Are you okay?"

He would've laughed if he knew how happy my heart felt to hear him ask that.

"Yeah." *I am now*.

He looked satisfied as he turned to Melanie and asked, "You wanna get out of here too?"

She nodded eagerly in reply.

"Okay," he said, turning toward the door and leading the way. "Let's go."

***

She lived down the street from Rob's house. Luke and I walked her home without speaking a single word, and when we reached her front porch, she thanked us both with a pretty, friendly smile and a quiet, "See you around, Luke," before disappearing behind her door.

Then, it was just Luke and me, and all I could think about was what he had been doing while I stood alone in his friend's living room, drinking gross beer and dealing with Ritchie.

We began to walk home in silence, the streetlights passing over us and the sound of our rubber-soled footsteps against the sidewalk filling the space between us. I felt like a little kid beside him, aware now more than ever that he was closer to being a grown-up than I was. Girls *liked* Luke. They wanted to kiss him; they wanted to do things with him. Girls looked at me and wanted to run away—like Melanie had when Ritchie told her to kiss me.

I sighed, training my eyes on the sidewalk. I hadn't ever cared about it much before, but now, I started to think that maybe I *wanted* them to like me. One day at least. And what if they never did?

"Charlie."

Luke sounded annoyed, and I didn't bother looking up at him.

"What?"

He didn't answer right away, and I imagined all the things he might say. Like maybe Ritchie was right, that I *was* weird and fucked up. I mean, kids had been saying it my whole life, so why wouldn't Luke agree? Or maybe he wanted to tell me how pissed he was that I'd been there, ruining his good time. He could've been getting drunk right now or spending more time with that girl—Becky, whoever that was. Maybe he'd even say that he wished he'd never had a little brother at all, and as much as it pinched at my chest to think about it, I didn't think I would blame him.

I wasn't sure I'd want me for a little brother either, if I were him.

Every possible reply weighed me down a little more until it felt like a six-thousand-ton brick was sitting on my shoulders, and all I wanted was to drop onto my bed to relieve myself of the pain. I'd probably cry, and I didn't want Luke to know about that either. He'd think I was a baby, just like Ritchie.

But then Luke finally said, "Don't let him get to you, okay?"

I was so shocked that I couldn't speak. I just continued to walk beside him as we turned the corner onto our street.

"You're not a freak, no matter what he says."

I swallowed, afraid I would cry right there on the sidewalk, and still, I said nothing.

"And just so you know, I didn't do it with Becky," he continued, like I had any idea who she was. "I mean, like, we made out a little, but we didn't *do it*. I just told Rich that. I've never … you know … done it. So …"

I was so confused. Why was he saying all of this to me? It felt more like old times, when we had been little kids, back when we would talk and hang out and the years between us felt more like inches rather than miles.

I didn't know what to say, if I should say anything at all, and before I knew it, we were nearing the lamppost at the end of our walkway.

"So, um …" Luke cleared his throat awkwardly.

That was when I looked up at him, acutely aware now of just how much taller he was than me, and I wondered if I'd ever stand eye to eye with him again.

"Do me a favor, okay?"

"Sure," I replied, finally speaking after a long ten minutes of silence.

"Don't tell Mom and Dad you drank beer. They'll kill me. Like, literally."

I couldn't help but laugh. "Yeah, I wasn't gonna say anything. They'd kill me too."

"No, they wouldn't. You're their favorite, and you know it." He slugged my shoulder, and I was so painfully aware of how much I missed him, even as he stood beside me. "Thanks, Charlie."

He turned and walked up the path, and I waited a couple of seconds, reflecting on the things he'd said as I watched him climb the porch steps. Thinking that maybe there was a chance we weren't so far apart after all.

And then I followed.

CHAPTER FOUR

MASSACHUSETTS, PRESENT DAY

I wasn't sure I'd slept at all, but that wasn't anything new. Sleep hadn't mattered much to me in years—the nightmares rarely allowed for it. So, hours before my alarm was set to go off, I jumped out of bed, ready to start my day without any desire to force myself back to sleep.

Besides, it would only be time wasted on lying there, doing nothing but battling against my mind and the things—and people—it kept insisting on bringing back from the dead. So, I made a pot of black coffee instead. Because sometimes, our memories were crueler than the ghosts that haunted us, and the only thing you could do to chase them away was to caffeinate and wake the hell up.

What the hell was wrong with me anyway?

Of course, I had thought about Luke over the years. Of course, I had occasionally relived the experiences of our shared and often colorful past. But I was skilled at tamping them down once they emerged from the cellar

I'd locked them in. It did me no good to remember, so why couldn't I stop myself now?

I sipped my coffee, wishing I could just administer the stuff via an IV line directly to my bloodstream. Doing much more than blinking and breathing felt like too much of an effort when I'd only gotten an hour or two of sleep, fractured by memories, but I managed to down the first cup in less than ten minutes while staring at the blank kitchen wall.

Then, I poured another cup and made my breakfast. I put on my black jeans, black T-shirt, black leather jacket, and black boots. Then, I grabbed the keys from the simple hook beside the heavy wooden door. The same routine I'd been keeping every day since I'd accepted the job of caretaker five years ago. Routine was good. It kept me grounded, kept the mind quiet and functioning like a well-oiled machine.

I rounded the stone cottage to Luke's motorcycle, keeping my eyes down and on the dew-dusted grass on either side of the stone path. It was too early to open the cemetery gate, but that didn't mean I couldn't head over to the maintenance shed and grab the mower.

With the keys dangling from my tattooed fingers, I grabbed the helmet from the seat and went to place it on top of the old tree stump behind the house. Never saw a reason to wear the thing when I was only driving a few miles per hour and just around the corner from the cottage with no one else on the grounds. Hell, normally, I would walk the distance if I wasn't being so lazy.

Then, with the helmet sitting on the stump, I turned to face the bike and immediately clutched at my chest because there, on the seat, was the butt of a cigarette.

I didn't spook easily. I had faced my share of torment throughout my thirty-eight years of life, and I had experienced more tragedy than any person deserved to be dealt with. I'd accepted the spiritual world for what it was and resigned myself to coexistence at a fairly early age. But what did have the ability to crawl under my skin was the idea of being followed, known, and watched when all I wanted was to be left alone.

With my hand still gripping the fabric of my T-shirt, I looked around the cemetery, surveying what I could see of the land from where I stood. The sun had begun to rise, casting a hazy light through the morning mist over the trees and headstones, but nowhere did I see the form of a person, lurking somewhere in the distance.

My fingers shook as I pinched the cigarette and dropped it in the garbage can against the back of the cottage.

It was probably some stupid, snot-nosed kid.

But when? How?

The alarm would've gone off if someone had come in after closing. I would've seen someone outside. Max, the night security guard, would've known, and the trespasser would've been caught.

No, maybe not. It gets dark out here. They could've been hiding somewhere when I locked the gates. Kids do shit like that.

I blew out a breath, calming my frantic heart, and rolled my eyes at my paranoia. It wouldn't have been the first time local kids had spent the night in the graveyard on a dare or a date. I'd caught them countless times before, but there was no telling how many times they'd gotten away with it under my nose. I did what I could, and so did the security guard, but some incidents fell through the cracks sometimes. Surely, that was what had happened.

Hey, maybe it was even that piece of shit who had dropped his tissue on Ellen's grave.

My nerves settled as I nodded to myself, feeling instantly stupid and silly for thinking it could be something else.

Or some*one*.

***

The cemetery was large, one of the biggest in the state, just outside of the Salem city limits. It was one of the reasons I had jumped at the chance to put in my résumé the moment I saw the job listing online years ago. Forty acres of land and burial plots, all for me to maintain and keep watch over. And it had given back in the form of shelter and a beautiful, glorious distraction. This place provided to me as much as I gave to it, and I'd grown more fond of it than most things I had in my life.

But today, I missed the people I couldn't get out of my head.

Mom and Dad.

Melanie.

Luke.

Dammit, I fucking missed Luke.

I stepped on the ride-on mower's brake and heaved out a sob that surprised both me and some birds in a nearby bush. They scattered, flying toward the sky, and I watched them leave, just as everyone else had.

Well, everyone besides Luke.

He never would've left if they hadn't made him, and I never would've left him if—

No, stop. Don't think about it. Not now.

My eyes dropped to the steering wheel. My hands ran over the rubberized plastic as a single rogue tear dripped from my eye and slid through my beard. A searing ache ripped through my chest, splitting my heart and pouring a lifetime's worth of agony all over my lap.

How long could someone carry this much grief and heartache before they buckled beneath such a tremendous weight?

Almost five years, apparently.

That was how long it'd been since I'd seen the last person who meant a fucking thing to me. Five whole fucking years since I'd left my life in Connecticut behind.

It had taken nearly half a goddamn decade for it to all catch up to me, and there, sitting in the middle of the cemetery I now called home, I sobbed for all of the people I missed and would likely never see again.

CHAPTER FIVE

CONNECTICUT, AGE FIFTEEN

It was weird how cold it was, even for a late September day in Connecticut. It felt more like October or even November, and I tucked my hands deeper into my armpits as I curled up tighter in the wicker couch on the deck.

I'd woken up with a sick feeling in my stomach. Mom had asked if I thought I was going to puke, but it wasn't that type of sick. It was more like an *I have a feeling something bad is about to happen* sort of thing. A kind of nagging in the pit of my gut that made my mind feel unsettled and my nerves feel on edge. It was a feeling I hadn't felt in a while, not this strong and powerful, and I didn't like it. Not at all. I kept looking for a distraction, something to make it disappear, but nothing worked.

When I'd told Mom about it, the way I'd mentioned the hurricane almost eight years ago, she had studied me for a moment. I could tell she was unsure if she should believe me or not, and I couldn't blame her. I'd been right about that hurricane, but I had been wrong about stuff too.

Like when Luke had gotten his driver's license and I suffered a string of panic attacks, so sure he'd die in a car accident ... but he hadn't. Well, not yet anyway.

No. Stop. No. Not ever.

"It's probably just your anxiety, hon," she'd said, smoothing the hair off my forehead. "Why don't you go outside and read or draw or something? Get your mind off of it."

So, that was why I was out here now, freezing my butt off and staring out toward the backyard with my untouched book in my lap. The dread of something bad happening had worked itself through my nerves, making my legs bounce and my fingers tap with every unsettled passing of a moment.

God, what the hell is it?

When I'd first heard about the hurricane, I had just known without a doubt that it was bad news for us. I couldn't tell my parents why or how—I'd just *known*. And it was that sincerity and fear that convinced Mom to talk Dad into leaving—and look at what had happened! Our old house had been crushed by two downed trees and flooded by the creek down the street. I thought Mom had assumed I was psychic or something, and for a while, she asked me regularly if I had any feelings regarding certain things. Like I could pick the winning lottery numbers or some crazy stuff like that. But that wasn't what it was. I wasn't psychic, and I wasn't told things by a foreign entity, like ghosts or something. I'd just get a feeling that something bad would happen ... and it did.

And, yeah, I'd felt similarly since. I'd had a bad feeling about that party I went to with Luke years ago, but it was sometimes hard to tell what a genuinely bad feeling was and what was just my nerves and anxiety disorder getting the best of me.

But, no, this feeling ... this sick, jittering feeling crawling beneath my skin and worming its way through my gut ...

This wasn't anxiety.

This was something else.

The sound of an engine rumbling down the street broke through the silence, and then it stopped. The black Dodge truck I knew well must've just pulled up to the house. Less than two minutes later, Luke exited the back door with Melanie following close behind. Then, through the corner of my eye, I watched their approach, their fingers interlocked all the while.

I half expected them to walk past without so much as a hello. I never knew what any particular day would bring to my interactions with my brother. Some days, he pretended I didn't exist. Other days, nothing seemed to exist outside of Melanie and cigarettes and his part-time job at the local pizza place. But today, he dropped beside me on the white couch, then pulled Melanie onto his lap.

"Whatcha reading, ass breath?" he asked, bumping his arm against mine.

"Oh God, Luke," Melanie scolded, smacking his chest playfully. "Don't be mean." She wrapped her arms around his neck and rested her temple against his.

"He knows I'm kidding." He wrapped his arm around her shoulders before abruptly turning to me and asking, "Right?"

"Sure," I muttered, still unable to calm my lungs or heart or the shakiness in my limbs and fingertips.

"Hey, Charlie," Melanie said, her voice gentle and soft, just as it always was. "You okay?"

As it had turned out, Melanie hadn't been into me the way Ritchie the dick assumed all those years ago, and she'd become a better friend instead.

As for her and my brother ... well, let's just say, they'd been together since that night. And funnily enough, it didn't irk me nearly as much as it had when I thought of him with other girls.

Maybe I'd just known Melanie was different, the same way I knew now that something was wrong.

"Yeah," I answered, but I wasn't so sure.

My breath continued to escalate as a barrage of possibilities pelted haphazardly through my mind—both realistic and absurd.

Dad losing his job and us going broke.

A meteor hitting the planet and wiping out the human race.

Someone breaking in and stealing my computer and video games and Mom's favorite necklace.

All of us contracting malaria and suffering a horrible death.

"Hey." Luke laid his hand against my upper back. "What's going on?"

I swallowed and finally pulled my attention from the yard to look into his eyes. Silently, I pleaded with him to be my big, brave brother and make the bad feeling go away, but unlike me, Luke was lucky and normal, and he failed to know when I was in the middle of a panic attack or having a deep-seated intuitive feeling.

"What's wrong? Do you need, um … you need medicine or something?"

"No," I said irritably, shaking my head. "I … I don't know. I just don't feel right. Something just … I don't know."

"Oh," he said, nodding. "You're, like, freaking out or something?"

He narrowed his eyes, staring at me for a moment like he didn't know what the hell to do with me. And, hey, that made two of us. But then sudden recollection dawned on him, and his mouth fell open.

"Wait … is this like the hurricane?"

I shrugged, my legs continuing to bounce against the floorboards. "I don't know. I just … I don't like it."

"Well, what is it about? What made you feel like this?"

Melanie looked between Luke and me, confused. "Can I help with anything?"

Luke lifted a hand, gesturing for her to wait a moment as he said with more urgency than I'd expected, "Did something happen? Did you, I dunno … hear something on TV? Like how you got freaked out when you heard about the storm?"

Luke had been ten when our house was demolished by the storm, and I thought it had traumatized him more than he let on that, if it wasn't for my panic and insistence, we might not have survived that night.

He was always too cool to admit when he was weak.

"No," I replied. "I just woke up feeling like something bad was going to happen."

"Like what?"

I shrugged, feeling just as clueless as Melanie, who was staring at us like she wasn't sure if she should run away or stick around to see where this episode of *The Twilight Zone* was headed.

Luke stared into my eyes and held my gaze for several seconds, and there was that thing I couldn't read again. A message I couldn't hear, one I couldn't quite figure out. God, I wished he'd just tell me what he was thinking. Things had changed a little between us over the past couple of years. The gap between fifteen and eighteen didn't seem as vast as between a thirteen- and sixteen-year-old, and our friendship seemed to have repaired itself a bit.

But even though Luke hadn't said it, I was pretty sure Ritchie was still his best friend, and that giant, asshole-shaped boulder did nothing to bridge the gap. In fact, if anything, it kept that chasm from closing, and I was certain it'd remain open until he just wasn't there anymore.

Maybe, one day, he just won't exist.

"Well, tell me if you figure it out, okay?" Luke asked with finality, giving my back a pat before removing his hand altogether. "We're gonna go down to see if Ritchie and Tommy wanna hang out. See you later."

And then he was gone, proving my point once again.

***

The topic had been dropped, and Luke had forgotten all about the feeling in my gut, but I never did.

Instead, I'd become obsessed and completely consumed by a desperation to stop anything bad from happening to the people I cared about.

Luke and Melanie, Mom and Dad, or any variation of the only four people I kept close.

Anytime any of them left the house, I'd beg them not to go. It was like I'd regressed back to preschool when I didn't want Mom to leave me alone in a strange classroom that smelled of sweat and paste and stale apple juice, minus the part where I wrapped my arms around her leg and dug my fingers into her skin to keep her from leaving.

But don't think I wouldn't have done it if I could've.

"Dad, wait. Dad!" I called, jumping up from my desk as Dad made his way down the hall and to the stairs. "Where are you going?"

"Oh God, Charlie," he groaned, shaking his head as he made his descent. "Knock it off, will you, please?"

"But where are you going?" I pressed further, hurrying behind him quicker than my long legs wanted to take me. I tripped forward at the bottom step, and I stumbled over my big feet.

Dad glanced over his shoulder and bit back a laugh, shaking his head again. "Your mom and I are going to a concert tonight, remember?"

"What? You didn't tell me you were going anywhere."

My heart raced straight toward panic, just as Luke plodded down the stairs louder than a herd of elephants. He was dressed in nice clothes—his going-out clothes—and that panic I was feeling only heightened.

"Wait, you're *all* going out?" I sounded shrill, so stupid and pathetic, but, God, I didn't want them to go. I didn't want them to leave me alone.

Dad looked around me at my brother. "Luke, I told you not to—"

"I'm just grabbing dinner real quick with the guys and Mel," he reasoned. "I'll bring some home for Charlie."

Dad was quick to resign. There wasn't much he could do when Luke was eighteen, but I could tell he wasn't thrilled.

That made both of us.

"All right. But make it quick, okay? And you're coming right back here. You understand? No staying out late."

"Yes, master," Luke grumbled, rolling his eyes and heading straight out the front door without so much as a goodbye or a mention of where exactly he was going.

"Listen," Dad said, drawing my attention away from the door. "You have our numbers. If Luke doesn't come back in an hour or two, give one of us a call, and we'll get on him to get his butt home, all right?"

I really didn't like being around people much. Strangers, Luke's group of crappy friends, the people from Dad's job who sometimes stopped by for a beer … I could do without ever seeing a single one of them again. But being without Mom and Dad, being without

Luke—even if he was a butthead sometimes—it didn't sit right with me.

Especially not when this urgent feeling of foreboding clenched around my gut, telling me my cozy, safe, sad little life was going to, in some way or another, be set off-balance.

"Dad," I began, but he ignored the tension in my tone as he pulled on his jacket.

"If you're worried about being alone, you can always go a couple of houses down and sit with Mrs. Wheeler. I'm sure she wouldn't mind."

Despite the anxiety pulsing through my trembling veins, I rolled my eyes at that suggestion. Something would have to be *seriously* wrong for me to go down the street to Ritchie's house and ask his mom to freakin' babysit me. I'd never live it down.

Mom came downstairs, wearing a dress and high-heeled shoes. Her hair was down and curly at the ends; her eyes were done up in sparkling silver and black makeup. Glittering earrings dangled from her ears—so much different from the little gold balls she usually wore.

I could count on only a few fingers the number of times I'd seen her dressed up like this in my life.

She looked like someone I didn't know.

"Oh God, it feels so good to look like a human being again," she gushed, pulling some lip stuff out of the little purse under her arm.

She twisted off the cap and put it on her lips, making them pink, sparkly, and shiny.

"You look great, babe," Dad said, offering her a rare compliment as his mouth curled up at the ends in a smile I wasn't sure I'd ever seen.

My parents were always nice people. They were cool within reason, and they rarely complained about life the way other people might. But these were people I didn't recognize—all dressed up and looking less like my parents and more like people who had fun.

It made me feel guilty, like it was my fault they didn't look like this more often.

So, even though my pleas for them to stay home were still clinging to the tip of my tongue, I kept my lips shut as Dad held Mom's jacket up and open while she slid her arms into the sleeves.

"Okay, Charlie. We left cash for pizza on the counter if you wanna eat," Mom said, zipping the jacket up and smoothing its front down over her dress.

"Luke said he'd bring something home."

She eyed him pointedly. "We're talking about Luke, hon. He says one thing and does another. Anyway, you have our numbers, and Mrs. Wheeler—"

"Yeah, I know. Dad already said this to me," I muttered, leaning against the wall.

I wasn't going to ask them again to stay, but, shit, I wished they would. They said it was separation anxiety— that was what a doctor had once said a couple of years ago—and, yeah, that was true sometimes. But that wasn't what this was, and nobody would listen.

My fists clenched at my sides as my lungs stuttered.

Mom stepped toward me with her arms outstretched, then pressed her palms to my cheeks. Her eyes widened a little with surprise as her hands rubbed against my face.

"Oh my gosh, we gotta have Dad teach you how to shave," she said with a light laugh before leaning in to press a kiss to my forehead. "You'll be okay, Charlie. Call me if you need anything, okay?"

I released an exhale and nodded. "Okay."

She gave me another kiss—this one on the cheek— as Dad groaned playfully.

"Come on, Sue. Let's leave so Charlie can throw a crazy party." He reached out and ruffled my hair before heading to the door. "Be good, kiddo."

"Yep," I replied, tightening my fists as Mom followed him. "Have fun, guys."

The door closed behind them, and I watched through the stained-glass window as they got into their car. Then, as they pulled out of the driveway and began their drive down the street, the anxiety continued to build.

***

It was nearly midnight, and I was still alone.

Luke hadn't called, but Mom had.

Just a little over a half hour ago, she'd let me know they were leaving the concert venue and going out for a late dinner. She asked if Luke was home, and I lied, saying that he was in his room.

"Okay," she'd said, a hint of relief in her voice. "Good. So, you're doing okay then?"

She was worried about me. Mom usually was, and most of the time, I liked it. I liked that she looked out for me and made my comfort a priority in her life, even if it was selfish and babyish of me. But tonight, I didn't want her to be worried. I wanted to pretend to be a normal kid, like Luke. Courageous and cool, unbothered by his parents taking a night to themselves. All for the sake of letting them be happy.

"Yeah, I'm fine, Mom," I'd answered, and I smiled. Because I had actually sounded like I was.

But, no, I wasn't. And now, forty minutes after hearing her voice, I was sitting on the couch, bouncing my legs and chewing on my nails while I stared ahead at some stupid show on MTV.

"Do people really like this shit?" I muttered to myself in a shaky voice as a bunch of college kids made out around a pool.

Then, the front door opened, and I jumped up from the couch to see who'd come home.

Luke walked into the living room, hair disheveled and eyes red.

"Oh, hey," he greeted me, his voice sleepy and gravelly. "Sorry I'm kinda late—"

"*Kinda*?!" I shouted, shrill, releasing every bit of panic I'd been suppressing all night. "Dad told you to be home *hours* ago!"

Luke furrowed his brow and crossed his arms over his chest. "Yeah, well, Dad isn't here, is he?"

"So?!"

"*So*"—he took a couple of steps toward me, reeking of weed and beer and Melanie's perfume—"I went out for a while and had some fun."

I clenched my fists and looked into his eyes. He wasn't much taller than me now—only a couple of inches. But he was still bigger, stronger. He probably always would be. But right now, I was ready to kick his ass, and, dammit, I wanted to.

"You were supposed to be here with me!"

Luke dropped his arms and rolled his eyes, already turning to walk away. "Oh, grow the hell up, Charlie. Seriously. Do yourself and everyone else a favor and—"

I lunged at him, throwing my body against his and knocking him onto the carpeted floor. My hands slapped at his face, my fingers gripped his hair, and I got in a couple of good tugs before he shoved me off and onto the coffee table.

"Fuck!" Luke shouted, rubbing at his scalp as he scrambled to get to his feet. "God, you little asshole. What the hell is wrong with you?"

"I was worried about you!" I cried, feeling stupid as my eyes welled up. I got off the coffee table and sat on the couch as I brushed the hair off my forehead. "You said you'd be home, and I didn't know where you were. I should've freakin' *known* you'd rather get high and have sex than be with me. Why the hell would I—"

"Charlie," Luke interrupted, his tone much softer than before. He took a deep breath, then continued, "I'm sorry, okay? I lost track of time, and, yeah, I was smoking and drinking and …" He scratched the back of his head, then brushed the hair off his forehead.

"Anyway, you're right. I should've been back. I said I would be, and I wasn't, so … I'm an asshole, and I'm sorry."

I sniffed and wiped my eyes. "It's okay."

"Did you eat?"

"No," I muttered. "You said you'd bring something for me."

His expression of guilt deepened. "Shit, I forgot."

"Mom left money on the counter for pizza, but …"

I didn't need to say that the pizza place wouldn't be open now. We both already knew. I should've called earlier, I realized, but I hadn't been hungry then, too distracted by my panic. But now, with Luke home, I was suddenly aware of the grumbling from deep in my stomach.

"Come on," he said, gesturing for me to follow him as he turned toward the kitchen. "I'm making some grilled cheese sandwiches. Want one?"

"Yeah, okay," I said, standing and letting him lead the way. "Sounds good."

***

We had found the censored version of a movie on cable TV—*The Shawshank Redemption*—and we'd been watching for twenty minutes as we ate our sandwiches. Then, we sprawled out on either end of the L-shaped sectional and tried to focus on Andy Dufresne and his escape from prison, but my eyes kept drifting toward the clock.

It had been one hour, then two since I'd last heard from Mom, and I was starting to wonder if I should call. Just to ask what they were doing and if they were on their way home.

"Luke," I said quietly.

"Hmm," he grunted, half asleep with his head flopped against the armrest.

"Should we call Mom and Dad?"

His chest inflated with a sigh, and then he opened his eyes to look at me on the other end of the couch. "You freaking out again?"

I shrugged, dropping my gaze from his eyes. "No. I just ..." I picked at a loose thread along the couch's seam and tried to come up with something reasonable to say, yet I came up empty. So, I shrugged again, unable to look at him.

"If it'll make you feel better, go ahead."

I couldn't snatch the cordless phone from the coffee table quick enough while trying hard not to seem too eager as I quickly dialed Mom's number. I pressed it to my ear and listened as it rang and rang and rang, but she didn't answer.

I hung up when it went to voice mail.

"She didn't pick up?" Luke asked.

His eyes were closed again.

I didn't reply as my stomach ached. Pinching and gnawing around those two sandwiches I was suddenly regretting.

"I'm sure they're fine," Luke muttered, slurring his words a little as he wrapped his arms around his middle and drifted closer to sleep.

"But ..." I swallowed, staring at the glowing screen on the phone. "What ... what if they're not?"

"Stop." I looked up to see him open one eye. "You know that's just your brain talking. Tell it to shut up."

And I tried. I really, *really* freakin' did as I forced my eyes to focus on the movie, but my mind just couldn't settle, even as I wrapped a blanket around myself and felt my lids getting heavy.

Where are they?

I grabbed the phone again, quiet as to not wake Luke up, and I dialed Mom's number. Still no answer. So, I dialed Dad's number, and the phone rang one, two, three ...

"Hello?"

I laid a hand against my chest and breathed out the biggest sigh of relief.

"Hey, Dad."

"Charlie, buddy! What are you doing awake?"

"I, um ..." I hesitated to tell him I'd been too worried to sleep. Mom, I could be honest with her, but Dad took my fears and feelings a little less seriously. But I couldn't think of anything better to say. "I was waiting for you guys."

"Tell him we're fine," I heard Mom say.

"Mom says to tell you we're fine," Dad repeated.

"Okay, good." I breathed a little easier.

"We spent longer than we'd expected at the diner with Bill and Addy, but we're on our way now."

"Okay." I pulled the blanket higher over my shoulder, not sure I remembered who Bill and Addy even were. But it didn't matter. Mom and Dad were okay.

"So, get some ... hold on." His tone changed, and my eyes snapped open. "Sue, watch out for that guy. What—"

"What the hell is he doing?" Mom's voice sounded frantic, urgent.

I sat up abruptly. "Dad, what's wrong?"

"Oh my God, Paul! Ho-hold on!" Mom was yelling, her voice panicked and penetrating through my eardrum.

"D-dad! What's happening?!" I was shouting into the phone now, waking Luke up.

He sat up abruptly, his eyes immediately bewildered and alarmed. "Charlie?"

"Sue! Don't—"

Tires squealed, and glass shattered, and the faint tinny sound of the radio continued to play some stupid Michael Bolton song. But despite my cries and my pleas for my parents to answer me, I knew I'd never hear their voices again.

CHAPTER SIX

CONNECTICUT, AGE FIFTEEN

Mom and Dad had died instantly in a head-on collision with a pickup truck driving too fast on the wrong side of the road, and on a cold and stormy day in the first week of October, they were buried.

I had heard them speak their last words, heard them take their last breaths, with the phone pressed to my ear, my knuckles turning white around the receiver. Luke had to pry the damn thing out of my hand, unwrapping my fingers as the tears poured from my eyes in a never-ending deluge of inconsolable despair.

"Charlie! Let. Go!" he had growled through gritted teeth, more from sheer panic than anger, before pressing the phone to his own ear with a trembling hand.

He called for Dad, he called for Mom, but of course, neither answered.

So, he'd hung up with only a hint of reluctance and dialed 911.

Despite being an idiot a good deal of the time, Luke always seemed to know what to do.

Even as we had planned the funeral—something that felt so, so, *so* surreal and strange and wrong and unnatural—Luke had handled it all with the help of our last living relative, Dad's mom, Nana. And the whole time, I just sat there, barely nodding or shaking my head whenever someone dared to address me by name.

I had been too afraid to speak, too afraid to look at anything but my own hands. Too scared I'd cry instead, especially when in the presence of my big brother, who hadn't shed a single tear yet. Not that I was aware of anyway.

Now, after the morning Mass and the burial at the cemetery, I sat in the house where my parents used to live. Nana had said it made the most sense to hold the funeral reception here because it was closer to all of my parents' friends than her house, which was two hours away. Luke thought she'd made a good point while I just shrugged and kept my head down.

To be honest, I didn't think it was a good idea at all. Why would I want to tie the memory of my parents' funeral to the place I'd last seen them alive?

But Luke had gone along with Nana's plan, and I'd followed because what else was I supposed to do? I was the younger one, the *weaker* one, and as far as I knew, my opinion didn't matter much.

After all, Mom and Dad had left in the first place, even when I'd begged them not to.

I had known something was going to happen. I had *known*, and they didn't care. Nobody had cared, nobody had listened, and it took every last bit of my waning strength to hold it together as I sat on the couch in the living room—the last place I'd seen them both alive, so happy and full of excitement—and stared ahead at the funeral guests.

They hugged, kissed, cried, and offered their condolences to each other. Occasionally, someone would stop, pat my shoulder, and tell me how sorry they were. I'd offer a faint smile and nod, like I was simply playing a part in a movie I'd been forced to be an extra in.

But mostly, they just whispered.

"That's one of Sue's sons."

"Poor thing. Life has been difficult enough for him with, you know …"

"I can't imagine how hard he's going to take this."

"He's always been so fragile."

Nobody whispered about Luke though. Luke was strong, they said. He'd get by. He'd be just fine. And I thought I could be fine, too, if I could stay with him.

God, what if I can't stay with him?

The thought struck my chest, and my lips parted in a choked gasp. There hadn't been any talk of what would happen to us. We'd been too busy with the funeral to even think about anything else, but that part was almost over. Soon, all these people would leave to go back to their lives, as if Paul and Sue Corbin had never existed within their lives at all, and we'd have to go back to ours. But what kind of life was there without Mom and Dad?

I swept my gaze around the living room as my heartbeat sped up to a frantic, out-of-control gallop.

Just four days ago, Mom and Dad had been here. Laughing and happy. *Alive*. Now, they were cold and concealed in their caskets, and I was never going to see them again. For the rest of my life, I would be an orphan, and, Jesus Christ, that felt like such a long time right now when I was still only fifteen, and, oh my freakin' God, what the hell would I do without Luke?

Where is he? Where did he go? What is he doing, and why isn't he with me?

I abruptly stood up, nearly knocking the drink out of some guy's hand.

"Hey, watch where you're going," he scolded, but was quickly reminded by the woman with him that I was one of the grieving sons.

Grieving sons.
My parents are dead.
I'm all alone.
Oh my God.
I'm alone.

My palms were sticky with a thick coating of sweat as I hurried blindly from the living room and stumbled up the stairs. I ran down the hall, passing my parents' room—closed and sealed off to everyone—to Luke's open doorway, only to find it empty, and I was certain my heart would explode.

"Luke!" I cried as I hurried past his gigantic laundry pile and back out the door, not caring who heard.

The bathroom was empty, he wasn't in my room, and I wouldn't dare check Mom and Dad's bedroom. I wasn't ready—not yet, maybe not ever—and I seriously doubted Luke would be either. He had even made Nana go in to grab some clothes for their bodies to wear. So, I ran back down the stairs, clumsily weaving my way through the crowded living room to the dining room, not bothering to apologize to the people I bumped into as I went.

"Luke!"

I shoved my sticky, shaking hands into my hair, gripping the strands as the panic quickly made it harder to breathe. I gulped for air, struggled to calm the nausea building in my gut. Everyone was staring at me—I knew they were—but panic didn't leave much room for self-consciousness, and I didn't freakin' care.

"God, where are you?!" My voice cracked as I made my way to the kitchen, only to find he wasn't there either.

There were so many people. So many eyes. So many bodies taking up the space and air in a house that used to hold a family and now only had room for two orphaned kids. And not a single one of these people was the one person I needed, and where the fuck was he?!

Nana spotted me from the sink. She didn't understand me or my panic attacks—I had heard her talking to my parents once or twice before about how I needed help and what the hell were they doing to fix it. But I guessed she had some compassion this time—maybe because my parents were dead, who knows—and she came over to me with a rare look of affection and sympathy in her eyes.

"Charlie, sweetie, what is it?"

"I-I-I ... I c-can't find L-Luke," I managed to say, my voice barely carried by a terrible tremor that would be humiliating later, but not now.

She nodded and gestured toward the basement door. "I saw him go downstairs with his friends a little while ago."

My lips parted with my heavy exhale, and my lungs began to find their rhythm. The basement—*of course*. Why hadn't I thought to go down there? Luke hung out downstairs a lot, especially when his friends and Melanie were around.

It had seemed to be a mutual understanding that as long as he was safe, none of us—Mom, Dad, or me—really questioned what he did in the confines of the basement. I'd overheard Dad say that it was better he did shit at home than on the streets, and although I wasn't always sure what he'd meant by that, I had never disagreed.

Luke was always better off at home.

Now, even though I seldom went downstairs myself, I hurried for the door. The hinges creaked as I pulled it open and closed it behind me. The stairs groaned beneath my feet as I made my way down, listening as the older teens talked.

"Hey, Zero," I heard Ritchie say. "Grab me a beer, will you?"

Zero. I rolled my eyes.

I had always hated that stupid nickname. So did Mom.

"Zero?" she had asked a couple of years ago when Luke demanded we all call him that—even though we never listened. "Why the hell would you want anyone to call you Zero?"

"Because he gives zero fucks," Tommy had replied before high-fiving my brother.

"You're all ridiculous," Mom had grumbled, even as she smiled, reaching out to shove against Luke's shoulder.

He had kissed her cheek before walking out the door, even in front of his friend, and she'd been so happy. She'd smiled all through cooking dinner, singing songs and dancing around the kitchen, and my heart pulsed now with such a tremendous, impossible ache at the thought of never hearing her sing again.

A sob forced its way past my lips as I plonked down on the last step. Then, with my arms folded over my knees, I leaned forward and tried to force the tears back.

There was no way I was going to cry in front of my brother's friends.

Especially Ritchie.

"What was that?" Tommy asked.

"I dunno." Ritchie. "Came from over there."

Footsteps approached, and then there was a quiet gasp.

"Charlie?" Melanie sounded worried, and she sat beside me, wrapping her arm around my shoulders. "Oh, honey."

God, I hated the way she talked to me sometimes. Like I was a little kid who needed coddling, and I hated even more that, sometimes, I did. But right now, it felt nice, and even though she was only a few years older than me, she felt as close to Mom as I was going to get in the moment. So, I let her press her temple to my head, and I continued to fight against my tears.

"Oh, Jesus Christ," Ritchie groaned without the tiniest hint of empathy.

More footsteps approached and stopped in front of me, but I didn't bother looking up to see who it was, afraid that Ritchie had come to torment me during the worst, most nightmarish time of my stupid life. I just kept my eyes closed, shielded by my arms, and waited for the crushing weight of grief to finally subside, even if just a little.

"Hey."

Luke's soft tone jolted my heart, and I looked up to find him crouched in front of me, looking back. The dark circles beneath his eyes reminded me that he hadn't slept much—if at all—over the past few days, and I felt even more like a baby as I fought against the urge to cuddle beside him and ask him to take a nap with me and forget all of this for just a little while.

I'm so stupid.

We used to take naps together as little kids. Why had it stopped? Why had things changed? Why was it that, just because we got older, we had to stop doing things like cuddle and nap and hug?

I'm such a freakin' baby.

"Luke," I whispered as if I could keep his friends from overhearing.

"Yeah?" he whispered back.

"What are we going to do?"

His shoulders dropped heavily with the weight of his sigh, and his gaze flitted from mine to Melanie's.

"We'll figure it out, Charlie."

"But what if—"

To my left, I heard Ritchie release a guttural, long-winded groan. Someone else—Rob maybe—whispered for him to shut the hell up, but Ritchie never could listen.

He stood up from the beat-up old couch and said, "God, you know, the least they could've done was take him with them."

Melanie took in a sharp breath of air in time with the metaphorical punch to my gut.

"Oh shit," Tommy or Rob muttered—I wasn't sure who.

All I could focus on was the overwhelming need to throw up and the look of horrified betrayal in my brother's eyes.

"What?" he asked, slowly turning his head to look at his oldest, closest best friend.

The kid he'd known practically since birth.

The kid he'd grown up with.

The kid who had, for all intents and purposes, been there through everything—regardless of if he was an asshole or not.

"You know, your parents, man. Obviously, it sucks they died—*obviously*. I mean, come on. But, like, they could've at least had Charlie boy in the car with them." Ritchie snorted like he had just made the funniest joke on the planet. "Would've made your life easier—that's for damn sure."

My nose sniffled uncontrollably, and there was no holding back the tears now. I had always known Ritchie was awful. I had always known he was an asshole. But I couldn't wrap my head around just how *terrible* he was. How he could stand there, grinning and laughing, like he hadn't just said the single most horrific thing I'd ever heard someone say—and it was about me. How he could wish that I were dead, just like our parents …

It hurt more than I wished it had.

"Rich!" Melanie cried, appalled, as she tightened her arm around my shoulders. "Oh my God, how can you be so freakin' awful?!"

"Say that again," Luke dared his friend, slowly rising to his feet, still wearing the black pants and white button-down he'd worn to the funeral.

He'd taken off his suit jacket at some point while I hadn't had the strength to even kick off my shoes.

Ritchie laughed lightly. "Oh, come on, Zero, man. I'm just playing around. You know that."

Luke moved toward him, one socked foot in front of the other. Taking each step carefully, slowly. "You think this shit is funny, huh?"

Ritchie shrugged casually, never wiping the grin off his face. "I mean, it's a *little* funny that he's taking it so seriously. Come on, Charlie boy. Don't cry, you little baby. Your mommy isn't here any—*fuck*!"

My head whipped toward the cracking sound of flesh meeting flesh as my brother's fist connected with Ritchie's mouth.

"Luke!" Melanie screamed, jumping to her feet and taking me with her.

She backed us against the wall at the bottom of the stairs, and together, we watched in a blend of horror and gratitude and amazement as Luke held tight to Ritchie's collar and repeatedly punched him in the face. Once, twice, three times, his fist met with Ritchie's mouth, cheek, eye, before Ritchie could gather his bearings and grapple with Luke's shoulders, shoving him back and into the side of the staircase. Luke's back hit the flimsy banister—something Dad had always intended on fixing, but now never would—and I heard something crack and splinter.

"Shit, shit, shit," Tommy chanted, jumping out of the way as Luke lunged at Ritchie again, knocking him down and onto the couch. "Luke, man, stop! Ritchie, come on! Guys!"

"Asshole!" Ritchie shouted when Luke's fist caught him once again in the mouth, causing a spray of blood to splatter against my brother's clean white shirt.

Ritchie threw Luke off him and onto the coffee table. The thin, cheap piece of furniture shattered beneath his weight, and Melanie let out a shriek. I could only stare, petrified, too stunned to cry as I held on to Melanie's arm. Afraid Ritchie would kill Luke, the only person I had left, and leave me with no one.

God, I don't want to be alone.
I don't want to be without Luke.

"Stop it!" I heard myself cry out, my voice cracking as Luke scrambled to stand up, but Ritchie stopped him with a winding punch to the nose.

Luke shouted in pain, cupping his hands against his face. "You piece of fucking shit!"

I hoped they were finished. I hoped beyond all hope that Ritchie would just leave and never come back. But something had snapped inside my brother. Something that had been lying dormant for days—hell, maybe even weeks or years, I didn't know—and it was now awake and angry, unable to be contained.

He stood from the wreckage of the coffee table on unsteady legs, took Ritchie by the collar, and hauled him against the basement wall. The back of Ritchie's head smacked against the concrete, and Tommy jumped into action and grabbed the back of Luke's shirt, trying to pull him off his older brother. But Tommy wasn't a big guy, not nearly as strong as Luke, and there was nothing he could do to keep him from rearing back and thrusting Ritchie against the wall again.

"You think this is funny?!" Luke repeated, spitting into Ritchie's face. "You think it's funny that my parents are fucking dead?!"

"Luke, stop it!" Melanie screamed, her nails digging into my arm.

Rob joined Tommy, grabbing for Luke's arm, and somehow, together, they were successful in prying him off Ritchie.

"The fuck is wrong with you?!" Ritchie shouted, rubbing at the back of his head. He pulled his hand away and found it coated in a sheen of blood.

"Me?!" Luke yelled back, his arms still held by Tommy and Rob. "I am sick and fucking tired of putting up with your shit! All the shit you say! You think you're so goddamn funny, but you know what, asshole?! You're not!"

"Yeah, well, fuck you too," Ritchie snarled, stepping in close to my brother's face, their noses barely touching. "I'm done putting up with *your* shit and your retarded little brother."

"Don't you ever fucking talk about my brother again," Luke replied, his voice low and close to a growl. "I swear to God, if you say one more thing about him, I will fucking murder you."

Ritchie only snickered at the threat. "Whatever."

He walked around Luke and headed toward the stairs. He didn't seem to notice me as he zeroed in on Melanie. He towered over her, his bruised and bloodied face tipped downward to stare into her eyes. His chest heaved with anger and adrenaline, his fists clenched at his sides, and while I couldn't meet his wild, crazy gaze, Melanie never faltered.

I wished I could be so brave.

"Go home, Rich," she muttered through a tight jaw.

A drop of blood dripped from his mouth and onto the floor as he asked, "You wanna come with me?"

"Don't you fucking talk to her!" Luke shouted, struggling against Tommy's and Rob's hold on his arms. "Jesus Christ, let me go, assholes!"

"Are you gonna hurt him again?" Tommy asked, sounding uncertain and worried.

Luke groaned, more frustrated than enraged. "Just let me go, okay?"

They listened, and to my relief, Luke stayed back, wiping the blood off his upper lip. I watched as he shook his head and sniffled, then turned his back on all of us. He raised his hand over his eyes, his shoulders shuddered, and he dropped to his knees beside the broken coffee table.

"Luke," I said in a whisper as I witnessed the crumbling of my brother's walls.

"All of you, go. Get out of here," Melanie demanded, her voice trembling with an urgent need, before quickly moving between Ritchie and me, hurrying to reach Luke's side.

I wanted to join her, to wrap my arms around my brother's hunched back and cry with him. But Ritchie was there, and Rob and Tommy came to stand beside him. A wall of older, bigger guys blocked my path, and there was nothing I could do about it.

"I meant it, you know," Ritchie said, his voice quiet and cruel. "You should've been in that car."

The basement door flew open, and there was Nana, staring down at us at the bottom of the stairs.

"What the hell is happening down there?"

I opened my mouth to speak, but Ritchie was quicker.

"Nothing. We're just saying goodbye to Charlie boy here," he said, never taking his eyes off me. Never allowing Nana to see the blood coating his bottom lip or the way his left eye was beginning to swell shut.

Luke had really done a number on him.

Good.

She didn't look convinced and narrowed her eyes at Ritchie, but still, she said nothing. Then, she stepped away from the door, leaving us alone.

Ritchie stepped in closer, ready to speak or hurt me or something, but Tommy grabbed his shoulder.

"Let's go home, Ritchie," he said, and for whatever reason, his brother actually listened.

The three of them left, parading up the stairs like defeated soldiers and shutting the door loudly behind them. I didn't bother to watch them go though and instead stared at my brother.

His arms were around Melanie, gripping her black dress with clenched fists as he pressed his face to her chest. His shoulders shuddered as he cried, sobbing and wailing like a lost, wounded dog against her. Melanie softly raked her fingers through his hair, whispering reassurances that everything would be okay even though I thought we all knew it was a lie.

How could *anything* be okay now?

How would we *ever* be okay?

I sank down onto the bottom step, silently watching my brother and his girlfriend. I didn't know if they wanted me with them. I didn't think I was welcome. Luke needed to cry, and I wasn't sure he wanted me to watch any more than I already was. I wasn't sure I even wanted to. Everything changed a little when the person you saw as Superman took off his cape, and that was exactly what was happening now as I watched my brother fall apart.

He'd become a little more human, a little more like me.

So, there I sat, giving him the space I assumed he wanted as his shudders eased and his cries subsided.

Then, his head lifted from her chest and his hands from her back. He pressed his palms to her cheeks, and he leaned in, slamming his mouth against hers, hard and fast.

I wrinkled my nose as he gripped her chin, tipped his head, and stuffed his tongue into her mouth. I turned away, not wanting to watch while being acutely aware of that thing between my legs, aching and twitching.

Dammit, I wished it would go away.

Now wasn't the time, and I didn't like Melanie like that. But I was curious, wondering what it was like to kiss someone, let alone with tongues, and it felt wrong to feel like that today, of all days—but somehow, I also couldn't help it.

But, *God*! How could he even be kissing her like that *now*? How could he ever want to kiss someone again when Mom and Dad were gone forever?

"Luke," Melanie whispered, trying to catch her breath. "No, we have to ... we have to stop."

She said it, but she didn't sound like she *wanted* to stop. She sounded like she wanted to keep going, to keep kissing. To do *anything* but stop.

Would a girl like it if I kissed her?

I shook my head, sending the thought away, immediately feeling guilty for thinking it at all.

"No, no, please," Luke begged. "I need you. Why—"

"*Your brother*," she hissed beneath her breath, as if she could prevent me from hearing, even as I sat less than ten feet away.

All Luke could say then was, "Shit."

Melanie cleared her throat, and there was some rustling behind me, but I wouldn't dare look. Afraid I'd see something I couldn't unsee.

Then, she said, "I'm going to get a washcloth for your face, okay?"

Luke sniffled. "Okay."

"Talk to him," she whispered, and then she was walking closer, stepping onto the staircase, and resting her hand against my head before ascending quietly and disappearing behind the door.

Luke and I were alone now. I was painfully aware of the fact that this was the first time we'd been truly alone together since the night our parents had died. I was so painfully, *acutely* aware that this was how our family would be from now on.

Luke and me. Just the two of us. Nobody else.

I hate this.

"Charlie."

I inhaled deeply, then answered, "Yeah?"

"Come here."

Just like that, I forgot all about kissing and girls, and I was instantly reminded of why I had come down here in the first place. There was so much of me that didn't want to go over there and hear what he had to say. What if he was about to tell me that we'd have to leave our house and go live with Nana in Mystic? What if he said he couldn't come with me?

I can't be without Luke.

Swallowing repeatedly at my quickly rising panic, I slowly stood from the stairs and walked over to where he now sat on the couch. Reluctantly, I took a seat beside him, facing forward, just as he did.

I guessed he couldn't look at me when he said whatever it was he needed to say.

"Ritchie is a piece of shit."

I nearly laughed. That wasn't at all what I'd expected.

"Well, duh. I could've told you that."

"No, I'm serious. He's not a good guy, Charlie. You have no idea. He's *bad*. He's …" Luke wiped his hand over his bloodied mouth. "I should've ditched his ass a long time ago. It's just …"

"I get it."

Luke glanced at me through the corner of his eye, a little skeptical. I figured it was hard for him to believe that I'd understand, and I guessed I couldn't blame him. It wasn't like I really had any friends of my own, outside of him and Melanie—if I could really consider my older brother and his girlfriend friends at all, organic ones at least. So, why should he have assumed I'd understand the difficulty in ditching a friend you'd had since you'd both been in diapers?

But the thing Luke didn't get was, I *did* understand it.

After all, it was exactly why I couldn't imagine a life without him in it.

It was hard to let go of someone you'd built so much of your life around.

"Anyway"—he wiped at the drying blood beneath his nose—"you don't have to worry about anything, okay?"

I scoffed, already beginning to choke on another wave of emotion. "I *have* to worry."

"Well, don't."

"Yeah, okay. Let me just turn it off."

Luke sighed, pushing his hands into his disheveled hair. "I'm just saying, I'll take care of shit, okay?"

Then, I asked the question I had been reluctant to ask. "But what if we can't stay together?"

Luke turned in his seat, and his bruised and blackened eyes came to mine with an urgency he hadn't shown before.

"That's not going to happen. That won't *ever* happen."

"But upstairs, they said—"

"Charlie, listen to me. I won't let it happen. Everything is going to be fine. *You're* going to be *fine*."

I wiped my hands against my cheeks and nodded, not sure that I believed him, but not wanting him to know that.

Then, I remembered one of the last things Mom had said to me, and knowing she was never coming home felt like a living nightmare. I turned to my brother, my heart full of pain and an overwhelming feeling of helplessness, and asked, "Luke … w-will you teach me how to shave?"

And I didn't know why that was funny, but Luke laughed despite the tears building in his eyes. He wrapped his arm around my shoulders and pressed his forehead to mine, then said, "Yeah, Charlie." His voice broke, and then he sighed. "I'll teach you how to shave."

CHAPTER SEVEN

MASSACHUSETTS, PRESENT DAY

I glanced at my bearded face in the motorcycle's side mirror at the stoplight. The wind blew against my back, whipping my hair forward against my cheeks. Thank God for the helmet, holding it down and keeping it out of my eyes.

"If you don't cut that shit soon, I'm gonna start calling you Jesus."

My chuckle rumbled up from my chest at the brief memory of Luke, but just as quickly as it'd come, it was replaced by an ache so deep that I knew nothing would touch it.

It had been two weeks since I'd had my breakdown on the mower, two weeks since I had cried. But grief had a funny way of being evergreen, no matter how much time had passed, and it was as fresh as it'd ever been now.

The light changed colors again, and I was on my way. I didn't know where I was going today, but I had woken up with that same longing to do something other than sit around the cemetery. So, I'd gotten onto Luke's bike that morning, opened the gates, and left. Hoping to come across something to scratch this persistent, new itch. I knew it was loneliness. I was familiar with the feeling. But I wasn't sure what to do with it when all I'd truly wanted since leaving Connecticut was to be alone.

Is that really what I want though?
I never used to like being alone.

The challenge was obnoxious, and I rolled my eyes at my stupid brain as I turned the corner and spotted a tea shop that looked whimsical and intriguing. Of course I wanted to be alone. That was why I'd come up here in the first place. Why the hell would that have suddenly changed a handful of years later? Other than the fact that I'd been more or less alone for that long. *Years*.

I parked the bike and pulled the key from the ignition, then headed across the street to walk through the door of Jolie Tea Company. Instantly, my senses were hit with the fragrant aromas of Earl Grey and lavender, and although I was more of a black coffee sort of guy, I'd never been known to say no to a nice cup of tea.

The shop was quiet and nearly empty. I wondered if that was normal for almost noon on a Wednesday as I pulled off the helmet and awkwardly approached the counter, where a woman was waiting with a beaming smile on her face.

"Hi!" she greeted me merrily. "What can I get you?"

I was already cursing myself. *Dammit*. Why hadn't I been more prepared? I should've checked the menu, rehearsed my order, or better yet, put the order in online to avoid this tedious exchange altogether.

"Um"—I cleared my throat, keeping my eyes on the menu on the wall and never on her—"I, uh ... don't really know. Uh, w-what would you recommend?"

I dug my fingernails into my palm, a silent punishment for the fumble over my words, while my face heated with embarrassment. She didn't seem to notice though as she glanced over her shoulder and pointed to the menu.

"Well, I guess that depends on what you're in the mood for. We have hot tea, iced tea—"

"W-what's your favorite?" I asked, both genuinely curious and desperate to not have to speak more than was absolutely necessary.

Her cheeks seemed to flush—maybe she was warm; it did seem like the temperature was too hot in here—as she turned again to address me. "Well, personally, I'm a big fan of the Wonderland Elixir, iced."

I nodded and pulled out my wallet. "Okay, y-yeah. I'll get one of those."

Her eyes danced over my face, settling on my mouth, and I wondered if I had something on me. Crumbs in my beard, leftover from breakfast? I worried my bottom lip as she brought her eyes back to mine.

"Okey dokey."

She smiled with her own lip trapped between her teeth—*she's mocking me*—and turned to make the drink while I peeked one eye over my shoulder at who else was sitting in the tearoom. Any excuse to look at anyone but this woman who was clearly finding amusement at my expense.

Because you're a loser, Charlie.

I swallowed at the insult and tried to ignore it as my eyes quickly frisked the room. The only other customers were a handful of heavily tattooed and pierced people—one man and two women.

I recognized the guy immediately as an artist from Salem Skin, the tattoo shop I'd gone to a few years ago. He was the same guy who had done the freehand spiderwebs on my hands, chest, back, arms, and shoulders a few years ago. It took three five-hour sessions to complete, and I appreciated his ability to communicate as little as humanly possible with the client, only stopping to ask if I needed a break or a drink a few times.

For the record, I hadn't.

I assumed the women worked with him to some capacity. The one with the dreadlocks looked vaguely familiar, like someone I could almost place in my memory somewhere. And the other …

"Here you go," the tea shop employee said, handing the cup and a straw to me. "Um, listen, I don't normally ask random guys—"

"Th-thank you," I cut her off, handing her the cash for the drink. "Keep the change."

Then, with my head down, I was out of there, not caring at all about what the woman behind the counter had to say—and maybe a normal guy would've. Maybe a normal guy would've stuck around to chat her up or defend himself or ask her out—whatever was appropriate. But I was anything but normal. I thought that much had been established by now.

And after my eyes locked with a hue of green so stunning and otherworldly for a second blip in recent history, I was reminded that there was a place for beautiful, perfect people in this world. People who could suck the air and energy from a room with just one look, and I wasn't one of them, nor was I deserving of a glance from her jade eyes.

***

"Things are looking good over here, my friend. Very good indeed," Ivan—the one and only person I could come close to calling a friend—said. He walked slowly past an open grave I'd dug that morning after receiving notice from a local funeral home. "You did that by shovel?"

I shrugged nonchalantly, then nodded. "Yeah, still waiting on the guy to fix the backhoe."

"He'd better show up soon. It's going to get mighty cold, mighty fast."

Ivan wasn't too much older than me at forty-six, but what little hair he had left was grayer than Nana's when she'd died, and he walked with a limp due to arthritis. Sometimes, he even sported a cane when the pain got to be too much to handle, reminding me of Mr. Monopoly, especially when he insisted on donning his top hat. I had taken over for him as caretaker after his condition got too bad for him to continue working such a physically demanding job, but he still made sure to stop by every so often, and I couldn't say I minded all that much.

I didn't care much for having friends, but Ivan was one I was usually glad to have around. Maybe it was because we had an understanding I hadn't found in most people.

Ivan appreciated the desire for little human interaction, and we respected each other's need for solitude. Phone calls and texts were infrequent, if they happened at all, and his visits were typically limited to once a month, if that.

"He said they were waiting on the new bucket," I explained. "It had to be back-ordered."

Ivan stuffed his hands into his pockets and shook his head. "What a nuisance."

"It'd probably be easier to just get a new backhoe."

"Yeah, but you know nobody's going to spring for that until the old piece of junk kicks the bucket." He snorted and glanced my way with a lopsided grin. "Get it?"

I reluctantly lifted one side of my mouth in a tight-lipped smile. "Sometimes, you have jokes."

"Wouldn't kill you to smile every now and then, Chuck. Might be exactly what the doctor ordered."

Ivan limped along toward the house. While I normally moved at a brisker pace, I never walked faster than he did. He never commented on it, but I knew he must have noticed because every so often, he'd try to pick up speed, only to wince and slow down again.

"Take it easy, old timer," I'd tease, never mind that he was only eight years my senior, and he'd roll his eyes and mutter something about getting off his lawn.

But today, he didn't bother moving faster than he was comfortable as we moseyed along to the cottage. Maybe it was the weather—delightfully cloudy and always two seconds away from raining—or maybe it was the company.

For me, surprisingly, it was both.

Ivan's visit today had caught me off guard, but it'd scratched half of that insistent itch to feel some semblance of companionship. I hoped it would be enough to refill my proverbial bucket before his next visit.

"I'm getting married," Ivan blurted out, completely unprompted.

I tucked my hair behind my ear as I glanced at him, startled by the news. "Why did I think you were single?"

"I was until a month ago," he explained, a whimsical smile on his face.

I widened my eyes, taken aback. "And you're getting *married*?"

"Kid, I'm forty-six years old. At the rate I'm going, I have far more years behind me than ahead of me. I met Lyla at a bookstore, and we … oh, I just don't know, Chuck. I always thought that whole love at first sight thing was a farce, invented by the same people who believed in Valentine's Day—"

"Because it is," I interjected, laughing incredulously.

"No," he argued lightly, shaking his head and keeping his eyes on the ground as we turned up the path. "It's not. You'd understand if it happened to you."

"Well, listen"—I pulled my keys out and unlocked the door to a place we'd both called home at one point or another—"if you're happy, I'm happy for you."

"Oh, I'm happy."

"Then, I guess I'm happy too."

I hung my keys beside the door and pulled off my jacket, just in time to catch the dubious look in Ivan's eyes. It was enough to furrow my brow as I hung my jacket up on the coat rack.

"What's that look for?"

"Well, no offense, Chuck, but I don't know that *happy* is the word I'd use to describe you."

A noise akin to a growl rose in my throat. "Ivan. Seriously. You know I hate it when you call me Chuck."

Ivan ignored the complaint—he usually did—as he pulled off his black-framed glasses and used the hem of his shirt to buff them clean. "I've known you for years, and I'm not sure I've ever seen you crack a *real* smile."

There was no reason to honor that statement with a reply. So, instead, I asked, "Coffee?"

"One cup. I have to skedaddle in a few minutes. Need to hurry home and cook dinner for my lady love."

Lady love? I released a huff that sounded more begrudged than intended on my way to the kitchen.

It wasn't that I was particularly against the idea of love or romance in regard to other people. I was accepting of the happiness others found in their lives, and I had witnessed my parents' devotion to each other up until the day they died. But I couldn't help my own miserable luck in that department—or Luke's for that matter.

"Been drawing anything good lately?" Ivan asked as I walked into the brick-walled kitchen and opened a cabinet.

"I haven't been drawing much, period," I replied.

"What's this then?"

I glanced through the open doorway into the adjacent living room to find Ivan peering down at the open sketch pad on the table between the wingback chairs.

Grabbing two mugs from the cabinet, I replied, "I did that a few months ago."

"Well, it's excellent," he said. "I know I've said it a hundred times, but you're very talented."

"More like a thousand times, but thank you." I grabbed the canister of instant coffee packets. "Decaf?"

Ivan groaned before replying, "No, but ... yeah. I have to be up early tomorrow. Going to Connecticut to check out some bakeries. Lyla and I both agree that a memorable cake is an absolute *necessity*."

Connecticut. My feet froze on their way to the kettle. My lungs stuttered and coughed. I wouldn't ask. I wouldn't demand an explanation as to why they were tasting cake in Connecticut and not Massachusetts when I was sure there were perfectly good bakeries here in Salem. But I wouldn't draw attention to my anxiety and panic. Instead, I forced myself to think about how strange it was that Ivan was suddenly in a relationship while the ghosts of past broken hearts clawed their sharp, spectral nails up my throat.

"Maybe we should double date. Lyla has a younger—"

"Oh, no," I interrupted, leaning my back against the counter and crossing my arms, grateful for this change in topic. "I'm thrilled for you; don't get me wrong. But I don't do that double-date stuff."

"All right." He smirked and lifted his shoulders. "I'm just saying, Lyla is quite the looker, and her sister is just as beautiful."

The kettle whistled, and I poured the water into the two mugs. The black powder billowed in the clear water before being swallowed into darkness. The scent of strong, bitter instant coffee hung heavy in the air.

"Milk?"

My friend hummed with contemplation, then said, "No, but I'll take some sugar if you have any."

I took the jar of sugar down from off the fridge and carried it into the living room with Ivan's mug and a spoon. I placed them on the end table next to the wingback chair he'd taken a seat in.

"Help yourself."

"Thank you kindly, my good man."

I went back to the kitchen to grab my own mug, and when I returned to the living room, Ivan had already begun sipping his coffee, then wincing and scrunching his nose.

"Oh Lord, that's sweet as molasses," he groused, smacking his lips and sucking his teeth. "Absolutely delightful."

I sat in the identical wingback chair across from his and crossed one leg over the other as I leaned back. While Ivan might've liked his coffee to be full of enough sugar to rot his teeth from his skull, I preferred mine to bite at my tongue with the strength of its sharp, nutty flavor. So much that while it might've been decaffeinated, the taste alone was enough to keep me jolted awake for hours.

Whatever it took to keep the nightmares away.

For the next ten minutes, Ivan and I drank our coffee and talked about recent books we'd read. Neither of us had found anything quite worth recommending, so instead, we critiqued and nitpicked until our mugs were empty. Then, he stood with decorum and announced it was time to head home to his better half.

"I'll give you a ride to your car," I said, already grabbing my jacket and keys.

"You're a gracious man, Chuck. Don't let anybody tell you otherwise."

"Nobody else tells me shit, Ivan," I muttered as I opened the door. "And nobody in my life has ever had the balls to call me Chuck."

Not even my worst enemy.

"You gonna cry, Charlie boy?"

Where the hell did that come from?

I resisted the urge to flinch at the never forgotten, but rarely thought about nickname as Ivan reached up and patted my cheek.

"That's because nobody else has ever loved you like I do," he said, smiling and making his round cheeks even rounder.

***

I pulled the utility truck into the lot near the front gate, where Ivan's car was parked. He opened the passenger door and carefully dropped himself out, wincing when his feet hit the ground.

"How's the hip doing?" I asked, offering an empathetic grimace.

"Not great," he replied honestly before shrugging. "But we can't do anything about the hands we're dealt, Chuck. All we can do is hobble our way through life and thank the man upstairs that things aren't worse. Because they can always be worse, my friend. *Always*."

For as long as I'd known him, Ivan's attitude toward life had always been one of nonchalant realism and aggravating gratitude. He rolled with the punches and tolerated each and every one, and I guessed maybe that was another reason we got along. I might not have been as grateful, but I was skilled at simply tolerating life and trudging my way through, even when giving up entirely seemed like a far more comfortable option.

"I'll come back soon," Ivan promised, looking up into the truck's cab. "I'll bring a wedding invitation."

The idea of attending a party of any size was enough to make the top three layers of my skin tingle with buzzing wasp-like nerves and red flags. But I forced a nod and wished my friend a good night. Then, he closed the door and limped away to his little sedan.

I waited as he got inside, making sure his hip didn't suddenly give out on him, and offered a half-hearted wave as he drove away. Then, I lingered for a moment, looking out the gate toward the hotel across the street from the cemetery, reminding myself, as I did every now and then, that there was an entire bustling world outside of my forty acres of quiet seclusion.

A woman with long black hair came into view, her face tipped downward as she looked at her phone. She wore an outfit of all black—sweater, lug-soled boots, and the tightest jeans I'd ever seen. A black leather satchel was worn across her chest, the bag smacking rhythmically against her hip as she walked.

I couldn't know for sure why I felt the need to watch her initially. Honestly, I felt a little like a voyeuristic creep, eyeing this beautiful woman as she walked alone just after sunset. But my gut felt the pull, felt the need to keep a watchful eye over her, and so I did. And that was when I spotted the tall, hooded man rapidly approaching her from behind.

My spine straightened as I narrowed my eyes at him, watching as he sped up. The woman quickly glanced over her shoulder, then hurried her pace, but she wasn't fast enough. The guy grabbed her by the arm, forcibly pulled her along as she struggled, and disappeared through the row of towering rhododendrons against the hotel's shadowed outer walls.

"Dammit," I grumbled as my hands clenched the steering wheel, simultaneously angry that pieces of shit like this existed in the world and angry that I'd have to get out of my car because of it.

But I did without hesitation, leaving the key in the ignition as I ran through the open cemetery gate and across the street, already dialing 911 for the second time in my life and narrowly dodging an oncoming car as I spoke to the dispatcher. I gave her the address of the cemetery, told her the hotel was across the street, then hung up as I listened for the woman's muffled pleas coming from behind the screen of bushes. I followed the sound of her voice as I slipped through the narrow crevice between the hotel's entrance and the trees.

Then, as my eyes adjusted to the shadowy dark, I spotted them. The front of his body was pressed against the back of hers. He held one hand over her mouth while his other worked to undo his jeans—hers were already pulled halfway down her thighs. Only a sliver of pale skin was visible beneath the length of her sweater, but I prickled at the sight. Violent fury rushed through my bloodstream, hot and angry. I didn't say a word as I made my quick approach, reached into my pocket, and pulled out the box cutter I kept on me. In one smooth, fluid motion, I released the blade and wrapped my arm around his throat, holding the box cutter's sharpened tip just beneath his chin with my other hand.

"Holy shit!" he cried through a surprised gasp, as if he had any right to be afraid.

"Let her go," I hissed into his ear. "Now."

The woman screamed beneath his palm when she realized they were no longer alone, and whether that scream was out of relief or an escalation of fear, I couldn't be sure. It didn't matter. She'd know soon enough that I wasn't someone to be afraid of.

Her assailant didn't move a muscle though, apart from his pathetic, fear-induced quivering. "I don't know what you want from me, man—"

"I want you to *let her go*," I repeated, enunciating every word as the tip of the blade pressed deeper and pierced his skin.

"Shit, shit, shit." He panicked, his breathing escalating close to hyperventilation. "Okay, okay, man. I'll let her go."

He removed his hand from her mouth, and she gasped, hiccuping with a sob.

I stepped backward, taking him along with me. What her sweater and dropped jeans didn't cover was now exposed to the elements and watchful eyes. With the blade still pressed to his chin, I turned us away, giving her privacy.

"We're not looking. Get dressed," I ordered, trying to tamp my anger down enough to speak gently.

"Thank you, thank you, thank you," she chanted in a quivering whisper, and I listened as she shakily pulled up her underwear and jeans.

Sirens sounded in the near distance.

"You hear that?" I said to the man I still held by the throat, my mouth moving against his ear. "They're coming for you."

"Ah, fuck, man," he wailed, and I realized he was crying. I almost laughed at the absurdity of it. "I'm on probation!"

"Then, I guess you should've been on your best behavior, but …" I sighed, feigning disappointment. "Oh well."

The flashing lights approached and stopped, a cascade of red, white, and blue broken by the shadowing trees surrounding us, reminding me of one Halloween night I'd rather forget entirely while knowing I never ever would. The guy continued to cry and shiver as I held the blade to his flesh, and I listened to the sound of car doors opening.

"You gonna be a big boy and go out there yourself, or do I have to take you?"

"I-I-I'll go."

"Well, okay. But just remember, if you run, the cops will catch you. And if they don't, then I will. I'm pretty fast." I gave his chin a nudge with the blade, turning his head to pin his wide, frightened eyes with my glare. "Do you understand?"

His head jittered with a nod. "Y-yes."

I released him from my hold and gave him a hefty shove forward. "Good boy. Now, go."

He shook his arms out and began to step out from the bushes. "F-fucking psycho."

"Hey, asshole, I wasn't the one grabbing women off the street," I countered with a roll of my eyes, turning in the direction of the woman with the black hair, still standing against the building's shadowed exterior.

Then, I asked in a gentler tone, "Are you okay?"

The flashing lights revealed more of her face to me now, and—*oh shit*—I recognized her. I'd recognize her anywhere. She was that woman from Jolie Tea this afternoon, the one who'd been sitting with the tattoo artist. I'd bumped into her weeks ago, right outside of that restaurant, Village Tavern. The one with the most ethereal green eyes I'd ever seen in my life. More vibrant than every emerald and peridot unearthed from the planet's crust.

Those eyes were wide and frightened now, like gemstones swimming in a sea of crystal tears, as she barely nodded.

"Th-thank you," she whispered, understandably shaken as she wrapped her arms around herself to grip her elbows.

"Just doing what anyone would have done," I muttered, retracting the box cutter's blade and tucking it back into my pocket.

"No," she replied, her voice breathless and hushed. "N-not everyone would've."

I held her gaze for a moment. It was a statement that begged a question, and it also held a truth I knew too well. My intuitive gut tugged, and my curiosity demanded that I continue the conversation, but she had to speak with the police, and I had to get back to the utility truck, and it was better for both of us if we went our separate ways.

The adrenaline from the altercation was already wearing off, and there were my nerves again. Reminding me that pretty women and I never mixed well.

"Come on, Charlie. Give her your number." Luke broke through the fog, and I huffed in reply.

"No," I said to her and the voice of my faraway brother, focusing on nothing but speaking that one simple word and taking a deep breath. "I-I guess not."

Then, I turned and slipped away, denying myself one more glance at a woman like her, too beautiful to deserve the attention of a monster like me.

CHAPTER EIGHT

CONNECTICUT, AGE SEVENTEEN

There was one time in elementary school when my art teacher had instructed the class to pick any color and draw any animal. I chose to draw a spider—always my favorite of all the creatures—with a black crayon because it was also my favorite color.

I was incredibly proud of that drawing and couldn't wait to show my mom, excited about how lifelike it looked compared to some of the primitive stick figures a few of my other classmates had scribbled on their sheets of construction paper. But when I showed my teacher, she gave me an F on the assignment before proceeding to hold my drawing up to show the rest of the class what not to do.

All because I'd chosen black instead of a *color*.

I was seven years old and made to look like a fool in front of a classroom of kids who'd already decided they hated me.

I'd thrown that drawing out on my way back to my seat, and I seldom allowed myself to draw again, no matter how much I'd enjoyed it then as a kid.

But the thing about experiencing immense trauma and grief was that nothing that had happened before seemed to matter anymore. And those horrible, soul-consuming emotions had a way of making a guy feel like a boiling pot, full and ready to bubble over, and that was exactly what had happened shortly after my parents died.

I had been fifteen years old and pulsing with unimaginable pain, desperate for a release that nothing else could provide. So, on a rainy night a few months after I'd last spoken to Mom and Dad, in a fit of tears and snot and blubbering sobs, I grabbed a black permanent marker from my desk and scribbled exactly what I'd been feeling inside onto the back of my white bedroom door.

Luke heard the outburst from down the hall—in the middle of fucking Melanie, I was sure, since that was all he ever seemed to do those days—and knocked, asking if I was okay. Of course, I wasn't okay—neither of us were—but when I let him in, I expected him to yell at me when he saw my ruined door. Toddlers weren't supposed to color on walls, let alone teenagers, and I had once again broken the rules.

But instead of getting mad, he was silent. He stared at that door with his hands on his hips, his eyes growing wide and his mouth hanging open, before breathlessly uttering only one word. "*Damn.*"

I didn't say anything in reply, unsure of how to take his single-worded response. He'd said it the way one did when they were impressed by something, and I tried to understand why. I stood back and stared at the graffiti—a black-and-white sketch of a long-legged spider trapped inside a wild and chaotic storm. Drenched in rain, surrounded by bolts of jagged lightning, the spider wore a look of devastating horror—and I knew exactly how he felt. But I still couldn't understand what Luke was so taken aback by. Yet, after the initial shock wore off, he told Melanie he'd be right back and took me out to buy a box of Sharpies and a few cheap sketchbooks. Then, on our way out of the store, he said to start drawing and never stop.

"But I'm not good at it," I had said, looking into the bag from the local craft store.

Luke snorted, shaking his head from behind the wheel of his truck. "No, Charlie, you're not *good* at it. You're fucking amazing, and that's something to hold on to. Shit, I wish I had something like that. I'm not good at anything but fucking up."

The compliment stirred something else inside me as my eyes welled up with unexpected tears. But these tears weren't like the ones I'd cried while destroying my bedroom door. These were pulled from a feeling that wasn't anger or grief or loneliness.

For the first time in months, I actually felt good.

Maybe even happy ... if I even knew what happy was anymore.

So, I had done exactly what Luke had said. I didn't stop drawing, and two years later, I was sitting on my bed, filling the page of my sketchbook with a black-eyed portrait of my mother. Ghostly in figure, she stared out from the page with sadness written in her unshed tears.

I liked to believe she missed me as much as I missed her.

I liked to believe she'd cry for me if she still could.

"Hey."

Luke's gruff voice startled me, and I looked up from my drawing to find him in my open doorway.

"Hey," I parroted, holding his gaze for a second before looking back to finish the damp, limp strands of her hair.

"You ready?"

"Not going."

He sighed and entered the room, dropping down onto the end of my bed with a huff. "Dude, come on."

It was only three o'clock in the afternoon, and I noticed that his breath already smelled like booze. Luke wasn't an alcoholic—I didn't think so anyway—but I was starting to wonder when it was he'd begun drinking for the hell of it and not just when he was hanging out with his friends. Come to think of it, I couldn't remember when he'd last hung out with his friends at all.

"Mom never thought I needed therapy," I countered, knowing that using the mom card was cheap and easy. But it was no less the truth.

Mom had looked at my anxiety and nerves as just being a part of who I was, and in what way was that a lie? If I was supposed to be an awkward loner, meant to deal with the occasional panic attack, then why should I push myself to be anything else? But Luke and Melanie didn't agree, and they thought they were the boss of me now.

"Melanie thinks—"

"Oh, is *she* my mom now?" I fired back, stilling my marker and glaring up at my older brother.

Melanie seemed to be calling a lot of shots lately. Some of them weren't all that terrible—like insisting we clean the bathrooms once a week and making sure we had dinner every night, even if those dinners were simple and cheap. But some of the shit she thought was a good idea was really starting to piss me off, like suggesting I see someone to manage the demons that'd had ahold of me since I was a child.

"Oh, knock it the hell off, Charlie," Luke grumbled, shaking his head. "Stop acting like she's a fucking bad guy, okay? I thought you liked her."

"I didn't say I don't like her," I replied defensively. Which, for the record, was true. I didn't dislike Melanie. But there had been a time when I liked her more than I did now.

Luke ignored me and continued, "She just thinks it would help you to talk to someone, all right? Like, I don't know if you realize this, but Mom coddled the shit out of you—"

"Don't talk about Mom," I warned him, leveling him with a look that I wished would make him decide to leave me alone.

He released a sigh and glanced at the drawing in my lap. "I'm not saying she did anything *wrong*, okay? I'm saying, we—*I* just think that maybe it's time to try something different. And would it honestly kill you to give it a shot? Like, seriously? Because if you really think you're gonna croak the second you walk into her office, then let me know 'cause I'll—"

"God, will you shut up?" I rolled my eyes and dropped the sketchbook on the bed and capped my marker. "I'll freakin' go, okay?"

Luke stood up, grabbed both sides of my face, and pulled me in to plant a sloppy kiss on my cheek. "Good boy."

I shoved him away and climbed off the bed, ready to stuff my feet into my sneakers when he stopped me.

"Wait. You're wearing that?"

I looked down at my black sweatpants and black Type O Negative T-shirt. "Uh ... yes?"

He raised an eyebrow. "Could you, like, I dunno, throw on a pair of jeans or something?"

"Oh, is that one of Melanie's rules too?"

"No, wiseass. I'm just thinking the doctor might appreciate it if you don't waltz into her office with whatever the fuck you have stuck to those pants you have on. Like, fuck, Charlie. When's the last time you changed your clothes?"

I sighed and trudged my way through the piles of laundry on the floor until I spotted a patch of dark blue peeking out from between a heap of black T-shirts. I pulled off the sweatpants, leaving me in nothing but boxers, and then I snatched the dirty jeans from off the floor—at least I thought they were dirty—and stepped into them.

"Happy?" I asked, zipping the fly and buttoning them up.

"Thrilled."

"Great." I stuffed my feet into my sneakers and brushed past him on my way out the door. "Now, let's go."

***

I hated to admit it, but talking to the psychologist—Dr. Sibilia—wasn't as bad as I'd thought it would be.

She walked into the room, wearing jeans, a Grateful Dead T-shirt, and Adidas sneakers. She didn't look much older than Luke or Melanie—even though she probably was—and she began the session by fanning herself with the sheets of paper in her hand and mentioning how much she fucking hated the heat.
　I barely laughed, barely curled my lips into a half smile, but dammit, it happened, and I knew she had noticed.
　"So, you are ... Charles Corbin, I see," she said as she plopped into the chair across from mine, her eyes scanning the paper.
　"Charlie," I muttered, leaning back and widening my knees.
　She looked up. "What's that?"
　"Ch-Charlie," I stammered, speaking a little louder. "N-nobody calls me Charles."
　"Gotcha." She plucked the pen from behind her ear and scribbled as she enunciated slowly, "Char-lee. All righty, great. So, Charlie, what brings you in here today?"
　"My stupid brother and his girlfriend made me."

Dr. Sibilia nodded as she continued to write. "Note to self: brother and brother's girlfriend are stupid." She looked up from the paper and offered a smile. "I see. So, why did they make you come in? There's gotta be some kinda reason, right? Other than them being stupid."

I lifted a hand off the arm of the chair and gestured in lieu of a shrug. "I-I don't know. They think I'm depressed o-or that I n-need to-to do something about my panic attacks or, um ... or something."

"Well, let me ask you this: do you think you're depressed?"

"Maybe."

She cocked her head. "And what makes you think that?"

"Both of my parents died in a car crash two years ago, and I was on the phone with them when it happened," I said easily for some reason I couldn't quite put my finger on. "So, I dunno. I think that's a pretty good reason for someone to be depressed."

Her eyes took on an expression of deep sympathy. "I'm very sorry to hear that, Charlie."

I dropped my gaze to my fidgeting hands and swallowed at the violent rise of emotion in my throat. I wouldn't allow myself to speak, afraid that I'd cry in front of her. So, I just lifted one shoulder in a pathetic excuse for a shrug, like my parents being dead didn't matter—but it did, and she seemed to know it.

"And I'd have to agree," she continued gently. "That's actually an excellent reason for someone to be depressed."

I gave her a little nod as I chewed on my bottom lip, waiting for the lump in my throat to drop back down to wherever it had come from.

"You know, Charlie, I understand that we just met and all, but I do want you to know that you are safe to do or say anything you want in here. I won't judge you if you wanna cry or scream or beat the living crap out of that really, really ugly chair you're sitting in."

The lump slowly began to ease up, and I sniffed a nearly silent laugh, then nodded.

"Cool. Okay. Now, why don't you tell me a little about these panic attacks? When did they start?"

Just as I'd started to feel comfortable, I began to tense up. Even though it had felt like a lifetime ago, I remembered that one time Mom had taken me to a doctor—that old guy who looked like Grandpa with a mustache.

He'd thought I was crazy.

Even now, I clearly recalled the word psychotic, *although I couldn't recall in what context.*

Dr. Sibilia cocked her head and eyed me with concern. "What's wrong? Is there something you'd like to tell me? Or something else you'd prefer to talk about instead? We're getting to know each other right now. You can say or—"

"No," I answered flatly.

"Okay," she replied, just as friendly as before. "Can you tell me what about discussing your panic attacks made you shut down just now?"

I picked at my jeans. They were definitely dirty. Something dry and crusty was stuck to one of the thighs, but I couldn't find it in me to be embarrassed about that.

"M-my mom took me to a doctor once," I said. The words came out mumbled, but she seemed to understand as she nodded and encouraged me to go on. "He thought I was crazy."

"And you're afraid I'll think you're crazy too. Is that right?"

I shrugged.

Dr. Sibilia laid her clipboard and pen onto her lap before resting her elbows on her knees and clasping her hands together.

"Charlie, I will never use that word in this office. Do you understand that? I will never think you are crazy."

My eyes met hers with a challenge. "What about psychotic? Do you like that word?"

"Is that what he called you?"

My silence was response enough, and she shook her head.

"I can see now why your mother never wanted to take you to another doctor," she said softly. "And she was right to protect you. But I want to protect you, too, Charlie, and I can promise you I will never make you feel bad for the way you are. You have my word."

And then the most amazing thing happened.

I believed her.

I knew in that moment that I could trust her, and I nodded before telling her everything I could in the two hours we had. I told her about my panic attacks. I told her about the anxiety I had in social situations and the bad feelings I'd get in my gut that often turned out to be founded in truth.

And you know what?

Not only did she seem to believe me, but she never once called me crazy.

***

After our parents had died, their life insurance policies had covered what was left of their mortgage on the house while still leaving a sizable chunk for Luke and me to split. We each opened bank accounts to use the money as we saw fit—and I know you're probably thinking that one or both of us blew it all on stupid stuff, but you'd be wrong. My money at this point had been left untouched, and contrary to what might be popular belief, Luke wasn't a complete idiot. He realized before I did that whatever money we'd gotten from our parents wouldn't last forever, so he made the very mature and very surprising decision to quit his job at the pizza place, skip his high school graduation, and go to work at Melanie's dad's auto repair shop.

He'd started in the office, pushing papers and organizing the files, while he went to trade school at night and moved on to fixing cars. And now, two years later, he was still enjoying the work he did there, even if Frank—Melanie's dad—still wasn't all that thrilled that his daughter was living with us instead of him.

Anyway, the money that Luke made at the shop was decent enough, but he pinched his pennies, ensuring he got the most out of every single one. It was because of this that we hardly ever got the chance to do frivolous things, like eat out unless it was a special occasion.

But I guessed Luke considered my first successful day of therapy to be a special occasion because after my appointment, we swung by Melanie's job at the local drugstore to pick her up, and then we were off to Friendly's for a rare dinner outside of the house.

I was in the middle of eating my cheeseburger when Luke kicked my shin underneath the table with his steel-toed boot.

"Hey!" I grunted and kicked back. "What the hell, dick? That hurt."

"Did you just kick him?" Melanie asked, shoving against Luke's shoulder.

Luke ignored both of our protests and complaints and leaned over the table, gesturing for me to come closer. I rolled my eyes and sighed before bringing my face to his.

"What?" I hissed.

"There's a chick at that table over there—"

I followed his gaze and looked over my shoulder, but Luke just as quickly kicked my shin again.

"Will you cut it out?! Fucking hell, Luke," I whined, reaching under the table and rubbing the spot that I knew would bruise by the end of the night.

"You're not supposed to *look*, you freakin' moron," he whispered harshly. "She's been staring at you since we walked in here."

I snorted, returning my attention to my dinner with a disbelieving huff. "Yeah, okay."

Melanie's blue eyes flicked toward the table Luke had been referring to. "Oh, no. She *definitely* likes you," she whispered in a teasing tone, reaching out to nudge my wrist. "And you know what? She looks like your type."

"Yeah," Luke agreed, bringing the straw of his Coke to his mouth. "Like she spends all day sucking the blood from her victims while deciding what color shirt to wear tomorrow—black or blacker."

I couldn't help my smile as it reluctantly spread across my face, knowing my cheeks were burning scarlet. Melanie wouldn't have lied. She might've crossed a couple of lines recently—making decisions that weren't her business to make, even if they were for the better—but she didn't lie. Luke might've just to tease me and feel bad about it later, but not Melanie. And the thought of a girl actually staring at me and maybe even liking what she saw ...

I didn't know how to deal with that.

It had never happened before.

"So?"

My eyes lifted from my cheeseburger to meet Luke's taunting gaze. "Huh?"

He glanced at Melanie, incredulous. "I dunno what to do with this kid." Then, he looked back at me and nudged his chin in the direction of the table behind us. "You gonna talk to her or what?"

My jaw fell open as I shook my head incessantly. "What? No, I'm not gonna talk to her."

Luke didn't look amused. "Seriously?"

"That'd be weird!" I glanced at Melanie, begging her with my eyes to back me up. "Right?"

But she didn't seem to agree. "Well, I don't know. I guess it'd be one thing if she wasn't the one interested, but ..." She shrugged helplessly, dodging her eyes quickly toward the other table and back again. "She looks pretty interested to me, Charlie."

"Oh God," I groaned, dropping my burger and thrusting my hands into my hair. "I can't just ... *talk* to her. What would I even say? I don't—"

With an impatient groan, Luke took a hefty bite of his sandwich before dropping it back onto the plate. Then, he stood up and began sauntering in the other direction before I could finish talking.

"Where are you going?" I hissed, turning in my seat to stare at his broad back. "*Luke*! What are you—"

My older brother stopped, and that was when I saw her. A girl, about my age, with shiny black hair pulled into a fancy, long braid cascading over one shoulder, dressed in a black sweater and black jeans and black boots. Her eyes were rimmed heavily in onyx, and her lips were painted a deathly shade of pale.

Melanie was right; she was my type. And really freakin' cute.

"Excuse me. I don't mean to bother you, but my name is Luke Corbin," my older brother said, pressing his hand to his chest before thrusting that same hand in the direction of our table. "I couldn't help but notice that you were staring at my freaky little brother, Charlie, over there, and because he's too shy to say something himself,

I'm here to ask what your name is and if you'd like to give him your number."

Her eyes looked about as surprised as mine, and then she looked at me. My heart hammered wildly, attempting to jump out of my chest and up my throat. I swallowed repeatedly before turning away, horrified and completely embarrassed, and looked across the table at Melanie.

"I hate him," I whispered—and why the hell was my voice so high?

Melanie smiled apologetically, but there was also excitement twinkling in her eyes. She found this amusing. She found it adorable. But, Jesus Christ, I was so humiliated and freaked out, and why would a girl want me to have her number anyway? She would probably go back to her friends and laugh about the loser at Friendly's in the Type O Negative shirt. Maybe they'd look up our house number and prank call a few times, come up with some ridiculous plan in which they'd torture me for a while with promises of dates and long walks on the beach or something, and then they'd forget all about me.

Girls didn't want guys like me; they wanted guys like my brother. Confident. Cool. Good-looking. I wasn't any of those things. I was the loner with the sketchbook, dirty jeans, and a brand-new shrink who apparently *didn't* think I was psychotic.

What a catch.

A moment later, Luke wandered back over to the table and dropped a napkin in front of me. "Her name is Amanda, and that's her number. She says to call tomorrow night when she's not at work."

I stared at the napkin and the handwriting scribbled onto it. It was bubbly and neat, so much nicer than mine, and she had written the first *A* in her name as a star. Something pinched in my chest, something maybe close to excitement, and I felt the good kind of nerves you got when you were about to do something you'd always wanted to do.

Luke dropped back in his seat across from mine and lifted his sandwich to his mouth, resuming his dinner. "Oh, and, hey, Charlie?"

"Huh?" I looked up, stunned and bewildered.

"You're welcome," he said with a smirk and a wink, then took a bite.

CHAPTER NINE

CONNECTICUT, AGE EIGHTEEN

Our first date had been in the living room.
Luke and Melanie had made themselves scarce that night, using the excuse to go out to the movies. I ordered a pizza and sat on the couch, biting my nails and feeling oddly similar to the way I had the night my parents died. Anxiously waiting with a gnawing ache in the pit of my stomach. My intuition was rarely wrong, and at that moment, I wondered what it was trying to tell me and why—if it was, in fact, my intuition and not just the nerves talking.

Dr. Sibilia had told me to try and listen when it came calling, but I couldn't seem to hear what it was trying to say then.

But after a little while, before I could allow myself to overthink and overanalyze too much, Amanda showed up, wearing a gauzy black dress and black boots, and I stopped thinking about anything but her and her lips and her boobs and her ability to make me stupid and single-minded.

And that was how it'd been for a total of six months. An entire half of a year.

She'd been with me through a Halloween, a birthday, a Christmas, and a New Year. I had given her a drawn bouquet of black roses for Valentine's Day, even though she'd said Valentine's was for losers, and we celebrated over a dinner of homemade lasagna and garlic bread.

I had cooked, but Melanie had helped.

Amanda had given me my first girlfriend and my first kiss. She'd taken my virginity, and with it, she'd taken my heart, giving me my first—but not my last—taste of what it was like to fall hard and fast.

It might've been silly of me, but I started to believe that we'd be like Luke and Melanie—perfect. Together through the best of times and the worst of nightmares. And even though I was only eighteen, I felt so certain that I could imagine myself with her forever.

Watching terrible movies for the sake of ignoring them to have sex on the couch while Luke and Melanie were at work. Cooking dinners I knew sucked, but she ate them anyway. Sketching her perfect, porcelain-like face while she was reading a book in my dad's old chair or focusing on the TV or looking up to the sky on a moonlit night.

I had never been in love before, but, dammit, this had to be it. The way I felt about her ... I couldn't put any other word to the emotion that flooded my chest any other time I looked at her.

Love.

I had to tell her. I knew it as I looked at her instead of watching *The Matrix*. She needed to hear the words, even though I was terrified she wouldn't say them back. I wondered if that was something I should mention to Dr. Sibilia. I wondered if she'd be able to help, as she had with so many other things in the months since I'd started seeing her.

Amanda glanced up at me and caught my stare, then smirked as her cheeks splotched red. "What?"

"You're beautiful," I said on a shaky breath, feeling my smile grow.

She rolled her eyes and rested her head back on my shoulder. "You're insane."

"My doctor doesn't think so, but maybe she's wrong. Either way, you're still beautiful."

She snorted. "You're just trying to get into my pants."

I laughed as my face heated and my dick began to swell. "I mean, I guess that'd be a bonus …"

Amanda lifted her head again and shifted to kneel beside me. She laid her black-nailed hand over my engorged crotch and leaned in to bring her lips close to mine. "Then, maybe we—"

"All right, kiddies, that's enough," Luke declared boisterously, entering the living room.

Amanda hopped backward a whole seat cushion and made no secret of her exaggerated eye roll. She crossed her arms and glared at my older brother as he walked past us and grabbed his leather jacket from off the back of Dad's recliner.

"Where are you going?" I asked as he put the jacket on.

"Gonna go down to Tony's and grab a beer with Tommy and Rob."

My brows practically shot into my hairline. I was immediately shocked and suspicious. "Tommy and Rob? Since when do you hang out with them again?"

Luke hadn't seen either of them since the fight he'd gotten into with Ritchie at Mom and Dad's funeral.

Come to think of it, he hadn't spent time with *any* friends, apart from Melanie and me since that day. He only ever made time for us when he wasn't working, and considering it now, I wasn't sure it was a good thing. Not for him. I might have been perfectly content, doing nothing but sitting in my room all day, but Luke? He thrived socially, and I thought it was time he made some new friends. But spending time with the old ones? That I wasn't so sure of.

Especially if the worst of them would be there too. And considering he was seeing Ritchie's brother ...

I highly doubted Ritchie would be far behind.

"They called me up to ask if I wanted to celebrate my birthday. So"—he patted himself down, making sure he had his pack of cigarettes, lighter, keys, and wallet— "I said yes."

I narrowed my eyes warily. Luke's twenty-first birthday had passed a couple of weeks ago. Why would they call him *now* and not then? And why the hell did I feel so betrayed that he was leaving me to spend time with *them*?

"Why would you say yes?"

"Because I wanted to, Charlie. Okay?" Luke's hardened glare pierced through my skin and straight to my heart. The way it used to when we were younger. "I'll be back later. Don't forget a condom, all right? I don't want any baby vampires running around here."

He shot me with a pair of finger guns and a wink before turning and heading out the door before I could respond. He closed it behind him, and maybe I should've let the subject rest, but I couldn't help the way my stomach turned sour. My insides twisted and ached at the thought of him seeing those guys again. Especially when the memory of them leaving with *him*—Ritchie—was still so fresh in my mind. Like it had happened yesterday.

They didn't stay to be with Luke on the day his parents were buried.

They left with Ritchie.

He was more important.

Do they even like *Luke? Does he realize that's not what friends do?*

But you know what? What the hell do I know? I don't even have friends. Luke's my friend. Melanie's my friend. And if I don't have them, then—

"God, finally," Amanda groaned, completely oblivious to the turmoil in my head as she crawled across the couch to unzip my jeans. "Now, I'm gonna make you hard again, and then we're gonna—"

"I ..." I dragged my hand over my face before brushing her away. "No, Amanda, not now. I-I can't focus, okay?"

She sat back on her heels, her hurt and rejection abundant and clear. "You seriously don't wanna do it now? Just like that?"

I gnawed at my bottom lip for a moment as I stared ahead at the TV, not quite processing what was playing, then sighed. "No, it's ... it's not that. I'm just ... I'm thinking, okay?"

She uttered a noise of disgust, and I watched her shake her head from the corner of my eye. "About *Luke*? You can't fuck me right now because you're thinking about your goddamn *brother*?"

"You don't understand."

She stood from the couch and crossed the living room to snatch her fuzzy leopard-print purse from Dad's recliner. I probably should've stopped her from walking away. I probably should've told her to stay, then pinned her to the couch and fucked her hard enough to forget what I was even worried about in the first place.

But what if Ritchie was at Tony's Bar with Luke? What if Luke forgave him for what he'd said the day of our parents' funeral? What if I had to see that asshole again after everything he'd done to me when I was a kid? The past couple of years without him around hadn't been perfect, but it'd been nice to not have him looming over my shoulder, whispering fucked-up nothings into my ear while he pulled my brother further and further away.

So, Amanda grabbed her hoodie from the arm of the recliner and pulled it on, and I remained on the couch, doing absolutely nothing to keep her from leaving.

"I'm going home," she said with a sigh. "If you change your mind and decide you *do* want to fuck me tonight, don't bother calling me. You can go ahead and jerk off yourself."

"You're mad," I stated plainly.

"Yeah, Charlie." She shook her head, incredulous. "I'm fucking mad."

"I'm sorry," I replied, meaning it.

"Right. Sure you are. I'll talk to you later or tomorrow or ... I dunno ... whenever."

She walked out the door, slamming it behind her, and I was alone in that living room once again, left to worry and obsess and panic about everything and nothing, all at once.

***

When Melanie got home from work, she found me sitting on the couch, bouncing my knees and staring at the TV. My thumbnail was wedged between my teeth; my bottom lip was chewed and peeling. She asked what was going on, and when I told her, she was about as suspicious as I'd been, but without the obvious panic.

So, we sat together until eleven o'clock rolled around and she made the decision to go get him herself.

"You wanna come with me?" she asked, but I declined, worried I'd have to face Ritchie. Worried I'd find he was still bigger, still taller, still as menacing as he'd always been. "Okay. I'll be back."

Another hour went by before I heard her car pull into the driveway. Two doors slammed shut, two sets of feet climbed the stoop steps, and then there was a key in the lock, turning and twisting the doorknob. The door swung open, and then a very drunk Luke stumbled inside, nearly tripping over his own feet as he entered the house.

"Charlie!" he crowed, lumbering over to where I now stood. "There's my baby brother!"

His words were slurred and sloppy, and the stench of sour booze attacked my nostrils as he draped an arm over my shoulders.

"Had a good time, huh?" I asked, unamused, now remembering all those times he'd come home drunk, and I had to help him into his room before Mom and Dad could find out.

"The fuckin' *best*, man," he replied, slapping his hand against my chest with every syllable. "*God*, it was so fuckin' *good* to see those guys again. I don't ... I don't even 'member why w-we stopped hangin' out, you know? Like, what did they even *do*?"

Technically, Tommy and Rob hadn't done anything, but wasn't that part of the problem? They might've groaned at Ritchie's commentary, they might've rolled their eyes, but they had never *done* anything to *stop him*. They had tolerated his bullshit, and by association, they were just as guilty.

But I wasn't going to say that to Luke. Not when he was hammered and barely able to keep his eyes open. It was better to let him talk, to smile and nod, and get him into bed so he could sleep this shit off. I could talk to him tomorrow, when his head was on straight, but not now.

Melanie apparently wasn't riding the same wavelength.

She closed the door and secured the lock. Then, with her arms crossed and her mouth downturned in a scowl, she shook her head. "Are you serious?"

He turned in her direction, his head bobbing like it was a ball of lead balancing on a toothpick. "'Scuse me?"

"I asked if you were serious."

Luke pursed his lips and nodded. "Yeah. That's what I thought you said. The fuck is *that* s'posed to mean? Am I serious about *what*?"

"They're *assholes*, Luke. All of them. Every single one of those guys you used to hang out with is a fucking *asshole*."

I shook my head with a warning. "Melanie ..."

"They're my *friends*!" he shouted, the sound cracking against my eardrums and making me flinch.

Clearing my throat, I slipped my arm around his waist and said, "Hey, come on. Let's get you upstairs, okay? You should sleep—"

"Those *friends* haven't called you in *years*, Luke! Those *friends* have done nothing but treat *him*—your *brother*—like shit." She jabbed a finger in my direction. "They talk crap about you behind your back, and they hit on me every single time they see me at work! Is that what *friends* do? Huh?"

Luke shook his head and stumbled, taking a step toward her. "Shut the fuck up, you fuckin' liar. They haven't hit on you. They wouldn't—"

"Oh, okay." She laughed sardonically. "*That's* unbelievable to you, but it's totally okay that they've talked shit about you and your family behind your back for as long as I've known you. *Totally* okay that they've treated Charlie like a piece of fucking trash for no reason whatsoever."

"You don't know any of this shit! God, what the fuck is *wrong* with you?! Why would you—"

"Come on, Luke," I begged, grabbing him around the waist and attempting to steer him in the direction of the stairs. "Let's go to bed, okay?"

"They come into the store sometimes," Melanie said, tightening her stance and nodding. "I hear them talk. They say shit to me. They make fun of you. They say you're *weak*, that you should've dropped Charlie into the system after your parents died instead of taking care of him."

The statement crashed against my chest, shattering my patchwork heart. God, was that true? Was that what people thought? Melanie wouldn't lie. Melanie never lied. What reason would she have now?

Luke startled us both by beginning to cry. Big, blubbering sobs broke through his drunken stupor.

"Shut the fuck up! Goddammit, shut the fuck up!"

"Is that what *friends* say, Luke?" Now, she was crying. Huge, fat tears slid down her cheeks and fell from her chin onto the floor. "Are you cool with your *friends* coming into my store and asking me out and saying they could fuck me better—"

"Go!" He thrust his finger toward the door. "Get the fuck out of my house, you bitch! You fuckin' liar! Get the fuck out!"

"Luke!" I shouted above them, desperate for this to end. "God, guys! Fucking stop, okay? Just stop!"

And like I'd possessed the power to command sound, the room fell silent, save for the ticking of the clock inherited from Mom's grandmother and Luke's heavy breaths. Melanie's lips pressed together as she seethed across the room. She stared at my brother, the tears continuing to fall from her big eyes.

What is going on?!

God, what the hell had happened? What had gone on at that bar? What had been said in that car? I wanted to ask, wanted to demand they give me the play-by-play so that maybe I could fix it, but I knew now wasn't the time. I needed to get Luke to bed. I needed Melanie to stop talking long enough to let me. I needed to draw and call Amanda, if she'd even answer, and I needed to think about everything I was going to say to Dr. Sibilia about this fucking night.

"Fine," Melanie finally said, turning on her heel and opening the door.

"Melanie! Where are you going?" I cried, not caring that I sounded shrill and pathetic.

She didn't look back as she stepped outside. "Sorry, Charlie," was all she said before closing the door.

Luke and I were silent for a minute, staring toward the oval stained-glass window and watching as the headlight beams flickered on, backed away, and disappeared down the street. For the second time tonight, I'd watched a girl I loved walk through that door, and we were both to blame.

I wanted to punch my brother for going out with Tommy and Rob, for getting drunk and saying the shit he'd said to her. Melanie had been nothing but good to us—despite her meddling. She hadn't deserved a word of his vitriol. But, I had to remind myself, he was drunk, and nobody could listen to reason when that very reasoning was impaired.

So, I said nothing as I sighed and steered him in the direction of the stairs, and this time, he complied without so much as a peep.

***

After he fell easily into a snore-broken slumber, I went to my room and closed the door. I picked up my phone and called Amanda, not caring that it was well after one thirty in the morning. I knew she had work the next day, knew she would likely be sleeping, but I didn't care.

I needed to talk to her.

I needed to apologize for everything. For my brother. For worrying and stressing and overthinking.

For being *me*.

I needed to tell her I'd do better. I'd *be* better because I wasn't Luke. I wouldn't make her feel the way he'd made Melanie feel tonight. I wouldn't make her cry, and I would never ever allow her to leave again.

I needed to tell her that I loved her. That I'd marry her if she wanted to. That we could have kids and a life, even if I had no idea how we'd make that happen right now. Nothing mattered. Just me and her and this hopeless ache sitting in the center of my chest.

So, when she answered the phone, I gasped with relief.

"Hi," she said, her tone short.

She was still mad. But that was okay. I understood it now. And after I said what I needed to say, she'd feel differently.

"Hey," I said, breathless and desperate. "Sorry I'm calling so late. It's been a long night, and things are ... things are kind of a wreck right now, but I need to talk to you."

"So, talk."

I didn't love talking to Amanda when she was angry, and she got angry a lot. Her anger made me nervous—I never handled confrontation well—but I wasn't worried in this instance. Because I was so sure that what I was about to say would calm her down and cool her off to the point that she'd forget she was ever angry in the first place.

"I'm sorry," I began, hurrying to get on with it. "I'm sorry about before and for, you know, turning you down. I was just ... y-you don't know ..."

I was stumbling on my words. My nerves were getting the better of me. I could hear Amanda sigh impatiently on the other end, and I squeezed my eyes shut, determined to get through this without making an ass of myself.

I took a deep breath and started over.

"You don't know what I've been through with Luke's friends," I feebly explained. "They were never nice to me, especially this one guy, so when Luke said he was going out tonight—"

"Do you know how sick I am of everything coming down to your fucking brother?"

I pinched the bridge of my nose. "W-what? No, that's not what—"

"It's your brother, or it's your nerves, or you have a stupid panic attack," she said in a mocking tone, and a knot tied itself so tight in my throat that I wasn't sure I'd make it through this call without suffocating. "God, I am so *sick* of it."

"S-sick of *what*?"

"You!" Amanda cried into the phone, and I dropped down onto my bed like a sack of bricks.

"You're sick of *me*?"

"God, we don't even do anything! You're always too afraid, or you don't want to deal with people, or you'd rather hang out with your fucking brother and his loser girlfriend. You don't even drive! What eighteen-year-old doesn't fucking drive?!"

I was under attack, and I didn't know how to fight. Shaking, heart hammering, and lungs struggling to keep up with the rapid puffs being pulled and pushed from my flared nostrils.

"Y-you know why I don't—"

"Right. Because your parents got into a car accident years ago and you're *scared*. Jesus fucking Christ, Charlie. People die every damn day. Get the hell over it."

I couldn't help the tears that filled my eyes at the hateful, belligerent comments she was throwing at me—and not even to my face. This girl—this *coward* I had been certain two minutes ago would be the woman I married—had to spew her hateful comments at me over the damn phone.

At least she can't see me cry.

"I was just going to tell you I loved you," I muttered pitifully, raking my hair back.

Amanda snorted with amusement like it meant nothing at all. Like it was *funny*. "Well, that would've been awkward."

I said nothing. I could only listen to the sound of my heart beating louder and louder with every passing second, knowing that this would be the last time I ever heard her voice.

The last time I'd heard Mom's and Dad's voices was over the phone too.

I swallowed relentlessly at the clotting panic in my throat and waited for her to speak or hang up first. I couldn't be the one to do it. I couldn't be the one to break my own heart.

"Well, I hope you and your brother will be very happy together," she said with a chill in her tone. "Do me a favor and lose my number."

***

My eyes were swollen, and my face was sticky with the tears I had only just stopped crying. It seemed like twenty-four hours had gone by since Amanda had hung up when it'd only been about sixty minutes.

I was thirsty, and my chest hurt with another loss, and all I could think about was grabbing some water from the fridge. I missed my mom. I missed my dad. I wished I could talk to them now and ask how the hell I was supposed to continue living without her when I hadn't yet figured out how to live without them.

I slumped my way down the stairs, not caring about being quiet. Luke was still passed out cold, and I knew a bomb would have to go off to wake him up.

Then, when I stepped into the living room, I found Melanie on the couch. I stopped in my tracks, stunned and relieved and grateful to find her there, awake and watching TV. She lifted her hand in a weak wave as she offered a little, almost-apologetic smile.

"Hey," she whispered, and I realized she'd been crying too.

"Hi."

"What are you still doing up?"

An odd but familiar feeling of being wrapped up tightly in a warm blanket came over me at the question, and I was struck with a revelation I probably should've realized months—no, years—ago.

Melanie might not have been my mom—God, of course not, and I knew nobody would ever, *ever* replace the woman who had loved me unconditionally, perhaps even to a fault, but she was the only female on this planet who made me feel the way Mom had. All of her meddling had simply come from a place of caring, and how could I have thought anything but?

God, I was such a fucking idiot.

"Amanda broke up with me," I stated point-blank.

The sadness in Melanie's eyes only deepened at the announcement. "I'm so sorry, Charlie."

"Yeah ..." I dropped my gaze to the carpet and shuffled my white sock-covered feet.

"Did she say why?"

"Oh, she had a lot of reasons," I huffed sardonically. "Mostly that I'm too anxious and sensitive and I can't drive."

Melanie didn't answer right away. She scowled, forming lines between her brows I hardly ever saw, then shook her head. But her silence remained, so I hung my head and turned to walk toward the kitchen, thinking about Amanda and how I'd never kiss her again. And what if I never got to kiss anyone again ... *ever*? What if I never had sex with anyone else? Hell, what if I didn't *want* sex with anyone else? What if I spent the rest of my life wishing for her and only ever her until the day I died?

God, forever felt like a long time in that moment, and I ached horribly for a thousand things and people I could never be with again, and no amount of wanting or wishing would ever change that.

"Charlie."

I had nearly reached the glow from the night-light in the kitchen when Melanie said my name.

I glanced over my shoulder and asked, "Huh?"

"She's a bitch."

It was my turn to scowl. "No, she's—"

"Yeah, she is. And I'm sorry Luke ever got her number because you are too sweet to deserve someone as nasty and judgmental as her."

It was the last thing I wanted to hear when I had just declared my love for the so-called bitch she spoke of. But Melanie continued speaking, and I was too angry, hurt, startled, and shocked to speak.

"There is nothing *wrong* with being sensitive, Charlie. A lot of guys would benefit from showing their feelings more often. Like your brother," she grumbled irritably and rolled her eyes in the light of the TV. "He could learn something from you."

"But she's not wrong," I argued, finally finding my voice and crossing my arms. "I'm messed up. I don't even go anywhere. I just … hang around here and do nothing all damn day."

Melanie snickered and swung her eyes toward mine. "Yeah, maybe you could learn how to drive at some point, and, okay, you have some anxiety issues, and could you get a job? Sure, and eventually, you will. But you know what? You're in college, you're *ridiculously* talented, and, like …" She lifted her hands from her lap and thrust them toward the ceiling. "You listened to your parents *die*, Charlie! God, the fact that you're able to do *anything* after going through something like that is a freakin' miracle. So many people would have let that completely destroy them. God, I mean, just look at your brother."

I pretended to ignore what she'd said. About listening to my parents die, even as it replayed in my head as I asked, "What about him?"

"He's a fucking wreck."

I shook my head. "No, he's not. He's … he's fine. He's—"

"He's far from *fine*," she cut me off, and at first, I thought she was mad, but … no.

She was worried. Hurt. Sad. "He wants us to think he's fine, but … he's so messed up, and he doesn't talk about anything. He just …" She pressed her lips together and shrugged. "Clams up. Smokes his fucking cigarettes and acts like he's all good. And I guess now, he stays out all night at the bar, getting completely fucking smashed, and—"

"Are you breaking up with him?"

She pinned me with her eyes and pulled in a deep breath before allowing her lips to twitch into a morose smile. "I don't know."

"I don't want you to leave," I admitted in a way that was probably too desperate, but I didn't care.

"I don't want to leave either. And I'm not, like, breaking up with him *now* or anything. I just have to think, and … he needs to get his head out of his ass, and …"

She sighed and leaned back against the couch, returning her attention to the TV.

"I don't know. Anyway, just promise me you won't change, okay? You can better yourself and learn how to drive and whatever you want to do, but just … don't become someone else. Don't change."

CHAPTER TEN

MASSACHUSETTS, PRESENT DAY

Nobody cared about the dead after the living they'd belonged to were gone.

When I had been a kid, I'd think about it sometimes while lying in bed. That, once Luke and I were also gone from this world, nobody would care about our parents anymore, as if they'd never existed. Even if he and I were lucky enough to have kids of our own, those children would never know their grandparents, and it was hard to truly care about people you'd never even met. It was hard to ever call them truly *yours* when your memories of them were made up of nothing but stories.

It was something that had drawn me to Salem. Because while people might not have cared much about the ordinary dead, they undoubtedly cared about those with profound history, and Salem was certainly full of that.

Hell, people from all over the world flocked to this city to remember and pay their respects to those who had been wrongfully persecuted and killed hundreds of years ago. Maybe they, too, felt misunderstood for simply being who they were. Maybe they, too, had faced extreme punishment for something they'd had no choice but to be a part of.

I knew that was certainly the case for me.

So many people cared for Bridget Bishop, Reverend George Burroughs, Martha and Giles Corey, and Elizabeth Howe—among many others—and rightfully so. They *should* be remembered. They *should* be exonerated and respected in ways they never had been in the final moments of their lives.

But nobody cared about Annabel Lee Croft Black. Nobody but me.

Born in 1663 and dead in 1734, Annabel was the oldest soul in my cemetery—the graveyard guardian, some might call her. Her small, flat little marker was tucked just on the other side of the stone fence separating my cottage from the graves. Why she'd been buried there instead of beside her beloved husband, Thaddeus Black—buried somewhere in one of Salem's other cemeteries—I wasn't sure I'd ever know, but I suspected it had something to do with Thaddeus's family disapproving of his marital bonds to an accused witch.

Once a week, while on my rounds, I made sure to leave a flower on her grave, knowing nobody else would. Nobody cared about a seventy-one-year-old felon who'd escaped the hanging rope. She hadn't made the history books like the rest of them. Her story had begun in a town outside of Salem, one no longer written on the map, and she'd gotten lucky and died in her bed, I'd learned after doing some research. Nobody ever looked at her grave, nobody knew it was there, and maybe that had been done on purpose—whether by Thaddeus or someone else—hidden by bigger, more impressive monuments and headstones. Hidden from the accusations, judgment, and torment.

But not from me.

Today, a Sunday like any other, I walked past Luke's bike and hopped the low fence—a shortcut to Annabel's grave I'd discovered on accident while trying to trim a low-hanging branch a few years ago.

"Hey, Anna," I greeted as I normally did while approaching the little worn headstone tucked away between a couple of bushes. "Found a nice lily last night on my way back to the house and thought you might—"

My words were cut short by the sight of a rose, lying precisely beneath the dash Annabel had filled with supposed witchcraft, love, and scandal. Its full bloom and deep, healthy color reminded me at once of the flowers Nana had instructed Luke and me to drop unceremoniously onto our parents' caskets on the day we buried them.

It had been a short while since I'd felt the viselike grip around my lungs, squeezing from me every breath of air I needed to survive. But there it was again—the panic. As strong as the day I'd found that cigarette on Luke's bike. The escalation of my heartbeat. The saliva flooding my mouth. The sticky sweat coating my palms.

"What the f-fuck?" I uttered in a high-pitched, squealed whisper as I turned on my heel, whipping my head this way and that to survey the land around me.

The landscaping went a little wild back here. The trees were fuller; the bushes grew wider. The shadows were darker, stretching long over the cleared but rarely walked path. It would be easy enough for someone to conceal themselves within the brush, cloaked in darkness and shrouded in mystery. Watching. Laughing. Taunting. *Planning.*

My lungs pumped harder, working overtime. My jaw began to tremble, my teeth chattering like I'd suddenly been submerged into the dead of winter. I thought about the cigarette butt left beneath the helmet, and now this.

Someone's watching. Someone knows. *They know who I am.*

The lily fell from my hand to the ground, glistening with the remnants of the morning's rain. And I ran, jumping the fence with the agility of an Olympic hurdle jumper and hurrying through the rarely used back door of my house.

With the dead bolt locked, I pressed my back to the door's surface, squeezed my eyes shut, and pushed the breath from my panicked lungs.

"Breathe, breathe," I coached myself, my voice hushed against the ticking of the clock I'd taken from my childhood home.

In through your nose, out through your mouth ...
In ... out ... in ... out ... in—

A floorboard creaked from deeper within the house, and my eyes flew open at the same time my lungs stopped working altogether. Then another creak, the sound of a light footstep.

Someone's in the house.

A swarm of dreadful, unwanted memories encircled my brain, and adrenaline blanketed over the panic. I knelt, concealed by the kitchen island, and quietly untied my heavy steel-toed boots. I slipped them off and stood slowly to ensure I was still alone in the kitchen, then grabbed a long chef's knife from the rack, still drying from breakfast.

I listened for the floorboards' telltale whispers, another needed clue of the intruder's whereabouts, as I tiptoed through the kitchen and into the living room, pressing my back to the wall and gripping the knife in a steady palm.

It was a small cottage, containing only a kitchen, living room, two bedrooms, and a bathroom. There weren't many places for a trespasser to hide—or me for that matter—and I spotted them easily from where I stood.

A woman with black hair, tied into two sloppily coiled buns on top of her head, like a haphazard attempt at Minnie Mouse ears. She wore a long black coat, black pants, and heavy lug-soled black boots. Her back was to me as she stood at the mouth of the short hallway, leading to the bedrooms and bathroom, and I snagged the opportunity to make my quick approach.

I walked swiftly, rapidly, and grabbed her by the shoulder, whipping her around to pin her against the living room wall and pressing my forearm across the top of her chest while holding the knife up high with the other.

"The fuck are you doing in my house?" I hissed before recollection settled in and her green eyes came into focus.

She was the woman from Salem Skin. The one who I'd saved from being raped across the street.

What the fuck is she doing here?

Her bold gaze held mine with a bravery I admired despite the frantic thrumming of her pulse, fluttering beneath my arm at the base of her throat. The only tell that she was, in fact, terrified.

Good.

"I'm sorry," she said with a held breath, fighting to maintain the calm in her tone. "Your door was open."

"And that gave you the right to trespass?"

She tried to shrug against my hold as she replied, "I tried knocking."

I furrowed my brow at her cockiness, even with the blade of a knife pointed directly at her throat. One swift thrust, and she'd be dead. She should be scared. If she knew what I was capable of, she would be. But she didn't, and I assumed that was why she maintained eye contact and a firm set of her jaw.

My nostrils flared, the adrenaline and irritation singeing against my veins. "You should've knocked harder."

"And *you* shouldn't leave your front door wide open. There're some crazy fuckin' people out there, buddy. Just be glad I'm not one of them."

"An oversight." I tipped my head at the fair challenge while internally berating myself for being so careless. I knew better.

"A stupid one." Her eyes dodged toward the knife, holding steady just above her head. "Are you still planning to stab me, or can you let me go now?"

"Why the hell are you here?" I asked, still maintaining my stance. Still putting pieces together. "Have you been following me?"

Her triple-pierced nose wrinkled as her single-pierced upper lip curled. "*Following* you? What the hell?"

"The rose!" I exclaimed, seeing its soft, perfect petals through my mind's eye. "Did you leave the fucking rose?!"

The woman blinked, startled by my tone, then shook her head. "Dude, I don't know what the hell you're talking about. I came by because it's my day off, and I wanted to thank you for saving my fucking life the other night—that's all. Okay? I'm sorry. If you let me go, I'll—"

I lowered the knife and released her from my hold, taking a step back and gesturing toward the open door. "Leave."

She seemed taken aback as she lifted her hands to dust off her chest, as if wiping my touch away. "Um … okay … I just—"

"*Go*," I stated more firmly, jabbing the knife toward the cloudy, dreary world outside.

"Jesus." She blew out a breath and walked carefully toward the door, keeping her eyes on me all the way. "Um … thank you … for stopping that guy," she said as she moved. "You didn't have to, so … thanks."

I swallowed, hating that I could feel my resolve shifting, even as I struggled to hold on tightly. Hating that I felt such a desire to be so *awful*. "Great. You did what you came to do. Now, please, *please* leave."

"Oh, so he does have manners. That's good to know." She smiled, the piercings through her bottom lip twinkling in the glow of a table lamp beside the door. Then, she turned and lifted her hand in a lackluster wave, wiggling her fingers. "See you around, Spider."

Spider?

I narrowed my eyes at her back, then dropped my gaze to the webs tattooed on the backs of my hands. I couldn't tell if the nickname was meant to be endearing or an insult, but it didn't seem to matter. That nagging desperation for contact and companionship was back in an instant, flooding my chest and warming my frozen, forgotten heart.

"She's kinda cute in a creepy way," I could hear Luke saying, and I twisted my mouth, willing him to shut up as I hurried to stand in the open doorway, watching as she coolly made her way down the path. Strolling along as if the sun were shining and the birds were singing, completely oblivious to the ominous black clouds hanging overhead.

A black four-door sedan was parked not far from the cottage, one that hadn't been there before, when I left through the front door to lay the lily on Annabel's grave.

She couldn't have left the rose.

Unless she had parked somewhere else ... but ...

No, that doesn't make sense. She'd have had to walk too far. It wasn't her.

"Hey," I called after her, and when she stopped to look over her shoulder, I added, "You're welcome."

She flashed me that smile again. "Glad you were there to stop him."

I pressed my lips together as I nodded curtly. "So am I."

She continued to watch me as she walked backward, nearing the bottom of the hill and the gate. She would get into the car and drive away, and why did that make me feel so horribly ... *sad*? I didn't know her, nor did she know me—but why the hell was there a small, nearly insignificant part of my brain telling me to change that? She had entered my fucking house without permission! She had snooped through only God knew what before I caught her! A sane man wouldn't *want* to know her. No, no, a sane man would call the fucking cops, maybe even insist on getting a restraining order. Yet there I was, wishing Luke were around to get her name and number because even as an almost-thirty-nine-year-old man with more than a little experience under my belt, I was no better at this shit than I had been at seventeen.

She turned out of the gate and headed to the driver's side of the car.

Then, after opening the door, before climbing inside, she looked in my direction and called, "I'll knock louder next time!"

I watched as she got in and drove away at the slow but required fifteen miles per hour, and one side of my mouth twitched until it lifted into a reluctant smile.

I hoped there would be a next time.

And I hoped for that so much that I nearly forgot about the rose on Annabel's grave.

CHAPTER ELEVEN

CONNECTICUT, AGE TWENTY

"Luke! I'm taking the car, okay?" I called up the stairs, pulling on my jacket and feeling more excited than I'd been in a long time.

I had a job interview down at the cemetery where my parents were buried. Luke and Melanie had thought I was insane when I applied for the position. They thought it was too weird, too creepy, too … *depressing*, working in such proximity with the dead—including those that meant the most to me.

But to be honest, I couldn't have thought of a better job for me to have.

Even Dr. Sibilia had agreed when I told her about the interview.

It had decent pay. It required only a high school diploma and the ability to handle physical labor. I was overqualified academically with my bachelor's degree, and physically, I wasn't too worried since I'd started hitting the gym with Luke a few days a week. The thought of working very little with the public was more than appealing, but—and Dr. Sibilia had been sure to point this out—whatever interaction with people I might have would help in building my social skills.

Not to mention, I'd work in close vicinity to my parents. I'd be able to ensure their graves were cared for, I'd be free to visit them whenever I wanted, and while the thought made me feel a little nervous—I hadn't seen their headstones since the day they'd been buried—Dr. Sibilia thought it might be a little cathartic for me to have that kind of closure.

It seemed like an all-around win to me, especially because I'd finally be able to help financially. It wouldn't all have to come down to Luke and Melanie, and I thought that, maybe, it could help to lift some of the strain off them.

With my jacket on, I checked the hook beside the door for the car keys. They weren't there.

Maybe Luke's pocket.

But after checking his leather jacket dumped sloppily over the back of Dad's recliner, I found they weren't there either.

"Luke!" I shouted louder this time. "Where are the keys?!"

There was no answer again, and sighing, I rolled my eyes and began the climb upstairs when Melanie came hurrying down.

"Hey," I said as she passed. "What the hell did Luke do with the car keys?"

She shrugged, her eyes exhausted and weighed down by the dark circles beneath them. "Who knows? He came home last night and passed out before I could even talk to him."

I shook my head and headed back down the stairs behind her. It'd become routine. Luke went down to Tony's to have a few beers with his self-proclaimed pals. I was glad, so far, that Ritchie never seemed to be among them—that I was aware of anyway—but still. I had yet to understand what was so appealing about Tommy and Rob, at least from what I remembered, and I had no desire to figure it out.

"So, he's still sleeping," I guessed out loud, checking the pockets of his jacket once more. Just in case.

"Yeah," Melanie replied, sounding as tired as she looked. "And whenever he does wake up, he's going to be hungover, so you know how that's gonna be."

Luke was insufferable when he was hungover. He was almost angrier than when he was drunk.

I checked the clock and groaned. "I'm going to be late for this damn interview."

Melanie reached out for her keys on the hook beside the place where Luke's were supposed to be. "Here. You can take my car."

"Are you sure?"

She nodded, passing the keys to my hand. "Yeah, I'm off tonight, so it's not like I have to go anywhere. All I have to do is clean up around here, do some laundry, and deal with your brother."

I didn't like the way she'd said that—*deal with your brother*—as if the very thought of spending any time with him wasn't unlike a trip to the dentist. And it wasn't that I didn't understand. Luke's bad days, the ones where he'd go right to the bar from work and come home late and drunk, were becoming more common than the good ones—times when he'd come home immediately after he was done at the shop and spend time with Melanie or me or both. Dealing with him was just that—*dealing*. Tolerating. Trudging through one day and into the next, only to do it all over again.

But if she was unhappy, then she was likely to leave. And I wasn't sure what I'd do if Melanie left.

Both of us really—God, would Luke have any reason to be sober at all if she left? Would he even *survive*?

But ... mostly me.

I'd be lost without her.

"I can help clean when I get home," I offered. "And I can make dinner."

Dinner was something I'd gotten decent at since the days of Amanda with a star. A gourmet chef I was not, but my meals were edible, and it left Melanie with one less thing to do some nights.

I couldn't imagine another twenty-three-year-old working as hard as she did, and I'd kick my brother's ass into next Wednesday for not appreciating her more if I realistically believed I could take him.

"That'd be nice," she said, finally smiling for the first time since she'd come downstairs. "I think we have the stuff to make pasta."

"I can grab Italian bread on the way home."

"Oh, that sounds good. Yeah, do that."

Her face was lit up now. A little less tired, a little more relieved, and that made me feel better. She was more likely to stay another day if she had something happy to look forward to.

"Anything else you need me to grab?" I asked, heading for the door.

She thought about it for a second with her hands planted on her hips. Melanie used to put so much effort into her appearance. She'd work out, do her makeup and hair, and wear nice clothes. These days, I couldn't remember the last time she'd dressed in something other than sweatpants and Luke's baggy T-shirts or one of her work uniforms—the one she wore at the drugstore or the one she wore as the receptionist at her dad's shop. And it wasn't that she was no longer pretty. Melanie was one of the most naturally beautiful women I'd ever known. But it was her lack of desire to make an effort that left me bothered, and I wasn't sure if it was that she didn't have the time or that she'd just forgotten how to care about herself while caring about us.

I hated the idea that Luke could make her feel that way. I hated it even more if the reason had anything to do with me.

"I don't think so," Melanie finally replied. "Just the Italian bread will be fine."

"Okay," I said on my way out the door, already knowing I was going to also grab a pint of her favorite ice cream.

***

The interview didn't take long, and I was given the job on the spot.

The old guy who conducted the interview—a bald man by the name of Marty—said most young guys weren't into the idea of spending time with a bunch of ghosts, and I laughed, thinking he was making a joke, until I realized he wasn't laughing with me.

"You don't believe in ghosts?" he asked, lifting one brow to eye me studiously.

"I didn't say that. But are there really ghosts here?" I asked, not at all startled by the talk of an afterlife.

He looked me dead in the eye and replied, "Son, it's a graveyard. What do you think?"

I shrugged and looked around the hallowed ground, then said, "I don't know. I think, when I'm dead, I wouldn't want to haunt the place where I was buried. I'd probably prefer to go wherever the people I cared about were."

He nodded slowly with what seemed like consideration, looking off into the distance, before saying, "Maybe they just don't have anywhere else to go."

That comment rolled around my brain on the ride to the grocery store and all the time it took to grab Italian bread, ice cream, and a case of Dr. Pepper. Just lingering and nagging me to mull it over, to obsess about what it might be like to die and not have anyone to care about you in your afterlife, let alone haunt.

Do the dead even give a crap about things like that?

As I'd already mentioned, I hadn't visited my parents' graves since they'd died. I hadn't been able to face their names, carved eternally into the stones Nana had paid for. But now that I had a job at the same cemetery and I'd have to care for the land their bodies lay beneath, a simultaneous battle between comfort and sadness crushed against my chest as I drove Melanie's car back home.

And why *hadn't* my parents haunted me? Why hadn't they sent me any of those signs people talked about all the damn time? I figured, of all people, I'd be the most susceptible to receiving messages from the beyond, so why the hell not? Did they think I didn't care? Or was it that they didn't care about me or the trauma they'd caused when they died?

Suddenly, I didn't want to cook dinner. I didn't care about eating or celebrating the job I'd gotten. All I wanted was to go inside, crawl into bed, and miss my mom and dad while their room stood dormant down the hall, still untouched after all this time.

But when I got inside, there was Melanie, vacuuming the carpet, keeping the house clean when I knew damn well, if she wasn't here, it'd all go to hell. I knew I'd try, but Luke wouldn't. The house was too big, my time would be spread too thin with the new job, and sooner or later, it would become too much for me alone to handle.

What am I going to do without her?

The thought nearly left me breathless. There was a calm, knowing certainty laced between the words. Like I already knew my time with her here was limited, the way

I'd known things in the past. I couldn't be sure of when or how, but I knew in that moment, one day, she would be gone.

I just hoped I'd be ready when it inevitably happened.

I'll never be ready.

"Hey!" she exclaimed when she realized I was home. "How was the interview?"

"Good," I choked out, closing the door behind me. "I got the job."

"Charlie!" She turned off the vacuum and ran toward me, arms outstretched. "Congratulations!"

She hugged me tightly, and I lowered my chin to touch the top of her head. It hadn't been that long ago when I could look straight into her eyes, but somehow, in the past seven years since meeting her, I'd grown over a head taller. How did that just *happen*? How had I not noticed?

"Thanks," I said as the hug ended and she took a step back.

"Are you excited?"

Her grin was contagious, and I grinned back.

"Yeah, actually. It's a pretty cool job, and I like the old guy I'm working for."

She reached out to touch my elbow. "Good. I'm so happy for you."

I nudged my head to the side toward the stairs. "Luke awake yet?"

Her happiness and excitement wilted immediately, like a flower denied rain and sunlight. "Nope. He's out cold. Still breathing though, so I guess that's something."

She said it with a lighthearted air, but I thought we both questioned if the day would actually come when Luke would go to sleep and simply not wake up. It was a problem neither of us ever talked about much, and maybe it was just that we didn't know what else to say that hadn't already been said.

How many times could you mention that someone needed help before you simply stopped mentioning it at all?

"I guess I'll start cooking," I said, then held up the bag. "And, hey, I got ice cream for dessert."

There was that happiness again, lighting up the room. Her eyes twinkled as she asked, "Double fudge brownie?"

"Would I get any other flavor?" I rolled my eyes as I walked past her toward the kitchen. "Come on, Mel. You know me better than that."

***

Luke did eventually wake up, just before dinner was ready, but he complained that he felt too much like dog shit to even think about eating.

So, he hung out in the bedroom he shared with Melanie while she and I had dinner. And even though it might not have been the first meal we shared in each other's company, it was the first one to begin with a strange discomfort and almost-complete silence.

She set the table while I brought over the pot of pasta, and we moved around each other in an odd, practiced dance but without a single word spoken. We sat simultaneously across from each other and filled our plates.

We chewed and buttered our bread and drank from our glasses, and the whole time, I wondered, *What is she thinking?*

Part of me worried that she was already planning her escape from this house. That my thought of forewarning earlier hadn't been a premonition of the future, but the present.

Don't freak out. Not yet.
It would help if she fucking said something.

Then, as if she were gifted with the ability to read minds, she said, "I don't know what to do with him anymore, Charlie."

The sound of her voice was so abrupt and unexpected at that point that I nearly jumped out of my seat as my eyes bounced from my plate to meet her gaze.

"Yeah, I know. I don't either."

Melanie pulled in a shaky breath as her bottom lip began to tremble. "I just …" She clamped down on that lip to stop it from quivering, even as her eyes flooded with tears. And then she just gave up altogether, allowing them to fall freely as she continued to speak. "I just miss him so much, you know?"

I did know, and I nodded. "Yeah."

"And that's crazy, right? Missing someone who is literally *right there*, right in front of you … but it doesn't *feel* like him. Sometimes, it does. Sometimes, I talk to him, and I'm like, *Oh, there he is. There's Luke.*" She gasped with a sob as she wiped her face with the backs of her hands. "And all I can do is hope that's the time he doesn't go away again, but he always does. And, God, Charlie …" She dropped her head into her hands. "I'm just so tired. I'm *so* fucking tired. I'm tired of missing him. I'm tired of hoping he'll want to talk to me. I'm tired of begging him for any kind of acknowledgment. I'm tired of lying in bed, wishing he'd fucking *touch me* the way he used to or that sex won't feel like a goddamn chore."

She groaned, lifting her head and letting her hands fall to the table. "I'm sorry. You don't want to hear about this shit."

I didn't. I didn't want to hear the details about my brother's sex life—or lack of, apparently. It was bad enough I'd had to hear them going at it down the hall all these years. The last thing I needed was for his girlfriend to confide in me about their premarital problems. But Melanie was also my friend, and it was obvious that she was desperate to talk, so I shook my head.

"No, it's okay. I get it. You need to vent."

"I just love him," she stated simply. "I love him so fucking much, and I want him to come back to me—to *both* of us, honestly. And I think that's what makes it so hard to leave. Like, I just think, *What if he's suddenly better after I'm gone, and I miss the chance to see him normal again?* Or worse, what if, I don't know, he … he is like this *because* of me? What if I did this to him?"

"No. You know that's not true," I insisted adamantly.

The truth was that our parents' deaths had fucked us both up. It was just that, for me, all that had happened was the amplification of my existing issues. But for

Luke, he'd been so focused on fixing me that he never stopped long enough to realize he needed to be fixed too.

Now, he was broken—maybe even beyond repair—and that was, in a way, my fault. Not hers. *Mine.*

If he hadn't been so damn concerned about me, he wouldn't have been so carefree with himself. He wouldn't have sought a Band-Aid to patch his wounds and instead taken himself to the ER to get stitched up.

Melanie sniffled and wiped her eyes again, nodding. "I know. I just ... I just hate this. I hate that I can remember a time when everything was so fun and easy, and I hate that I know nothing will be like that ever again. And yet"—she laughed beside herself, shrugging—"here I am, because I love him too much to give up."

Nobody will ever love me like that, I caught myself thinking as I stared at the tears drenching her face.

We ate the rest of our dinner, and then I excused myself to shower and hang out in my room with some Nine Inch Nails and my sketchbook. My feelings and fears of living a loveless life felt too big to keep them stifled, so I let the Sharpie do the talking.

Big, sweeping circles and jagged lines formed the spider, standing in the middle of a field, barren of everything but countless, nameless headstones. He wore an expression as vacant as the dark, cloudless sky, save for one rogue tear clinging to his cheek.

Destined to care only for the dead because nobody alive cared for him.

I swatted a tear from my own face at the same time the door down the hall opened.

Melanie had gone to bed a while ago, and those footsteps now didn't belong to her.

I listened as Luke quietly walked past my room and down the stairs, and I dropped the sketchbook and marker to go after him and see what he was up to, where he was going.

He was already down the stairs by the time I caught up with him, and he was heading in the direction of the kitchen.

"Oh, hey," he mumbled, glancing briefly over his shoulder.

His eyes barely met mine for a second before looking away.

He didn't bother to ask how my interview had gone. Didn't even express any interest in what I was still doing awake. His lack of care for anyone else dug beneath my skin, deeper than ever before. And when he reached the fridge, opened the door, and pulled out a bottle of beer, I smacked it right out of his hand.

He hadn't expected it. Neither had I. The glass clattered loudly against the tiled floor, but didn't break, resounding through the otherwise hushed kitchen. Luke stared at the amber glass, nearly black in the lack of light, before turning to me. Fuming and insulted.

He took a step toward me. "What the fuck is wrong with you, Charlie?"

"What the fuck is wrong with *me*?" I jabbed a finger at my chest.

"Yeah," he challenged, shoving hard against me, sending my body backward toward the wall.

I regained my footing and shoved him back. "I can't believe you even have the balls to ask me that fucking question when you should be looking in the fucking mirror."

His back hit the refrigerator. The impact left him stunned, confused as to how to react. The years separating twenty and twenty-three weren't that big. They had made us nearly the same height—I was taller now—and the hours at the gym had made me stronger. He might've been able to lift more than me, but that didn't mean I couldn't put up a good fight against him—even if I knew he was likely to win in the end.

"You stay out of my way, asshole," he warned, pointing a finger at my face. "You understand me? If I wanna have a beer, I'm gonna have a beer. Now—"

"Yeah? And what does your girlfriend say about that? Does *she* have to stay out of your way too?"

Luke's jaw tensed for a moment before saying, "Melanie has nothing to do with this."

"Oh, no? That's news to me. Probably to her, too, considering she was crying earlier about how much she wished you'd stop fucking drinking."

His nostrils flared at my combative tone, and then he bent to snatch the beer from off the floor. He stomped, barefoot, past me toward the living room, as if he'd had the final word, but he was wrong about that.

I trailed close behind, and he pretended not to notice. When he dropped onto the couch, kicked his feet up, and grabbed the TV remote, I didn't move from his direct line of sight. Instead, I stared down at him, defiant and stubborn.

"Will you fucking move?" he asked coolly.

"No."

He used the coffee table's edge to pop the top off the bottle before getting up and flopping to the other side of the L-shaped sectional. Then, with a smug little smirk on his face, he turned on the TV, now unperturbed by my presence.

"What the fuck happened to you, Luke?" I asked, shaking my head.

He flipped the channels mindlessly, keeping his gaze diverted from mine.

"You know, Melanie says she misses you. Did you know that? She says she'd fucking leave if she didn't love you so goddamn much."

"Then, she should fucking go," he muttered, shrugging like it all meant nothing.

"You know what?" I slammed my hand against my chest. "I agree with you! She should! She doesn't deserve this shit. And if you had any fucking decency left in you, you'd let her go. Fucking break up with her! Because she's wasting her life on you. Do you realize that? She's wasting her fucking life waiting for you to get your head out of your ass. And she deserves better than that. She deserves someone who *loves* her. She deserves—"

"Do *you* love her?"

He turned to level me with a narrowed glare, and I could see it there, something possessive and alive flickering somewhere within his otherwise indifferent expression. I had awakened that tiny piece of the old

Luke, the Luke we—Melanie and me—had been holding out hope for.

So, I risked bodily harm by shrugging and lying. "Maybe."

Just to see what he'd say.

Just to see what he'd do.

And what he did was get up quicker than I could blink and grab my shirt by the collar to bring his face close enough for me to feel the heat emanating from his skin.

"Look me in the eye and tell me you fucking love her, and I swear to God, Charlie, I'll fucking beat you so hard—"

"I don't fucking *love* her, you idiot," I said, relenting easily. "Not like that. But what if I did? Why does it even fucking matter to you? It's not like you do."

His grip on my shirt loosened as the anger etched into the lines on his face eased, just a little. "Yes, I do."

"Well, you have a really fucked-up way of showing it."

He released his hold on me altogether and dropped back down to the couch, pushing his hands into his hair.

"You've spent years worried about me," I said, standing over my older brother. "Now, how about you start worrying about yourself? And stop pushing Melanie away unless you really want her to go. Because one day, she will, and if it's because you're too busy drinking yourself to death to see how lucky you are to have someone like her, I'll never fucking forgive you for that."

My heart hammered wildly as I turned around and headed back upstairs, the adrenaline flowing through my veins. I'd said exactly what I'd needed to say, and I hadn't allowed for him to reply. All I could hope was that he thought about what I'd said. All I could hope was that it'd make a difference.

And I guessed it had, even if for a while. Because the next day, Luke went to his first AA meeting. Two weeks after that, he asked Melanie to marry him.

She said yes, and I prayed that she wouldn't regret it.

And I prayed that, one day, someone might love me as much as she loved him.

CHAPTER TWELVE

MASSACHUSETTS, PRESENT DAY

The sun peeked from around its blanket of clouds, then disappeared again just as quickly. I shielded my eyes with my hand and peered up toward the sky as two crows cawed and disappeared between the branches of a nearby tree.

I had read that autumn in Massachusetts would be cold. But this wasn't what I'd consider cold. I couldn't even call this cool or comfortable even. I was approximately two degrees away from sweating through my long-sleeved shirt, even while on the back of Luke's bike on my way to the gate, and if the sun decided to show itself fully, I knew I'd have to roll up my sleeves.

But as much as I preferred days that were dark and dreary, I could also appreciate that days like this were meant to be taken advantage of. So, after unlocking the gate and using the recently repaired and returned backhoe to dig a few graves for upcoming funerals, I decided to head back home to chop some wood in preparation for the impending winter.

My backyard wasn't much of a yard at all. A small patio that contained an even smaller grill, two lawn chairs—even though I could count on one finger the number of times Ivan and I had sat outside—a place to park Luke's bike, a pile of firewood, a handful of logs waiting to be chopped, and a wide, flat tree stump on which to do said chopping.

A little garden Ivan had started during his time at the cottage was tucked into the corner of the walled-in yard. I hadn't understood the purpose of it when I first accepted the job, even though I made it a point to maintain its vibrant greenery.

But one day—the only time we'd taken our coffee outside instead of staying in—Ivan had commented on how nicely I'd kept his garden, and I laughed, mentioning how ridiculous it was to have kept it at all when I was surrounded by well-maintained landscaping and flower beds on all sides of the cottage.

"But that's all theirs," Ivan had said, unamused by my teasing. He swept his arm out, addressing the surrounding acres of greenery and headstones. "This tiny piece of land was *mine*, Chuck. All mine. Now, it's yours, and it's important to remember that. It's yours to keep for *you*. Take pride in what you do for them, but always take more in what you do for yourself."

I had taken that to heart. Nothing had ever been truly mine before. Not after spending the first thirty years of my life in a house with members of my family and three years struggling to maintain the shell of something that had once existed.

Not once had I forgotten to water that garden ever since that conversation. There'd been days I was too bogged down by thoughts and memories and sadness to mow a section of the cemetery or times I'd overlooked trimming the bushes on my to-do list simply because of how daunting of a task it seemed to be. But that garden was always tended to.

So, after giving the flowers and shrubbery a good sprinkle of water from the hose, I wiped my hands against my jeans and turned to grab a log off the pile. Then, with it positioned on the stump, I wrapped my hands around the axe handle, lifted it up and over my head, and grunted as the axe came down hard, splitting the log in two.

It was primal, a connection to my oldest ancestors. The ones I knew nothing about, apart from the fact that I wouldn't be here had they never existed. I wondered what they would've thought about me now. Rapidly approaching middle age and unmarried. No children to speak of, nobody to pass my legacy on to. Reclusive and tending to the graves of the remembered and long forgotten.

What would they have thought about my past? Or better yet, Luke's?

I sniffed a laugh at that as I shook my head, repositioning one half of the log on the stump.

THWACK! Another swing of the axe.

My nose burned at the thought of Luke, and the backs of my eyes prickled with an abrupt but heavy-weighted sadness. It always came on out of nowhere—the pain of missing my brother. It crept up on me when I least expected it, hitting hard and fast with such precision that I could barely see the log in front of me as I brought the axe over and down.

The pieces split and fell off the stump to meet the others.

My back dripped with sweat beneath my shirt, and with the weight of sadness sitting heavily against my chest, I planted the axe blade into the stump. Then, I pulled the shirt off and threw it aggressively to the ground, as if it alone were the distance and time separating me from my big brother.

Another log was set in place. The axe handle was gripped tightly in my palms. I squeezed the worn wood until my knuckles turned white, gritted my teeth, and set my jaw. An angry roar scraped against my throat as I swung, and upon impact, the log splintered, breaking into four pieces and falling to the ground at the base of the stump.

Relax. Let it go.

I let my lungs heave for one, two, three breaths before clearing my throat and shaking my head, chasing the pain and rage away. Reminding myself for the millionth time that this—being here—was for the better, that it was what we had both felt was best, given the circumstances. If only he—

A nearby tree erupted with the scattering of crows, taking to the sky in a burst of black and echoing calls. My heart hammered at the disruption to the quiet, sunny day, and I stared as they flew off, focusing on their beating wings and the heaviness of my breathing.

"Jesus," I muttered, clasping a hand to my bare chest before turning to grab another log from the pile.

And that was when I saw her.

That woman.

The one I'd saved across the street, outside of the hotel.

The one who'd broken into my house.

The one with the longest, prettiest onyx hair I'd ever seen before in my life.

The one who emanated an aura so bright and tempting, beckoning me to investigate its glory, while the nerves in my gut and the panic in my brain told me to stay as far away from her as I could possibly get.

If only I could convince her to comply ...

I said nothing as she walked toward me slowly, her heavy black boots thunking against the brick. My hands remained tight around the axe handle, although I wasn't sure I intended to use it. Not on her. But it made me feel better to keep it there between my palms, held in front of me, warding her off and forcing a distance I knew was best.

"Oh, come on, Charlie," I imagined Luke saying. *"Like you don't wanna see what else she has pierced."*

Shut the fuck up.

"I knocked louder this time," she said, approaching me like one would a wild animal. A sly smile tugged at her lips, painted black and glossy. "You didn't answer."

"Obviously, I'm a little busy," I replied in a low tone I thought—I *hoped*—sounded menacing to her ears.

But still, she came nearer.

Her long black coat hung to her knees. The buttons were undone, leaving it open to reveal a sheer black top embroidered with spiderwebs. The coincidence of our coordination—her in cloth and me in flesh—wasn't lost on me as I struggled to not stare at the black patent bra, bejeweled navel, and heavily tattooed skin beneath the patterned fabric.

She turned her head toward Luke's bike, and a light breeze lifted her ebony hair from her shoulder, revealing her left ear. Between the countless piercings and gauged lobes, there was enough metal there to set off airport security, and I fought against an amused smirk at the thought.

"Nice bike," she commented, nudging her chin toward the Harley.

"It's not mine," I felt the need to say.

She looked back at me with a raised brow. "No? You stole it?"

"No."

"Hmm," she muttered, nodding at the bike again.

"What?"

"Oh, I'm just thinking, I wouldn't be surprised if you had." She looked back to me, her mouth twisted to one side before saying, "I mean, you're a pretty scary guy."

I snorted a sardonic laugh and shook my head as my hands loosened just a bit from my grip on the axe. She had no idea just how scary I was capable of being, and suddenly, I didn't want her thinking that side could—or would—come out around her.

"No, seriously," she went on with widened eyes, like I needed clarification, "that guy was ready to piss himself when you had that knife to his throat. And, man, you're *fast*. You just came out of nowhere, like a fucking ninja."

I pulled in a breath while giving myself a quick reminder that I wasn't here to make friends. Hell, I wasn't even here to make casual acquaintances—Ivan not included. I was living my life as quietly as I'd always wanted it to be, away from everyone who'd ever wished ill on me or my family. Conversation with this strange, gorgeous, and disturbingly brazen woman didn't fit into that plan.

"What did you—" I began, only to be cut off again.

"So, whose bike is it then?"

She turned to run her hand over the polished handlebars, and my shoulders stiffened as a protective streak bristled the hairs at the back of my neck.

"Hands off," I demanded.

She pulled back her fingers. Not with the hurriedness of someone frightened though. She looked back at me with an apologetic nod of her head.

The gesture was at least appreciated, and to show her as such, I responded, "It's my brother's."

Just acknowledging him out loud to someone was enough to scrape at the wound on my heart, barely beginning to scab. Mentioning I had a brother, mentioning he existed, brought on a consecutive thought that she would look at him the way I knew I'd looked at her just moments ago.

Lustful. Longing.

Pathetic.

Women had always loved Luke. They'd always been drawn to him like the night moths to the lantern outside my door. He might've been my brother, but I understood his appeal. He wasn't the type of man women made a family and a life with—he'd made sure of that, the fucking asshole. But he was the one they wanted an experience with. The bad boy with the cigarettes and motorcycle, the one with the tattoos and a love affair with recklessness. He reeked of it, and women wanted to bottle it up, wear it for a night, and leave after it faded, long before their disapproving daddies could find out that it'd ever happened.

I was nothing more than a shadow, lurking in the distance and fading with the absence of his fiery light.

"I didn't know your brother lived here too," the woman replied, seemingly surprised. "I thought you were all alone here."

"I am." I swallowed hard against the pain of missing my wonderful asshole of a brother. "I'm just looking after it for him."

She lifted her chin as she acknowledged me, and for a second, I thought maybe she could see the ache glowing bright and hot beneath my skin.

"Where is he?"

"Prison," I replied through a tense jaw, the word spoken as a dare for her to continue with her questions. To ask what he'd done, why he was there, how long he'd been there, and how many years he was meant to rot behind bars before he'd be sent back out into the wild, like a fucking animal.

He did it to himself, I had to remind myself. And that was the truth, but, dammit, I didn't have to like it.

Especially when he wasn't the only one who'd deserved that fate.

But she didn't ask. She just took on a certain look of empathy I hadn't expected, and then she nodded with finality. A period at the end of the sentence, the closing of the book, and just like that, my soul dared to look out from the cold, dark cell I'd shut it in, and with slender, shadowy, tangled fingers, it reached out.

Stop it.

She tucked her hand into the black leather satchel at her hip and pulled something out—a white envelope—then handed it to me.

I looked at it skeptically before slowly accepting. "What is this?"

"An invitation."

I narrowed my eyes at the heavy paper in my hand, unable to meet her gaze with mine. "To what?"

"We're throwing my boss a birthday party the weekend before Halloween," she explained, my flesh zinging with anxiety at the word *Halloween*. "A bunch of people are coming. Nothing too crazy, but I asked if I could invite someone, so …" She gestured toward the envelope with splayed fingers. "You're my someone."

My eyes flitted up toward hers for just a brief second as I asked, "Why?"

"Your charm and warm, welcoming personality, of course." She tipped her head in the direction of the axe. "And your penchant for carrying sharp objects."

My smirk was reluctant, and I tried desperately to fight it, but there it was as I thought about the box cutter and chef's knife I'd also wielded in her presence.

"Everybody likes free food and booze," she added, her tone softer now.

"I don't drink," I muttered as the memory of too many of Luke's drunken nights came to mind.

I looked at her face in time to see her smile.

"Well, that would make two of us then."

"Hmm," I grunted, otherwise unmoved.

"But you do eat, right?"

Then, just like that, before I could say anything more, she turned and began to walk away toward the open gate.

I stared at the envelope in my hand for a second, taking note of the word *Spider* written in swirly cursive. Then, as I was about to crumple it in my hand and stuff it into my pocket, another murder of crows scattered through the sky. Cawing and calling, startling me from the task of discarding the invitation I never intended to use.

Three black birds took purchase on the roof, just feet from where I stood. They looked at me, cocking their heads in jerky, surreal motions. Their dark eyes watching as I swallowed and took a deep breath.

Then, for some stupid reason, I sneered at the trio as if responding to an unspoken message and begrudgingly left the axe against the stump as I stomped my way back into the house with the only party invitation I'd ever received in hand.

CHAPTER THIRTEEN

CONNECTICUT, AGE TWENTY-ONE

When I was twenty-one, Luke was twenty-four, and in most ways, that three-year gap had seemed to disappear entirely.

Except in the way that he looked like he'd lived decades longer than me.

And in the way that, a lot of the time, it was me who felt like the older brother.

More responsible. More put together.

Luke's skin wrinkled in ways that a lot of twenty-four-year-olds didn't; his voice sounded hoarser, throatier; and his eyes held more experience and street-smart wisdom. I'd known it was from the years of smoking, questionable socialization, and alcohol abuse, yet it never ceased to surprise me every now and then when I caught a glimpse of him across the dinner table or in the upstairs hallway, passing him on my way to the bathroom.

Sometimes, I'd wonder if it was because of me, as I had for years. If he'd still look like that if he hadn't had to look after me for as long as he had.

I had mentioned it to Dr. Sibilia during one session, the week before my twenty-first birthday.

"Charlie, why do you think you blame yourself so much for Luke's poor choices?" she asked, sliding her thick, black-framed glasses off her nose. She held them by one arm in her pinched fingers, tapping them against her bottom lip.

She had recently gotten a labret piercing, and I liked it. I thought it suited her, and I'd told her so. But I wasn't thinking about that now as my legs began to bounce and my fingers began to scratch at the threads holding my jeans together.

"I don't know. I guess because ..." I shrugged, lifting my hands. "Because he needed to cope somehow?"

I sounded unsure because I was. It just seemed like the right answer. What other reason was there?

Dr. Sibilia sucked in a deep breath and nodded, raising her gaze to the ceiling tiles.

"I'm not saying you're wrong," she said even though it seemed an awful lot like she was, in fact, saying I was wrong. "But did you ever consider that Luke was already a legal adult when he took over as your guardian? A legal adult in control of making his own choices?"

My legs bounced quicker in short, erratic little movements as I looked away from her and argued, "He was barely an adult when Mom and Dad died."

"No, I know that," she reasoned, laying the glasses in her lap to scratch at the side of her neck. "But, Charlie, didn't Luke already drink and smoke before they died?"

"Yeah, but no more than the usual stupid teenager."

"And was that by choice or because he was forced to"—she pursed her lips and clasped her hands together—"to cope with ... what, being a stupid teenager?"

I knew she was testing me. I knew she was only helping me to navigate through my discombobulated brain and the shitty, tragic circumstances of my life. But her condescending tone pissed me off. That she would insult my brother like this and make him sound like the loser I hated to think he was pissed me off even more.

"Grown freakin' men become alcoholics because of their circumstances. Their kid dies, or they lose their job or whatever. So, I don't know why you think it's so damn impossible for him to have used booze as a—"

"Charlie, I'm not saying he didn't turn to alcohol as a way to cope with his circumstances," she interrupted, her tone a bit gentler as she leaned forward in her seat across from mine. "All I'm asking is, at what point do you stop blaming yourself for the choices he's made? At what point do you stop believing that it's your fault and start holding him accountable for his own actions?"

I'd been seeing Dr. Sibilia for years now. I knew I had been lucky to find a therapist I clicked with on the first shot, but that was all Melanie's doing. I couldn't take credit for that. But as good as I'd felt about my sessions with the doctor—and as much of a positive impact as she'd made on my mental health—she also had a way of pushing my buttons, of making me think. And I guessed that was the point, right? She made me think, recalculate, and look at things in a different way.

But this ... believing that Luke was solely to blame for his poor choices ... I was too stubborn—too *guilty*—to release my fault in that.

But it was fine now.

Because Luke had been sober for a year. He'd been attending his meetings, and he'd been at least somewhat present in the planning of his wedding.

So, whether he was solely to blame or not was moot at this point. Because he was better—we all were. And whatever had happened before no longer mattered.

***

"My little Charlie's all grown up," Melanie cooed in an overly dramatic, babyish tone as she pinched my chin in her grasp and pressed a wet kiss to my squished cheek.

I brushed her away and rubbed where she had squeezed. "I don't wanna break it to you, but I've been grown up for a while."

"You know what I mean." She walked away from the table to head for the fridge in the kitchen. "Twenty-one is, like ... there's nothing else, you know? All restrictions are lifted now. You're free to do anything."

I grabbed the pepper shaker and dashed my scrambled eggs as I asked skeptically, "Like what?"

"Well, like ..." She produced the bottle of orange juice from the fridge and pursed her lips as she shut the door. "Um ... you could rent a car ..."

Luke entered the room with the grandeur of a hungry and sleep-deprived toddler, his boots clomping loudly against the hardwood floor. He gripped my shoulders from behind and gave me a hearty shake.

"You can get legally wasted," he chimed in, an air of wistful delight heavy in his tone.

As if on cue, Melanie and I both froze in place, and I held the breath within my aching lungs. Being around Luke in the year since he'd decided to get sober had been mostly great, but every now and then, especially during times like this, it felt like we were precariously walking over shattered glass. Afraid to take a step, afraid to slip, afraid of what jagged fragment might wedge itself into flesh, only to fester, infect, and eventually require antibiotics and amputation. Neither of us wanted to say the wrong thing. Neither of us knew exactly what the right thing was.

Melanie's eyes dodged quickly to mine and narrowed.

Say something, they said.

No, you, mine said back.

Her brows lifted with a stern demand to man up and intervene, and Luke broke our silent, private conversation with a groan and a *thwack* of his palm against the side of my head. Hard enough to send a message, not hard enough to inflict pain.

"Will you guys knock it off?" he grumbled irritably in the same tone he always used when we questioned his strength and sobriety. "I didn't say *I* was gonna get wasted."

"Well, I'm not going to either," I declared.

While it might have sounded like a noble gesture of camaraderie—and it was—Luke wasn't my only reason why I had no intention of drinking. I hated the taste of alcohol. Hated the way it made me feel. I'd only ever been tipsy on one occasion—on New Year's with Melanie and Luke when I was eighteen—and the lack of control I felt after only a few glasses of shitty wine had scared me enough to never want to do it again. Especially after witnessing firsthand how toxic it could be to your life and the relationships in it.

But Luke didn't like my answer, and he proved as much later that night, when he came to pick me up from work at the cemetery.

Ever since I'd started driving a couple of years back, Luke and I had been sharing Dad's old car. Luke had said on many occasions that he was going to take the money he got from the sale of his old truck and get himself a motorcycle, and once he did, he'd give the keys to the car to me for good. But he hadn't yet saved the extra money he'd likely need for his dream Harley, and so, whenever his shift at Melanie's dad's shop aligned with mine, one of us picked the other up.

It had been a fine system, until that night, when instead of turning onto our street, he kept on driving.

"Where are we going?" I asked, not intending to sound as worried as I did.

But I was a creature of habit. I liked my days to go as planned. It felt safe, it felt comfortable, and if something was even remotely out of place, I worried.

"I'm buying you a drink," he said matter-of-factly, not taking his eyes off the road.

That was when I realized he was driving in the direction of Tony's, and I ran a hand through my hair and held my palm to the crown of my head.

"No. *What*? No, come on. Melanie's making dinner, right? And w-we're having cake, and—"

"Relax, will you? Jesus." He shook his head. "It's one drink. Can't I buy my little brother *one* drink on his twenty-first birthday, huh?"

It didn't feel good. Nothing about it did, and I grimaced as I replied, "Shit ... I don't know. Let's just—"

"Being in a bar isn't gonna miraculously ruin everything I've done in the past *year*, okay? One drink. That's all I'm asking. Just one. It's what Dad would've done, right? So, just ... just give this to me, okay? *Please.*"

He was begging, and it made me waver. It was cheap, using Dad like that. But he wasn't wrong. I knew that was exactly what our father would've done—for both of us. He would've taken us down to Tony's, bought us a beer, clapped us on the back, and told us how proud he was. And given that Luke had been the person to help me survive these past six years, I started to think that maybe it wouldn't hurt to let him buy me that one drink. Never mind every warning I'd ever heard about letting an alcoholic walk within the vicinity of a bar.

I realized that what I wanted was to pretend that everything was fine for a couple of minutes. I wanted to pretend that we—all of us—were fine. That life was good. That Luke's alcoholism wasn't a giant fucking elephant sitting in the corner of every room, and my anxiety and penchant for premonitions weren't a couple of shit-talking demons sitting on my shoulders.

So, I agreed.

I was going to let my brother buy me a beer. I *wanted* to. Because it was what Dad would've done, and right now, Luke was the closest I was going to get to our father.

***

The thing was, I had always considered myself a smart guy.

I'd flown through school, thanks to being taught at home and being allowed to work at my own pace. Mom and Dad had set up college funds for both Luke and me, and while Luke had spent his on bills and food, I'd spent mine on getting my GED and taking college classes online at sixteen. I'd graduated with my bachelor's degree just a few months before my nineteenth birthday, and I could run circles around nearly anyone in a game of Trivial Pursuit.

My point is, academically, I was a pretty smart guy. Book smart. Intellectually intelligent. A fucking nerd, as Luke would call it.

But I was also naive, and although my intuition had always been strong to a fault, I wanted to believe so badly that I could knock back a beer beside my brother without the fear of him sliding face-first off of the wagon.

But of course, that wasn't what happened. And anyone else would've seen that coming from three hundred miles away. Hell, I did, too, when I really thought about it. But hope had a way of making us do dangerous, stupid things sometimes. And stepping foot into Tony's Bar was a dangerous, stupid, stupid, *stupid* thing.

It started with one beer. Just one, and it was mine.

Luke watched me take a pull in a way that looked serene and desperate at the same time.

"How is it?" he asked, and I grimaced, choked, and barely swallowed before croaking, "Horrible."

We laughed, and, fuck, it felt so normal and good to laugh with him. His hand on my back, moisture collecting in both of our eyes as we fell into silly hysterics. And why the hell we were laughing so hard, I had no idea, but there we were, bellied up to Tony's polished bar and unable to stop laughing until our stomachs hurt and the tears were flowing into our nearly identical beards.

"Ah fuck," Luke muttered, running his palm over his mouth and chin. He sighed audibly and pushed his fingers into his hair. "What a crazy fuckin' life it's been, huh?"

The joy and laughter wilted like a dying flower as I nodded and quietly replied, "Yeah, it has been."

"We did okay though," he said with reassurance, and I wasn't sure if that had been for him or me. "I mean, all things considered, we turned out all right. I'm getting fucking married, I have a good job, and you ..." His hand clapped against my back once again. "You're working, you're fucking *driving*, and you're not nearly as neurotic as you used to be."

I chuckled with melancholy at that. Luke always had a harsh way of speaking the truth, but that didn't make it any less true. I was doing better—Dr. Sibilia told me frequently. Panic still had a way of choking the life out of me sometimes, but it wasn't nearly as debilitating as it had once been.

"So ... yeah, man." He nodded to himself, his fingertips tracing a knot in the mahogany wood. "All things considered, I'd say we did pretty fuckin' good."

"Mom and Dad would be proud," I said, unsure why I had even spoken it out loud. I didn't like to talk about them like that—and especially not with Luke.

He swallowed hard, the muscles in his throat shifting. "Yeah," he replied in a whisper.

I realized too late that it'd been the wrong thing to do—mentioning Mom and Dad—because that was when Luke uttered a rasped curse and grabbed the neck of my beer bottle.

Then, without a second thought, he took a sip.

I watched in horror, like I'd just witnessed a homicide. He'd been sober for over a year—a whole fucking *year*—and it had taken my birthday and a stupid comment about our dead parents to tip him over the edge.

"What the hell, Luke?" I hissed with a gasp.

"Relax," he said, then cleared his throat and sucked at his teeth.

He stared at that bottle, looking down its gaping mouth as he licked his lips. His eyes were glazed over, in a trance, gazing into the amber glass like a junkie who'd just gotten a sought-after fix—and, I guessed, that was technically what my brother was.

A junkie.

An addict.

And after a year of fighting to shake the hold his poison of choice had on him, he'd given in.

And it was all my fault. Always, *always* my fucking fault.

"Luke," I said, already sliding off my barstool. "I think we should go. Melanie—"

"Hey!" he called the bartender. "Bring me another one of these, will ya?"

The bartender nodded, and I could only stare at my brother, horrified, as a turbulent wave of nausea barreled over me.

No, no, no.

"It's one beer, Charlie," he muttered, giving me the nastiest side-eye glare I'd ever seen.

"You shouldn't have *one beer*," I murmured just as the bartender slid the bottle over.

Luke caught it like a seasoned pro and knocked it back without a second to spare.

"God, we never should've come here," I said, shaking my head as he guzzled the whole damn thing down in three hearty gulps.

He sighed and smacked his lips, then wiped the back of his hand across his mouth. His eyes rolled toward mine, and I could see it already. Sober Luke was gone.

Just like that. One stupid little fucking sip was all it had taken to wipe away every bit of his progress.

Why didn't I drive the fucking car?

"Oh, shut up, Charlie. I'm fine, okay? Fucking *relax*."

And, hell, you know what? Maybe it could've been fine. Maybe in some other dimension, we walked out of that bar with one celebratory beer under each of our belts without any lasting damage to my brother's journey of an alcohol-free life. But that wasn't what happened.

Tommy and Rob walked into Tony's then. It had been years since I'd laid my eyes on either of them, and with just one glance, they reminded me instantly of my brother.

Only twenty-four, yet they bore the look of men ten years their senior. Tall, muscular, and I bet they each had their fair share of women. But their skin crinkled where mine didn't, and they laughed with a throaty rasp, like people who'd spent the past ten years of their lives sucking on cigarettes and guzzling down booze. Because they had.

"Holy fuck! Is that little Lukey Corbin?!" Rob crowed from the door.

I suppressed my eye roll. Dealing with Dumb and Dumber had never ever been on my list of plans for my twenty first birthday. But neither had been Tony's Bar to begin with.

Tommy whooped at Rob's side before quickly barreling in our direction. He wrapped his arms around my brother's shoulders and gave him an enthusiastic shake.

"Zero! What the hell happened to you, man?! You fuckin' disappeared!"

Luke laughed in a way he never did with Melanie or me, clapping his hand against Tommy's arm. His eyes twinkled with happiness and mirth, like he'd spent this past year hibernating and finally came back to life in the presence of his shitty friends.

Displeasure coiled tightly in my gut, and I palmed my phone in the pocket of my jeans, readying myself to call Melanie to tattle on her fiancé.

"Life, man," Luke answered with a shrug and a plastered-on grin. "You know how it goes."

Rob came to join the reunion at the bar when his eyes landed on me. He tipped his head, his lips curling upward in a smile that didn't quite meet his eyes.

"Charlie?" he asked as if he wasn't sure it was really me. Like he couldn't believe that, as he'd aged, so had I.

"Last time I checked," I muttered, rolling my eyes away to stare at the half-empty bottle of beer in front of me. I was surprised Luke hadn't finished it.

Tommy glanced in my direction, suddenly aware of my presence. "Whoa, is Charlie boy *drinking*?"

Charlie boy. The nickname pierced my skin and hit a nerve that made me flinch. Memories of Tommy's brother, Ritchie, and the fucked-up shit he'd done to keep me away, to keep me scared and quiet, came rushing in like a tidal wave I had no chance of escaping.

God, was he coming too? Would I have to face my mortal enemy after I'd managed to keep his shadow from falling over me for so many years?

"Charlie's twenty-one today," Luke said, grinning with pride in my direction.

For just a second, he was back, my big brother. Not the guy who put on a persona for his friends. Not the alcoholic who'd depended so much on poison to get through his days and nights.

He was Luke, and for the faintest glimmer of a moment, I thought, *God, he looks so much like Dad.*

I could almost hear my father in his voice. The inflections I'd nearly lost in the worn, faded memories. The gruff, throaty tone I'd spent so many nights reminding myself I'd never hear again. They were there now, all of it, living inside my brother.

Then, it passed, that bright moment of comfort and clarity, and *Zero* was back with his stupid fucking nickname and his stupid fucking friends.

They ordered another round of drinks, and Luke never protested. He clinked the neck of his second bottle against those of his friends' before glancing at me with a silent plea.

Don't tell Melanie, it said, as if she wouldn't figure it out herself when he came home, stinking of Budweiser.

Please, it said again and again when that second bottle turned into three, then four, and by the fifth, I was tired of meeting his gaze with mine. I was tired of this night. I was tired of checking the clock, watching the minutes and hours tick away, knowing damn well that Melanie was wondering and worrying and making herself sick while dinner grew cold.

He's such a piece of shit, I thought to myself as I left my barstool. *But I am, too, for letting it go on for this long.*

Luke grabbed my arm. His eyes weren't his anymore; they had lost all focus, lost their clarity. I shook him off.

"Where are you going?" he asked as his sixth bottle was placed in front of him.

"The bathroom," I snapped louder than was maybe necessary.

God, I was so *mad*.

"Why?"

I scoffed with a roll of my eyes, shaking my head. "To piss, Luke. I need to fucking piss. Is that okay with you? Am I allowed to fucking piss?"

He narrowed his eyes, their hue darkening by the second. A storm was rolling in. I could feel it, I could see it in the clenching of his fists, and I didn't fucking care. He could come at me if he wanted. He could pummel my face into oblivion, and I didn't give a shit because suddenly, this entire thing—going to the bar, the drink, the celebration—it no longer felt like something he'd done for *me*. He'd used me as an excuse to get a fix, and, okay, maybe he hadn't planned on his buddies being here, but he'd known exactly what he was doing when he passed our street.

He'd ruined my birthday, and he didn't give a shit.

"What's with the fucking attitude?" he demanded as his friends sniggered beside him, guzzling down their own beers.

Losers. They were all losers—my brother included.

"I don't have an attitude," I fired back. "I just need to fucking piss, and I want to fucking go home. So, I'm going to the bathroom, and when I get back, you're giving me the keys, and we're getting the fuck out of here."

Tommy snorted and leaned toward Rob's ear as he said, "Looks like Charlie boy finally grew a pair."

"Go to fucking hell, Tommy."

I stomped away in the direction of the bathroom, wishing I could be the one to send him there myself.

I threw the door open, slammed it behind me, and jabbed at the lock with my thumb. The small room was grimy, reeking of shit, stale vomit, cheap cologne, and piss. Yet I welcomed the calm I'd found inside. The noise of the bar was muffled within these graffitied walls, and without much thought to the diseases I was almost definitely contracting, I gripped my hands on the discolored sink's edge and stared at my reflection in the mirror streaked with only God knew what.

This is your fault, a little voice in my head said. *If you'd taken the car to work this morning, if you had been the one driving, if you had picked Luke up, we'd never be here.*

My lips pressed in a thin line as my head shook slowly from side to side. Dr. Sibilia's voice came to me, insisting that, no, this wasn't my fault. This had nothing to do with me—not really—and all to do with an illness Luke had contracted somewhere along the line. He was struggling. I'd known it, and Melanie had too. We'd questioned his strength every single time he was late coming home and every time he made a joke about wanting a drink.

Maybe I should've seen this coming.

I released a shaky breath and smacked the automatic faucet. A weak stream of tepid water sputtered from the tap as I pumped soap into my hands and scrubbed them until they ached. Then, I pulled my phone out of my pocket and dialed Melanie's number.

***

I had thought it'd feel more like tattling when I called my brother's fiancée and confessed where we were when we should've been at home. I had thought it'd feel wrong. But instead, I felt like I'd finally done something right in a string of wrongs.

I hadn't convinced my parents to stay home from that concert when I knew something bad was going to happen.

I hadn't kept Luke away from Ritchie before the damage could be done.

But I had called Melanie—the one person I knew who could make him leave the bar—and *that* felt good despite the way he glared at me when she showed up at Tony's and demanded he get into her fucking car. Like a mother to a child.

He didn't protest though, and I took solace in that. Even when his friends glared at me as I snatched the keys from the spot at the bar where my brother had sat.

"You've always been a little shit—you know that?" Rob muttered, his words loose and on the brink of slurring.

I stopped from leaving and looked at Tommy, waiting for whatever bullshit he was about to spew at me. And why I waited, I didn't even know. Maybe I just wanted to see if their words could still knock me down or make me cry.

Tommy shook his head, struggling to stand up straight. "Some babies don't ever fuckin' grow up."

"Too bad Ritchie isn't here. He'd kick his whiny little ass."

That was the last thing I heard as I walked toward the door, surprised that I was able to. Surprised that their bullshit hadn't left me curled up on the ground, wishing my big brother would come along to save me.

And it wasn't that it hadn't stung, and I knew their callous comments would swarm through my mind and leave me sleepless. But I was able to walk away, and that …

That felt like something.

Or maybe I just hadn't had the time to care about what Luke's friends thought about me when I couldn't stop thinking about what would happen once we got home.

***

"It was a few fucking beers, Melanie! I'm not even drunk," Luke shouted, his voice ringing from upstairs.

I sat at the table, alone, eating the reheated cottage pie I'd requested for dinner.

I doubted anyone would sing "Happy Birthday" to me.

There were bigger things to deal with. Like Melanie once again threatening to leave and Luke trying to convince her that what he'd done wasn't a big deal.

I wished she'd go. I wished she'd get herself a new, better life.

I wished he'd get his head out of his ass. I wished he'd realize he had won the lottery when she agreed to stick around—over and over and over again.

I wish Mom and Dad were here.

I sighed and breathed through a wave of emotion that threatened to pour into my mashed potatoes and beef.

"God, you really don't fucking get it, do you?" Melanie cried, desperate and exasperated.

"No! No, I don't. So, why don't you explain it to me, huh? Explain to me why it's a big fucking deal that I had a drink with my brother on his—"

"You and I both know this has nothing to do with Charlie. So, keep him the hell out of it, okay? Don't even go there. You used his birthday as a fucking excuse to get your drink on with your loser buddies, and you know it."

"I had no fucking idea that Rob and Tommy would be there!"

"Luke! Oh my God!" Melanie exclaimed. "They're there every single fucking night!"

God, she was right. I knew it, and I'd bet anything that Luke knew it, too, judging by the momentary pause in their heated fight right above my head.

I poked my fork around the plate, rolling a single pea around the edge. Just waiting for them to continue while praying Melanie didn't leave, but also hoping she'd finally let this be the straw to break the proverbial camel's back.

It was strange to be so simultaneously selfish and selfless. My heart and mind were in constant war, and I wished I could turn back the clock to this morning. Things hadn't been perfect for the year Luke was sober, but it sure as hell had been better than this.

"I thought we were done with this shit," Melanie finally said, her voice quiet but still loud enough for me to hear through the ceiling. "I thought … I thought you were doing better."

"Babe, I *am* doing better," Luke replied, gentler than before.

I at least had to give him credit for that. His anger was quicker to dissipate now, and that was somewhat of an improvement. Maybe he was growing up after all.

"Luke, you drank when you were supposed to stay sober."

"I'm not drunk though. I stayed sober." He paused, then said, "Well, kind of."

"But you *drank*! God, the definition of staying sober, Luke, is that you *don't drink*. Period. End of conversation. Do you not understand that?"

"I just had a couple of beers, Melanie. That's all."

Six, but who's counting?

"And you would've continued if your brother hadn't called me."

Right again.

I shook my head, finally done with the game of tag between the pea and my fork. I dropped the utensil to the side of my plate and held my head in my hands. A nauseating rush of trepidation speared my gut as that old feeling of knowing something bad was about to happen made itself at home, and all I wanted was to kick it out, knowing damn well that would be impossible.

She's going to leave.

"I'll go back to AA tomorrow," Luke said, determination in his voice. "Okay? I'm done. No more."

"I've heard that before, Luke." God, she sounded so weak, so tired.

"No," he nearly shouted as footsteps crossed the floor above. "Babe, I'm serious. I won't ever have another drink. That's it. I swear to fuckin' God. I love you, okay? And if giving up booze is what it takes to keep you around, then ..."

His voice drifted off and the conversation died. Before I could hurry and get my dish washed and put away, they began to fuck—and I was all too aware of it, thanks to the telltale signs of the mattress springs singing their favorite song. I guessed she'd forgiven him, and I was both happy and disappointed—as usual.

But we were both quick to learn that Luke's promises—no matter who he swore to—were meant to be broken.

Because two weeks later, he got into a fight at Tony's Bar.

It was with Ritchie. They were both drunk, and although Ritchie later decided not to press charges after Luke broke his nose—*again*—my brother had still spent an entire night in a cell.

And I wished I could say it was the only time he'd been arrested, but Luke was the liar in the family. Not me.

CHAPTER FOURTEEN

MASSACHUSETTS, PRESENT DAY

It wasn't quite Halloween yet, but in Salem, that didn't matter. The streets were packed with decorations and costumed amblers. Tourists and spooks, the real and the posers.

It was easy to tell the difference. The genuinely dark souls carried their shadows with comfort, whereas the posers pranced around in an awkward, giddy display, like they were getting away with something naughty when they'd probably never done anything truly naughty in their lives.

I kept my head down as I weaved my way through the crowded sidewalk toward the house of Blake Carson, the tattoo artist I'd gone to years ago and owner of Salem Skin. Even the side streets in the residential parts of the city were packed with people, and the way my skin prickled with nerves to be around such a large mob was nearly enough to make me slink back into the shadows and disappear.

God, I wanted to. But there was that silly fact that I'd been invited to this party—*me!* I was *wanted*. And I had told myself that I wasn't allowed to back down from it, no matter how badly I swore I didn't want to be there, sharing the same oxygen as all the people I didn't know. Shit, even now, standing outside and struggling to control the panic racing through my bones, every ounce of my body told me to turn around and run back to my cottage, where it was safe and secluded.

But a much smaller piece of me, so much tinier than my monumental panic, yelled through the static of anxious thoughts and told me to just step inside the house. Just one foot. Hell, one *toe* would suffice, the very tip of my boot. Just to say I had done it.

All because nobody in the entire world had ever invited *me* to a stupid party.

I took a deep, shaky breath and pulled the black hooded mask from my jacket pocket with trembling hands. The invitation had strictly stated that it was to be a costume party, so I tugged the hood—imprinted with a skull—over my head, ensured that my ponytailed hair was tucked underneath and hidden by the collar of my jacket.

Then, I headed up the cobblestone walkway to the open door, where I entered Blake's house, officially attending a party by myself for the first time in all my thirty-eight years on this earth.

If you could only see me now. I sent the thought off to Luke and smirked sadly behind my mask, not at all surprised to feel the familiar tug of emotion against my heart and lungs. I was quick to recover, clearing my throat and feeling the rush of embarrassment scorch my cheeks, until I realized nobody here could see me.

None of these people crowding this living room had any idea whatsoever who I was, and with that epiphany came an unusual surge of confidence.

I could be anyone.

I could be any*thing*.

Anonymous.

My head was held higher now as I moved through the crowd of people, all in costume. All unknown to me. Just as I felt I could be anyone, so were they, and none of them mattered.

Blake Carson showed up in the doorway of what seemed to be the dining room, wearing a leather jacket, a black T-shirt, and black jeans. He didn't appear to be in costume, and I thought that was peculiar when the invitation to his own damn party had made it a requirement.

"Hey, man," he said by way of greeting, extending a hand to me. "Thanks for coming."

Taking his hand in mine felt like the most daring thing I'd ever done. Forming a smile I knew he couldn't see felt reckless. We shook, and he smiled, and that was when I took note of his elongated canines.

"Nice costume," I complimented without hesitation. No stutter. No fear.

Maybe I should wear a mask more often.

"Don't encourage him," a blonde woman—dressed as Dorothy from *The Wizard of Oz*—said as she hurried past with a plate of food in hand. "He wears the same thing every single year."

I watched briefly as she brought the plate to the couch, where she handed it to a man who looked nearly identical to Blake—the only difference being that Blake sported a beard and a longer, more polished hairdo. This other man was clean-shaven with short, mussed-up hair, and he was dressed as Captain America. There was chocolate smudged on one of his cheeks and an innocence in his eyes, one I hadn't seen in my own reflection since childhood.

"That's my brother, Jake," Blake said, and I turned back to him to see he'd followed my gaze.

"Twins?" I asked, surprised by my own bravery in prying, continuing a conversation with a person I hardly knew.

Blake nodded curtly. "Yeah. Anyway, food's in the kitchen; booze is in the fridge and the cooler by the back door. Make yourself at home."

He slapped a hand against my shoulder as he walked past before I had time to process his abrupt change in demeanor. There'd been a defensiveness in his tone when speaking of his brother, I realized after the fact, and although I couldn't say I knew his personal reasons for that, I also understood the need to defend and protect well.

Having a brother incarcerated for ending someone's life would do that to you.

I moved into the kitchen, watching the world through a sheer screen of black mesh. I looked for the woman who'd invited me, scanning the crowd around the buffet table and the few people standing by the mentioned cooler.

Exactly why I wanted to find her, I wasn't sure. To avoid her maybe. Or perhaps, with the help of my mask, I'd finally found the courage to ask for her name.

When I didn't find her in the dining room or kitchen, I moved silently like a specter, following a witch and Ghostbuster through the back door and into a backyard bordered in English-style gardens. Purposefully chaotic and meticulously overgrown.

It felt fitting to find her there, standing to the side of a weeping willow, a black cup in her hand as she spoke with a woman donning a head of purple dreadlocks. She was oblivious to my presence at first, and I was grateful, as the gown she wore stopped me dead in my tracks, reminding me instantly of embarrassing Victorian goth wet dreams I'd had in my late teens.

The ribbons laced through the corseted top were cinched tightly enough to emphasize her waistline and the voluptuous, rounded swell of her breasts, accentuating a cleavage I was struggling to tear my eyes from. The full, flowing skirt dusted the ground, only revealing quick glimpses of the sparkling black heels she wore on her feet. Her jet-black hair was piled into a cool and purposefully messy nest that would've made Helena Bonham Carter proud, and to it, a veil was pinned, distorting my view of her face.

I hated that I couldn't stop staring.

I hated the thoughts that were going through my head.

The things I wanted to do to her. The things I wanted her to do to me. Things I never should've wanted in the first place, and I knew without a shred of doubt that it was then that I should turn around and leave.

I'd held up my end of the self-imposed bargain. I'd entered the party; I could say that I'd gone. It was time to go, yet not only did I not leave, but my damn feet kept on moving toward her. One foot in front of the other, walking as if I were floating on air through the yard.

She turned from the dreadlocked woman to watch me stalk in her direction, and although the night was dark and the veil kept her features soft and shadowed, I could clearly make out the curve of her black smile.

"You came," she said, both genuinely surprised and—dare I say it—happy.

"You knew it was me," I stated, my voice low, and not at all paying attention as the dreadlocked woman smirked like she knew something I didn't before walking toward the house without announcing her leave.

My mystery woman in the Victorian gown didn't falter for a second as she reached out and lifted my hand in hers. Instinct warned me to pull back, to snatch my hand away, and still, I didn't listen to an intuition I'd seldom ignored in the past.

I let her impossibly smooth fingers clench lightly around mine as she said, "You don't exactly blend in."

She was talking about my tattoos, of course, but the comment dug deeper beneath my skin, grazing against something I'd kept locked away and guarded. I was reminded then of my heart, as if I needed to be, and, God, it was beating so loud.

Can she hear it?

"I try," I muttered, watching the way her long black thumbnail traced one thin strand of ink etched along my middle finger.

A shock of electric heat zapped my nerves, and the hairs along my arms stood on end. I swallowed audibly, and she must've heard because she looked up to where my face was. Her eyes struggled to meet mine through the barriers of her veil and my mask, and yet she managed to succeed.

"You should try harder," she replied, her voice not unlike a satisfied cat's purr.

I caught myself chuckling before I could stop the sound from rumbling up from my chest. "I thought I was doing a pretty good job, to be honest with you."

"Well, I can't speak for anybody else, but ..." She released a deep breath as she nodded, lowering our conjoined hands, her thumbnail still tracing that webbed line. "I see you."

I lifted my chin, looking down at her through hooded eyes concealed from hers. "And what if I don't want to be seen?" I challenged past my heart, thumping an irregular tune in my throat.

The woman tipped her head with consideration before laughing gently through her nose. She shook her head slowly—hardly noticeable to anyone who wasn't paying attention, but I was. She tightened her hold on my hand, reminding me she hadn't yet let go and neither had I, as she took a step closer. There were mere inches of space between us, and a breeze blew past, carrying with it a spicy blend of cinnamon and black pepper, filling the gap between our twin black forms.

With her chin tipped up, her face aimed toward mine, I was glad for her veil. I was even gladder for my mask. Glad for the things that kept her from witnessing the turmoil on my face and the hope in my eyes as they dropped to stare at her full black lips.

"But I think you do, Spider," she said quietly, using that nickname again that I both loved and hated, only for the fact that she had nothing else to call me. "And I'm glad that, of all the witches in this city, you chose to catch me in your web."

My lips parted softly to speak, though my tongue ceased all ability to form words as she released my hand and walked back toward the house, daring me with a crook of her lithe finger to follow.

But if I could've, I would've told her I hadn't chosen her. I would've said she'd come along when I least expected, landing on one silvery strand of my carefully crafted life of secrecy and solitude when my back was turned. I would've mentioned that she possessed the ability to leave, to fly away and never see my face or speak to me again, and I would've gladly let her.

Unless I just forgot where I'd laid the sticky shit down, I thought as I followed, lured by lace and tulle, cinnamon and black pepper.

Maybe, if I'm not careful, I'll get caught with her.
And would that really be so bad?

CHAPTER FIFTEEN

MASSACHUSETTS, PRESENT DAY

Somewhere in my mid-twenties, I'd met a girl named Morgan.
    She'd bumped into me during my shift at the cemetery. I had just finished weeding the area surrounding my parents' graves when I spotted the pretty young woman, weeping over the grave of her sister's stillborn son.

"I feel so weird," she said through her tears, *accepting a tissue from the pack I always kept in my pocket for moments like this. "I didn't even know him. And it's such bullshit that I never will."*
    "We often mourn for two different reasons," I replied while thinking about her poor sister, unable to comprehend how it must've felt to carry a baby for months, only to bury him before getting the chance to hear him cry. *"We mourn what once was, and we mourn the possibility of what could've been. Sometimes, we only*

mourn one or the other, and unfortunately, in your case, it's obviously the latter. And you're right; it is bullshit."

I hadn't intended anything to come from saying what I had. It'd been as much for her as it was for me, shedding a few tears myself for the parents who'd never been allowed to witness me becoming a somewhat-stable man with a college degree, driver's license, and steady job. But my words touched something inside of her, and she collapsed into my arms, sobbing for her sister's pain and the nephew she'd never get the chance to hold and know. I wiped her tears, surprised that I possessed the power to be so brazen with a stranger, especially an attractive member of the opposite sex.

And then, in a moment that was unexpected and unprovoked, she kissed me.

A full-blown make-out session ensued right there in the middle of the cemetery I worked at, only yards away from where my parents eternally lay. A chaotic frenzy of snaking tongues and tangled limbs, the taste of salt and sorrow mingling between our open mouths. She wove her hands into my hair, pulling tightly, holding on for dear life, almost as though if she let go, she'd be the next one to join those in their infinite slumber. In a breathless moment of sheer desperation, she asked if I had a condom, and of course, I didn't because why would I? Sex with random women wasn't something I'd engaged in ... well, ever.

"Never mind. That's okay," she replied, panting as she quickly undid my belt buckle. "I'm on the pill."

It'd been the most exciting, most careless, most insane thing I'd ever done in my life at that point, having unprotected sex with a woman I didn't know in the shadows of the cemetery. But I couldn't find a damn thing wrong in what we'd done together.

We'd needed a release. We'd needed fun. We'd needed the exhilaration of engaging in the most primal of things, the very lifeblood of what it meant to be a living, breathing human. Even if we'd both known we'd never see each other again—and we hadn't.

And now, this woman—the one I still had yet to know the name of—reminded me of that moment in my life. Of Morgan and that blip of time in which our paths had crossed. Of excitement and scandal and everything good about being alive when there was otherwise nothing good about it at all.

I had felt it the moment her hand grabbed mine and her pointed nail traced the lines embedded into my skin, like her intent was to commit every touch of ink to memory. I hadn't wanted to feel it—God knew I'd spent long enough resisting this very thing. Connection. Interdependence. Intimacy on any point of the spectrum. But to deny that she'd reignited something that I had long ago left to die would've been a waste of time and proverbial breath.

It was there. I didn't want it to be, but it was.

She sees me.

I had learned early in life that hope was often a foolish thing, meant only for those who hadn't yet gotten sick of being let down. I knew better, and I couldn't allow myself to want anything more than this time here, in this yard.

And yet ...

It was so nice to sit with her on this bench in Blake's backyard. To feel her presence, to share the air with someone else. And as the minutes passed, my comfort expanded, and my knees spread further, pressing my thigh deeper against hers almost absentmindedly until the fabric of my jeans was flush with the threads of her dress and the warmth of her body seeped through every fiber to awaken my nerves and heat the life pumping through my guarded heart.

It wasn't good. I *knew* it as I barely heard what she'd said, too deafened by the blood whooshing through my ears, and still, I nodded, not wanting her to think I'd been ignoring her.

I shouldn't care.

Oh, but, God, I did.

It was already a beautiful night. The perfect example of autumn in New England. But the cinnamon and incense she'd injected into the air, combined with the smokiness of her voice, cocooned me in a serenity I'd never known before. There was an awareness that, once I emerged from this chrysalis, I'd remember this as the most gorgeous night of my life despite the cluster of guests who had just wandered out into the yard, chattering loudly and barking with abrupt bursts of laughter.

Our party of two on the bench fell as silent as my neighbors, both of our attention turned in the direction of the stragglers. And I found that even our silence was comfortable when it shouldn't have been, too comfortable for two people who didn't yet know each other's name, and the warning sirens in my head were ringing louder than any church bell in the city.

The group seemed to take particular interest in one of the flower beds, nodding with approval for a few moments before turning around and heading back inside without sparing a second to notice our presence.

When they were gone, the woman at my side said, "So, this might surprise you because I'm obviously the definition of everything sunshiny and sweet, but I really don't like parties."

"Neither do I," I replied.

"And yet you came anyway." She laughed with a tiny shred of triumph and the tiniest, almost-undetectable bit of disbelief.

"I had nothing better to do," I replied nonchalantly, trying so hard to act casual and cool while knowing I was probably failing miserably at both.

It was hard to act anything but neurotic and shaken when I knew, as sure as I'd known something terrible would happen the night my parents died, that my world was never going to be the same as it was before I came to this party.

"From saving my life to threatening to kill me to offering stellar compliments." She added a wistful sigh for good measure. "I don't wanna say anything, but I'm getting some mixed signals over here."

The words were said in jest, sarcastic, but there was truth to them, and I said nothing, as they were allowed to marinate.

Am I intentionally pushing her away?

The wind answered with a gust of rustling willow branches. Of course I was. I knew myself enough to see that, and I knew myself well enough to know why.

"So, what exactly do you do all the time? I mean, when you're not ... doing whatever it is you do in the graveyard," she said, stealing me away from my thoughts and changing the subject.

I chuckled quietly, splaying my hands over my knees. "I maintain the grounds. I open the gates, dig the graves, mow the lawn—"

She snorted and nearly choked around a laugh. "That's one *big* fuckin' lawn."

Beneath my mask, I smiled easily. "Keeps me busy."

"Too busy to work on those social skills—that's for damn sure."

My smile broadened. "That's kinda always been the idea."

"But, like ... why?"

"Why do you want to know?" I asked, amused.

She shrugged. "I'm curious! You're, like, a mystery, and now, I finally have my chance to talk to the elusive *Spider*." She said it with amazement and awe. "I wanna know more about you, other than how much you love threatening people."

"I don't *love* threatening people," I corrected, fighting the urge to clench my jaw and grow rigid with the need to defend myself.

She huffed a laugh. "Sure had me fooled."

"I do what I have to do to get by and do the right thing, but I don't *love* it." I snickered, giving my head a slight shake at the audacity.

"Oh, I see." She nodded, an air of sarcasm fueling the motion. "That makes me feel better. You were about to sever my jugular, but you wouldn't have found pleasure in it."

"You *broke into* my *house*," I pointed out for what felt like the thirtieth time. This time though, it was said teasingly with a smile.

"And I *said* I was *sorry*!" She laughed, her cheeks darkening beneath the blush she wore.

Shit, she was pretty. Absolutely stunning. She looked like one of those alternative-style models with pale skin, a generous number of piercings glittering in various parts of her face and ears, chaotic black hair, and a certain rebellious quality, carried with every lift of her hand or quirk of her lips.

What she wanted from a loser like me, I had no idea.

"Anyway"—I cleared my throat, attempting to send the unwanted negativity away—"I draw, read … that's sort of it."

It seemed pathetic now that I'd said it out loud. But the truth was, a part of what kept me loving my job so much was how little time I had to do anything else. Little downtime meant little time to think. Little time to mourn. Little time to miss people I couldn't be with.

"You draw?" She seemed intrigued. "Are you any good?"

I shrugged. "My brother always thought so," I said, already knowing how lame that sounded before it even came out of my mouth.

"Does your brother lie a lot?"

I huffed a laugh, thinking of all the blunt truths Luke had thrown my way. "No. Not particularly," I said, even as I thought about all the promises he'd unintentionally broken.

She quirked a half smile, bumped her shoulder against mine, then said, "Well, you must be pretty good then."

I swallowed at the thought and replied, "Maybe."

"I hope you'll show me sometime."

My half smile matched hers as I muttered once again, "Maybe."

***

She was from Connecticut, not too far from where I'd lived up until several years ago. But I didn't tell her that.

She had a younger sister and a couple of nephews, and I thought about how nice it would've been to be an uncle. Not that it was likely for me to be a cool one. I was too weird and reclusive for that, and then the thought of being the weird uncle seemed all at once fitting and shitty. But I would've loved whatever kids Luke might've had in a different, better life, in my own weird, crappy way, and the pain twisted like a dull knife to know it would never ever happen.

I told her none of that either.

In response to her talk of where she'd been and who she'd left behind, I nodded and threw in various sounds of acknowledgment. Just so she knew I was listening with the hope that it would be enough. In the same way that the simple joy of sitting beside her in an intoxicating cloud of smokiness and cinnamon was enough for me.

"Do you like living at the cemetery?" she asked, steering the conversation away from herself for the first time in about a half hour.

"I do," I replied, keeping it simple.

"Seriously?" Her eyes twinkled with delight, her voice incredulous.

I nodded. "It's peaceful—well …" I paused, unsure if I wanted to continue. Unsure if I wanted to be so brazen—unsure that I even possessed the ability. But then, after taking a moment to carefully choose my words, I continued, "Except for when mysterious women show up, looking for me in unethical ways."

It sounded rehearsed and cautious, almost robotic in tone. I hated myself for it immediately. Hated myself for thinking I could actually talk to her in a way that teetered on the edge of flirtatious.

But it didn't seem to bother her as she snorted with amusement.

"Does that happen often?"

"I can say with confidence that you were the first."

She turned to me, narrowing her eyes with skepticism, like she had a hard time believing that I didn't have women lined up at my door.

"What?" I chuckled, diverting my gaze even though she couldn't see through the mask I still wore.

"I just can't believe nobody has ever tried to get their hands on you yet."

It was her own attempt at flirtation, and it was far more effective than mine. My face heated as my collar made the abrupt decision to strangle the life out of me, leaving little room for a response. And when it was obvious that I wasn't saying anything, she cleared her throat, as if to close the door on another awkward exchange.

Nice job, moron.

She turned away and said, "I love cemeteries. Like, what they stand for. I *appreciate* them. But I don't know that I could live *in* one."

I huffed a laugh as one side of my mouth twitched upward. She couldn't have known, but Luke had said roughly the same thing to me when I told him about the job in Salem.

"Dude, I know you've always been into the cemetery thing, but, like, I don't know how you could live in one. It gives me the fuckin' creeps, just thinking about it."

I could hear him now and the incredulity in his tone, like he had legitimately thought I'd finally lost my damn mind.

I had told him I had already accepted the job. I watched the furrow of his brow as I worried my bottom lip, my hands shaking and my legs jouncing wildly beneath the table. I waited for what felt like years for him to beg me not to go, even though it was his idea in the first place for me to get the fuck out of Connecticut. I desperately wanted him to take it all back ... but he hadn't.

I released a morose sigh, and my shoulders hunched against the bench. The black-haired woman at my side turned to study me with the strangest blend of curiosity, pity, understanding, and an affection I felt was undeserved. I half expected her to ask what was wrong, what had once again shifted my demeanor, but what I was noticing about her was that maybe, just maybe, she had the same ability to read people and situations as I did.

So, she said nothing about that and instead continued to talk. And I sat on that bench, reluctantly allowing my lips to smile again, as I listened to her go on about nothing against the backdrop of crickets and muffled chatter coming from the house.

Shows she had been watching on the hotel TV.

A brand of cereal she'd been craving for weeks, but would never be able to find because it'd been discontinued for years.

Her love for a pair of platform boots she'd seen at a local clothing shop and not stopped thinking about since.

It was all so mundane and pointless. I had no idea why she was talking to me about any of it. But I sat there and took it all in because I was also listening to what she wasn't saying.

She was anxious and nervous, displayed only in her penchant for rambling and bouncing her legs beneath the full, lacy skirt. Her words flowed easily enough; she didn't stutter the way I sometimes had a tendency to do, but there was something about the night that left her feeling uneasy.

Is it me?

I speculated as she went on about her appreciation for Luke's bike and how she'd always wanted a motorcycle, but never gotten around to getting one.

No, I thought, narrowing my eyes. *If it were me, she wouldn't have invited me. She wouldn't have allowed me to sit with her all this time.*

I wondered if there was one person inside who made her feel this way—nervous, internally on edge. I wondered who it might be and if there was anything I could say—or do—to put her at ease, finding that I wanted to be that person to make it better.

But then again, maybe it was *everyone* who made her anxious. After all, she had mentioned that she hated parties, so perhaps that was all it was.

Do I make her feel better? I wondered as she laughed at something she'd said, something I'd missed while navigating through the twists and turns of my stupid brain. *Am I arrogant enough to believe that I could?*

I wasn't sure about that, but as I watched the jittering of her knee, concealed only a little by the layers of black and tulle, I was sure about something.

She was far more like me than I'd initially expected.

And perhaps not allowing this to develop into anything more was going to be harder than I'd thought.

***

Blake wandered outside with the blonde Dorothy in tow. She was on the phone, veering off to stand in a quiet corner of the yard while Blake approached. He walked in a way that reminded me instantly of Luke—casual and effortlessly cool—with his hands tucked deep into the pockets of his leather jacket. He stopped beside the mystery woman I'd spent the night with and playfully patted the bouncy, knotted mess of hair on the top of her head.

"You good out here, Stormy girl?"

My eyes narrowed beneath the cover of my mask while my heart galloped at an alarming speed as another bit of information fell into my lap. I curled my fist at my side, as if to hold on to the nickname, pressing the letters and syllables against my palm and forcing them to burrow beneath my skin.

Stormy girl.

"You came out to check up on me, huh?" she replied, tipping her head back to look up at the man who looked as at home in the shadows as I did.

"Me? Never," he denied, shaking his head, then flicking his eyes in my direction. "Just needed to get some air."

She jabbed her elbow against his thigh. "I'm a big girl, Blakey boy. You don't need to watch over me."

Their penchant to use nicknames—*pet* names—bristled a part of me that had no reason to be bristled at all. Jealousy was swift to kick in though, and I didn't have time to tamp it down before it reared its ugly head. I didn't like how close they seemed, how familiar and openly affectionate. Questions of what their relationship entailed bit ferociously at my tongue while my brain screamed reminders of how it was none of my damn business, and why the hell did I care anyway?

Blake pulled in a deep breath and pressed his lips into a flat, thin line. He wasn't happy with her response. He wanted to protect her, like she needed to be guarded at all costs. Whether it was for romantic or platonic reasons, I couldn't tell, but there was something in the way he glared at me with question and skepticism that made me realize he didn't trust me.

He was right not to, yet, suddenly, there was nothing in this world I wanted more than for this guy to know I wasn't someone he needed to worry about. So, in a fleeting moment of furious determination, I pulled off my mask and was greeted by a flurry of crackling static as the knitted material ran over my mess of ponytailed hair.

The mystery woman—*Stormy girl*—stared intently while her body remained still; even the jitters of her legs had ceased through the duration of my unveiling.

Blake watched, too, but his stare was less excited and more satisfied.

The night air was cool on my face, and my skin began to breathe again, even as my lungs were already on their way to anxiety-induced failure. Now bare and vulnerable, I forced my gaze to meet Blake's, and he acknowledged the gesture with a subtle nod of his chin.

A man up to no good was unlikely to reveal himself to witnesses.

"There you are," Stormy girl said, finally introducing a voice to the moment.

I felt her green gaze on me, and my eyes dodged toward hers before looking down at the mask wrenched between my hands.

"It was getting hot in there," I felt the need to explain, my voice barely above a whispered mutter.

The blonde Dorothy headed in our direction, a wide smile on her face as she came to stand at Blake's side.

"My mom's going to be bringing the kids back in about an hour," she said, looping her arm through his.

"Shit," he muttered, clapping a hand to his forehead. "I forgot to put their sheets in the dryer before—"

"I'm way ahead of you, babe," she said, patting her hand against his chest. "I washed Jake's too."

I quickly put the pieces together and realized Dorothy must've been Blake's wife or girlfriend. Relief swept over me, as if any of it had any bearing on me at all.

Blake blew out a sigh as Stormy girl jabbed her elbow against his thigh.

"You should thank the universe for thinking you're worthy of someone like her," she teased. "She's a saint for putting up with your cranky ass."

"I fuckin' know it," he replied before resting his hand over Dorothy's and kissing the top of her head.

Another rush of jealousy pushed its way into my veins and heated the apples of my cheeks. I looked away from Blake and his significant other and tried to remember when I'd last had any kind of intimate contact with anyone.

I couldn't.

"Babe, is that your work?" Dorothy asked.

"Yeah, I did those. How long ago was it?"

When nobody else replied for a few seconds, it occurred to me that they were talking about me. With a start, I followed Dorothy's gaze to my hands lying in my lap.

"O-oh," I stammered, feeling like a socially inept jackass. "Um ... three years maybe?"

I dropped the mask to my thighs and lifted my hands, splaying my fingers for them all to get a better look at the chaotic design of webs embedded into my skin.

"They still look good," Blake complimented.

"Of course they do," Dorothy said softly, her voice full of love and adoration and everything I was unlikely to ever know again. "You did them."

Blake grumbled in protest, then said, "Well, yeah, but that doesn't mean jack shit if they're not cared for after the fact. Even the greatest tattoos will look like trash over time if they're not taken care of properly. But these, they still look really good. Nice job, man."

"Thanks," I replied, not knowing how else to react.

"So, is that how you two met then?" Dorothy asked, her eyes volleying between me and the woman at my side. "At the shop?"

She thinks we're a couple.

A cold, aching panic arose in my gut, and I immediately wanted to correct her. What if she didn't want anyone to think we were together? Fuck, what if *I* didn't?

Do I?

But Stormy girl wasn't fazed at all by the question as she shook her head. "No, I was never around when Blake did Spider's tats. But we sort of ..." She glanced at me and lifted one shoulder. "We just … kept bumping into each other."

Her eyes pinned mine as one side of her mouth lifted into a half smile, sickly sweet and painfully adorable, and the thought of kissing her hit me like a punch to the gut.

"Spider? Is that your name?" Dorothy asked.

Stormy girl's laughter was abrupt and nervous, her eyes never leaving mine. "Actually, that's just what we call him down at the shop. Um, I don't, um—"

"Charlie," I interrupted quickly before I could think better of it. My eyes held Stormy girl's for a moment before going back to Dorothy's. "M-my name's Charlie."

After all these years, they were the first people in this city, apart from a few colleagues and Ivan, to know my name. I guessed Blake had technically already known it, after doing my tattoos years ago and needing my driver's license to do the work, but I figured it was unlikely that he'd remember after all this time.

"Ah, that's right," he said, proving my assumption correct. "Charlie. Not as badass as Spider, but what can you do?"

He was teasing, offering a friendly smirk. The more of myself I gave, the more at ease he seemed while I stressed that it was all too much, like I was diving in too deep and too fast.

"Anyway, we'd better get back to the party," Blake said, already beginning to walk back inside. "Don't keep her up too late, Charlie. She's got work in the morning."

The woman beside me groaned lightheartedly. "Whatever, Dad."

Dorothy tossed a friendly wave over her shoulder while keeping up with Blake, her arm still wrapped around his as they disappeared inside.

"So, Ch—"

"What was—"

We spoke at the same time, and then we both laughed. Hers a giggle stifled by closed lips, mine a gruff chuckle. Her cheeks deepened in their blush as my face was set on fire.

"What were you gonna say?" I asked.

"No, you go first."

I shook my head, furrowing my brow. "It wasn't anything. I, um, I was just wondering what her name was—Blake's—"

"Audrey. She's Blake's wife," Stormy girl replied. "Sorry. I don't know why I thought you already knew. I should've introduced you, but ..." She laughed again, and I reveled far too much in the smokiness of the sound. Like sitting beside a bonfire on a cool autumn evening. "Okay, I thought about it, but I felt a little stupid, not knowing your name. And Blake was already going all big brother on me ..."

I shrugged with forced nonchalance. "No big deal."

"He gets like that. Maybe a little *too* overprotective for his own good, but ... it's nice," she went on, plucking at a loose thread in her lacy skirt.

She liked to talk. Far more than I did. I wondered if it helped her nerves, to fill the dead air with the sound of something. I was the opposite; I clammed up when I was even remotely anxious. It was for the better, knowing damn well that I was likely to stutter my way through whatever stupid nonsense I was trying to say, only to fuck it up and spend the night in a puddle of sweat while keeping those humiliating moments on repeat in my mind.

But I liked listening to her.

I didn't want to, knowing I would probably spend many sleepless hours replaying the way she'd said certain words in my head. Slowing them down, speeding them up, memorizing the inflections. But it was happening. I knew it in the way my heartbeat hammered an erratic beat at the sound of her voice while my shoulders loosened just a little, relieving the tiniest amount of tension.

She relaxed me, and, fuck, it wasn't good.

But … I liked it.

"Why?" I bit out the one-worded question just to keep her talking, and, sure, I was curious.

She replied with a huffed laugh. "Why what?"

"Why does he, you know"—I gestured with a hand—"get like that?"

I hadn't known it at the time, but I soon learned that it was the wrong thing to ask.

Stormy girl stiffened at my side, her leg frozen mid-bounce. Her hands clenched together; her lips puckered and pulled to one side. She pulled in a deep breath and cleared her throat.

"Never mind," I was quick to add. "Don't—"

"Let's just say, I don't have a great track record with men," she replied and released the air in her lungs. "And Blake, Cee—the lady with the dreads—they're my best friends, they're practically family, and they know all about it."

"Ah."

It wasn't the answer I'd wanted or expected. My brain automatically envisioned her sleeping with a slew of questionable men. Threesomes. Full-blown orgies. Her body among a massive heap of tangled limbs and nameless faces contorted in immense pleasure. It was ridiculous and irrational, but that never stopped my brain from working itself to death before.

"Maybe I'll tell you about it someday," she quietly added.

"If you want."

"A man of many words," she jabbed, relaxing again with a snarky retort.

"Not a lot to say."

She sighed wistfully. "Gonna be really awkward when we spend the drive back to the hotel in total silence."

My brow furrowed as my eyes quickly narrowed with suspicion and protest. I thought about Morgan, that girl in the cemetery all those years ago. It'd been my one and only random hookup, as Luke had called it. I had no intention of doing it again—and especially not with Stormy girl. I couldn't put my finger on why, but she seemed worth more than that.

She *deserved* more than that.

I shook my head. "I don't—"

"I just meant I don't want to walk through the parking lot alone," she quietly explained. "Blake's been taking me back every day since … you know … and, um,

I just figured since you live across the street, you could—"

"Oh. Sure," I interrupted brashly, feeling stupid for assuming anything otherwise. "Yeah, I can do that."

She sighed as her lips curled in a soft smile. "Thanks, Charlie. I appreciate it."

"Yep," I replied as I read between her lines, aware of the things she wasn't saying, confirming my earlier suspicions.

Despite not knowing me, I made her feel protected—*safe*—and I wanted to find comfort in that.

But, God, if she only knew how wrong she was to believe those lies …

Man, she probably wouldn't want to be alone with me at all.

CHAPTER SIXTEEN

CONNECTICUT, AGE TWENTY-TWO

Luke's AA meetings were held in the basement of a church, which was conveniently located just across the street from where I worked at the cemetery.

After breaking Ritchie's already-crooked nose a second time in a bar fight, Melanie and I had held yet another intervention with my brother, begging him to get his shit together. He accused us of not truly giving a fuck about him and that we only wanted him to clean up his act for our own benefit. And okay, sure, there was some truth to that. Melanie still wanted to marry him for some reason, and I had no desire to bury the last living member of my immediate family.

We loved the hell out of him—there was no denying that, so we didn't even try.

But what we truly wanted, more than anything, was for him to find enough love for himself to get better and not die of alcoholism before the age of thirty.

We wanted him to want to live, and somehow, we were convincing enough for him to give sobriety another shot.

Now, one of the stipulations was that he wasn't to drive himself anywhere. Not until we all—himself included—could trust that his desire to survive was louder than the beckoning call of his addiction. So, on the days he attended his meetings, Melanie would drop him off, and after work, I'd pick him up.

It was a workable system, one we'd easily slipped into comfortably with surprisingly few complaints from Luke.

That was, until I met Jersey.

***

I left work early one day due to a stupid, minor cut on my hand from the hedge clippers. Marty, my boss, had insisted he could handle things on his own despite being older than the dirt we shoveled, and I'd left reluctantly, only to avoid his crochety attitude.

But there was a half hour to kill before Luke would be done at his meeting, and so I stepped inside the coffee shop next door to the church to grab something quick to drink.

I spotted her stark-white hair the moment I walked in, and I was lured to its light like a moth to a candle's flame. I didn't mean to stare as I stuttered stupidly through giving her my order—which should've been easy, given I was only getting a small black coffee—but I couldn't help myself.

I'd never seen someone so stunning before in my life, and all I wanted to do was burn her image to my brain, just so I'd be able to remember her later when I had the chance to bring the tip of my marker to the drawing pad.

But to my surprise, she was also taken by me, and she gave me her number before I could leave.

And in the weeks that followed, Jersey brought out a side of me I'd never known before, and for that, I saw her as a savior.

I fell *hard*. I fell *fast*. And so did she.

But the problem was, for me, love always came with the side effect of blindness.

With Amanda, I couldn't see that my love for her was unrequited.

With Jersey, I simply lost the ability to see anything else *but* her. And, God, what a sight she was.

Tall, only an inch or two shorter than me, with slender legs that stretched on for miles. Pale, icy-blue eyes that were only ever emphasized by thick black lashes and a clean sweep of blacker eyeliner. Long, voluminous white hair. Manicured fingernails painted a permanent shade of deep, dark blood red—the same signature color as her full lips.

I felt like an imposter with her on my arm. Like at any moment, she'd snap her crystalline eyes open, take one look at me, and wonder how the hell she'd spent three months sleeping naked beside me without ever noticing what a spastic, skinny, socially idiotic ass I was. Because that was exactly what I couldn't stop thinking anytime I caught a glimpse of her in her bed, in her kitchen, in her shower, in her car …

What the hell is she doing with me?

But also …

God, I fucking love her.

"So, when are you finally going to introduce us to whatever chick has you looking like that all the time?" Luke asked as we sat down to dinner.

Oh, right.

And I had yet to bring Jersey home to meet my brother and his fiancée.

"Huh?" I asked, feigning cluelessness as I reached across the table for the pepper.

"Right?" Luke asked Melanie, gesturing the tines of his fork in my direction. "He always has this dreamy look on his adorable widdle face."

I glanced at Melanie, who I knew would back me up if Luke was just being a jackass, but she smiled and gave a little shrug.

"You kinda do," she answered, her eyes glistening with that type of affection I had grown accustomed to over the years.

It was one of the things I missed most about Mom, but I was grateful it hadn't died with her.

"So, what's her name?" Luke asked, chomping down on the end of a carrot stick like he'd decided to start moonlighting as a Bugs Bunny impersonator.

"Jersey," I replied, dropping my gaze back to my plate.

"Ooh, Jersey!" he teased, raising his voice a few octaves. "Exotic! What is she, a stripper?"

"Oh Jesus, Luke," Melanie groaned. "Stop. I like it. Jersey is a cool name."

"Is she?"

I looked up at my brother, instantly defensive for no fucking reason I could explain. "Is she *what*?"

He lifted one side of his mouth in synchronicity with his shoulder. "Is she cool?"

"Cooler than you, dumbass," I replied.

Luke cackled obnoxiously. "Babe, look at him. He's blushing, and his feathers are all ruffled. Aww …" He folded his arms on the table and grinned, waggling his brows. "So, you really like her, huh?"

"Yes," I answered simply because it was a lot easier—and less likely to earn me more of Luke's obnoxious torment—than to say that I was in love with her.

"So, uh, why haven't we met her then? Why don't you bring her over?"

I sniffed a sardonic laugh and shook my head, avoiding his questions for as long as I could.

The truth was, I wasn't sure I wanted to bring Jersey into the house I'd grown up in—ever. The house that had once belonged to my parents, the house that still encased their untouched room like a dust-encrusted tomb. The house I shared with my wreck of an older brother and his incredible, saintly girlfriend-now-fiancée, who was more blinded by love than I'd ever been.

There was a lot of baggage there, a lot I wasn't sure I wanted to unpack when Jersey knew so little about my familial life and the things that had so far formed the foundation I now sat upon.

And, hell, maybe it wasn't about her at all.

Maybe I just didn't want to admit that it was my baggage to begin with.

"What, are you ashamed of us?" Luke jabbed, and I looked up to see the hurt darkening his gaze.

"I'm not *ashamed*," I defended myself. "I just don't know that I'm ready to bring her here."

"I get it," Melanie was quick to interject. "You don't want real life to burst your happy little bubble."

Exactly.

I offered a small smile her way, but said nothing.

"Bullshit," Luke replied angrily, shaking his head. "Life is a shit show, Charlie, okay? Don't pretend like you've forgotten that just 'cause you've been getting your dick wet by some chick you really like. And the sooner you rip off the Band-Aid and show her who you *really* are, the better. It'll suck a lot less if she finds out she doesn't like what she sees."

He winked and dived back into his dinner. Rotisserie chicken, carrots, mashed potatoes, and gravy. It was one of Melanie's quick and easy dinners. Everything was either prepackaged or frozen, but it always tasted good, and I never complained.

Tonight, I couldn't find it in me to eat.

Because what if he was right?

What if I was just prolonging another inevitable heartbreak? What if I'd been spending months thinking I was protecting her from my chaotic life when, really, I'd only been trying to protect myself from being hurt?

I was beside myself with the revelation, and I sat at the table, staring into a puddle of canned gravy as it spread between the island of instant mashed potatoes and pile of canned carrots.

What if I just never tell her? I wondered in foolish desperation. *What if she never knows what things look like here?*

I glanced up from my plate and looked at the old clock on the wall. At some point, it had stopped ticking. None of us could remember when it had happened, and we would comment on it occasionally, yet none of us seemed to care if it was frozen at 10:22 forever or not. Just like none of us cared enough to do anything about the peeling paint in the living room, or the cracked crown molding around the basement door, or the upstairs bathroom mirror that had been broken since one of Luke's black-out-drunk nights three years ago.

For fuck's sake, the carpet in the basement was still stained with the bloody evidence of Luke's fight with Ritchie the day of my parents' funeral.

We had allowed the place to go to hell, and why would I want Jersey to bear witness to that when her little apartment was clean and pretty and nice?

But maybe Luke's right, I thought, rolling my lips between my teeth, while he and Melanie jumped into a conversation about her father's auto shop and how Luke's work schedule conflicted with his next AA meeting. *Maybe I should just call her up, invite her over here, and rip off that crusty, old Band-Aid.*

So, that was exactly what I did.

I left the table without ceremony and hurried through the living room and out the front door with determination. The moment I was standing on the stoop, I pulled my phone out and dialed Jersey's number.

She let it ring twice before she answered. "Hey, babe!"

She always sounded happy to hear from me. I closed my eyes and pictured her contagious smile. The way her crystal blues twinkled with joy. The way her lips curled upward, as if attempting to reach the crinkles at the corners of her eyes.

I inhaled deeply, wistfully, at the ache pulsing through my chest, spreading outward through my limbs and anchoring in my gut.

When it came to Jersey, I was completely fucked. Both literally and figuratively. And how I was supposed to survive the wreck she'd undoubtedly leave in her wake, I had absolutely no clue.

"Charlie?"

"Y-yeah, hey," I stammered, pulling myself away from thoughts of a breakup that hadn't even happened yet. "Sorry. Hi."

She giggled. She always laughed whenever I sounded nervous and stupid, as if I'd done it to be cute or something. "What's up?"

"I, uh ..." *God, just fucking say it. It's not a big deal. Invite her over and get it over with.* "I was just thinking, um ... you've never been to my house, so ..."

"Babe, are you finally asking me to meet the family?" she teased, that smile still evident in her voice.

"It's just my brother and his fiancée."

"Yeah, and? Are they not your family?"

I pushed the hair off my forehead, raking my fingers through it. "Well, I mean, yeah. I just, you know, don't want you thinking it's a crazy-big deal or something. It's just ... Luke and Melanie."

Jersey came from an enormous family. Happily married, living parents. Two sets of grandparents and a great-grandmother. Three sisters, two brothers. Nieces, nephews, cousins. Eight sets of aunts and uncles.

My family wasn't as grand or as wonderful.

No parents. No other siblings. No grandparents.

Just ... Luke and Melanie.

"Well, you love them, don't you?"

I swallowed and ran my fingers down the length of my face. "Yeah, of course, but—"

"Then, that's all I need to know. When do you want me to come over?"

"Um ..." *Oh God, this is a mistake.* "This Friday okay for you?"

"Actually, Friday ..." She was quiet as she considered it, then said, "Yeah, this Friday isn't good. I have Mia's birthday party. But Saturday is okay for me, if you're not working too late."

"Saturday's fine," I replied quickly.

"Oh my God, okay. I'm so excited," Jersey said, and I truly believed she was. "What should I bring? Wine or—"

"No," I cut her off with a harsh bite. "No wine."

"O-kay," she slowly drawled, both startled and mildly amused. "Your family aren't wine people. Noted. What about a six-pack of b—"

"No alcohol, period."

She giggled again. "Are they, like, crazy religious or something?"

Fucking hell.

I had hoped I'd never have to divulge the information about my brother's alcoholism. I hoped he'd never quit his AA meetings and that it was all behind us, like we could just continue with our lives and look back on that time with awkward laughter and comments like, *Well, thank God that shit's over, right?*

But I couldn't avoid this.

"My brother goes to AA meetings," I confessed, keeping my voice low and hoping Luke couldn't hear me talking about him.

"Oh God! Charlie, why didn't you tell me? I feel like such an asshole now!"

No judgment. No cruel commentary. Just sweet acceptance.

How could I have expected anything less?

"You're not an asshole," I assured her, wishing we were together to make out and make love and pretend that the outside world didn't exist. "I should've said something a while ago. I'm sorry I didn't."

"No more secrets, babe. Okay?"

I breathed out a sigh of the most incredible relief and nodded as I pinched the bridge of my nose and closed my eyes. "Okay."

"I love you, Charlie, and I cannot wait to meet Luke and Melanie."

I grinned, my heart thumping the syllables of her name. "I love you too."

***

After I left work on Friday evening, I headed to the grocery store to grab what I needed to make one of Jersey's favorite dishes—lemon chicken and rice.

With a smile on my face, I shopped and gave myself permission to buy the name-brand stuff, even if it did make me wince at the cost at checkout. Then, I drove home, grinning like a lovesick fool as I tapped my fingers against the steering wheel and ironically hummed along to The Cure's "Friday I'm in Love" playing on the car speakers.

Since inviting her over, I'd managed to crawl away from my pit of anxiety and held tight to something daringly close to excitement. I wanted so, so, so badly for Jersey to love Luke and Melanie. I imagined future double dates and movie nights, and maybe, if we could climb out of our collective financial hole, we could even take a trip together at some point. Not anywhere crazy. Boston perhaps or maybe Salem. I'd always wanted to go, and I'd bet anything that Jersey would be into it too. Maybe Luke and Melanie would be down for it also. Maybe ...

I narrowed my eyes as I slowly pulled into the driveway, feeling like I was suddenly moving in slow motion as recollection cleared my mind of the dense cloud it'd been living in.

Luke.

I gasped, staring wide-eyed at the garage door. "*Fuck*," was the only word I could utter as my hands gripped the wheel tighter.

I had forgotten Luke.

Shit, shit, shit.

I was supposed to pick him up after work. He was supposed to go grocery shopping with me. We were supposed to come home together to make dinner for Melanie. She was working late, and we were supposed to do all this shit together so she didn't have to worry about it, and—

Dammit!

I had forgotten him, and all because my mind had been too fixated on Jersey and forever and the chicken I was surely going to blow her mind with at Saturday's dinner.

Fuck, how did I forget Luke?!

I sucked in a deep breath and exhaled, trying to push myself closer to a level of calm.

Okay, I coached myself as I shot off a quick text to my brother, letting him know I was on my way. *It's only been an hour. He's probably chatting with a couple of guys from the meeting. No big deal. It's fine. It's not a problem. It's* fine.

But as I drove, the heavy weight in my gut told me it *wasn't* fine. And when I reached the church, only to find the door leading to the basement locked, I was even more aware of just how not fine the situation was.

"Fuck," I whispered, my voice taking on a higher pitch as I fumbled with my phone and dialed Luke's number.

Ring.
Ring.
Ring.

Ring.

"Hey, it's Luke. Obviously, I can't answer the phone, so leave …"

"Dammit!" I dropped my phone to the center console and pushed my hand over my forehead and into my hair, pulled into a short, low ponytail at the base of my neck.

I swept my gaze across the parking lot and around the sidewalk. He might've taken a walk. Maybe he'd taken to pacing, allowing his anger toward me to grow, knowing damn well I'd forgotten all about him, like a dad who'd forgotten his kid at school.

But he wasn't anywhere to be found in the nearby vicinity.

"*Fuck*!" I smacked my hand against the steering wheel.

Okay. Think. I gritted my teeth at the silent command as The Cure began to sing "Cut Here." *What's around here? Where would Luke go?*

There was Jersey's coffee shop, but unlike me, Luke was more of a tea guy.

There was a discount card shop, an abandoned shell of a building that had once been a 7-Eleven, and a thrift store that seemed to specialize in ugly clothing nobody but the confident eccentric and the blind would wear.

And then there was the bar. Not Tony's, but a bar nonetheless.

A harrowing feeling of dread corroded the lining of my gut as I stared across the street at that bar with its tinted windows and blinking neon advertisements.

Goddammit, Luke. Please, please, please don't be in there.

The thought was on repeat as I got out of the car and crossed the street. My hand clenched around my keys, the metal digging into my palm as fear built higher and higher and higher. By the time I reached the door, my teeth were chattering, and my lungs were stuttering, barely able to hold on to a single breath of air.

Then, as I opened the door, I saw him.

Hunched over the bar. His hands in his hair. A half-empty glass in front of him.

Tears and disappointment bit angrily at the back of my eyes as I cursed for the hundredth time through gritted teeth and took the first step toward him.

The bartender—a middle-aged guy wearing a vest and more gold chains than a Mafia boss—nodded his chin in my direction.

"What can I get ya, boss?" he asked in a thick Brooklyn accent.

"My fucking brother," I replied, mad, but not at him, as my hand landed heavily on Luke's shoulder.

He was surprised to see me, his eyes rounded and his mouth open. "Charlie, I—"

I shoved at the shoulder in my hand. "Are you fucking kidding me, Luke?!"

The bartender's brow crumpled with agitation. "Hey, man, if yous wanna fight, I don't give a shit, but you're not gonna do it in here."

Luke looked back at him. "We're not fighting."

"The hell we aren't!" I shouted, struggling to maintain control over my emotions and fists. "Jesus Christ, what do we have to—"

"Charlie, will you just fucking listen to me? I'm not *drinking*."

I guffawed and thrust my hand toward the glass on the bar. "What the hell do you call that then?"

"Yo! Guys!" the bartender cut in, smacking his hand on the bar to get our attention. "I don't fuckin' care if yous wanna kill each other. Just—"

Luke lifted the glass from the bar and shook it in my face. "It's fucking water, okay?"

I didn't believe him. I wanted to—God, I did. But I *didn't*. How could I? His track record was piss-poor, and he had to understand that it was going to take time for that trust to rebuild—if ever. For crying out loud, Luke had barely been sober—*again*—for six months, and here he was, sitting in a bar with a half-empty glass in front of him.

I grabbed it from his hand and sniffed the liquid inside.

It smelled like nothing.

"You didn't show up," he said quietly. "I thought you were just late, finishing up at work or something. So, I waited."

I took the tiniest sip from the glass. The cool liquid evaporated on my tongue. No flavor. No burn.

Water.

He was telling the truth.

I hung my head as I slid the glass back onto the bar.

"After a while, I got bored, just sitting in the parking lot, so I came in here. I thought about going to that coffee shop, but …" He spun the glass in a puddle of condensation. "I wanted to see if I could do it."

I didn't ask him to elaborate.

I knew what he'd meant.

"And you did it?" I offered, and he only shrugged.

"It's so fuckin' hard, Charlie," he admitted in a weak whisper.

The bartender was silent as he walked away to busy himself with drying glasses at the other side of the empty bar. Satisfied that there wouldn't be bloodshed in his bar today.

"I know," I said.

Luke closed his eyes and shook his head. "No, you don't. You have no *idea* how hard it is. It's like having a devil on your shoulder every second of every fucking day, always fucking talking to you. Just yammering on and on and on and *on*. Saying your name, daring you to just do it, giving you every reason on the goddamn planet to just say fuck it all."

I felt sick, listening to him talk, witnessing for maybe the first time how unbelievably vulnerable and defeated he felt against the substance that held the leash tied to the collar around his neck. All this time, I'd thought he was just an asshole, stubborn and only focused on himself. But that wasn't the case at all.

Luke had lost his power somewhere along the way.

He had given it all away to an illness he'd never asked to have.

"So, why don't you?" I asked, not intending to sound so snarky, but genuinely curious. "If everything is so difficult, why don't you just give in?"

He sighed and lifted one shoulder in a limp shrug. "Because she'd leave, Charlie. And I don't know what the fuck I would do without her."

He was talking about Melanie, of course, but as he spoke the words, I thought about Jersey. Because, holy shit, I *loved* her, and I did so with such a force that I had to slump onto the stool beside my brother and stare ahead at the shelves of multicolored liquor bottles behind the bar.

What would I do if Jersey left me?

Sure, it had only been a few months, and, sure, I knew we were both fairly young without a whole lot of experience under our belts. But I'd always heard that when you knew you had found the coveted *one*, you simply *knew*, and did the amount of time and experience really matter in that equation?

"Luke."

He glanced at me, looking like a lost, sad dog. "What?"

"How did you know Melanie was it for you?"

His dark, thick brows lowered over his eyes as he studied me for a moment. Staring in an intense, indecipherable way that made me feel defensive and embarrassed at the same time. Suddenly, I wished I had never asked, and I swallowed, ready to run away when his lips slowly spread in a big, stupid grin.

"Ho-ly *shit*," he drawled. "Charlie, are you telling me I'm about to meet the girl of your dreams?"

I began to backpedal. "No. I—"

"Does she make your creepy little black heart go pitter-patter?"

Groaning, I slid off the stool. "Oh, for fuck's sake. Forget I said anything."

"Wait, wait, wait. Am I about to meet my future sister-in-law? Because, dude, if I am, maybe I should actually try to make a good impression."

"I hate you," I grumbled, shaking my head and turning to head toward the door.

Luke was chuckling, enjoying himself too much as I blushed and wished I had seen this coming before opening my stupid mouth. We made our way to the door and crossed the street together to the car, all while Luke giggled to himself and I wondered if it was too late to back out of this dinner altogether.

It wasn't until I started the car and began to drive that Luke sighed away the remainder of his laughter. He reached over to jab at the radio buttons, ditching The Cure's album of hits to scan the stations for something to listen to until finally settling on something I wasn't sure either of us knew.

Then, he scrubbed his palm over his mouth and said, "It was when I realized my life would be nothing without her in it."

I remained silent as I turned to glance at him.

"That's how I knew," he said, his voice low and gruff, like he was ashamed to speak the words out loud. "Is, uh, is that how you feel about, um ..."

"Jersey," I offered.

"Right." He nodded, patting his hand against his thigh. "Jersey. You love her?"

"Yeah," I admitted. "I really do."

"Then, do yourself a favor and hold on to her. Do whatever you gotta do. Just don't let her go," he said, nodding affirmatively, like he knew best.

And, hell, for all I knew, he did.

"Okay."

He clapped his hand against my shoulder and squeezed, and I couldn't help but smile. It was moments like this that I missed most of all, and even as it passed, I was aware of how precious and fleeting it was.

"Hey, Charlie."

"Yeah?" I asked, all too mindful of how much I had grown to miss my brother, even while living under the same roof.

"Don't tell Melanie you found me at the bar."

I locked my jaw tight, clenching my teeth and biting back my protest. Melanie never lied to me, so I made it a point to never lie to her, and come to think of it, I could say the same for Luke—not recently at least. The idea of lying to her now and about something as serious as this settled in my gut like a three-ton brick.

"I didn't drink," he pointed out, staring at the side of my face with his plea written in every line around his eyes and the downturned tip of his brows.

"Luke …" I rubbed at my chin, shaking my head.

"Fucking hell, Charlie. I'm not asking you to *lie*," he said, raising his voice and sounding desperate. "I'm just asking you to not tell her. If she fucking *asks*, then go ahead, spill your guts. Just don't go running to her as soon as we walk through the door, okay? Can you do that?"

I gripped the wheel, still unsure. It didn't feel right; that was what my intuition was saying. It wasn't good. But Luke's panic was clear, and I knew that if Melanie were to ever know where I'd found him, she'd never find trust in him again. I wasn't even sure if it had ever been rebuilt to begin with, but this would surely be another nail in the coffin.

Hell, maybe even the last.

"Come on, man. *Please*," he begged, and finally, I nodded.

"I won't say anything," I muttered. "But if she asks …"

He breathed out with relief and nodded, settling back in his seat and returning to the radio buttons.

"Right, yeah," he replied. "If she asks."

CHAPTER SEVENTEEN

CONNECTICUT, AGE TWENTY-TWO

The chicken cutlets were roasting in the oven, swimming with diced potatoes in a lemon butter sauce Melanie had helped to prepare.

The table was set, and the house was as clean as it was going to be. Although there wasn't a whole lot I could do about the chipping paint or loose floorboards at the moment, the place didn't look all that bad, and the clock had been wound.

Luke had even trimmed his beard and ironed a button-down shirt to wear with his jeans. "In case I'm about to meet my future sister-in-law," he said with a wink, and as he passed me in the upstairs hallway, I knew my cheeks had turned three shades deeper.

I was nervous and—dare I say it—excited.

Melanie left their room, wearing a pretty pink dress and white high heels. Her hair was curly, her lips were glossy, and out of nowhere, an image of my mom crashed against me, hard and fast.

I thought of the last time I'd seen her alive. All made up and happy. I couldn't remember ever seeing someone more beautiful. I couldn't remember the last time I'd seen her like that—if I ever had before—and that was how I felt now, looking at Melanie.

Pretty and happy, and those attributes never should've become a rarity.

Tell her he was at the bar.

Give her the fuel she needs to finally leave.

"What?" She laughed awkwardly, fastening a necklace behind her neck.

"You look really nice," I complimented, lifting one side of my mouth in a small, melancholy smile.

Her smile rounded the apples of her cheeks. She glanced down at her flowy dress, pinching the fabric between her fingers and spreading it wide, like a princess about to curtsy.

"It feels good to get all dressed up for once," she replied, hints of excitement and disappointment in her tone.

Like she enjoyed channeling this part of herself.

Like she hated that her life didn't allow for it more often.

"And, hey"—she looked up to gesture toward me and my black button-down and black slacks—"you look pretty nice yourself."

I chuckled. "I mean, honestly, I feel kinda stupid, but since you guys were getting dressed up …"

Melanie shrugged and stepped forward to loop her arm through mine, steering us toward the stairs. "Nothing wrong with pretending to be something you're not every now and then, Charlie. Makes the rest of it feel almost bearable."

I worried my bottom lip between my teeth as we descended the stairs. It was all I could do to keep the secret I held from spilling from my mouth with the lifeblood of her relationship with my brother.

***

Jersey drove a hearse.

Its sleek black paint job and matching leather seats had been a dream come true for the past few months we'd been dating. But now, seeing it pull into the driveway of my childhood home, I wanted to puke.

Melanie and Luke were busy in the kitchen, making sure everything was ready and just right. They reminded me of how my parents had been when Luke first brought Melanie home to meet them, and to see my brother and that same girl giving me the same treatment warmed my heart, but did nothing to calm my raging nerves.

So, with an entire army of butterflies alive and well in my stomach, I slipped outside to greet my girlfriend.

Jersey climbed out of the driver's seat, wearing a black-and-white striped dress—very *Beetlejuice*-esque—and black creeper shoes. Her mile-long legs were bare, every one of her traditional-style tattoos on full display, and it took everything in my power to not forget all about dinner and demand we go back to her place. The only thing I'd like more than that dress on her—with its corseted back and strappy neckline—was for it to be lying on the floor, forgotten.

I walked slowly down the steps, keeping my hands tucked deep in my pockets. I watched her smooth out her bleached-white hair in the driver's side mirror. She checked her blood-red lipstick, running the tip of her long fingernail around the edge of her mouth before sliding off her cat-eye sunglasses to assess her makeup.

That was when she noticed me approaching, and that was when she smiled.

God, I loved her smile.

I loved everything about her.

"Hey, babe," she whispered breathlessly, speaking like she never thought she'd see me again, as if she hadn't just seen me a few nights before.

"Hey."

"You look nice." She reached out to trace one finger down the seam along my buttoned front.

"You look …" I let my eyes roam over her hourglass figure, then back up again to her ice-princess eyes. "Wow."

Jersey laughed, her eyes twinkling like diamonds in the setting sun. "Is that the best you can do? *Wow*?"

"I'll do better later," I mumbled, sliding my hand around her waist, pressing my palm to her lower back, and pulling her toward me.

Her hands flattened against my chest, and her head tipped back. "Why not now?"

"Because"—I lowered my mouth to hers, allowing my eyes to close before impact—"I'd rather do this first …"

Kissing Jersey was nearly as good as the sex we had, and if I hadn't known how good the sex was, I would've been content to kiss her for the rest of my life.

She kissed with passion, like every moment might be the last. She held the back of my head, gripped the front of my shirt, and plunged her pierced tongue into my mouth the moment my open mouth met hers. Every tug of hair, every stroke of metal against flesh, caused an ache so deep that I throbbed with it and wished she would take that hand against my chest and lay it over the front of my pants instead.

Her body was flush against mine, and as she slipped her tongue from my mouth, she hummed with salacious delight.

"Poor baby," she whispered, tracing my lower lip with her fingernail. "Too bad we have to go inside and have dinner with your family. Otherwise, I'd get on my knees right here and—"

"Charlie! Where the fuck did you—oh. My bad."

I squeezed my eyes shut at the sound of my brother's loud, obnoxious voice, followed by the door closing behind him, and shook my head as Jersey took a step back.

"Sorry," I grumbled for some reason.

"No, it's fine," she said, laughing gently. Her cheeks were flushed, her lipstick smudged. "I'll take a rain check. Show me your room later."

"Oh shit," I said, grinning like an excited teenager as she checked the mirror once again to fix her makeup. "I've never had sex in my room before."

She turned to me with mischief and anticipation, taking my hand. "Oh, no? I thought you had a girlfriend before."

"Yeah, but we never did that in my room. Usually the living room or basement when my brother wasn't home," I said, remembering Amanda for the briefest moment and pushing her away just as quickly. "Luke would've tormented me back then."

We climbed the steps to the door as she laughed, and I found myself chuckling along with her.

"Oh, but he won't torment you now?"

"Oh, he will," I said along the waves of laughter. "But I'll mess with him right back. The guy sounds like an ape when he's getting laid. It's about time I told him."

I took a page from Luke's book and winked at her as I pushed the door open. She was grinning and holding my gaze with a desire I couldn't believe would be directed at me, and yet there it was. It never failed to astound me. Someone so beautiful, so confident, so put together in ways I could only dream to be ... she could've chosen anyone. Yet she had chosen *me*, and I knew I'd never stop thanking the fates at hand for making that happen.

But then we stepped into the living room. Her sparkling eyes left mine to survey the room, only to land on something—or someone maybe—and that smile dropped immediately, and the twinkle in her eyes dulled to nothingness.

"What?" I asked, turning to follow her gaze, only to find Luke standing there with his hands stuffed into his pockets.

"Hey," he said as he walked toward us, pulling one hand out to extend toward Jersey.

I didn't know what was happening. Didn't know why she was so instantly taken aback by the sight of my brother. But I pretended not to notice as I placed a hand on her back.

"Jersey, this is my brother, Luke. Luke, Jersey."

"Nice to meet you, Jersey," he said.

She was slow to accept his hand, but when she did, they shook. "Hi, Luke. Nice to meet you too."

He pulled away, tucking the hand back into his pocket, and turned to me. "Dinner's almost ready."

Then, he walked away.

No goading.

No jabs about making out in the driveway.

He just ... walked away, leaving me there to wonder if I should thank him for being normal for once or demand to know what the hell was wrong with him ... or was it something else? Something I didn't want to acknowledge, something I knew would break my heart and obliterate my soul. And if that were the case ...

Maybe I was better off not knowing at all.

***

Luke was a lot of things, but a good actor had never been one of them.

I'd realized that when we were kids and he shattered the glass panel in Mom's clock. The baseball had ricocheted off the pendulum and rolled beneath the dining room table, causing it to stutter, but it kept on ticking as shards of glass sprinkled all over the floor. Luke had stammered in the face of our enraged mother, trying weakly to blame something else, including a ghost that never existed within our walls.

His skills in bullshitting hadn't improved since. But he probably wished they had though, as he now tried to act like nothing was going on while going out of his way to not look in Jersey's direction.

And honestly, it wasn't as if she was any better. I could count the number of words she'd spoken on two hands since we'd sat down to eat.

Melanie and I had so far carried the entire conversation with mundane, robotic small talk neither of us gave a single fuck about. Things like, "What's the weather going to be like tomorrow?" and, "Did you see that the McDonald's on the highway got a new sign?" and, "How're things?" and, "Seen any good movies lately?"

We spoke like strangers. Like people who hadn't seen each other every day for nearly a decade. It was weird and uncomfortable. But I guessed there wasn't much else to be said when our focus was more on our significant others and their sudden inability to act like the people we knew them to be.

Every so often, Melanie would meet my eye with raised brows and a gentle nudge of her head in Luke's direction. I'd shrug in response or shake my head, then focus my attention on Jersey and her vow of silence.

"Hey, so, Luke," Melanie said with ceremony, folding her arms on the table and clearing her throat, like she was about to say the one thing that would break the spell, "I thought we could look at that country club we talked about."

He shoveled more food into his mouth before turning to her and nodding, never once allowing his eyes to land on the woman sitting across from him. "Yeah, yeah, sure. Sounds good," he mumbled around a heaping amount of chicken and potatoes.

I nudged Jersey with my elbow and said, "Luke and Melanie are getting married. I can't remember if I mentioned that or not."

Melanie nodded happily, her lips spread in that wide grin she'd worn earlier that evening.

Before Jersey came and things got weird.

Why did things get so fucking weird when she showed up?

I swallowed and forced a smile as Melanie replied, "We've been engaged for a couple of years, but we only recently got serious about planning the wedding."

What she didn't say was, she'd been too busy worrying about Luke and keeping him on the wagon to focus on their big day.

What she didn't say was, she'd been unsure if they'd ever make it to their big day in the first place.

"O-oh, wow," Jersey replied with an awkward stammer, her eyes flitting rapidly between Melanie and Luke. "Married. That's … that's, uh … that's really cool."

Does she not want to get married?

The thought flicked angrily at my heart. I would've married Jersey yesterday, if she'd have me.

"I'm the best man," I chimed in for no real reason other than to say something.

Jersey mumbled a gentle, acknowledging, "Mmm," as she poked around the plate of her favorite meal that she'd barely touched.

Every second that passed, I berated myself more and more with insults. Things like:

This was a fucking mistake.
What the hell was I thinking?
Why did I let them talk me into this?

And the biggest, baddest, worst one of all: *She doesn't really love me.*

Nobody could ever love me. I always knew it. Why did I think she was special?

By the time Luke stood up without saying anything and headed into the kitchen, I couldn't take the mental insults anymore and pushed my chair back, following closely on his tail, so close that I knew I had to raise suspicion in the women we'd left at the table.

I cornered my brother at the refrigerator and whispered in a low growl, "You wanna tell me what the *hell* is going on?"

Luke shrugged nonchalantly. "I dunno what you're talking about."

"No. You're gonna tell me *right now* why the fuck you're acting so weird."

He grabbed a bottle of Coke, then closed the fridge door and turned around to meet my eyes as he called, "Hey, babe! You want some more soda?"

I crossed my arms and held his cool, stony glare as Melanie replied, "Yeah, sure, thanks!"

My brother stepped around me, but before he could pass, he stopped at my side, brushed his shoulder against mine, and whispered, "Just drop it, okay? It's nothing."

"You know, that's really funny because it doesn't *feel* like *nothing*," I replied, equally as quiet. "It feels fucking *weird*. It feels like you ... like ... I don't know ... like you ..."

It was when she walked in. When she saw him. When her eyes landed on him.

My gaze widened as my heart plummeted straight to my stomach. "Do ... do you *know* each other?"

"Charlie. Trust me. Drop it."

Then, the asshole walked away, leaving me to stand there alone in the kitchen while my brain raced blindly, and my heart hammered, and my hands began to shake so badly that I could feel the tremors in my bones.

I spun on my heel and hurried after him.

"Luke," I hissed, reaching out to grab his shoulder the moment he left the kitchen. "What the f—"

"Don't worry about it, man," he said, adding a dose of cheer to his voice as our respective significant others turned to look at us.

And that was when Jersey's face fell, and her fork dropped to her untouched plate with a resounding clatter.

"What did you tell him?!" she shrieked, her voice shrill and sounding too unlike her to feel right. "Charlie, it was nothing, okay? I swear it—"

"It *what*?" I shouted back, desperate and panic-stricken. "What the hell are you talking about?!"

"Oh my God," Luke groaned, scrubbing his hand over his face while the Coke bottle dangled at his side.

"Luke, what's going on? What is she talking about?" Melanie asked, her voice and hands now trembling nearly as bad as mine.

With a sigh of resignation, Luke dropped the hand from over his eyes and placed the bottle on the table. Then, he looked at Jersey and pointed a finger right at her. "For your information, I hadn't told him shit. But now, since you've given me no choice, I *will*. And honestly, he deserves to know since you seem to be incapable of telling the truth," he spat at her, speaking like the Luke I knew for the first time that night.

Speaking like he *knew* her.

Then, he turned to me, ignoring the look of wide-eyed shock and growing despair on his fiancée's face.

"When I was at the bar yesterday, some chick walked up to me and didn't even give me her name before laying one on me. Just"—he slapped a hand against his thigh—"grabbed me and started making out with me like it was totally fuckin' normal to just grab some random dude and shove her tongue down his throat. And I'm sorry to break it to you, man, but that chick, unfortunately, was her." He jabbed his thumb in her direction. His features softened as he dropped his hand back to his side and shrugged. "I didn't know what to say when she walked in tonight and I got a good look at her. I thought I could get away with saying nothing and just leave it alone, but I can't. That might be who she is, but it's not me. I'm sorry, Charlie. Seriously, I am."

He laid his hand on my shoulder, but I shook it off violently. I couldn't be touched right now—I *wouldn't*. Not while I was letting his words settle in beneath my goose-pimpled skin. Not when all I could envision was her mouth on his. My *brother*.

God, how the fuck could she do this to me?
God, please don't let it be true.

"Is he fucking lying?" I asked Jersey, knowing damn well that Luke wasn't typically one to lie to me. He might've stretched the truth. He might've *withheld* the truth. But he never *lied*.

And Jersey didn't deny it as she stood from the table, looking now like a succubus and less like the angel I'd thought she was.

"It was Mia," she tried to explain.

I could only scoff and push my hair back with my hands. "Mia," I said with a snicker, shaking my head. "*Mia* didn't fucking make out with my *brother*!"

Jersey flinched, and I couldn't find it in me to care.

"W-we went to the bar after work, and we saw him sitting there alone. We had a couple of drinks, and we thought it would be funny if—"

"So, it's true," I accused, hardly able to compute the words I was hearing. "You fucking cheated on me."

"Charlie, I—"

I thrust my hand in the direction of the front door. "Leave."

Her icy-blue eyes swam in an ocean of tears as she parted her blood-red lips, letting them flop open and closed a few times before saying, "B-but I-I love—"

"No," I cut her off, shaking my head and sneering at her gorgeous, perfect, horrible face. "Don't you dare say that you fucking *love me*. Get the hell out of my house."

Stunned, she blew out a deep breath and turned toward the door, unable to look at me, my silent brother, or his defeated fiancée.

For a second, I thought about stopping her. I thought about giving her a second chance and sweeping her stupid, drunken misdemeanor under the rug just this once, like it didn't matter when it very much did. I barely lurched forward, ready to make a run for it, ready to cut her off before she could make it to the door, when Luke shot his arm out. Blocking me from moving and knocking that last bit of needed sense into me.

She disappeared into the living room, her creepers plodding quietly against the squeaky hardwood floor, and then the front door opened and closed behind her.

That was when it dawned on me that she'd never stalled. She'd never turned around. She'd never begged me to reconsider.

She had just left.

Everyone fucking leaves. Except Melanie.

Melanie never fucking leaves.

Fuck. Melanie.

She had been so quiet ever since the proverbial bomb had dropped, and when I turned to her, I found her still sitting at her place at the table. A dead stare had fallen over her eyes, but her hands shook, and her throat worked relentlessly, swallowing over and over again.

Luke was just as silent, gripping the back of his chair and hanging his head.

"Melanie," he finally said, and it hurt to hear the magnitude of his pain, thick in his gruff voice.

She didn't reply, but she closed her eyes and slowly shook her head as one lonely tear escaped from between her lashes.

It fell onto her plate of barely touched lemon chicken.

The last supper.

Panic rose in my throat at the thought.

No, she won't leave. Melanie never leaves. She's never too mad at Luke to not forgive him. She's never mad enough to fall out of love.

"Mel." Luke lifted a hand to brush the hair off his forehead, only for it to flop back down again. "Come on. Talk to me."

Yes, please, God, talk to him.

She opened her lips to speak, and nothing but a little whimper passed through. She laid a shaky hand over her eyes and swallowed again, taking a deep, quivering breath, then said, "Luke, I think ... I think we've talked enough."

He turned abruptly to look at her, but she didn't look back.

"What does that mean?"

"It means"—she licked her lips, then gasped on a sob—"I'm done talking."

He didn't comprehend. He couldn't.

His head shook as he turned to me, his eyes begging for help as he said—to her or me, I didn't know—"I-I don't get it. We *need* to talk. We ... we need—"

"What the hell is there to say, Luke?" Melanie's hand hit the table as she turned to face in his direction, and still, her eyes wouldn't reach his.

"We can talk about what just happened, o-or, um, we can—"

"You didn't tell me!" she cried, springing to her feet and thrusting her hands against his chest. "You want to fucking talk *now*, but you didn't tell me when it happened!"

Tears fell from her eyes, streaming rapidly over her face and dripping from her chin to the floor. And with every one, my heart broke a little more. I wanted to go to her. I wanted to wrap her in my arms and let her cry. I wanted to be there for her, just as we'd been there for each other for so many years.

But I didn't.

I stayed at my brother's side. Because I thought, for some reason, he needed me more.

"I didn't tell you because it didn't matter," he admitted in a hushed tone. "She kissed me, and I was caught off guard, but I pushed her away. I *never* kissed her back. God, you *know* I wouldn't, Melanie. You know that. I would never—"

"But you didn't tell me! Another woman fucking *kissed* you, and you didn't say anything! You don't see that as a problem, Luke?"

He didn't reply.

Damn him. Why the hell couldn't he just say something at the right time for *once*?

Melanie shook her head, disappointment ablaze in her eyes as she took a step back from my brother.

"What were you doing at a bar?" she asked, and I knew then where the betrayal and disappointment truly lay.

"I wasn't drinking," he whispered, telling the truth.

"Oh, bullshit, Luke. Don't—"

"I'm not lying," he snapped, thrusting a hand toward me. "Ask Charlie!"

"He didn't drink," I was quick to say, taking a step closer to the table.

"I had some water—that's it. I just needed to—"

"*You* knew?" Melanie asked, stunned by the betrayal, her eyes burning a hole right through me. "You knew, and you didn't tell me?"

"I—" I stopped myself, shame and anger igniting beneath my skin, and I hung my head as I silently cursed my brother for making me promise not to tell.

Melanie had nothing left to say. She was right; she was tired of talking. Instead, she turned on her heel and hurried out of the dining room and up the stairs, where I assumed she went to pack her things.

I could only drop into a chair, staring at the meal left uneaten as my eyes glazed over with the pain of losing the only person who had kept us together, and asked, "Why aren't you stopping her?"

"Why didn't you fight to stop Jersey?"

Fury dried my tears away as I twisted my lips into a snarl and clenched my fists against the table. "Because I don't want to waste my life on someone who would do shit like that, let alone not tell me—"

"*Right*. And don't you think Melanie deserves to be with someone who feels like that? Because I do, Charlie." His voice broke as he jabbed his chest with his finger. "I fuckin' do, and I'm not too blind to see that guy's not *me*."

A torrent of terrible emotion swept over me, and I struggled not to let it take control. I swallowed relentlessly until I was able to reply, "I thought you couldn't see your life without her."

He cleared his throat and shrugged, sniffling a little and rubbing his nose, before saying, "That's because I *can't*. But blood is thicker than lies, Charlie. And I wasn't gonna just"—he gestured at the table—"sit back and wait for that bitch to tell you the truth, knowing damn well it was probably never gonna happen. You needed to know, despite the consequences, so I told you."

I deflated with my exhale, my heart breaking more with every passing second. "Melanie deserved to know too."

Luke nodded. "Yeah. She did. And now ... we live with the aftermath."

***

I had left Luke at the table, using the excuse that I needed to get something from my room before creeping upstairs. I passed my room, the bathroom, and the door that always remained closed. When I reached Luke and Melanie's bedroom, I hesitated before gently rapping my knuckles against the door.

A soft, broken, "Yeah?" came from inside, and I pushed the door open slowly, allowing it to creak quietly against its hinges.

I found her sitting in the middle of the floor, several full garbage bags and a suitcase surrounding her. In her hands was a stack of pictures and pieces of paper.

The top picture was of the three of us—Luke, Melanie, and me—taken a few nights after Tommy's party.

Before my parents died.

Before Luke and Melanie were much more than friends.

Before adulthood and alcohol and life and pain.

She looked up at me from the picture and barely smiled before looking back at the faces of three kids I hardly recognized now.

"Look at you," she whispered, warbled by tears.

I suspected she hadn't stopped crying since entering their room.

Luke's. It's just Luke's room now.

"Look at all of us," I muttered, folding my legs to sit beside her on the cluttered floor.

"Yeah, but you ... you've changed the most."

I wasn't sure I agreed with that. We had all gone through one transformation or another. Some worse than others. But we had all grown up, and with growing up inevitably came change.

"I'm proud of you," she added. "I mean, you're still that nervous worrywart you've always been, but ... you handle it better. You've become such a good guy, Charlie."

The way she was talking ... it sounded like a goodbye, and I hated it.

"Stop talking like you're never going to see me again," I said, wrapping my arms around my knees.

She managed to huff a soft laugh, but she didn't correct herself. I thought she knew as well as I did that our lives were at a crossroads. She was going one way, and I, another, and the likelihood of us crossing paths again was slim.

I knew her leaving was for the better. I knew I'd been wishing for it for years—for her sake. And still, I wished it were different. I wished he—*Luke*—had been *different*.

I just wished she wouldn't leave.

"Thank you," I found myself saying, unable to look at her.

She swallowed, then quietly hiccupped on a sob. "For what?"

"For staying as long as you did. For cooking, for cleaning, for getting me into therapy, for"—I batted at the single tear that had worked its way from my eye—"being around for me—and Luke, obviously—when no one else was. You did more than anyone your age should've had to do, but you did it anyway, and I wish I had thanked you more for that. So ... thank you."

Her head hanging, she sniffled and nodded. "You're welcome."

My throat constricted around a hot, heavy knot of emotion as I croaked, "I wish you didn't have to go."

"I know. But you're gonna be okay. I know you will be. I'm not so sure about your brother though. I do love him so much, and I don't want to leave him. I just—"

"I know."

"But you'll be okay," she repeated, as if it made it better. As if it helped to settle the ache in both our hearts to know that, at the end of the day, at least I'd be fine … even if he wasn't.

And that was all because of her.

***

I had left her alone to finish packing, and Luke had remained in the dining room, doing only God knew what.

At some point, I'd somehow fallen asleep, thinking about heartbreak and the people I'd been forced to let go of before I was ready. I woke up to Luke tripping up the stairs and cursing angrily beneath his breath.

That was how I knew she was gone.

He wouldn't have come upstairs if she were still here.

An ache so deep and great pierced my heart. An emptiness threatened to swallow me whole. God, what would I do without her? What would either of us do? What the hell would our lives look like tomorrow or next week or next year?

I stared at my ceiling long after Luke closed his door at the end of the hall, allowing my tears to silently drip over my cheeks and into the pillow beneath my head. I thought about Jersey. I thought about how none of this would have happened if I'd just picked Luke up when I was supposed to, if I'd never invited her to dinner, if I'd never walked into that coffee shop in the first place.

It was *my* fault Melanie was gone.

It was *my* fault we were all hurting.

It was *my* fault for being too blinded again by love to see that I'd neglected the most important people in my life.

I clambered from my bed to walk down the hall. I needed to apologize to Luke. I needed to tell him that this wasn't his fault, that Dr. Sibilia had been wrong once upon a time, and this had all once again come down to *me*. I was the problem here, not him, and even if it wouldn't bring Melanie back, he had to at least know that I accepted all of this damn blame.

So, I stood in front of the door, ready to knock, when I heard something coming from inside.

Something I hadn't heard since the day of our parents' funeral.

Luke was crying, and this time, Melanie wasn't there to hold him.

And that was also my fault.

I didn't open the door, didn't want to intrude on his grief and mourning. So, I sank to the floor, sliding my back against the wall, and pressed my forehead to my knees. Then, I cried with my brother, mourning the woman who'd kept our pieces together and wondering what would happen to us once they inevitably fell apart.

CHAPTER EIGHTEEN

MASSACHUSETTS, PRESENT DAY

Dozens of girls had been on the back of this motorcycle with their arms wrapped around my brother's waist. Most of them had ended up at our house, and some of them had even managed to stay the night. Yet what nauseated me wasn't the number or the memories of listening to Luke fuck random women in various parts of the house while I locked myself up in my room with markers, paper, and very loud, very angry music.

It was that Melanie had never been one of them. She should've been the only one.

But now, it was Stormy girl. And she was the first woman to ever sit behind me on this seat, her arms wrapped tightly around my waist and her chin perched atop my shoulder.

I had agreed to give her a ride back to the hotel with all intentions of dropping her off and never allowing my path to cross hers again. I'd even quit my job and find a new city to hide in if I had to.

Except I hadn't expected this to feel so nice, her body tucked around mine. I hadn't expected her to smell so good as we zipped through the dark streets of Salem toward the road that stretched between her hotel and my graveyard.

I was so acutely aware of a part of me, pulsing and weeping with needs I had kept silent for a long, long time.

The need to be touched.

The need to be in the presence of a beautiful woman and remain there for as long as she wanted me.

But before I could allow that miniscule, stifled part of myself to regain too much control, I pulled into the hotel parking lot and remained silent as I waited for her to dismount. All while reminding myself that I had never had the best of luck with relationships and I couldn't afford another heartbreak.

The last one had nearly killed me.

Stormy girl stood beside the bike, looking out of place in her Victorian gown while holding the helmet she'd borrowed from Blake's wife. She looked like she was hesitating, holding back the things she wanted to say, and I was beginning to get nervous. I wouldn't leave until she was safely inside, but my brain was racing with every possibility of what words were about to pour from her mouth. I didn't want to hear any of them. I'd already let this night go too far by just attending the damn party.

"Do you think—"

"No," I reflexively fired at her, interrupting in a way that was immediately embarrassing.

"What?" She was taken aback, and I refused to give myself room to care.

"Whatever you're going to say, the answer is no."

"Wow. Okay," she replied, huffing a belligerent laugh.

She turned away, releasing a deep breath, but she didn't walk away.

Her reluctance to leave made me groan inwardly as I tipped my head back and asked through gritted teeth, "What were you going to say?"

"Never mind, Charlie. Don't worry about it." Cold and distant—a stark contrast to how she'd been all night.

It bothered me. But it bothered me more that it was a direct reflection of how I had treated her.

Would it kill me to not be an asshole?

It might actually, I thought as I undid the helmet and tore it off as my heart screamed at me to stop.

"I'm sorry, okay?" I snapped, not sounding sorry at all. But it wasn't her I was annoyed at, and now, for some reason, I needed her to know that.

"You know"—she turned around and crossed her arms over her chest, glaring down at me through eyes heavy with makeup—"this hot and cold shit is seriously getting old."

"Dealing with people isn't exactly my forte," I grumbled back.

"Oh, really? Well, shit, you certainly had me fooled." Stormy girl shook her head and rolled her eyes. "Like I said, never mind. Thanks for the ride, Charlie."

She turned around once again, and this time, with a deep breath and her head held high, she took a few steps, walking away with purpose driving her every move. I groaned out of frustration and climbed off the bike, dropping the helmet on the seat.

"Stop! I'm sorry, all right? Seriously, I'm *sorry*."

She did stop then, and she looked over her shoulder. "You know what? I might actually believe that apology."

I shrugged and offered a single nod. "Great," I muttered. "Now, can you please tell me what you were going to say?"

Her tough-girl attitude withered a bit as she bit her bottom lip before asking, "I was going to ask if you'd just bring me up to my room. You don't have to come in—I'm not asking you to. I just get really creeped out, and Blake usually—"

"Yeah," I replied, feeling more like a jackass with every passing second. "Sure. Come on."

Her lips twitched upward in a small, grateful smile before she turned again to head from the asphalt to the sidewalk where she'd been attacked just weeks before. I followed close behind, making my presence known without walking beside her, until I heard Luke's voice in my head.

"Dude, what are you doing? Do you like her or not?"

I think I like her.

"Then, stop being such an asshole. Jesus fuck."

I furrowed my brow as I watched her move toward the hotel doors. I didn't know what I really expected to take from this ... *thing*, but still, I quickened my pace to walk by her side. She glanced up at me, and one side of her mouth quirked into a half smile, and still, we didn't speak as we approached the place where I'd found her and held a blade to her attacker's throat. Stormy girl swallowed and pulled in a sharp breath of air as we walked by, and on instinct, I lifted my hand to touch her elbow—a little reminder that I was there, that she wasn't alone—and she settled with an exhale.

We headed into the lobby of the old hotel. It smelled a bit musty beneath a disguise of overpowering floral, and I wrinkled my nose.

Stormy girl laughed. "I know. It smells like a funeral home in here." I lifted a brow, and her laugh escalated into a fit of giggles. "I guess I don't need to tell you that."

"Actually, I don't make a habit of going to funeral homes," I replied, remembering in an instant every moment of my parents' final send-off.

"Oh, I thought that came with the territory."

"Not in my position." Then, I reconsidered and said, "Well, I guess it also depends on the cemetery. Back home, I—"

I caught myself and clamped my lips shut. I was unsure if I wanted to tell her anything about myself, especially my life before Salem.

"Anyway," I muttered, deciding I wasn't ready to unearth that particular grave, "duties differ depending on the cemetery. I don't do much in the line of office work. Every now and then, I deal with funeral directors, but it's usually over the phone. My job is more physical—"

"Yeah, I could tell." She waggled her brows and grinned up at me.

I smirked and pretended the comment didn't faze me even though I knew my cheeks were blushing.

I never could take a compliment well.

"Well, trust me, it smells like a funeral home in here," she continued as we reached the elevator.

She jabbed her finger at the upward arrow and stood beside me as we watched the flashing numbers count their way down to the lobby.

When the elevator doors opened, we stepped inside, and Stormy girl hit the number seven. The doors closed, leaving us in complete seclusion, and I stiffened my spine as a memory of Luke popped into my head.

"You ever fuck a girl in an elevator?"

I cocked a brow. "Do I seem like the type of guy who fucks girls in elevators?"

"No, but you don't look like the kinda guy who would fuck a girl you don't know against a headstone either."

"Touché."

"So, have you?"

"Have I what?"

"Fucked a girl in an elevator."

"No," I said, unable to control my incredulous burst of laughter.

Luke sighed mournfully and went back to flipping channels. "Yeah, me neither."

I imagined grabbing Stormy girl right then and there, kissing her and hiking up that heavy-looking skirt. I imagined pressing her back against the elevator wall and wrapping her legs around my waist, all to live a fantasy Luke had never gotten the chance to fulfill.

I smiled to myself despite the heat rising from the collar of my sweater, and Stormy reached out to nudge my arm with her knuckles.

"What are you thinking about?"

I let the smile fall from my face as I shook my head mournfully. "Nothing."

She studied me for a moment, like she wanted to ask something, but wasn't sure she should. I could only imagine what that question might be, and thank God the elevator didn't allow her to ask it.

We reached her floor, and I immediately stepped out. She quickened her pace to keep up, her heels echoing a hollow sound through the empty, monotonous hallway.

"I hate hotels," she muttered, staying close to my side. "Did you know, like, roughly a hundred thousand people die in hotels every year?"

"People die everywhere every single day," I replied.

"Well, thank you for that, Mr. Morbid," she grumbled sarcastically. "I think what gets me about hotels is how empty and eerie they feel. Like, I've never stayed at a hotel that felt warm and comfortable. They're all just ... *cold*."

"Well, yeah. They're not home," I said as I thought about *my* home. The house I'd left. The house that held every memory that meant something to me. The house I would never see again.

"Right. And when you think about how many people died in all those hotel rooms, it just makes it so much worse. I can't stand it."

I glanced at her through the corner of my eye. "You don't like death much, huh?"

That earned me an amused laugh. "Does anyone *like* it?"

"I mean, I wouldn't have a job without it."

She snorted. "Interesting take, but okay. Anyway, no. I don't like death. When I was in my early twenties, I watched a guy my age die." She stopped at a door and quietly added as she dug her key card from her purse, "I never really got over that."

"I'm sorry," I said, not knowing what else there was to say.

She shrugged, pulling the white card out and flipping it over in her fingers. "I mean, I'm okay, for the most part. It just changes you, I guess."

"Yeah, death has a way of doing that. It never leaves you the same as you were before."

Her eyes met mine with a touch of intrigue and a dash of sadness. "Is that what happened to you?"

"I've never died before, no," I countered with a smirk while avoiding a question way too personal for my liking.

Stormy girl murmured a contemplative sound, those green eyes holding mine for just a moment before she turned to swipe her card above the door handle. It clicked open, and I contained my relieved sigh as she stepped inside.

"So, can we see each other again?" she asked.

I shook my head and diverted my gaze. "I don't date."

She lifted one side of her mouth. "Who said I was talking about dating? What if I just want to be friends?"

"Nope. Sorry." I stuffed my hands into my pockets as I took a step back from her door, bringing my eyes back to hers. "I don't do friends either."

A grin broke out across her face as she laughed, shaking her head. She brushed a few strands of her long black hair off her forehead, then let that hand fall heavily against her side as she blew out a breath.

"Okay, then how about if I just stop by every now and then to annoy you? Would *that* be okay?"

Somehow, we'd both turned rejection into something flirtatious, and I found my own reluctant grin tugging at the corners of my mouth. I heard Luke telling me to go for it. To let her in, let her shake me up a bit before setting her free.

Luke had always been right until the day he wasn't, but I knew in my gut that he would've been right about this. Even if I wasn't sure I was wrong in resisting either.

So, as I took another step back, I found my head nodding. "I guess I could deal with that."

Her smile softened as she leaned against the door. "Cool. Then, I'll annoy you soon."

"Can't wait," I grumbled, my tone sarcastic as I stared at her in that corset, accentuating the depth of her cleavage and the length of her neck and the delicate curvature of her collarbone.

God, Luke would've kicked my ass for leaving her to spend the night alone in her room.

"Neither can I."

She smirked with those deep red lips. There was a dare in her eyes. A come-hither glint that beckoned to me every moment I stood in the middle of that hotel hallway. But I was stubborn, my resolve firm, and I ignored every desire that coursed between where she and I stood.

"Have a good night," I concluded, bowing my head like I wasn't of this century before turning on my heel and walking as fast as I could to the elevator.

"You too, Charlie," she called to me. "Thanks for keeping me safe."

Don't turn around. Don't turn around, I silently commanded, my eyes set on the bronze doors at the end of the hall. *Let her close the door first. Let her get inside.*

I jabbed my thumb at the arrow and tapped fingertips against my thighs as I watched the flashing numbers above the doors roll around to the seventh floor. But it was too slow, and Stormy girl never closed the door.

Why didn't I ask for her damn name?

The thought pulled at my mind until I turned, glancing over my shoulder to find her leaning against the doorway. Her smile had disappeared, leaving room for a lonely, longing sadness I was too familiar with. Her eyes met mine, and her lips quirked for the briefest second before the little glimmer of a smile faded again.

The elevator arrived. The doors opened.

"What the hell are you doing, man?" Luke's voice said. *"Are you out of your fuckin' mind?"*

Maybe, I answered, glancing at the empty elevator car and swallowing against the lead ball in my throat. *I don't want to go.*

"So, don't, you idiot."

What if she doesn't want me to stay?

"Her door's still fuckin' open. She's still standing there. God, have I taught you nothing?"

"Fuck it," I muttered aloud.

Then, with a puff of my chest, I turned on my heel and barreled down the hallway with only one thing on my mind. Stormy girl pushed off the doorframe, leaving her arms loose at her sides, curiosity and expectancy burning like chaotic wildfire in her emerald eyes. A warning sounded from down the hall as my palms framed her face. She tipped her head back, and my neck craned to bring my mouth to hers in a moment of uncharacteristic spontaneity.

"The elevator," Stormy whispered breathlessly, her eyes fluttering closed as her hands wrapped around my wrists.

"Okay," I replied.

But as my lips met hers and our mouths simultaneously opened to lick and taste and savor, she dared to take a bold step backward into her room, taking me with her …

I knew I wasn't leaving anytime soon.

And you know what?

Nothing told me it was the wrong thing to do.

Not my intuition. Not my tormented brain. Not Luke's disembodied voice.

For once, with Stormy girl in my webbed grasp, everything felt okay.

CHAPTER NINETEEN

CONNECTICUT, AGE TWENTY-THREE

It had been a year since we'd last seen Melanie.
    It'd been about that long—minus a day—since Luke had left his job at her father's auto repair shop, and it'd been just as long since we'd heard anything about how she was doing. *What* she was doing.

Not that her father had offered much information to his daughter's ex-fiancé when my brother stopped by the shop to quit and grab his things, other than to let him know that she would be fine.

I wondered often if she actually was—fine, I mean.

Because we sure as hell weren't. Yet we were getting by.

Somehow, the world hadn't stopped turning the moment Melanie walked away, no matter how much I felt like that spider on the back of my door, caught in the middle of a storm he couldn't imagine weathering.

Somehow, Luke had quickly found himself a new job at another mechanic's shop. My work at the cemetery was still going strong, and I could say with absolute certainty that my brother hadn't stepped foot inside a bar.

Over the past year, the wins might've been few and far between, and I might've had to squint a bit to see them at all. But they were there, and that had to count for something. I just wasn't sure I could say we were *fine*. Not in the way I hoped Melanie was. But I hoped we would be eventually, and apparently, Luke did too.

"We should go out. Do something," he suggested one night after I picked him up on the way home from work.

I raised a brow with a blend of suspicion and shock. "Uh, what?"

He and I never went out. But there he was, in his grease-stained coveralls and backward hat, motor oil beneath his nails and smeared over one cheek, asking if I wanted to do something.

"We should. You know, just to get out of the house for once."

I actually laughed. "You're kidding, right?"

He lifted one shoulder and glanced at me, his gaze nonchalant. "Why? You don't wanna do anything?"

"I didn't say that. I just …" My lips turned downward as I shrugged. "What would you even wanna do?"

"Well, I'd suggest a bar if I didn't think you'd rip me a new asshole."

I lowered my brows and slid my unamused glare in his direction.

Luke smirked and huffed a laugh. "I dunno. What would you wanna do? Grab some dinner? Go to the library? Pick up chicks at a comic store? I mean, what kinda shit does a guy like Charlie Corbin even like to do?"

It was my turn to smirk as a chuckle rumbled through my chest. "Is that something people do? Pick up chicks at comic stores?"

"You tell me, man. You're the nerd around here."

"Hate to break it to you, but I don't go to comic stores."

"Get the hell out of here. Yes, you do." Luke stared at me, incredulous.

Now, I was laughing and shaking my head, unable to remember the last time any moment between us had been this lighthearted and—dare I say it—sort of normal.

"No," I said, "I really don't. I think I went to one once, but that was back when … God, I think I had to be ten, maybe eleven? I don't remember, but it was forever ago. Dad had taken me."

Luke scoffed, disbelief crinkling the corners of his eyes. "The fuck do you read then?!"

"Not comic books!"

"Since when?!" He sounded shrill, the words squeaking out between bursts of his own laughter.

"When the hell have you *ever* known me to read comic books?"

"Oh, come on. You used to read, uh … what was it?" He snapped his fingers, commanding the words to come to him. "The one with Pinhead. It was a movie. Uh …"

"*Hellraiser*?" I supplied as mirth continued to tug at the corners of my mouth.

My face began to hurt; I was smiling so much.

"That's it! And, uh, *Sandman*, right? Oh! And, uh, *The Crow*! No, wait, that was a movie ..."

My laughter settled as one side of my mouth curled up in a soft, almost-melancholy smile. I had never realized Luke paid so much attention to the things I'd been into over the years—apart from my drawing.

He always paid attention to that. Even when he had been drunk.

"No, that was a book before it was a movie," I corrected quietly. "And they're graphic novels, not comic books."

He groaned and shoved my shoulder. "Oh, shut the hell up. Same fuckin' thing."

I didn't bother suppressing my eye roll. "Graphic novels are longer and more complex than comics."

"Oh God, whatever," he groused, followed by a chuckle. "And where do you buy those?"

I raised a brow. "The bookstore?"

He raised one back. "The ... *comic* bookstore?"

I snorted. "Just the bookstore, you dick. Or the library."

He harrumphed and turned his attention to the radio. Neither of us had been paying attention to it since I'd picked him up, but now, it seemed to matter. Or maybe he was just trying to think of something else to say. Something to keep the moment of normalcy from fading, to prevent the usual air of sadness and monotony from filling the space between us.

He settled on Kansas's "Carry on My Wayward Son" before leaning back in his seat, staring out the window and tapping his grease-stained fingertips against his thigh.

Then, after the second verse and I turned the car onto our street, he asked, "So, uh … where do you pick up chicks then?"

Surprised, I glanced in his direction and stared at the back of his head for a moment before replying, "I don't."

When the hell did he think I had the time to pick *anyone* up, besides him? My days consisted of waking up, driving us both around, working, cooking dinner, and going back to bed, only to wake up and do it all over again. There wasn't room for anything—or anyone—else, and it was for the better.

Nothing good ever came from me letting my guard down and allowing myself or others to *live*.

"Hmm," Luke replied with a short nod before dropping the topic altogether as we pulled into the driveway.

I cooked us a box of cheap pasta and sauce for dinner, and Luke carried his bowl back to his room, where he did God only knew what while I sat at the table and read that week's book. Knowing damn well I wouldn't see Luke again until the next morning, when it was time to drive him to work again. Wondering if we'd ever find that normalcy again and if it would ever stick around.

***

"Hey, so I need you to take me somewhere," Luke said the next morning, interrupting my breakfast.

It was his day off, and the fact that he entered the dining room dressed, complete with his black leather jacket and boots, startled me from Stephen King's *Bag of Bones*.

"Where?" I asked suspiciously, holding a spoonful of oatmeal midair, still unable to believe my brother had woken up before noon on a day when he didn't have to be awake at all.

Usually, if he didn't have work, I'd come home after work to find him draped over the couch in his underwear and nothing else, snoring while the TV played an old action movie or '90s sitcom.

He proceeded to pull something out of the pocket of his leather jacket, unfolded it, and slapped it down on the table in front of me. I leaned over my bowl of oatmeal to peer at the crumpled piece of paper to find a picture of a motorcycle staring back at me.

"Guy's selling it for an amazing price," he explained as I read the paragraph of information beneath the picture.

It was a two-year-old Harley. The person selling it could no longer keep it and was looking for someone who'd appreciate it the way he did. He was selling it for just ten grand after buying it for thirty, which only made the deal seem too good to be true—a trap my brother was likely to fall for.

I dropped my spoon into its bowl as I shook my head and said, "I dunno, Luke …"

"I know what you're thinking. But I talked to the guy on the phone last night." He pulled out the chair across from me and plopped down, folding his arms on the table. "He's a tool. Fucked around behind his wife's back, so she kicked him out, and now, he's looking to make some quick cash. He doesn't *want* to get rid of the bike, but he can't afford to sell his car 'cause he's living out of it right now or something, so ..." He grabbed the paper from beneath my eyes and folded it back up. "I told him I'd give him eight thousand for it, and he accepted."

I slowly lifted my spoon again and shoveled the oatmeal into my mouth, then chewed as I replied, "Where the hell did you get eight thousand dollars from?"

"I've had it," he muttered nearly defensively, lowering his gaze. "It's left over from Mom and Dad."

"Oh," I replied before dropping my eyes to the gloppy oatmeal I no longer had the stomach to finish.

I still had most of mine too.

It always felt wrong to spend it, never knowing when I'd really need it one day. I always thought I would use it on something important, something I knew my parents wouldn't have thought twice about helping me with—like fixing the car a couple of years ago when the belt snapped and needed replacing.

Luke's half was to be spent on whatever he wanted, just as much as mine was. Honestly, I had thought he'd blown it all on booze. But now, knowing he still had some left, I couldn't help but judge a little.

Would Mom and Dad have really wanted him to get a motorcycle? Was that the most necessary thing when the house was looking more and more like shit every day?

Why should I have to hold on to my money for the things we needed when he got to blow it on a fucking *toy*?

"Don't look at me like that," he spat at me.

"Like what?"

"Like I'm a fuckin' idiot."

I shook my head and dropped my eyes to the bowl of golden-brown mush on the table. "I'm not—"

"Yeah, you are. I don't give a shit what you think, Charlie. It doesn't matter. I've thought about this, and I think it's a good idea."

"I didn't say—"

"I can't keep relying on you for everything. You need a fuckin' life, okay? And you're never going to have one until I get my own wheels."

My gaze shot back to his. "You'd better not be doing this for me. I don't mind—"

"Oh, trust me." Luke sniffed a laugh, leaning back in his chair. "I *want* the bike. I've always wanted one. And that has absolutely nothing to do with you. But if it means giving you a little of your freedom back, then I'll consider it a solid selling point."

I lifted one corner of my mouth into a helpless half smile. "I don't really care about having freedom or not. It's not like I'm really missing out on anything."

Luke groaned and tipped his head back against the chair, staring at the ceiling as he shook his head.

"What?"

"Bro," he muttered on a sigh, looking back at me with an expression that said, *What the hell am I gonna do with you?* "Neither of us has gotten laid in over a fuckin' year, and if you say you're good with that, I'm calling you a goddamn liar."

I kept my lips shut about that one.

"Now, I'm getting that bike, and you and I are going out. We're gonna get our asses back out there, maybe find a couple of chicks and live our fucking lives a little. Because, I dunno about you, man, but I'm sick of moping around this place like I'm just waiting around to fuckin' die or something. Shit needs to feel normal again, and the only way that's gonna happen is if we act like it. So, finish your shitty breakfast, and let's go."

CHAPTER TWENTY

MASSACHUSETTS, PRESENT DAY

My old therapist, Dr. Sibilia, would have a field day if she knew that the first time I made out with a woman in years, I struggled to keep my brother from infiltrating my mind.

I just couldn't stop thinking about that first night after Luke had bought the bike and we'd gone out to a local burger place. We played the part of each other's wingman, pointing out girls who were both hot and interested. I got a kiss in the parking lot while Luke got a blow job in the restroom, and both of us went home feeling more confident and free than we had since Melanie had left.

But we were also sad. Because even though we'd allowed ourselves a couple of hours to forget that she was gone, we'd still had to go home to a house just as empty as we'd left it, and we'd had to remember all over again that we were orphaned bachelors.

I thought about that now as my hair knotted around Stormy girl's fingers and our tongues coiled like snakes.

I hadn't felt this kind of good in who knew how long, and every inch of my body pulsed with an impossible, needy ache. But I had been aware since too young of an age that these moments were fleeting, and before I had a chance to commit them all to memory, they would already begin the process of fading.

God, at this point, I could barely remember the sound of my own mother's voice. How the hell was I supposed to remember the sweetness of this rare woman's tongue?

But she kissed so well and with so much passion, forcing a memory of Jersey to come to my mind, only to think that she—that cheating, home-wrecking bitch—paled in comparison to *this*. Stormy girl held me captive within her grasp, steering me toward the bed and pushing me down. Straddling my waist and letting those skirts of lace and tulle to spill over us. She took control, never giving me a chance to hold the reins, and, shit, I liked it—*a lot*.

I let my hands roam along her back to her bottom. My palms molded over the curved mass of fabric, and I dug my fingers into the flesh hidden beneath. Stormy girl groaned into my mouth, and I moaned back, our tongues never slowing in their battle for more.

"What's your name?" I asked in a breathy whisper, never pulling my lips from hers. Desperate to stop calling her by some silly nickname that wasn't mine to use.

She smiled against me. "That's the first real question you've asked me all night."

I responded with a huffed chuckle, realizing she was right.

"Stormy." Her fingers flitted down to the hem of my shirt, disappearing beneath the fabric to trace the faintly defined lines of my abs. "My name's Stormy."

"Really?" I was taken aback. I hadn't expected the nickname to be at all similar to her real name, and I opened my eyes to half-mast, only to find hers looking back.

She offered a silent nod, and my heart took off galloping as I remembered that old drawing scribbled on the back of my door.

The spider caught in the middle of the storm.

It had always been a metaphor to describe the shit show that was my life, the misunderstood creature forced to weather every bolt of lightning and crack of thunder.

I had always considered that storm to be full of bad and terrible things. Death, destruction, heartbreak, and pain. But now, looking into those wild green eyes, I wondered if maybe the storm could offer something good, just this once. And how could I deny that possibility when this woman had been given such a name?

The spider and the storm.

Me and her.

"You wanna know a secret?" she asked, her lips moving against mine.

"Hey, can I tell you a secret?"

I swallowed and closed my eyes to Luke's long-ago trembling voice. "Huh?"

"I'm scared, Charlie. I'm really fuckin' scared."

"I've been thinking about your body since the other day," Stormy confessed, pushing her hands further upward to my chest. "Like, I had a feeling you'd look good, but *this* good ... I wasn't expecting that."

I opened my eyes again to watch her sit up, straddling my hips and moving her hands over my chest and shoulders. I tried to focus only on her. Tried to see her breasts, straining against the confines of her corset. Tried to take in the crimson shade of her blushing cheeks and the fading hue of her lipstick. But while my body was here, on her hotel bed, my mind had one foot in the present and another in the past. I saw the flashing lights flooding the living room of my childhood home. I saw my brother break down in front of me before the cops knocked on the door to take him away.

He would never know *this* again. I wasn't supposed to either, but there I was, and it felt so *wrong* and *backward*.

Stormy's hands slowed in their movements as her head cocked slightly, her eyes pinned to mine. "You're sad," she said with a hint of wonderment and realization in her tone, like she'd finally figured something out after a long time of questioning. "I always thought you were angry or something, but ... no. You're *sad*."

The image of Luke faded enough for her empathic eyes to come fully into view. I pressed my lips together for a moment, searching for my composure.

Then, I replied, "Deep down, we're all sad about something."

"I guess, yeah, but most of us can compartmentalize our emotions. You know, like, there's a time to be happy, a time to be angry, sad, whatever. But you ..." She shook her head and, to my horror, removed her hands from beneath my shirt. "I'm pretty sure you're just *sad*."

I furrowed my brow. "I'm pretty sure you don't know me well enough to make that assessment."

The words held a playful quality as my fingers roamed from her ass to her thighs, still stretched and spread over my lap, but I meant it. She didn't know me. And for her to pretend that she did pushed me dangerously close to shutting down again, even if I didn't want to, and I was already starting to wish I had gotten onto that elevator.

Stormy smirked, clearly amused, but her eyes gave her away. "Here's the thing though, Charlie. Misery doesn't just love company; it knows it when it sees it. And like I said, I see you, and no amount of broody grumpiness is going to make you magically disappear now."

I had known this woman for the equivalent of a few days, if that. I knew little about her, outside of what she'd already told me, and she knew even less about me. Yet here she was, making declarations like she *did* know me, and it was getting beneath my skin.

"You seem a little too confident for someone who doesn't know a damn thing about me," I countered.

Her lips quirked into a smug smile as she slid from my lap.

I guessed the moment was over with little thanks to my brain and apparently sad eyes.

"I don't need to know your favorite food or the name of your mom's dog to feel like I know you," she said.

"Sorry to break it to you," I replied, sitting up and folding my arms across my knees, "but my mom's dead."

I didn't know why I had said it. Not even Ivan—my only friend in the entire world—knew about my parents. It had never come up—I'd never had a reason to divulge the information. Yet I had said something to Stormy with little reason at all. In fact, it was almost as if I'd *wanted* her to know, to invite her to weather the torrential downpour with me, and that was terrifying the hell out of me.

The grin dropped from her face. "Oh shit. I'm sorry."

I shrugged nonchalantly even though the familiar pain of a forever heartbreak was already searing through my chest. "It happened a long time ago."

"How did she die?"

"Car accident."

Stormy nodded somberly. "That sucks. What about your dad? Is he still—"

"He died with her," I offered too easily.

Stormy watched me momentarily, chewing her bottom lip before replying, "Wow ... I don't even know what to say."

"Most people don't."

"No wonder you're sad."

It was my turn to smirk as I waggled my brows. "And that's just the tip of the iceberg."

She opened her mouth to say something, and I could only imagine what inquisition she was about to throw at me. Because at that moment, I glanced at the clock on the nightstand, taking note of the time after being oblivious for too long.

"*Shit.*" I got off the bed and walked past Stormy to the door while patting my pockets down to make sure I still had my keys.

"What's wrong?" she asked, panic and concern in her tone.

"The gate. I have to unlock the gate."

My heart hammered in my chest. I reached out to grab the doorknob, bothered by how the cool metal felt against the coating of fresh sweat on my palm.

God, what an idiot I was. I had been going to bed every night at the same time to unlock the gate in the morning. But the moment I allowed a woman to catch even just a glimpse of my life, I forgot all about my responsibilities.

I never should've kissed her.

"The gate?"

She sounded clueless, and for a second, I was irritated by it. That she could have such a total disregard for my career and the things I was trusted—not to mention *paid*—to do. I was ready to put her in her place, to snap and ensure she'd never bother me or get in the way of my regimented life again. But I stopped myself, reminding myself that it wasn't her fault.

She hadn't been the one to kiss me first.

"I have to unlock the gate in the morning," I further explained, staring out into the empty hallway. "If I have any hope of waking up in the morning, I need to get to bed."

Her silence was damning. The hallway, her room, the hotel surrounding us ... it was all too damn quiet, and I was too damn aware of how fast and loud my heart was beating as I waited for her response.

"It's not really that late," she finally offered, unsure as she spoke.

"I'm on a schedule. If I don't go to bed at a certain time, I won't wake up. It's how I work; it's how it's always been."

She uttered a thoughtful, "Hmm," from behind me. "I guess you probably know better than I do."

"About this? Yes, I do."

"I'm pretty sure you don't know me well enough to make that assessment," she mocked, throwing my words back at me in a playful tone that made me long to have her body back within my hands.

"Fair enough. Anyway, have a good—"

"Charlie, wait," she interjected hurriedly, her footsteps matching her urgent tone.

I braved a glance over my shoulder to watch her approach. She had kicked off her heels at some point, and I was reminded of our height difference. With her, I liked it. Not that I'd never been with shorter girls before—at six foot three, it wasn't exactly common to find women close to my height. But with the others, I'd always found our vertical differences to be awkward and more of a nuisance. For a short time, Jersey had felt like my ideal in every way imaginable, including our modest four-inch height difference. We had felt like puzzle pieces, perfectly complementary and proportionately balanced, until she went ahead and soured every characteristic she'd held in my mind, to the point where I found it difficult to even look at women with platinum hair without the phantom pains of heartache tearing through my chest.

But Stormy didn't feel awkward. She didn't call out old pains lingering in the shadows of my past.

Instead, she reminded me of every reason I always hated to be alone, and in the moment, that was so much worse than anything else.

Her cool hand lay over my shoulder, and her other reached up to my cheek. With little persuasion, she lured me in, like a siren at sea. My mouth was drawn to hers, and as her fingers danced lightly over my bearded jaw, her lips moved against mine in feathery, dreamlike touches.

The kiss ended, but her hands remained where they were, one cupping my jaw and the other on my shoulder, as she tipped her head back and stared through my eyes, straight into the soul I'd kept hidden and silenced for what now seemed like an eternity.

"I don't know what it is about you, but for some reason, kissing you feels like a privilege," she whispered in the open doorway of her hotel room. "Thank you for that and thank you for tonight. Even though you're still sad, even though you might shut me out again tomorrow, I hope that, somewhere in your heart, it means something to know that this was the best night I've had in a really, really long time. Because, honestly, as lame as it sounds, for me, it means a lot. Probably more than it should."

Her voice weakened in strength the longer she spoke as her eyes misted and gleamed in the hallway light.

It hurt me to know that I—a man she hardly knew—could inspire such emotion. That she'd been denied something as simple as a good night for so long that this—a night of mixed signals and a push and pull I couldn't help—was enough for her to feel grateful when, from where I stood, she deserved perfection.

I wrapped my hands around hers, lowering them away from my face and shoulder, as our foreheads touched, and my gaze looked to her lips, all to avoid seeing the hope in hers.

"The privilege was mine," I replied in a voice hoarse and unused to talking.

Then, before she could reply and distract me again, I released her hands and hurried out the door and down the hallway to the elevator.

This time, I didn't turn around.

CHAPTER TWENTY-ONE

MASSACHUSETTS, PRESENT DAY

I had learned about the Salem witch trials when I was nine.

Mom wasn't thrilled when I insisted on taking the book from the library. She thought I was too young and emotionally sensitive to handle the truth of what had gone on back in the early 1690s, and she wasn't wrong. Because after staying up all night, devouring that book and educating myself on what had become of those men, women, and children, I snuck from my bed to find Mom downstairs on the couch, watching Cheers.

"Charlie, honey, what's wrong?" she asked after seeing my face, sticky and red from crying.

"Why did they have to kill them?" I demanded to know, remembering the horrors from the book as I tucked my body around hers and rested my head on her shoulder.

Mom sighed in the way she always did when she was about to explain something she'd rather not explain at all. Then, she said, "Because they didn't understand them, Charlie, and people ... sometimes, they're afraid of the things they don't—or can't—understand. They think it's easier to fear than to accept."

"But they just wanted to be left alone," I muttered, knowing, even then, exactly what that was like.

God, I *still* knew.

My entire life, that was all I'd ever wanted—to just be left alone to live my quiet life in peace.

That was what all those misunderstood, prosecuted people had wanted then too. To be left to live in the way they saw fit without judgment or mistreatment. I had felt that kinship ever since I'd read that book, and when it was time for me to leave Connecticut, Salem was the only place I'd thought to go. To a place that now honored those who were different, those who were misjudged, and those who simply wanted to be left the fuck alone.

Then, Stormy had walked into my life.

I hadn't wanted her to; I'd never asked. But she had. And five days ago, she'd said she'd come back to annoy me, yet there'd been no sign of her since I had left her hotel room.

To be honest, her absence was annoying me more than her presence ever had.

What was annoying me more was that it was now Halloween, and I hated Halloween. I hated the memories it stirred, the panic and anxiety it instilled, and I hated it in Salem.

I'd always thought it was the influx of tourism, the increase of groups traipsing their way through my cemetery to ogle at the graves of people long since passed. And, hell, maybe that was still part of it. I didn't love that the souls of the wrongfully condemned had somehow turned into a spectacle in death when all they'd wanted was solace in life.

It angered me more today than ever as I cleared a crumpled fast-food bag from the tucked-away grave of Annabel. The woman had been rumored to be a legitimate, magick-wielding witch who'd escaped execution, helped by her law-breaking lover, Thaddeus. And now, all these years later, this was the respect she was given. Greasy garbage and a muddied cup of soda, emptying at the base of her flat, simple stone.

"Fucking assholes," I muttered to myself and Annabel's ghost, piercing the grease-coated paper sack with the long-armed trash picker and stuffing it into the bag in my other hand.

Disrespect angered me. *People* angered me, and that was exactly what infuriated me so much about knowing I was also soul-crushingly *lonely*. That hollow, aching feeling I hadn't been able to shake for weeks was now amplified tenfold since the night of Blake's party.

My mind, flooding with images of Stormy in that dress. My lips, wanting to relive the memory of kissing her. My fingertips, craving to skate along her paper-smooth skin one more time. My body, pleading for the chance to be pressed against hers once again.

But I hadn't seen her in five days.

She probably realized what a fucking psycho loser I am and decided to find someone else to annoy.

I walked along the path with my picker and garbage bag, turning my head to look in the direction of her hotel. Was she there now? It was unlikely. The sun was still shining, and although I didn't know her work schedule or what she did when she wasn't working at all, it seemed too early to be sitting in a hotel room, hunkering down for the night.

Unless someone else is with her.

I approached the truck, sitting idle on the cemetery's one-lane road near the cottage, and threw the trash bag and picker into the bed before climbing in the cab. I gripped the steering wheel in tightly clenched fists and stared ahead at the dashboard, working my jaw from side to side as I plunged deep into a black abyss of intrusive, terrible thoughts.

I should've gotten her number. I should've given her mine.

But what if she didn't even want it? Wouldn't she have asked if she did?

She doesn't like me. Her friends saw through me and talked some sense into her. They told her to stay the fuck away.

God, what if they googled my name?!

The secrets I'd been holding tightly, locked safe in the crevices of my brain, were just an internet search away. And while, no, I didn't think Stormy had my last name, it would've been easy enough to find it out.

What if she knows?
What if she's scared?
Could I blame her?

I looked up from the ink embedded in my flesh to stare out the windshield, my brow furrowing as I tried to muster whatever was left of my confidence and bravery.

Maybe I should go down to the tattoo shop and see if she's there.

Right, yeah. Excellent idea. Freak her out even more. Maybe she'll slap a restraining order on my ass.

I clapped a hand over my eyes and groaned loudly. Fucking hell, it had been years since my anxieties had screamed this loudly, and they bled out now in tremors and a fresh sheen of sweat coating my skin.

I tipped my head back against the seat and curled my bottom lip between my teeth as I begged my mind to give it a rest. If she showed up, she showed up. My life wasn't affected either way. And to never see her again would be for the better, right? I could go back to the way things were. This loneliness would eventually fade like everything else in life, and things would be fine. Hell, maybe they'd even be good.

But ...

Dammit, NO. I like her. I fucking like *her, and any normal guy who likes a woman would just go and see her, so fuck it.*

I turned the key in the ignition, and even as my brain screamed obscenities and every single imaginable reason why this was the worst idea I'd ever had, I tried to believe for a second that I was a *normal guy* with a normal past and didn't stop driving until I reached Salem Skin.

***

"Hey! What can I help you with?"

The girl at the counter was cute. Petite, dusted in freckles, and dressed up in a Winnie the Pooh costume. Some might consider her choice of outfit to be lame, especially given her occupation and the fact that the whole place was heavily laden in gothic decor and black paint, but that only made her sunshiny disposition and costume that much more ironic.

If I could've pulled myself from the task at hand long enough to compliment her, I probably would have.

"Is Stormy here?"

She smiled cheerfully and nodded as she began pulling a clipboard from beneath the counter. "Yep! She's with a client right now, but if you'll fill this—"

"I really just want to talk to her," I interrupted, trying my hardest not to sound like a crazed maniac.

"Oh! Well"—she laid the clipboard onto the countertop—"if you'll just wait here, I'll let her know you're here for a consult—"

"No. I'm just here to *talk*." I emphasized the last word, my patience growing thinner as the seconds ticked on by.

The young girl seemed unsure now, wringing her mittened Winnie the Pooh gloves together and eyeing me warily, like she wasn't sure if she should do as I'd asked or call the cops.

"Um ... okay, well, uh ... who should I say is here?"

"Spider."

The girl narrowed her eyes, studying me with even more suspicion before saying, "Just wait here, okay?"

I nodded before she quickly disappeared through a black velvet curtain. I smirked to myself, unable to believe the stupid nickname had fallen from my lips so easily. It made me think about Luke and his own ridiculous nickname. *Zero*. God, it had been forever since I'd even thought of that stupid name. It had been so dumb, but the guy had used it anyway with more pride than he ever should've had.

Zero. I huffed a laugh and shook my head. *Always such a moron.*

My momentary confidence wilted to make room for a deep, pulsing pain. He might've been a moron, but, fuck, did I ever miss him. I missed him more than I missed anyone or anything, even my parents and Melanie and the innocence I'd known for only a brief stint of time.

We were supposed to be together now. We'd been all each other had for years, and it was meant to remain that way until we were old men. But he was there, back in Connecticut, locked away behind bars of steel and walls of concrete, and I was here.

Alone and pretending I deserved to be anything but.
I should be with him.
I should be exiled and left to rot too.
Don't forget that Halloween night five years ago.
Don't forget the knife. The blood.
Shit. I glanced toward the door, wondering if it was too late to make a quick getaway. The girl dressed as Winnie the Pooh was already back there, telling Stormy I was here, but was I really in any position now to talk to her when my brain was on a warpath and my heart was on the brink of combustion?

Then, there was a smoky voice behind me.

"Charlie?"

My head lifted at the sound of my name. My lungs filled with a deep breath, slow and controlled. The beating of my heart was lulled into a calmer pace, the jittering of my veins and fingers relaxed. My soul felt lighter as my shoulders slumped with the weight of impossible grief and guilt.

I turned to face her and swallowed as I took in the sight of her in a formfitting, long-sleeved, ankle-length black dress, nearly knocking me on my ass.

Stormy's eyes met mine with a gentle smile, but when I opened my mouth to speak, another woman passed through the velvet curtain.

Stormy turned away almost immediately to address the woman now standing at the counter. "Ashley, Melissa will ring you up, okay? You remember your aftercare?"

Ashley replied, "Of course."

Stormy smiled, and although it wasn't directed at me, I wanted to pretend that it was. "Cool. Come back and see me when you wanna get those snakebites."

"I wouldn't go to anyone else. Thanks again, Stormy."

"Anytime, girl."

I stood there, waiting. Staring. Focusing on nothing but her and the silver flecks gleaming against the deep emerald of her eyes. Like lightning illuminating a cloudy sky from within, and I was the spider, unexpectedly desperate to find shelter within her storm.

She returned her focus on me, tipping her head as her heavily lined eyes danced across my face, like she was trying to figure me out.

"Hey, mister," she said, curling one side of her mouth into a half smile as she crossed her arms over her chest. "What brings you to my side of town?"

Before I could speak, my gaze quickly dodged toward Melissa and Ashley, still engaged in the transaction. As much as I wanted to spill my guts to Stormy—to tell her that I hadn't stopped thinking about her since Blake's party and that it had been many years since I'd taken the time to think of anyone new—I didn't want to do it in front of these women.

Stormy followed my gaze, then sniffed a soft laugh before taking my hand in hers.

"Come back here," she ordered, as if she wasn't already dragging me through the heavy velvet curtain.

We entered a hallway adorned with framed pictures of tattoos. It branched off into workstations, sectioned off from the hall by more velvet curtains. With Stormy's hand wrapped around mine, she led me into a station at the end of the hall and pulled the curtain shut behind us. I took a moment to sweep my gaze over the small space. A heavy chest of drawers, an autoclave, and a cluttered countertop with a sink took up two walls of the room while the other housed a padded black chair and a matching stool on wheels.

I had gone with one of my ex-girlfriends to get a few piercings, and this room looked much like that one had nearly a lifetime ago. But this one was better; it was *hers*. The wall toward the back was painted black, the wall behind the chairs was accented by a gallery of various framed pictures of skulls, and the mirror on the opposite wall was surrounded by black bats.

"Well, it's not exactly soundproof, but we're the only ones here for now," Stormy said as she walked past me to the counter, where she turned to pin me with her gaze and gripped the black laminate edge. "So, what's up?"

She had said before that she saw me, and I didn't think I'd fully understood what she meant by that until this very moment. I stared at her for perhaps a moment too long while I allowed her understanding of my social issues to burrow beneath my skin.

Is it possible that she really gets it?

Nobody ever has before. But what if she truly does? Could she really be that special?

God, this is going to hurt so much when she inevitably leaves.

Stormy cocked her head and eyed me with more patience than I ever deserved. "Hey, you good?"

I cleared my throat and stepped forward as I shook my head. "No, actually, I'm not."

"Oh?"

"I seem to remember you threatening to annoy me, yet it's been five days, and"—I shrugged and dipped my hands into the pockets of my jeans—"I haven't been annoyed once."

She accentuated a furrowed brow and a black-lipped pout. "Oh, has it been five days already? I didn't peg you to be the counting kind, but I guess you're just full of surprises, huh?"

"There's a lot of stuff you wouldn't expect about me," I countered. Or, hell, maybe she would. I wasn't quite sure yet.

"Well, you know, you could've called—oh, wait." She snapped her fingers. "Damn, forgot you didn't ask for my number."

I took another step and another until my toes were touching hers, her chin aimed up toward mine. Still, her arms remained at her sides, and my hands stayed within my pockets, but I caught the anxious tapping of her fingers, and there was no mistaking the clenching of my fists.

"Thus the reason for this visit."

"Oh, is that the only reason? Because you realize, you could've just called the shop."

I shrugged. "Don't like calling people I don't know."

"Hmm." She nodded. "Neither do I. I'm just surprised you came down here at all. You do realize the sun is out, right? And that there's, like, people everywhere outside?"

"Oh, believe me," I huffed with agitation, "I'm aware."

"Oh, okay. Because I thought you might spontaneously combust if you ventured outside in anything but darkness."

I tried to fight my grin, tried to suppress my chuckle, but it was hopeless. My lips split with a smile as I shook my head and sniffed a laugh through my nose.

"Ah, so you *do* think I'm funny," Stormy teased, reaching out to poke my chin.

I caught her hand in mine. "I find you endearingly annoying. There's a difference."

"But you *missed* me," she pointed out, dropping her voice to a teasing whisper as she flipped her palm within mine to interlock our fingers.

My poor, battered heart sped up, hammering against its brittle, bony walls, as I nodded and tightened my grip on hers. "Yeah, so maybe I did."

"Hmm," she uttered again, nodding. "Well, I'm sorry for ghosting on you."

"Don't do it again," I replied in a low, gruff whisper.

Stormy giggled, pressing her other hand to my chest. "Oh, yes, sir. I'll—"

"No ... Stormy ..." I shuddered with a relenting sigh, my resolve to keep it together crumbling by the second. I dropped my forehead to hers, squeezing my eyes shut to the world and her piercing green gaze. "Listen to me, okay? You wanted me to let you in. I didn't want to, but it happened, so I'm here, accepting this for whatever the hell it is. But you can't disappear on me, and if you do, it can't be out of the blue. I can't handle it, as fucking pathetic as it sounds. I just can't do it."

We were blanketed in a concerning silence, and I was left to regret ever saying anything. What woman in her right mind wanted to dive headfirst into something with a man she not only knew little about, but one with apparent abandonment issues?

Yet there she was, breaking the silence with a hushed, "It's not pathetic, Charlie," as she tipped her head back and stood on her toes.

At the touch of her lips against mine, I inhaled deeply, sharply. My nerves were snapped into overdrive at the impact before being lulled toward desperate lust as her lips parted—a silent invitation to deepen the kiss. I answered with a groan at the reacquainting of our eager, wandering tongues. My hands moved to cradle her face, my fingertips skirting her raven-colored hairline. She gripped my shirt, pressing her fists to my heaving chest, as we made out like desperate teenagers against the countertop in her workspace. Both of us too wrapped up in the moment to hear the footsteps coming down the hallway.

"Hey, Stormy. You in—"

Metal rings slid along the curtain rod, and Stormy reluctantly pulled away but kept my shirt within her grasp.

"Oh shit. Sorry," a man's voice said.

I glanced over my shoulder to see Blake standing there in the now-open doorway. His eyes were already cast downward, aimed toward the floor.

"I thought we had a rule, Blake," she snapped as a deep blush spread from the collar of her dress to her cheekbones. "Knock on the wall before opening the curtain, right?"

He cleared his throat and still made no move to leave. "My bad."

She furrowed her brow and cocked her head as she glared at the man behind me. "And whose rule was that? Hmm ... let me think ..."

"I said I was—"

She unraveled her fingers from my shirt to tap her temple. "Oh! That's right! It was *yours*."

Blake sighed. "Melissa told me you weren't with a client. It hadn't occurred to me that you might be back here, sucking face with some guy." He met my eye with an almost-apologetic raise of his brows. "Sorry, Charlie."

I cleared my throat and smoothed my shirt over my chest, feeling a lot like a kid who'd just been caught doing something he shouldn't have been doing. "It's fine."

"Anyway," Blake said, clearly changing the subject, "there's someone up front, looking to get pierced."

Stormy didn't even try to not look disappointed as she nodded. "Okay. I'll be right out."

"Cool."

He turned to leave when Stormy stopped him.

"Can you do me a favor though?"

He sucked in a deep breath and turned slowly, like the last thing he wanted to do was hear what she needed from him, but still, he nodded. "What's up?"

"Give Charlie my number."

I caught her gaze, and her smile touched her eyes with every bit of reassurance she thought I needed.

"Yeah, sure," Blake replied before gesturing for me to follow. "Come on, man. I gotta get paper and something to write with."

Stormy's brow creased with what looked like suspicion, but she didn't say anything more. She gripped my arm, smiled, and told me to shoot her a text as soon as I could. She promised to annoy me when she got the chance; I told her I was looking forward to it, and I meant it.

Then, I followed Blake down the hall, through the waiting room, and down another shorter hallway to what appeared to be an office.

He closed the door behind us and gestured for me to sit in a chair on one side of an old wooden desk. I complied, and as he sat across from me on the other side, I was struck with an unwelcomed memory of speaking to the school principal after Ritchie Wheeler had used his seniority and popularity to torment me in the second grade.

Blake didn't look at me as nicely as the principal had that day.

He grabbed a pad of paper and a pen and began to speak without wasting another moment. "Listen, you seem like a good guy, and Stormy's apparently really into you."

He scrawled something onto the paper without glancing up at me while my blood burned to the temperature of molten lava at the thought of her being *into me* at all, let alone talking to her friends about it. But there was something else in his tone that had me sitting on edge, like he was about to drop a bomb onto my head.

"But, look, I gotta say this because I care about her. She's a good friend—practically family. She's been through some shit. She's been *hurt*."

"We've *all* been hurt," I countered defensively while also listening intently to what he was trying to say.

He looked up to pin me with a stern glare. "It's not my story to tell, and I'm guessing that when she's ready to tell it to you, she will. I'm not telling you not to go out with her or ... whatever you guys are doing—it's not really my business. All I'm saying is, be careful with her. And I'm telling you, man, if you hurt her—"

"You're gonna come for me?" I offered, leaning back in my chair while wondering how the hell I always found myself in situations where some asshole thought it was okay to threaten me with violence.

But Blake shrugged as he passed the piece of paper across the desk. "I can't speak for other people she knows, but no. Revenge isn't really my thing. I'd just be disappointed. Like I said, you seem like a good guy, and she really likes you, and ..." He sighed. "She deserves something good, is all I'm saying. And if she can find it with you, then ..."

I took the paper from his hand and tucked it into my jacket pocket. "I'm the last person you need to worry about," I replied, removing any hint of defense from my tone.

He nodded. "I hope that's true."

I forced a tight smile to form across my lips as I stood and left the room without another word. When I left the hallway, I found Stormy was still in the waiting room, handing a nervous-looking young man a clipboard with a consent form and instructing him to fill it out while she went to make a copy of his driver's license. She kept things professional at the sight of me but offered a small, glittery-eyed smile.

"Don't forget to text me, Spider," she said, her voice even and cool.

One side of my mouth curled upward as I replied, "Only if you don't forget to drive me crazy."

Then, I left the shop, feeling good about the future for maybe the first time in an incredibly long while. I knew better than to be too hopeful. I knew better than to expect too much.

But for once, I felt lighter, happier, and I thought, *Blake has nothing to worry about.* I knew what it was like to hurt, and I had no intention of inflicting pain on her.

And that was the kind of good feeling I held on to all the way back to Luke's bike. I picked up the helmet and was about to put it on when I stopped in a fretful stupor.

I could do everything to not hurt Stormy. But there wasn't much I could do to keep the past from breaking her heart. And once she inevitably learned about those skeletons hidden in my closet—stuffed deep and coated under an inch of dust—would she find it in her to stay?

And that was the question that swarmed through my mind and festered in my gut all the way back to my cottage in the middle of the cemetery, where I parked Luke's bike in the back and headed for the door.

Only to be stopped by the faintest hint of cigarette smoke lingering in the air and an empty pack of a familiar brand of cigarettes, sitting precariously in the center of the mat right outside the door.

CHAPTER TWENTY-TWO

MASSACHUSETTS, PRESENT DAY

It was hard to deny the possibility of an afterlife after I'd spent nearly half of my life working in a cemetery. There were things I couldn't explain as being anything but otherworldly, and I accepted those things without argument.

Perfectly timed gusts of wind, the casting of shadows when there was otherwise nothing there, unintelligible whispers carried along a breeze when there wasn't anyone else around, and the indisputable feeling of being watched. Those were just a few of the things I was used to. Those were the things I could brush off as being occupational hazards, and they never ever scared me.

But this empty foil package had my heart and lungs in a viselike grip. And when I remembered the other recent incidental findings—the cigarette butt and the mysterious flower on Annabel's grave—I was downright terrified to do anything more than blink against my will.

Someone knows. Someone knows who I am, and they know what I did. The thought crept into my mind like a digging, wriggling worm, and I shuddered at the very real possibility that I'd been found out. That I could've been *followed*. But who? Who would've cared enough to dig into the past of a withdrawn cemetery caretaker?

I couldn't even begin to guess.

Over my shoulder, a twig snapped, and my hair whipped against my cheek as I spun on my heel to look in the direction of the sound. A squirrel dashed between headstones to scurry up a nearby white oak, but apart from that one small creature, I was alone.

"Shit," I whispered, my voice cracking.

A flood of memories came rushing back as if a dam in my mind had been broken. The things I kept tucked deep inside, things that only crept up to haunt me in my nightmares.

The creaking of the floorboards outside my bedroom door.

The weight of the knife in my hand.

The heat of the blood pooling against my fingers and dripping onto my bare feet.

I gave my head a rapid shake and turned back to the cigarette packet, crushed and lying on the doormat. I wouldn't touch it, wouldn't dare add my fingerprints to the cursed thing, but I nudged it with the toe of my boot until it was away from the door. Then, after making a mental note to dispose of it later, I hurried to unlock the door and took cover inside, praying that whoever had come looking for me would understand that all I wanted—God, all I had *ever* wanted since Luke had gotten himself in more trouble than I could do anything about—was to be left alone.

And yet ...

***

"Wow. I gotta say, Charlie, when you asked for my number earlier, I didn't expect to get a phone call a couple of hours later. I thought you'd be more of a text kinda guy."

I huffed a laugh as I got out of the truck to approach one side of the iron gate, keys in hand. "You didn't *have* to answer," I pointed out.

A cluster of laughing kids, all dressed up for Halloween, walked by with a couple of adult chaperones following close behind. I mustered a smile at them and nodded my head in greeting. The kids scurried along, not daring to look at the creep who lived in the cemetery, but the adults with them acknowledged me with tired smiles and wishes for a good night.

Despite the eerie finding outside my door, that was the plan and the very reason for my call to a certain body piercer.

Stormy scoffed, feigning offense. "What kind of monster do you think I am? Of course I had to answer. I finally got a hot guy's attention after pining over him for weeks. I'm not gonna just ... I don't know ... play hard to get now."

The frozen metal of the gate sent an ache through my bones as it creaked loudly against its hinges. I swung it into the center of the driveway and headed for the other side as my flushed cheeks warded off the chill in the air.

She thinks I'm hot?

"Cool, uh ... so ..."

What am I, twelve?

I leaned my forehead against the heavy iron and squeezed my eyes shut. Up until this point, Stormy was one of the few people ever in my life to somehow leave me relaxed. I wasn't going to let my nerves get the best of me now that she'd called me *hot*.

"Anyway"—I cleared my throat and went back to closing the gate—"I was wondering if you had plans tonight."

The speaker was flooded with Stormy's forlorn sigh. "I wish. Normally, I'd be at my apartment, handing out candy to trick-or-treaters, but I'm stuck in a hotel room this year, watching shitty reality TV. Why do you ask?"

I unlocked the padlock hanging from the heavy chains as I said, "Just wondering if you'd maybe wanna hang out or—"

"Wait. Are you actually asking me out, or is this a hookup situation?"

She wasn't going to be satisfied until my face was completely set on fire—I was sure of it.

"Um, I—"

"Because honestly, I'm down for either. Anything to get out of this freakin' room. I'm pretty sure it's haunted, by the way."

I know the feeling. I glanced behind me down the dark, winding driveway, disappearing into the cemetery.

"Well, I—"

"I just need to know what I'm wearing. If we're going out, I can throw something on. But otherwise, are you good with shitty old leggings and my brother-in-law's sweatshirt? It doesn't scream sex appeal, but I can promise a good time once I'm naked."

Holy shit. I choked on a blend of nerves and amusement. "Um ... your brother-in-law?"

"My sister and her family visited a few weeks ago, and her husband left his hoodie at my place, so I called dibs. The guy is *huge*. It's like wearing a fuckin' blanket."

Her penchant for cursing and lack of filters tugged at the corners of my mouth, pulling it into a sad, nostalgic smile.

In a way, she reminded me of Luke.

"Ah, I gotcha," was all I said, my voice soft and wistful, even if a little melancholy.

"Anyway, so, yeah, whatever you wanna do, I'm down. Just let me know, presentable or bridge troll, and I'm good."

I snorted a laugh. "Bridge troll works for me."

"You know, I had a feeling it might."

"If you wanna run out now, I'm just about to lock up," I said, looking across the street and lifting my eyes to her floor of the hotel. "I'll wait for you."

"I'll be right out," she said in a softer tone. "And, hey, Charlie?"

"Yeah?"

"Is it weird that I can't wait to see you again when I just saw you a few hours ago?"

***

I was leaning against the stone pillar outside the cemetery gate when Stormy emerged from the hotel's front entrance. She was dressed just as she'd described—tight black leggings, an enormous black hooded sweatshirt, and black high-top Chucks—with her raven-colored hair gathered on top of her head in what seemed to be her signature style. Her eyes lit up at the sight of me, standing with my back to the stone and my arms crossed tightly over my chest, but she kept her gait purposely casual and controlled, like she didn't want to seem as excited as she felt.

She looked both ways before running across the street, dodging a bicyclist on his way past the cemetery.

"Hi," she said, breathless. "Sorry it took me a few minutes to get down here. I had to help some old lady get into her room. I was gonna just leave her standing there, struggling with her key card, but, man, she started to cry and how the hell was I supposed to leave her like that? Felt like bad karma."

"It's fine." I shrugged as I turned to unlock the side gate.

"I mean, I probably could've just let her stand there, weeping, but I would've felt like an asshole."

I snorted a laugh as I worked the key into the lock. "Abandoning a crying old lady in a creepy hallway *is* an asshole move, I gotta agree."

"Oh, that's nice to know." Stormy bumped her shoulder against me. "How a guy would handle a crying old lady says a lot about his character."

I held the gate open for her to walk inside as I said, "I take it, I passed the test?"

She met my eye as she grinned. "With flying colors."

We both entered the cemetery grounds, and I locked the gate behind me. Stormy didn't take a step further as she shivered and wrapped her arms around herself, sweeping her gaze over the moonlit headstones.

"You cold?" I asked, doubting it. It might've been the very end of October in New England, but her sweatshirt looked too heavy and warm for her to be shivering like it was the middle of February.

"No, not really," she easily admitted. "I'm just wondering how you walk around here at night without shitting your pants. That's all."

I grunted a laugh as my palm found the small of her back. "Actually, this is where I feel safest," I admitted as I led her along the path to the waiting truck in the parking lot. "When there's nobody here but me, the ghosts, and the security guard."

And even though I said it without any qualms, my nerves jolted at the mention of those ghosts. Or was it only one in particular?

Is it even a ghost at all?

"Where's the security guard?" she asked, turning her head in one direction and then the other, as if she might catch a glimpse of a man I seldom saw myself.

I pointed into the distance. "He's in the office over there. We don't cross paths much. I think I can count on one hand the number of times I've even seen or spoken to the guy."

Maybe I should talk to him now, I thought. *Maybe he'd have some insight into who's been leaving shit around my house.*

"You're not scared of the ghosts?" Stormy asked as we reached the truck.

She quickly glimpsed toward the first row of headstones and visibly shivered. She was obviously terrified, yet she had still come.

To be with me.

"Ghosts can't hurt you," I assured her, unlocking the car and opening the passenger door.

Stormy leveled me with an incredulous look. "That's not what those ghost hunters on TV say. They're always walking through some haunted cemetery or some shit, dealing with pissed-off spirits that like to throw random shit around."

I draped my arm over the top of the door. "And you believe everything you see on TV?"

She crossed her arms, leaning against the truck. "I didn't say I *believe* it. I'm only saying I don't have a reason not to."

"Fair enough." I nodded my chin toward the shadowed headstones in the near distance. "Well, I can tell you with a decent amount of certainty that the ghosts here don't wanna hurt anyone. They just want to be respected and left to rest in peace."

She pursed her lips and muttered a thoughtful, "Hmm," before climbing into the cab of the truck.

I shut the door behind her and got into the driver's side, immediately struck by how weird and also nice it was to share the truck's confines with another person who wasn't Ivan.

When the seat belts were buckled, I started the engine and pulled out of my usual parking spot, ready to get back inside my house. Because while I might've told Stormy that the ghosts didn't want to hurt her, I wasn't so sure anymore that they didn't want to hurt *me*.

We drove in silence for a moment, slowly rolling beneath a canopy of branches and falling leaves. I stole quick glances at her through the corner of my eye, unable to believe that she was here in my truck, going to my house by invitation. My tongue was tied into a thousand knots; I was unsure of what to say or if I should say anything at all. This type of thing—inviting a woman back to my place—wasn't my area of expertise, and I was already failing miserably.

Not knowing what else to do, I reached out to turn up the radio when she asked, "Do you like being here because you feel connected to them?"

I narrowed my eyes at the black road ahead. "What?"

"The ghosts. Do you feel a connection to them?"

It was a weird question, one I didn't quite understand. "Why would you think that?" I asked, my tone flat and teetering on the edge of defensive.

Stormy didn't seem to notice. "Because that's all you want too, right? To be respected and left to be at peace."

Had I told her that? I couldn't remember now, and I held my breath, unsure of how to respond, until I decided that the best way was to say the things I'd avoided in every other interaction I'd had in the past several years—the truth.

"I didn't always want to be by myself," I answered, already feeling lighter from being honest. I allowed a huffed chuckle to rumble from my chest as I added, "God, I fucking *hated* being alone when I was younger."

Nostalgic melancholy barreled over me as I remembered a time when just the thought of being alone would push me deep into an uncontrollable panic.

In my peripheral vision, I watched her turn her head and regard me with a soft, curious expression.

"So, what changed?"

"Life," I answered simply with a helpless shrug.

Stormy scoffed, like the answer wasn't good enough. "Life happens to everyone, Charlie, but not all of us make a complete one-eighty when it happens to us."

Her tone was almost harsh, and it stung, like she was speaking from some kind of experience—her own trauma perhaps. I thought about what Blake had said earlier, that she had been hurt, and I resisted the urge to ask her what he had meant by that.

"Yeah, well, losing everyone who ever meant anything can do that to a guy," I said, the words leaving a bitter taste on my tongue.

Stormy shook her head. "I think there's more than that."

I smirked to hide my surprise. "Oh, that's not enough?"

"I'm not saying that. And I think that's part of it, sure, but I think something really serious happened. I mean, you said your brother is in prison, right?"

My jaw clenched at the mention of Luke, my knuckles whitened against the steering wheel, and I regretted ever saying something about him to her.

"So, maybe it has something to do with that, or maybe it's something else. I don't know. But"—she nodded thoughtfully, her eyes glinting with empathy—"there's definitely more."

"And how are you so sure about that?" I challenged, my voice cold and even as I pulled the truck into the driveway and parked without so much as glancing at her.

"Because a drastic change requires a drastic reason."

"You say that like you're speaking from experience," I muttered, wondering further about her past and the pain she'd endured.

"I think you already know that I am."

I pursed my lips and swallowed as I killed the engine and pulled the key from the ignition. Stormy followed my lead—unbuckling and getting out of the truck—but instead of going straight to the door, I rounded the hood to meet her somewhere in the middle in front of the truck, the toes of her shoes nearly touching the toes of mine.

"What happened to you?" I asked, deciding on the spot to stop with this stupid dance around the truth and get right to it.

There was little light to speak of, but a sconce hanging beside the door was enough to illuminate the look of cool disregard on Stormy's face. The tilt of her head; her stony, bright green glare; the firm set of her pouty lips. There was a dare in her eyes that lit a flame somewhere deep inside my gut, and I knew, if I wasn't careful, I was likely to combust if I stared for too long.

I just wasn't so sure I cared much about being safe anymore. Not with her.

"Why do you care?"

"I don't fucking know," I nearly shouted. Helplessly. Honestly. "But something tells me that I should."

Green eyes darkened by the night flitted over my face in a dance as erratic and graceful as a butterfly, swooping through the wildflowers planted along the cemetery path. They filled with tears, twin crystal pools, and my fists clenched at my sides as I seethed, hating the way her face fell with distress and a pain I understood yet couldn't touch without knowing exactly why she hurt so badly.

Her gaze landed on my lips, and there was no time to think or speak before her hands were reaching up to grip the back of my neck, to anchor herself to me, like it was she who was drowning in this life and I was the saving grace keeping her from going under.

Then, she kissed me.

At this point, I thought I'd had somewhat of an idea of what it was like to kiss Stormy. She'd radiated passion, and her lips and tongue had moved with only the purpose of keeping that fire burning for as long as we were allowed. It had been intense and exciting, a taste of what it meant to be alive in something as simple as a kiss, and every time, I left the moment drunk and already craving the next.

But *this* kiss ...

There was no passion or lustful need to be found in the fuel that drove her mouth to press against mine. In this moment, when she trembled and sniffled and my hands pressed to her cheeks to collect her tears within my palms, I could sense nothing but a raw and tremendous pain. One that sliced so deep that I could do nothing to stop my brother's voice from permeating my mind.

"I know you don't believe it now, but one day, you're gonna learn to live without me, Charlie. And I promise, it's gonna be okay."

Was this it? Was I finally living without him? Because nothing about it felt okay, yet it felt *right*. Her lips and her cool hands around my neck felt so, so fucking right, and the more I thought about it, and the more my palms grew wet with the tears she couldn't seem to stop crying, the more my mind warred with how much I wanted it to feel wrong.

"I promise, it's gonna be okay."

Leaves rustled from behind where we stood. My eyes snapped open, and my hands dropped away as I took one quick step away from Stormy, both of us breathless and panting. The pounding of my heart echoed against my eardrums as I whipped my head in the direction the sound had come from. But the night was dark, and I saw nothing.

Another rustle, and Stormy closed the gap I'd created, pressing her trembling hands to my thundering chest.

"Wh-wha—"

Hoo-hoo!

An owl burst from a nearby tree, and I slid my arm around her shoulders as I pointed my gaze skyward. I urged my heart to calm as I watched the bird take flight against the deep, blackened sky.

"Shit." Stormy groaned before laughing, shaking her head as she wiped her palms over her face. "I'm sorry. That was ... that was freakin' weird of me."

"It happens," I said, blowing out a deep breath, still watching that owl beat its wings against the backdrop of a moonless night. "You get used to it though. The sounds—"

"Not ... that. I mean, crying. I shouldn't—"

"No," I interjected. "Don't ever apologize for that."

The owl flew overhead. And maybe I was seeing things, but I could swear it had peered down at me before it passed.

Stormy cleared her throat and sniffled again, taking a step back and wiping her palms against her sweatshirt. "I honestly can't even remember the last time I really *cried*. Probably not since Soldier was in the hospital and—"

"Soldier?" I looked back to her as the bird disappeared from my sight.

Stormy brushed a few strands of hair from off her forehead as she nodded. "Sorry. Um ... my brother-in-law, his name is Soldier. He almost ... well, actually, he *did* die several years ago, but they brought him back."

"Wow." I blinked, tucking my hands into my jacket pockets. Unsure of what else to say.

Where I had come from, nobody was brought back from the dead. Nobody was saved.

They only left, disappearing to vanish from my life altogether.

"Yeah, it's a, uh ... it's a long story." She shifted from one foot to another to hide her discomfort as she lifted her hand and waved the topic away. "Anyway, that was probably the last time I cried, so I guess I was due or something."

She tried to force a laugh, leaving the moment as awkward as we both seemed to feel. But I guessed that was what happened when two souls were stripped naked after being wrapped in impenetrable armor for so long.

She saw me, and I knew now that I saw her.

Without another word, I turned to head for the door, still spooked by the owl, still reeling from words I'd wished Luke had never said, still remembering the empty foil cigarette pack. Stormy followed just as quietly as I fished my keys from my pocket and unlocked the front door.

I pushed it open and gestured inside. "Ladies first."

She laughed, smoky and hoarse. "Such a gentleman when you're not threatening to slit my throat."

But she walked inside, and I followed, closing the door behind me and ensuring twice that it was locked before turning to watch her assess my small but cozy cottage.

Stormy walked slowly around the living room, taking in the wingback chairs in front of the stone fireplace, sliding her fingertips over the upholstery.

"No couch?" she asked, sweeping her gaze around to answer her own question.

"Never saw a reason to have one," I admitted as fantasies of laying her down filled my head.

"Why have two chairs then?"

"Sometimes, my friend Ivan stops by."

Stormy looked up to meet my eye, one side of her mouth lifting in a barely there smile. "You have a second chair just for him?"

I shrugged before nodding.

"That doesn't sound like the kinda thing a cold, axe-wielding murderer would do."

My fingers twitched, and I could feel the chilled handle of the knife in my hand. But even though I couldn't force a smile to my lips, I chuckled brusquely and dropped my gaze to the floor, relieved I didn't see a pool of blood at my feet.

"No. Guess not."

"Honestly, I'm surprised you have a friend at all."

I lifted my gaze to find her unabashedly raking her eyes over my small desk and the clock on the wall that had once belonged to my mother.

"He was kinda built into the job," I explained, my voice roughened by memories I wished I could erase. "He was the caretaker before me."

She turned, her head cocked and her smile growing affectionate. "And you stayed in touch?"

"He didn't give me much of a choice."

That smile was a full-on grin now. "I like him already."

The table between the two chairs held my sketch pad and marker, and it caught Stormy's eye, like a brand-new shiny penny to a magpie. She hurried over from the desk and ran her fingers over the drawing I'd done of the trio of blackbirds that had perched themselves on my roof just a little over a week ago. Their presence had left an impression on my mind, and I'd sketched them down onto the page when I couldn't take their black-eyed stare any longer.

Stormy stared at their feathered forms, her lips parting with her hushed gasp before she shook her head and uttered, "Damn."

She could've had any other reaction, she could've used any other word, and it wouldn't have fazed me. But it was *that* one—*damn*—that sent me back in time like a slingshot, and I could see Luke staring at the back of my bedroom door. At the spider trapped inside his storm. Shaking his head and muttering that one little word.

"Damn."

"Your brother was right," she said, as if she could see the scene in my head. "You are one talented motherfucker, Charlie."

"He never said it quite like that," I replied with a melancholy chuckle.

Her fingertips brushed gingerly over the spider at the bottom of the page, looking up from beneath the perched birds. "This is you?"

I narrowed my eyes with startled intrigue and tipped my head to watch as she grabbed the pad and flipped the page. "How did you figure that out?"

"Doesn't take a genius to figure out how you view yourself, Spider," she muttered absentmindedly before looking up at me and raising a brow. "You wear it, literally, on your sleeves."

"Maybe I just love spiders."

"Hmm …" She puckered her lips and flipped another page. "I'm sure you do. But they're also your spirit animal."

She presented the book to me, flashing a sketch of a black widow, surrounded by towering headstones. Ghouls swept from the graves, clouding the sky and shielding the spider from the world outside.

"These aren't just drawings," Stormy assessed with enchantment twinkling in her eyes. "This is your diary."

It had never been described that way before, but she wasn't wrong. She had me figured out, more than I could've ever expected. My chin lifted in a fake display of confidence as the little boy in my heart prayed she wouldn't turn the page. But she did, and her eyes widened before softening with the simultaneous parting of her lips.

I knew what she was seeing—the long-legged spider, curled inside the storm cloud, in deep, peaceful slumber, like a baby in a womb. The page beyond that cloud was blacked out, but that darkness couldn't breach the shield of lightning, illuminating the clouds' edges. The spider wore a smile as he slept. He was finally comfortable, and even as the world outside was drenched in chaos and tragedy, he'd somehow found comfort in the most unlikely place. As if all those years of being trapped outside, all he'd needed was for one of those clouds overhead to invite him in.

Stormy raised her eyes from the page to pin me with her gaze. "Is this me?"

I swallowed, struggling to not allow my embarrassment and anxiety to take hold. Still, I dropped my chin in a single nod and replied with a quiet, "Yes."

"Oh," she whispered, looking back to the page, too stunned to do anything but stare.

She hates it.

My palms started to sweat as her eyes continued to dance across the page.

God, she thinks I'm insane.

I turned my head, diverted my gaze. All too aware of the uptick in my pulse and the raging in my heart.

Probably for the better, but ... shit, why didn't I put that fucking thing away?

I swallowed relentlessly at the prickly ball in my throat, certain I was about to choke on nothing but my shame and panic.

I don't want her to le—

"Hey, Charlie?"

A harsh whoosh of breath escaped my lungs as I replied, "Y-yeah?"

I looked in time for her to lower the sketch pad back to the table. She still stared at the open page, tracing her fingers over that cloud and the spider held within its shelter as she cleared her throat.

"I really hope you plan to show me your room. Like ... now."

My brow furrowed as my brain struggled to compute what exactly she was saying. "My room?"

She lifted her eyes back to mine, strong determination and lustful need coalescing in the sea of green. "And I swear, if you end up only having a twin-size bed or some weird bachelor shit like that, I'm dragging your ass back to my hotel room."

I laughed while my entire face heated with the understanding of what she was alluding to. "I haven't slept on a twin-size bed since I was, like, seventeen."

"Thank God." Stormy's eyes held mine as she moved around the chairs and across the room. Her palms pressed to my bearded cheeks, and I touched my forehead to hers, struggling to find my confidence and breath. "Lead the way, Chuck."

My eyes squeezed shut, and I shook my head with my groan.

"Just one thing," I grumbled.

Stormy giggled, already steering me without an idea of where she was going. "What's that?" Her voice was flirtatious and eager, like she couldn't imagine being anywhere else than here with me.

She wants *me*, I realized, driving it home with a certainty I hadn't known or understood since the early days of my relationship with Jersey. And, Lord, *I* wanted *her*.

My eyes opened with new confidence, new purpose, and I stared into hers, moving her backward toward the hall, toward my waiting bedroom. Her breath hitched, and the green in her gaze popped with excitement and carnal anticipation as she bit her lip.

"Don't ever—and I mean, *ever*—call me Chuck again."

CHAPTER TWENTY-THREE

MASSACHUSETTS, PRESENT DAY

It had been a long time since I'd done this. Not as long ago as my relationship with Jersey. There'd been others in between then and now. The number of women I'd slept with couldn't begin to rival Luke's, and I had never developed a taste for casual sex the way he had. And now, I was here, miles away from where I'd started, heading to my bedroom with a woman I couldn't believe was still here.

God, I had tried and tried to scare her away. But she'd only seen my resistance as a challenge, and now, I was grateful for it. Because as she crossed the threshold of my bedroom, I realized with heart-stopping magnitude how badly I needed this. Not *this*—sex, I mean. If I was being honest, sex had been the furthest thing from my mind in the years since leaving Connecticut, when all I'd been trying to do was survive without being discovered.

But it was *her* that I had needed—Stormy—and my soul exhaled with relief the moment I finally made my peace with that.

I had no intention of turning on the light as we entered the bedroom. Somehow, I always felt like light had a way of making a moment like this feel less sacred, like it was its own a separate entity, watching and prying and capable of revealing our secrets to others.

But Stormy spun around to loop her arms around my neck and said, "I want to see you."

A lump formed in my throat as I held her around her waist. "I thought you already did."

"You know what I mean."

I did, and I considered saying no. The truth was revealed to me then that it wasn't that I was so much afraid of the light itself, but scared of her and what she might find. That she would leave, and right now, in this moment, all I wanted was for her to *stay*. But whether I turned on the light now or the sun did it for me in the morning, she would eventually, inevitably, see. She'd see it all, and I had to believe it was better to do it now and get it over with when I was drunk on lust and the excitement of allowing myself to *want* again than when the sobering daylight arrived.

So, I reached out for the floor lamp between the door and my dresser. With a yank of the chain, the room was blanketed in a warm glow. Stormy's arms remained around my neck as she turned her head, taking in my small but comfortable bedroom. To avoid watching her perusal of my choice in interior design, I dipped my head to bury my face in her neck, to breathe in the lavender she held in her hair and the cinnamon and black pepper she wore on her skin.

I inhaled so deeply that I almost believed I could get high on her scent. She was the embodiment of warmth, and in my haze, I pressed my lips to her neck, desperate to hear her moan in the quiet of my room.

When my lips didn't work, I tried with my tongue. Tasting her skin, working my hands over the small of her back. But she was too distracted, too entangled in what I'd originally thought was a mundane corner of my world, and I still didn't have her attention.

I pulled my lips from her neck as one hand lifted from her back to glide over the swell of her breast, concealed by her oversize sweatshirt. Moving upward over the long, smooth column of her slender throat to her defined jaw, where my grip firmed and guided her eyes back to mine, hooded and greedy. Jealous of her interest in my space and not in me.

I was met with a mirrored desire, her lust alive and thriving. There wasn't enough time to appreciate it before my mouth pressed hard against hers, my hand still gripping her jaw. Guiding the tilt of her head, thrusting my tongue against hers, deepening the kiss and fueling the fire I needed to move her backward toward my bed.

Stormy moaned into my mouth, tangling her fingers into the hair at the back of my head and loosening my ponytail as she pulled. I responded with a moan of my own, removing my hand from her jaw to grab her ass and lift her up against me. She wrapped her legs around my waist, and my pulsing, aching erection pressed firmly between her open thighs, pulling desperate groans from both of our open, slack mouths.

"Oh my God," she gasped against my lips. "I hope you fuck as good as you kiss."

I grunted a strangled chuckle as we tumbled together to the mattress in a knotted heap of limbs. "Not making any promises, but I'll try my best."

She pressed another kiss to my mouth as her lips twitched into a smile, and then she scooted back, untangling her legs from my hips and her arms from my neck. I settled on my side, propping my cheek in my palm as she sat up, pulling the sweatshirt off in one fluid motion without a second of hesitation. She'd worn nothing underneath, and my lips parted, my mouth drying in an instant, at the sight of her topless form.

"What?" Stormy smirked, reaching out to nudge my chin, closing my mouth. "Never seen a pair of tits before?"

An amused grin spread across my face as I lifted my eyes lazily from her chest to her eyes. "Not these."

She glanced down at the breasts in question—the nipples pierced and bejeweled with black barbells, the curved sides tattooed with black-and-gray florals and bats—and screwed her lips to the side. "I've never liked them," she said almost to herself. "They're kinda lopsided, and the right one sags a little more than the left." She looked back to me as I tried to unsuccessfully find the imperfections she was pointing out. "Right? I got, like, weird *Frankenstein* boobs."

I guffawed and shook my head. "Can't say I agree with that at all, but okay."

"Oh, whatever." She rolled her eyes away from mine as she stretched her legs out to untie her Chucks. "I forget all men care about is seeing a chick naked. You're not really seeing my body for what it is. You're just thinking with your dick, and listen, that's cool. I get it. You're simpleminded. You can't help that."

She prattled on as she undid the laces while my brow furrowed and my head shook softly.

"Uh, that's not true at all. Not always," I replied, my voice low, nearly offended by the accusation.

One shoe was pulled off as that intense green gaze shot toward me sidelong. "Oh?"

I sat up and moved to face her, pulling her other sneakered foot onto my lap. One corner of her mouth barely lifted into a smile as I began to untie the knot.

"My brother, Luke …" I cleared my throat after uttering his name aloud for the first time in years, keeping my eyes on my hands, slowly undoing the black laces. "He was the kind of guy you're describing. Single-minded, only cared about sex … you know. But I never was. And don't get me wrong; I like sex as much as the next guy. But I was never like him, sleeping with whoever would look at me. Honestly, I always had a hard time with stomaching the idea of sleeping with someone I didn't at least have some connection with, but he didn't seem to have that problem, and I couldn't understand if there was something wrong with him or me or … I don't know … both of us.

"So, anyway," I continued, loosening the laces, "one day, after this woman left our house, I asked him about that. I said, 'How the hell do you do that so easily?' And he looked at me like a second head had just sprouted from my neck and said, 'The hell are you talking about?' So, I told him, and he stared at me like his heart was breaking all over again right in front of me. Then, he said, 'It's only like that for me because *I* know and *you* know that it'll never be more than just fucking for me. You still have a chance to find more than that; you still have hope. But there's no hope left for me, Charlie, and I don't want it. I'm just fucking until I can't anymore, but you …'" I pulled in a deep breath as I tugged her shoe off and dropped it to the floor. "'You keep looking.'

"So, that's what I'm doing," I said, finally looking up to her eyes, never once stopping to take in the sight of her bare breasts or the tattoos etched into the skin of her chest or sternum. "I like sex, and believe me when I say that seeing you naked is a fucking honor. But I'd never be so arrogant to assume I was privy to either without your invitation. Because at the end of the day, all I'm looking for is something more than just this."

She stared at me for several loud, booming beats of my heart, and to my horror, a tear worked its way from the corner of her eye to slide over her cheek. Then, she blinked, laughed, and swatted that crystal drop away as she rolled her gaze to the ceiling.

"Jesus Christ, Charlie. You'd better stop doing that shit," she said with a groan, holding her palms to her eyes and shaking her head. "I don't fucking cry. I don't *like* crying. But, God, you're just …" She groaned again in lieu of words.

"Cheesy?" I offered, quirking one side of my mouth in a self-deprecating grin. "Lame? Stupid? Stop me when I hit on something accurate."

"No!" She dropped her hands to her lap and bit her bottom lip before saying, "You're sweet, and you're nice, and you're not at all what I expected, and you deserve more—"

"Stop." I pressed my hands to her knees. "I'm not going to pretend there isn't a lot I don't know about you or where you've been, but don't take who I am right now, in this room, as any indication of who you think I was before. Don't assume you know what I deserve."

I hadn't removed a single article of clothing yet, but I felt more naked than if I'd been stripped bare. Stormy's eyes narrowed for only a second with questions ablaze. I knew there was an invitation in the things I'd said, and if she asked now, I would answer as best as I could. I'd told you I was done running, and I had meant it.

But where I expected questions, she only nodded and replied, "Okay," as if, right now, none of it mattered. Maybe it would in the morning or in the middle of the night, when the euphoria eventually slipped away, but in this moment, we settled for acceptance.

She stood on her knees before me, hooking her fingers in the waistband of her black leggings. I pressed my palms to the microdermal piercings adorning her hip bones, twinkling in the glow of the lamp, and leaned closer to pepper kisses over the detailed serpent, coiling up from beneath her leggings to slither toward her rib cage.

I lowered my hands, laying them over hers. My head tipped back, meeting her gaze. Asking silently for permission to assist, and with a deep swallow, she nodded.

She wasn't wearing anything underneath the soft, stretchy fabric—a fact that no longer surprised me but instead just turned me on to the point of discomfort. As every inch of her smooth, inked, bejeweled skin was revealed to my hungry eyes and salivating mouth, she watched me, power crackling in her stare and beneath her flesh.

"You're overdressed," she stated, casually lying back to kick her leggings off the rest of the way and dropping them beside the bed.

"I think maybe I'll just look at you for a while," I countered, struggling to maintain my composure as she leaned against my pillows, stretching her arms out wide and bending her knees, crossing one thigh over the other.

No woman had ever lain in my bed, but if there was to be a first, I was grateful it was her, with every one of her piercings glimmering in the light and every one of her tattoos stark against the pallor of her porcelain skin. I had never felt luckier in my fucking life.

"Is this the something more you were looking for?" She cocked her head, addressing me with a cool, teasing smile.

I only sniffed a quiet laugh, hanging my head to conceal the warmth in my cheeks. Knowing that the something more wasn't in her nudity or the sacred place between her legs, but I couldn't say that. I couldn't tell her that I felt so certain that something was very likely concealed within her heart, and I suddenly found myself afraid that I'd be undone if I ever had to be without it.

So, I said nothing as I pulled my T-shirt off, refreshing her memory of what she'd already seen when she caught me chopping wood. Then, I stood at the side of the bed, keeping my eyes locked on hers as I undid my jeans and let them hang around my waist.

Her eyes took the opportunity to roam then, frisking over my arms and chest before dropping to my softly defined abs and waist.

"How did you get that?" she asked in a hush, and I dropped my eyes to follow her gaze to the neat scar along my lower belly, just above my groin.

It was five years old now, whitened with the passing of time, but any attention brought to that puckered line of skin always brought with it the memory of feeling cold metal slice through my skin in the upstairs hallway, just outside my bedroom.

"I, um …" I dared my fingertips to touch the two-inch line of silvery white. "I was … I-I was stabbed."

"Shit, seriously?" Her eyes widened with horror and concern. "How bad was it?"

"Not as bad as it could've been," I admitted, my voice suddenly gravelly.

"What about the person who stabbed you?"

I pressed my lips into a tight line and raised my eyes to the ceiling. I swallowed at the pain and guilt and every other vile, disgusting feeling I didn't want to feel right now and cleared my throat before replying, "Not as good."

She closed her mouth and nodded once, as if the questions hanging in the air weren't worth asking right now, and I was grateful for that. She outstretched her arms, welcoming me into the bed, and I joined her. Half covering her body with mine, pressing my face to her neck, and finding my calm once again in her garden of lavender and spice.

Then, she took my hand and placed it between her legs. Evidence of her desire had pooled there, her paper-like skin wet and slippery against my fingertips as I groaned into her shoulder.

"You've done that to me since the first time I saw you," she admitted, her tone husky and wanton.

I choked out a laugh, lifting my head to smile into her eyes. "Why do I feel like I should apologize for that?"

"God, don't," she replied before releasing a gasp as two fingers slid inside easily. "You have no idea how hot you are, and for some fucking reason, that only makes you hotter …"

Her words faded, and her teeth clamped down on her bottom lip as she closed her eyes. But I continued to watch, gliding my fingers in, gliding them out, my timing slow and lazy and deliberate. Keeping her wanting, but never pushing her over the edge. Rolling my thumb over the barbell through her hood and wondering if she had any more piercings I didn't know about.

Her hand reached out for the elastic waistband of my briefs and tugged downward, failing to pull them off, and she whined out a desperate, "Fucking hell, Charlie."

"You could just ask," I teased.

"But that would mean making you stop, and I dunno if anyone has ever told you this before, but you're pretty good with your hands. A very pleasant surprise, I might add."

She opened her eyes then to waggle her brows at me, and I laughed while thinking, *This is nice.*

It was nice to joke and laugh while simultaneously maintaining the rhythm of my fingers and thumb, keeping her on the edge of desire. It was nice to *talk*, to build on a sexual connection with both bodies and voices and communication.

It was all so fucking *nice*, and I knew without a doubt that this was what I had always been missing before, without ever knowing I was missing anything at all. It was this that I had needed all along, and was it too soon to be thinking that? Yeah, maybe, but I *knew*. I knew everything I needed to know.

I knew, when I did reluctantly stop, pulling my hand from between her legs to tug my briefs and jeans off and onto the floor. I knew, when she pushed me onto my back, straddled my hips, and wasted no time in replacing my fingers with my desperate, throbbing erection. I knew, when she gasped on a sob and laughed away her embarrassment, commenting on how I'd put a curse on her ... and I knew she knew it too.

Is this what Luke knew about Melanie?

Did he know right away like this, or was he too young?

Is this why it took so long for her to leave?

I shuddered when Stormy's lips clashed with mine, her hair coming undone and spilling around us in a waterfall of shimmering black. She held my wrists in her grasp, pinning them down to either side of my head. Taking back her power, regaining her control. Reminding me that she still held the reins, even after she melted like softened clay in my hands, and I didn't mind, not for a second. Not when she commanded the speed of our movements, not when her hands left my wrists to pierce my shoulders with her fingernails, and not when she moved one hand between our bodies to drive her own orgasm while the other palm held to my throat.

I had become hers the moment I'd stopped that asshole from taking her against her will. It had taken me this long to accept it, but now, I was a willing participant in any way she wanted me, for as long as she wanted me, and I didn't mind. Not one fucking bit.

"I'm close," she announced, panting and breathless. "I want you to come with me."

My nod was erratic, even as I asked, "A-are you sure about that?"

"I wouldn't have said it if I wasn't," she replied before adding, "I'm on the pill. It's fine."

I nodded again. "Okay."

Then, as if on command, we came undone, spilling over together in coordinated chaos. Our moans and screams rang through the walls and the cemetery beyond, unheard by anyone but us and the dead. And when she collapsed against my contracting chest, her nails scraping lazily against my ink-webbed skin and leaving their mark, the sky opened to baptize what I knew was something different, something special, something *more*.

Rain pelted the roof, lightning stretched the sky, and thunder joined the sound of our booming hearts.

And I didn't mind.

Because, maybe for the first time in my life, I was safe.

CHAPTER TWENTY-FOUR

MASSACHUSETTS, PRESENT DAY

An infuriating stream of sunlight had broken through the blinds to lay across my partially downturned face, ensuring that, if my alarm had somehow failed to wake me up, the blinding light wouldn't have given me a choice.

I grumbled an incoherent curse, my voice thick with sleep and aggravation, as I reached out and smacked my hand against the nightstand until I found my vibrating, shrieking phone. That one eye, assaulted by sunlight, cracked open as I turned off the alarm, catching the date.

It was November. Winter would make its approach quickly. The new year would arrive before I was ready. It always happened that way, and this time last year, I'd been grateful, as I had been the year before that and the year before. One year closer to being free of this world, one year closer to ending my sentence of living alone with my sadness and guilt.

But it was a new November, a different one from before, and I was reminded of that by the shift of weight on the mattress and the arm lying across my back and the lips brushing against my shoulder.

"What time is it?" Stormy mumbled, groggy and barely awake.

I glanced at the time once again on my phone screen before dropping it back on the nightstand. "Few minutes after seven."

"Fucking Christ," she groaned and rolled over. "Wake me up when the hour is in the double digits, 'kay? Thanks."

My lungs emptied with a sigh as my lips spread in a smile. I said nothing as I remembered how much Luke hated mornings. How reluctant he always was to wake up for work, how he'd spend the entire day in his underwear on the days he didn't have to work at all.

"Why does she remind me so much of you?" I sent off to a prison in Connecticut, wondering what he'd say if he got the message.

"Charlie, man, I love you, but, like, I don't wanna fuck you. I mean, no offense, but ... yeah, no. You're too hairy and weird for my tastes, thanks."

I chuckled to myself before I pulled myself up to sit naked at the edge of the bed, brushing the hair off my forehead and scrubbing that same hand over my face. With a peek over my shoulder, I saw Stormy, her hair as wild and chaotic in the morning as mine. The blanket was pulled up tight over her shoulders, concealing everything but that big poof of black, and I couldn't help but laugh again.

"What the hell is so funny?" she grumbled from beneath the covers, clearly agitated.

"Your hair looks like a ... a ..." Another chuckle rumbled up from my chest uncontrollably. "An electrocuted cat."

She rolled over quickly, flipping the blanket back to stare me down with a murderous glare as she fired back, "Oh, yeah? Well, you look like a fucking bridge troll."

I snorted and grabbed my briefs from off the floor before standing up and turning to face her, her eyes still shooting daggers in my direction.

"I mean," I said, bending over to tug the underwear on, "that's not an entirely inaccurate assessment. But I don't have a bridge."

"No. But you do have a whole freakin' *graveyard*, which probably makes you worse than a bridge troll." She was speaking more clearly now, even though the circles under her eyes were deepened by smeared makeup and exhaustion.

"That's fair."

I snatched my jeans next, pulled them on, and then went in search of my T-shirt while Stormy watched, narrow-eyed and disbelieving.

"How the hell are you so awake? We only got, like, four hours of sleep."

I found the T-shirt at the foot of the bed and shrugged before slipping it over my head. "I don't usually sleep much. I'm used to it."

"You're used to having sex all night and waking up a few hours later to go to work?"

"No." I shot a smirk in her direction. "I don't sleep well on a normal night. I'm in bed at a certain time, for routine's sake, but I'm not usually sleeping."

Her smile was touched by too much sympathy for my tastes. "Why doesn't that surprise me?"

"Because I'm a bridge troll. No time to sleep when I'm always on guard."

I stuffed my feet into my boots on my way to the side of the bed, bending over to grip the headboard and press a quick kiss to her lips, immediately startled by how normal it felt.

"I'm making coffee," I announced quietly, staring into her eyes.

She didn't reply right away. She tightened her hands around the blanket at her shoulders, looking back with dancing eyes and breathing deeply for a few beats of my heart. Her lips parted gently, as if she'd seen something within my gaze she hadn't expected to find, and then she nodded.

"Okay," she whispered.

I kissed her again, then left the room to begin my day as I normally would. But …

It wasn't a normal day, was it?

Because today, I hadn't started the morning beneath a rain cloud of despair and loneliness. I had been pulled in from the storm, within the shelter of an impenetrable cloud, and for the first time in I didn't even know how long, I was happy. Truly and honestly happy.

And there really wasn't anything normal about that.

***

Stormy had dragged herself from my bed fifteen minutes later with her wild hair tied into an even messier knot and one of my T-shirts hanging over her frame. She sat at my little kitchen table with a cup of hot black coffee held within her hands, sipping periodically and closing her eyes, as if to will the caffeine to hasten its journey through her veins.

"So, when do you have to open the gate?" she asked, clearing her throat and taking another sip.

"Eight thirty," I said, flipping the first omelet onto a plate and placing it in front of her.

"God, you cook too." She shook her head as she poked at it with the provided fork before taking a bite. "*And* it's edible. What the hell kinda bridge troll are you?"

"A domesticated one," I muttered, followed by a laugh, as I set to preparing my own breakfast.

"Were you married?" She narrowed her eyes suspiciously. "Are there any psycho ex-wives I need to worry about?"

"Nope." I shook my head. "Never been married."

"I mean, you had to have lived with a woman before at least," she accurately guessed, her mouth full as she pointed the tines of the fork in my direction. "And your mom doesn't count."

I added diced peppers to the egg mixture in the frying pan and slowly nodded. "My brother's fiancée. She lived with us for a while."

"God, I'm good," she said triumphantly, pumping her fork-holding fist into the air before taking another bite. "They never got married?"

"Nope." I took a deep breath and pressed my lips together, swallowing against a disappointment I had never been able to do anything about. "He had his issues, and after a while, she just ... couldn't deal with them anymore. Not without losing herself."

Stormy slowed her chewing as she stared at me, her green gaze heating with every passing second. "So, she what? Left you to clean up after him?"

It was a bold accusation for someone to make, and I began to shake my head, to defend the people of my past. But then I stopped myself and said, "I don't know that I'd put it that way. Luke and I ... we kinda looked out for each other. He always looked out for me, and then when we were older, I looked out for him too. It was fine. It's ... you know, we did what we had to do. It's just how it was."

"And what about her?"

I thought about Melanie and where she might've gone after she left Luke. "I don't know," I replied quietly while hoping she had wound up in a place where she always had time for herself, to do the things that made her happy.

I hoped she was *always* happy.

"You had feelings for her?" Stormy guessed, and I glanced at her, startled, before lifting one side of my mouth in something I hoped looked like a smile.

"For, like, two days a long, long time ago," I admitted aloud for the first time. "Back when I had first met her and we were still kids. I thought she was pretty, and she was always nice to me, which definitely wasn't the norm. But that was very fleeting. She was never for me, and honestly, she became more like a mother figure to me once my mom wasn't around anymore."

I turned off the stove and plated the omelet before taking it to the table. I sat across from Stormy, who had slowed her eating to watch me with intrigue. I pretended not to notice at first as I sprinkled my eggs with pepper and a dash of hot sauce. I sipped my coffee and set to eating, keeping my eyes from meeting hers. Had I said too much? Had I revealed more than I should've? Was it too soon to delve so deep into my past, and what the hell would her reaction be if I ever delved deeper?

Just stop thinking.

Stop talking.

Pretend it's a normal day.

I dived into my breakfast, cut a piece of omelet with the side of my fork, and began to shovel it into my mouth, when Stormy started to speak again.

"You asked me last night what had happened to me."

My gaze lifted back to hers then as the fork hovered somewhere above the plate on its way to its destination. "I did."

Her demeanor had changed. That comfortable, confident woman was gone, and, in her place, there was this small, timid creature, hunched over and unable to look me in the eye. This was the version I'd met at Blake's party, the one whose legs jittered and hands shook.

I saw myself in this side of her. The parts of me I tried to keep contained, the parts time had helped to stifle. But not everything died that easily, and I suspected that to be the same for her.

"I wasn't sure I wanted to tell you."

"You don't have to," I assured her, lowering my fork back to the plate, untouched.

She clenched her hand around her fork several times and pushed a chunk of red pepper around the plate. Her eyes never stopped watching it skate around between bits of egg.

"I've never told anyone other than Blake and Cee."

"You don't have to tell me anything you don't want to," I pressed further despite the flaming hot rage building beneath the surface of my skin and the urge to destroy whatever the hell could render her this terrified in a matter of minutes.

"But I *want* to tell you," she said, her voice firm. "Because I see how hard it is for you to talk about yourself and your life. And I'm with you, Charlie—you don't have to tell me anything you don't want to. But the thing is, I trust you. I don't even know why when I barely know you, but I do. Like …" She lifted her green eyes back to mine. "You ever just get a feeling about things? Like your intuition is doing the talking?"

I couldn't help but huff a sardonic laugh. "Oh, you have no idea."

She barely bobbed her head. "Well, that's how I feel about you. Like something *bigger* is pushing me toward you, and I'm not fighting it. So, I want you to know what happened to me, okay? And I'm not going to tell you because I want you to then spill your guts to me. I'm not, like, bargaining trauma for trauma … nothing like that. But if I tell you my story and you then wanna tell me yours, I'm here to listen."

When she finished talking, the room fell silent, save for the ticking of my mom's wall clock. Stormy was offering a gift; it didn't take a genius to understand that. She was declaring her commitment to whatever thing we had going on. She was inviting me into her world, and logic told me that the least I could do was return the favor.

And truthfully, I *wanted* to tell her. The weight I carried on my back was a heavy one, the type of load that hunched my shoulders and ached more with every passing year. But the thing that stopped me from baring my soul to her entirely right then and there at my kitchen table was this: not all nightmares were created equally. And while I knew with certainty—call it confidence, arrogance, whatever—that I could bear the weight of hers, I was too afraid that mine would keep her up at night.

So, I just nodded, unsure of what else to do or say that wouldn't chase her away or at the very least insult her.

"Um, so …" She diverted her gaze and glanced at the clock. "Oh, it's almost time for you to go."

Her shoulders sagged with disappointment, like she wasn't ready for this morning to end so soon. And even though I might not have been ready to unveil the monsters hiding in the shadows, I wasn't sure I wanted to be without her just yet either.

So, as I once again lifted the fork to my mouth, I asked, "You wanna come to work with me?"

***

The sun was shining as the wind blew cold, and I gritted my teeth to the chill coursing through my bones as I held on to one side of the iron gate. But Stormy didn't seem to be bothered at all with her hands wrapped in the long sleeves of her brother-in-law's sweatshirt. She pushed the other side of the gate open and wasn't at all fazed as another gust of wind bit at our cheeks.

In the truck, I had instructed her on how to open and secure the gate, and now, I watched from the other side of the wide-mouthed driveway, making sure she followed my directions.

With the hood over her head, she crouched and flipped the drop rod into the ground just outside the tall stone wall surrounding the perimeter of the cemetery. I knew it wasn't a difficult task, and honestly, an untrained monkey could probably figure it out. Yet I couldn't stop one side of my mouth from lifting, feeling an odd sense of contentedness and pride at the sight of her.

She looked up, peering at me from beneath the shade of her hood. "Making sure I'm not fucking up?"

My lips spread in a grin as I dropped my chin and shook my head, both at her and myself. Then, I stuffed my wind-bitten hands into the pockets of my leather jacket and walked slowly across the driveway.

"What do you think?" she asked as I pretended to assess her handiwork. "Am I bridge-troll material?"

"Well ..." I cocked my head, pursing my lips and making a show of this pretend critique. "You could use some practice, but ..."

"Oh, shut up!" She laughed, rolling her eyes as she turned to walk back to the truck, her sneakers plodding against the asphalt. "You're just jealous because it's taken you years to perfect the art of gate opening. Me? One and done. I'm just that—"

"Top o' the mornin' to ya, Chuck!"

I was mid-laugh when I heard Ivan's enthusiastic greeting bellow over Stormy's teasing. Surprised, I turned to watch him climb out of his sedan, parallel parked on the side of the road. How I hadn't noticed him pull up, I didn't know, but then again, I'd always been known to become distracted by a woman I was seeing.

"Shit," I grumbled as Ivan limped his way toward me.

I hadn't anticipated introducing Stormy to him or anyone … well, ever, let alone the morning after we'd slept together for the first time.

She glanced over her shoulder at me, her eyes flaring with instant panic.

She doesn't like strangers, I noted and walked coolly toward her to wrap my arm around her shoulders, caring more about her comfort than the transformation in Ivan's observant gaze.

"I told you I had a friend," I said, inclining my head toward hers.

"Oh, right. Your one friend." She nodded, her nerves unwinding just a little against my touch.

She took a step closer to my side when Ivan came to stand before us, his eyes alight with an excitement I both loved and wished I could extinguish.

"Well, well, well," Ivan exclaimed, clasping his hands over his rounded belly as he looked between Stormy and me from behind his black-framed glasses. "I guess I'm not the only one with happy news this morning!"

My sigh was accompanied by the closing of my eyes as I scratched an invisible itch on my eyebrow. "Uh, Ivan ... this is Stormy. Stormy, Ivan."

"It's a pleasure to make your acquaintance, m'lady."

Ivan scooped Stormy's hand in his, bringing her knuckles to his lips. She tensed against my side and made an attempt to inch backward, and I cleared my throat loudly with a warning. He looked into my eyes before his lips could touch her hand, and I shook my head. Like a pro, he straightened his back and laid his other hand over hers, giving her knuckles a warm, friendly pat.

She relaxed with instant relief.

"It's nice to meet you too, Ivan," she finally said after an uncomfortable few seconds.

He released his hold on her hand, lacing his fingers together once more over his middle, and looked up to meet my eye. "I have to say, Chuck, this is unexpected. You've been busy!"

"And you weren't supposed to be here until next week," I reminded him, glowering into his beady, taunting gaze.

"Well, I was in the area—"

"You're *always* in the area."

"Well"—he lifted his hands in a helpless shrug—"I just happened to be driving by—"

"You pass by here every single day. You literally work down the street." I gestured in the direction of the real estate office Ivan had gotten a job at once he could no longer handle the physical labor at the cemetery.

"Okay, fine," he finally relented, rolling his eyes at his own expense. "I saw you out here with this very lovely, very *you* specimen and thought I'd stop and say hi. But!" He held up one finger and waited approximately two seconds to continue, dramatically building anticipation. "That's not the *only* reason for this little impromptu visit."

He reached into the pocket of his long, oversize tan coat and handed me an envelope adorned in silver ink and a matching wax seal.

Without giving it a further look, I raised a brow at him and asked, "What is this?"

"An invitation to my wedding, of course." He grinned up at me with the expression of a man who'd found permanent residence on cloud nine.

Stormy peered over my arm as I ripped the envelope open.

I scanned the details quickly, then stated, "It's the day after Thanksgiving."

"Yes, well, we wanted to hurry things along a bit, and we got a good deal on the venue," he explained a little defensively.

I grunted a reply as I read further, my nerves kicking into high gear. "And it's in Connecticut."

"That's where Lyla's family lives," Ivan replied. "Her parents are too old to travel far from home, so we thought, why not bring the festivities to them? Plus, we'll already be in the area for the holiday, so"—he presented his hands in a gesture of grandeur—"why not make a weekend of it?"

Without saying a word, Stormy took the invitation from me and read over it as I struggled to work the boulder from my throat. I didn't want to raise suspicion, didn't want to express my current anxieties, but ... *Connecticut*?!

"You're from around those parts, aren't you?" Ivan asked, revealing a fact that Stormy didn't yet know about me. "Maybe you could stay with a family member, if you didn't want to—"

"There is no family," I quickly interjected, brash and on the defense.

Stormy looked up at me, surprise and shock widening her eyes. "You're from Connecticut?"

"Lots of people are from Connecticut," I grumbled.

"*I'm* from Connecticut," she said, as if this common ground somehow meant something, and she said it as though she couldn't believe I'd kept it from her after she told me at Blake's party.

But things had been different then. I hadn't wanted her to know anything about me in those moments in his backyard. Hell, I wasn't sure I wanted her to know now, but this time, it had nothing to do with her and keeping my distance.

Now, all I wanted was to not scare her away.

"I do hope you'll come," Ivan said, his eyes on the card in Stormy's hands. "I understand if you can't, but if you do decide to, I'd be honored if you'd also be my best man."

My heart leaped into my throat as my gut plummeted straight to my feet. "Best man? You don't want to ask someone—"

"There is no one else, Chuck," he gently interrupted, offering an embarrassed smile, his dark eyes jumping toward Stormy.

She took the hint that maybe this was a private moment between us, and she asked for the keys to the truck. I only turned my attention from Ivan to watch her walk away, that enormous sweatshirt hanging from her frame in a way that would've made anyone else look ridiculous, but she managed to pull it off effortlessly. When she got in and closed the door behind her, I looked back at my friend, not at all surprised to find a wistful little smile on his face.

"Don't say anything," I warned, but I had never known Ivan to heed my warnings.

"She's good for you, Chuck."

"You have no idea what you're talking about."

He tapped one finger against his temple and nodded. "Oh, but I do, my friend. My devotion to my Lyla might be new, but the roots of my love for her feel like they've been growing since the beginning of time."

I narrowed my eyes and crossed my arms over my chest, guarding my most battered organ from whatever he was going to say. "You talk like a crazy person sometimes—you know that?"

"And you're not as cold-blooded as you pretend to be. I see the way you look at her. She puts a light in your eyes I haven't seen in all the years I've known you, and I gotta say, Chuck, it looks good on you."

I glanced toward the truck to catch her swaying along to something on the radio, her lips moving to the song's lyrics, and one corner of my mouth twitched into an involuntary smile. Ivan caught this, of course, and wagged his finger at me.

"Like I said," he said as I shot him a sidelong glare, "she's good for you."

He was right, of course. I knew it more than he ever could, but I was too stubborn to satisfy him with my agreement.

So, as per usual, I said nothing.

He nodded anyway, as if he could read my mind and hear the truth in every beat of my heart, and he turned to head back to his car.

"Come to the wedding, Chuck," he said over his shoulder. "Bring your Stormy. Be my best man because you're my best friend."

Best friend. I had never had a best friend before, nobody outside of my family, and the declaration brought an ache to my chest I hadn't expected. Suddenly, I found it hard to breathe, and the backs of my eyes pricked with a humiliating rush of emotion.

"Yeah," I replied, clearing my throat. "I'll, um ... I'll think about it."

"Well, don't think too long," Ivan called over the engine of a passing car as he walked away. "I'm getting married in three and a half weeks, you know!"

I kept a watchful eye over him, making sure he got into his car safely before I headed back to the truck. Stormy's eyes grabbed mine as I rounded the hood, and her face lit up brighter than a thousand flames, like she hadn't expected I'd come back.

Is that what I look like when I look at her? I thought, hardly able to believe someone could be that happy to see me.

I opened the door, and Nirvana's "Heart-Shaped Box" poured out as I climbed into the cab to find Ivan's invitation on her lap.

"Are you gonna go?" she asked point-blank.

"I don't know," I replied honestly, starting the engine.

"You should."

I scrubbed a hand over my chin as I drove toward the maintenance shed. "I'll think about it."

"I'd go with you."

An exhale escaped my nose, and I tightened the line of my mouth. I didn't want to feel so aggravated by her well-intentioned insistence, but she had no idea what those state lines held for me. Was that her fault? No. But did it make it any less difficult for me to pretend there was nothing wrong? Also no.

"Why didn't you tell me you were from Connecticut?" she asked as if she could read my mind.

I had decided I wouldn't lie to her, so I sighed and said, "Because I was afraid."

"Afraid of what?" she pressed.

"Stormy …" I propped my elbow onto the window ledge and pressed my palm to my forehead.

She stared at the side of my face, eyes narrowed like she was trying to fit the puzzle pieces together herself.

Then, she cocked her head, her brows rising with realization, and I braced myself.

"Is this about your brother?"

That palm slid down the length of my face. "It's part of it," I replied. Not a lie.

"I don't care about your brother."

I shot a glare at her. "Don't say that. You have no idea what he did, or—"

"I don't care," she repeated, enunciating every syllable. "And if you think that me knowing where you're from is going to make me suddenly want to run a Google search on you, think again. I mean, for fuck's sake, I don't even know your last name—"

"Corbin," I offered, and it didn't rattle me nearly as much as I'd thought it would to say it aloud.

"Corbin," she repeated on a soft exhale, bobbing her head gently. "Well, Charlie Corbin, I won't be running a background check. But I do hope you'll go to your friend's wedding, and if you need a plus-one—"

"Why are you staying at the hotel?" I asked, parking the truck outside the shed that housed the ride-on mower.

She was taken aback by the abrupt change of subject, and honestly, so was I. I guessed the question had been nagging at me for too long, and I finally couldn't take it anymore.

"The house my apartment is in is under construction," she explained with an exasperated sigh.

I nodded, looking out the truck window in the direction of my cottage. I thought about what Ivan had said, about how she was good for me, and, God, I knew how right he was. Waking up, going through my usual routine, and beginning the day with her at my side had been easy and comfortable, like I'd been doing it every day for the past thirty-something years of my life.

Ivan had mentioned that, while his relationship might've been new, the roots of his feelings for her felt like they'd been growing for a long time. It had sounded crazy to me at the time, and, fuck, I still thought it was crazy ... but then why was I also starting to think it made at least a little sense?

If soulmates existed—and I believed they did—wasn't it possible for that affection to have been there, manifesting and building, over the course of ... well ... forever?

Now, I'm starting to sound crazy too.

"Hey, you okay over there?"

I blinked and turned to Stormy, realizing I must've gotten too wrapped up in my brain, probably staring into space.

"Yeah, sorry."

She smiled, tipping her head and sweeping her gaze over my face. "What're you thinking about?"

"Check out of your hotel," I blurted out before the thought had a chance to circulate my brain, before I had the time to reconsider. "Stay with me until your apartment is ready."

The smile fell from her face as shock took over, her brows lifting and her eyes widening. "You're serious?"

I nodded, now certain this was an excellent idea. "It just seems silly to pay for a hotel room when I'm right here."

"But ... where would I leave my car?" she asked quietly, as if she was trying to find a reason this wouldn't work out while a spark of hope ignited in her eyes. "I do have a job I have to get to, and you lock the gate for the night before I'm—"

"I'll let you back in," I quickly replied.

"And my stuff—"

"We'll make it fit. And remember, it's not forever."

She inhaled deeply, staring into my eyes with her lips locked tight, then sighed. "Right. It's not forever."

One corner of my mouth quirked into a forced smirk before I abruptly got out of the cab, not giving her the chance to change either of our minds. I flipped through the ring of keys, looking for the one to unlock the shed, when Stormy exited the cab to come stand by my side.

"So," she said as I crouched to fit the right key into the lock.

"So."

"I guess I'll check out of the hotel and grab my stuff."

I glanced up at her as I turned the key and unlocked the shed.

"I have to go to work today, but when my shift is over, I'll come here and call you at the gate. And then, tonight, I'll tell you a story."

As I stood, rolling the garage-style door open, the scent of grass clippings and earth pummeled my senses. I stepped onto the concrete floor and grabbed the work gloves from off the seat of the mower, then turned to Stormy as I put them on.

"Text me your schedule, and I'll make sure it's open by the time you get back."

CHAPTER TWENTY-FIVE

CONNECTICUT, AGE TWENTY-FIVE

There was a car in the driveway, parked behind Luke's motorcycle. I leaned my head back against the car seat, squeezing my eyes shut and sighing, already dreading whatever sights and sounds of transient passion might be awaiting me on the other side of the door.

I could just wait here until she's gone.

Yeah, I could, but God only knows how long that's gonna take, and I need to throw a load of laundry in before I go to sleep.

Begrudgingly, I released another sigh and climbed out of the car. If I'd known Luke had company, I would've asked Marie—the woman who I'd just slept with—if I could hang out for a while. Maybe used her shower or watched TV for a few hours until I could be certain Luke had passed out. But that also would've been ridiculous, and I knew it, yet it still felt preferred over hearing my older brother yelling for his bedmate to "take it all."

"Great," I grumbled, closing the door behind me.

"Oh my God, oh my God, oh my God!" a woman chanted loudly from upstairs, and I rolled my eyes as I slowly began to ascend. "You're so good. Oh God, you're gonna ... oh God ... you ... GOD!"

I rolled my eyes to the paint chipping off the ceiling. "Oh, that's exactly what he needs. To think he's *God*."

I moved my feet quickly up the stairs, knowing there was no reason to be quiet. Neither of them would hear me over the noise they were making, and, yeah, maybe I was a little jealous of that when the woman I'd just left couldn't reach her orgasm and simply told me "not to worry about it."

"Shit, baby," my brother groaned as I reached the landing. "You take that dick so fucking good."

She actually screamed in response, and ... Jesus, was she *crying*? "God, o-oh God, oh God ..."

At the end of the hallway, the light shone from beneath my brother's door. I was at least grateful he'd had the foresight to close it this time as I headed in that direction, walking past my room and hanging a right into the bathroom.

I shut the door as she let out another scream, accompanied by my brother's telltale primal shout, like he was heading out to hunt with his fellow tribesmen. I rolled my eyes and shook my head as I unzipped my jeans and used the bathroom. I never knew if Luke's ability to not give a shit was admirable or not. I'd been trying to decide for ten years now, and—

My lips parted with a surge of overpowering distress as the stream slowed.

Ten. *Years?*

It had been ten years since my parents had left the house and never returned. Ten years since I'd heard their voices, ten years since I'd listened to them perish in a fiery crash. God, how had I allowed this day to arrive without hardly thinking about what it was? How had I managed to have sex—to *come*—without once remembering that my parents hadn't been given the chance to watch me grow up?

I tucked myself back into my jeans and flushed the toilet, moving now in a dreamlike haze as the events of that night rolled in like they'd happened yesterday and not a decade ago. The sound of my mother's cries. The crunching, twisting metal. The nothingness that followed. The uncontrolled sobs that had racked my body as Luke pried the phone from my whitened knuckles.

Pain pricked the backs of my eyes as I stared ahead at my reflection in the broken mirror. My hair was longer now, brushing the tops of my shoulders. My beard had filled in. My dark eyes wore the circles of someone overtired and overworked. I'd reached adulthood somehow without the guidance of my father and the comfort of my mother, and still, in this moment, I felt so helpless and unsure of what the hell to do next.

How the hell was I supposed to get through the next ten years without them? How the hell was I supposed to get through the rest of my life?

I told myself that at least I had Luke. At least we had each other, for whatever it was worth, but I knew Mom and Dad wouldn't have approved of our fumble through the past ten years. Alcoholism. Sexual encounters with a myriad of random women. Motorcycles. Allowing the house to go straight to hell.

They hadn't taught us enough, I decided angrily, bitterly. They hadn't taught us how to survive like grown-ups in a world that expected too much from us. They hadn't taught us how to cope with the bullshit trauma life would inevitably throw at us.

It's not their fault.

I shook my head at my reflection and pulled back a loud sniffle. No, it wasn't their fault for dying. But it was their fault for coddling me too much, for not coddling Luke enough. For keeping me hidden beneath their shelter and not giving a shit about anything he did in his spare time.

Stop.

I blew out my breath and nodded. Anger never led to anywhere good, and everything Mom and Dad had done, they'd done out of love. They'd always done what they thought to be right, and wasn't that all any of us were doing?

After splashing some cool water on my face, I exhaled once more and turned to leave the bathroom when the door flew open to reveal my brother and a woman I didn't recognize.

Both of them grinning and laughing.

Both of them naked.

"Shit," I uttered as my hand quickly clapped over my eyes. I'd seen Luke in the nude plenty of times, but I didn't need to know the size and shape of this woman's boobs before knowing her name.

"Oh, hey, man," Luke said casually, neither of them bothering to move out of the way. "I didn't know you were home."

"Who's this?" the woman asked, her voice still breathless from the exertion. "You didn't tell me you had a roommate. He could've joined—"

I shook my head rapidly. "Nope. Not going there."

Luke laughed boisterously. "Charlie's my little brother."

"Well, he's cute. I like his hair—"

I retreated back into the bathroom as I felt her fingers touch the ends of my hair, still a mess from being in someone else's bed not even an hour ago.

"Look, I just wanna get back to my room, and then you guys can do whatever—"

"I thought you had a date," Luke said, his voice full of concern and question. "With, uh, Bethany? Right?"

"Marie."

"Right." His hand hit something—the wall maybe. "Marie. That's it. What happened? You good?"

That was just like Luke. He might've been a sex-crazed idiot who made shitty choices when it came to addictions and money and women, but he always cared about me. He always put me first. Even when he was standing naked in the hallway with a woman I didn't know, keeping me from fleeing to close myself behind my bedroom door.

I sighed. "We can talk la—"

"Nah, we're good. You can tell me now. What's up?"

Pressing my lips into a tight line, I blew out an exasperated breath through my nose, then relented and said, "She broke it off."

"*What?*" he asked, like he could hardly believe it. "The fuck, man! I swear to God, these freakin' women."

"Hey!" the nameless woman cried, and I heard a hand hit flesh. She must've slapped him.

"Sorry, babe. Not you."

I rolled my eyes behind my palm. I knew my brother, and I knew there was little chance of him ever seeing her again.

"Luke, I really just wanna get to my room, okay? So, if you could just move—"

"Oh, right. Yeah, sure. Okay. Well, listen, once Samantha—"

"Sarah," she corrected with a giggle.

"Right, sorry. Sarah." Luke cleared his throat, and I tried to bite back a smile. "Once Sarah here goes home, we can talk, all right? If you want, I mean."

"Sure," I said, nodding.

Then, there was the shuffling of feet against the hallway carpet, and I quickly made my escape. I hurried to my room, moving even faster past my parents' vaulted bedroom, and shut my door. Then, I grabbed my sketchbook and marker and turned on my music, just in time to block out the sound of Sarah screaming in the shower.

***

Luke let himself into my room a little over an hour later, and this time, thank God, he was dressed.

"Hey," he said, waltzing in like he owned the place.

I glanced up from the drawing I'd been working on to watch as he crossed his arms and flopped onto my bed, stomach down.

"Hey."

"Samantha left."

"Her name was Sarah," I corrected, looking back down to continue my scribbling.

"Shit, why can't I remember that?"

I knew why. The guy had been hooking up with a new girl every week for the past couple of years, or so it seemed. Sooner or later, naturally, they'd started to blur together. Names and the experiences tied to them had to eventually become meaningless.

It was sad, and no matter how much time had passed since Melanie had left, I couldn't help but think, *It wasn't supposed to be like this*.

For either of us.

"But anyway"—the back of his hand slapped my leg—"what happened with that chick you were seeing?"

"I told you," I replied, not bothering to look up now as my marker moved across the paper in fluid strokes. "She broke it off."

"Yeah, I got it, but why?"

I lifted one shoulder in a shrug. "She said I was a nice guy, but it wasn't working out."

Through the corner of my eye, I watched Luke's mouth press firmly into a terse line as his eyes dropped to the plaid blanket I'd been using for nearly a decade. I wondered if his thoughts mirrored mine—that it was never meant to be this way. That we weren't supposed to be perpetual bachelors in our mid-slash-late-twenties without any hope of that changing anytime soon.

"Her loss," he finally grumbled after a handful of seconds passed.

"I think ..." The felt tip stopped moving against the paper as I stared at the rainy scene I'd drawn. The car driving away on a wet street, the expanse of road ahead leading nowhere. "I think maybe I'm the problem."

Luke's gaze swung to mine. "What? Why the hell would you think that?"

"Come on, man. I know I come on strong, and I know I'm ... you know—"

"Weird as fuck?"

My eyes answered first with a slow blink. "Thank you for that. Yeah, I mean, maybe I'm just ... a lot to handle or something. I don't know. I'm not exactly normal. None of this shit is."

"None of what shit?"

I lifted my hand to gesture at the ceiling. At the house. At the life we kept locked inside. "This!" I exclaimed in a huff of exasperation, already on the edge of spiraling.

He lifted a brow. "You mean, the house?"

"I mean, everything!" That same hand swept over the entire room, making sure to pass over him in the process.

He reared his head back as his brow furrowed. "What's wrong with everything? Wait, are you talking about *me*?"

That hand now pressed to my forehead, my fingers rubbing against my brows. "No ... I ... I don't fucking know." I dropped my hand to the pad in my lap and dragged my eyes back to my brother's. "You're gonna tell me you're just fine with life? You're happy?"

Luke scoffed like it was the most asinine question I could've asked. "Of course I'm not happy, Charlie."

My mouth fell open to reply, only to close again. Had I really believed he was content to do what he'd been doing for the past couple of years?

"But here's the thing about me," he continued, leveling me with a stern glare. "I don't *need* to be happy. I just need to get from one day to the next, and that's exactly what I'm doing. I need to eat, I need to work, I need to sleep, and I need to fuck. That's what I *need* to get by."

"And you're good with that?" I asked as my eyes narrowed with skepticism.

His gaze shifted from mine to the comforter. "Never said I was *good* with it, but it's what I have. And anyway, this isn't about me right now. We're talking about you. If you need more than that, if you *want* more than that, then fucking get it, man. Don't sit there, getting all mopey, and act like this"—he lifted his hand toward the ceiling in a mock gesture—"is holding you back. If you want things to change, then fucking change it. And just because you struck out with this chick doesn't mean the right one won't come along eventually. Jesus fuck, Charlie. You're twenty-five, not ... fucking ... forty or some shit."

It had been my choice to hold myself back and only look out for my brother. To devote my nights to cooking dinner and my mornings to waking him up, out of fear that he wouldn't do either himself.

But he would've done the same for me, wouldn't he?

Hadn't he done it just by not ditching me with our grandmother when we were teenagers?

I pushed past my questioning brain to say, "You're assuming there is a right one."

He nodded encouragingly, glaring at me like I'd lost my mind. "Uh, yeah, idiot. There is. So, don't go thinking you need to change everything for these women, okay? Change if you want to, but not for them. 'Cause the right one's gonna come along one day and fuckin' love that you wanna get married after a couple of dates."

I couldn't help but chuckle at that. "I didn't ask Marie to marry me."

"Yeah, but with the right one, you fucking would, and you know it."

He was teasing, but somehow, somewhere deep in the pit of my rolling gut, I knew he was probably right.

"And she'll go running for the fucking hills."

"Man, are you kidding? The right chick's gonna be like, *Yes, Charlie, I will be your bride of Frankenstein. Let me just go sew myself a dress made from the skin of my victims, and I'll meet you down at the courthouse*," he said in a mocking, high-pitched tone.

"You're an asshole," I said, but I was laughing and feeling better somehow, lighter. Grateful that he had barged into my room and insisted on talking.

"Ah, there's that smile I love." He reached out to clip his knuckles against my cheek. "You're gonna be fine. I'm telling you. Like, ten, fifteen years from now, you're gonna look back on this little bitch moment. And then you're gonna look at your wife, Morticia, and your three freaky little kids and think, *Damn, Luke was right … again.*"

"Oh, yeah, you think so? And where the hell are you gonna be?" I looked at him with an incredulous, disbelieving cock of my brow while also hoping that he was right despite my devotion to him and keeping what was left of this family together.

Luke smirked with a faraway look glinting in his eye as he lifted one shoulder in a shrug before swinging his gaze back to mine with a laughing, forced smile. "I dunno, man. At this point, I'll just be lucky if I'm not dead or in prison."

CHAPTER TWENTY-SIX

MASSACHUSETTS, PRESENT DAY

"*I guess I wasn't so lucky, huh?*"

Luke's somber, melancholy voice woke me from an otherwise dreamless sleep that had been deeper than any I'd had in recent years. My eyes snapped open to stare at the wooden beams stretching the length of my living room, and I lifted my head to drop my bleary gaze to the sketch pad in my lap. Dingy bars of a blackened cell and an unintentional squiggled mark from my open pen looked back at me.

Disoriented, I tried to remember falling asleep, tried to remember when my lids had grown too heavy to keep open. But I shook my head, unable to piece together the last moments before my unintentional nap.

"Weird," I grumbled to nobody before grabbing my phone from the table between the two wingback chairs.

Darkness had blanketed the sun, and it was almost time to open the gate for Stormy.

Stormy.

Luke's sad chuckle disappeared with my easy smile as I thought about her and her promise to return. I couldn't wait to see her again. Couldn't wait to get my arms around her and press my lips to hers, to crack my chest open and beg her to defrost the barely beating organ hidden inside its frozen cage. She had the power to do it—I knew she did—and the desperation to let her buzzed wildly through my veins like a separate lifeforce from my own.

Careful. You know what happens when you lose control too fast.

"But the right woman won't run away."

My inner voice and Luke's warred for power, and I shook my head at them both. Neither was useful right now; neither mattered when I'd already made the decision to roll with whatever this was for now.

I capped my marker and laid it with the sketch pad on the table between my chairs. I left the house, locked the door behind me, and headed down to where I'd left the truck parked at the bottom of the hill. I dug the keys out of my pocket on the way, anticipation tingling in my fingertips as I imagined what it'd be like to have her things beside mine, even if temporary. Then, I turned out of the gate, keeping my eyes down as I shuffled through the key ring, only looking up when I approached the driver's door.

That was when I saw him.

The toe of my boot kicked my heel, and I stumbled forward, slamming hard against the side of the truck. But the pain in my knee was dulled by the sight of the man standing across the road, between a pair of headstones.

He was only illuminated by the lamppost in front of the house, his back to me as he blew spiraling tendrils of smoke into the chilled night air.

The cigarette.
The flower on the grave.
The empty pack.

A scrapbook of imagery flashed before my mind's eye as I watched him from over the roof of the truck, my jaw shaking and my hands trembling.

Go after him! What the hell are you doing?!

"Hey!" I shouted, my voice slicing through the silent night.

He barely shot a glance at me over his shoulder, too quick for me to get a good look at him.

And then he ran.

"Son of a bitch," I gritted through my teeth, taking off after him.

I pulled the box cutter from my jeans pocket, clenching the cool metal against my palm as I hurried over the asphalt road to race between the graves, following the sound of pounding footsteps against grassy hallowed ground. I didn't want to hurt someone, didn't want to do it again—but I would if I had to. I knew I had it in me for the right reasons, and the sporadic torment I'd been put under over these past several weeks was enough if he wouldn't talk to me.

The shadowed figures of bushes, monuments, trees, and headstones zipped by, blurring in my peripheral vision. I knew these grounds like the back of my hand, and he didn't, yet he hadn't slowed. He hadn't stopped, hadn't tripped or faltered once.

What the fuck?

I slowed my gait to a halt in front of a towering Celtic cross, my lungs burning a hole through my chest as I struggled to force the air in and out. I doubled over, pressing my hands to my thighs.

"Fuck, fuck …" I chanted with every huff of labored breath. "Goddammit … where the fuck did you go?!"

I forced my burning lungs to quiet and held my breath, listening to the night around me. Silence. No footsteps. My back straightened, and I turned to my left to face an angel with a wide wingspan, spun to my right to glare into the face of the Madonna holding her newborn child. Searching the surrounding area for any sign at all that the intruder had been there. He could've been hiding, could've ducked behind any one of these holy monuments that I now saw as demons, and with my weapon held tight in my fist, I peeked behind every one, only to come up empty every time.

With my teeth clenched and bared, I spun in a circle, then shouted, *"Where the fuck did you go, asshole?!"*

Of course, I didn't receive a reply. He was hidden too well, maybe even gone, and I was alone.

But now, I knew for certain that he existed, and that put me one step closer to catching him and finding out what he wanted from me.

***

Stormy drove her black sedan through the open gate, and as soon as she cleared the driveway, I swung the gate shut once again, making sure to take a few quick glances over my shoulder while doing so.

The adrenaline from the chase had dissipated quickly once I got back to the truck, and I spent the drive to the gate anxious and wide-eyed. Just waiting for him to jump out from his hiding spot and show his face. But it never happened, and by the time I reached the gate, where I'd kept Stormy waiting for a few minutes longer than intended, I had finally drawn the conclusion that the guy had gotten back to the stone wall and made his way over. But that didn't make my spine any less rigid or my shoulders any less tense, and I hurried to Stormy's car with hastened purpose, eager to get to my next stop—the security guard's office.

"Hey," she greeted with a smile as she climbed out of her car, and for just a second, I forgot all about the intruder.

She approached and slipped her hand into mine, gripping softly as she stood on her toes and pressed a gentle kiss to my lips. I closed my eyes, aware of my nerves unraveling just a little, and my lungs released a sigh.

Stormy took a step back, her hand still in mine. I opened my eyes to see hers narrowed, studying my face with concern.

"You okay?"

A twig cracked somewhere to my left, and my heart leaped into my throat as my eyes darted in that direction, but still, I replied, "Yeah, I'm good."

"You sure? Because I'm not gonna lie—you don't seem good. Like, at all. What's wrong?"

My hand squeezed around hers in forced reassurance while I kept my stare on that spot for two beats of my heart until I realized it was likely nothing but an animal. My lungs deflated, the gust of air passing through my nose, and I looked to Stormy's backseat. There were several large bags stuffed in there and another couple in the front passenger seat.

"Is there anything in the trunk?" I asked, intentionally avoiding her question.

To acknowledge that I wasn't okay only made it that much more *not okay*.

Her dubious gaze remained on my face for a moment before she slowly turned away to acknowledge her things. "No, this is it."

"All right."

It took only a few minutes to get everything loaded into the bed of the truck, and I tried to not concern her with my paranoia. But it was difficult to not spin around at every abrupt noise, and after the third snap of my head in the direction of a hooting owl, Stormy had decided definitively that she was not convinced by my feeble attempt at a tough-guy act.

"Okay, listen." She held her hands up, palms out, after we put the last bag into the truck bed. "You are seriously not helping me to feel good about sleeping in a fucking graveyard, even if I do really like you and I've spent all day looking forward to playing house for a little while. So, can you please just tell me what the hell is going on before I throw all this shit back in my car and check back in to that hotel?"

For good measure, I glanced behind me once more before nudging my chin toward the cab.

"Get in, and I'll tell you."

So, I told her about the man across the path from my truck. About how he'd taken off the second I apprehended him and how I'd lost him in the darkness of the graveyard. I chose not to divulge the details that I believed he could've also been the one leaving me personal, sacred mementos scattered around the vicinity of my house, only to avoid rattling my bones even further when I'd been shaken enough.

When I was finished, I glanced sidelong at Stormy as we neared the security guard's office, expecting her to look as terrified as I felt. But instead, she only wore the look of understanding and sympathy.

"Do kids break in here often?" she asked quietly.

I furrowed my brow, eyeing the door to the structure no bigger than a large storage shed. "It happens sometimes, but this guy wasn't a *kid*." I shook my head, allowing his image to fill my mind. His leather jacket and hood. "This was a full-grown adult."

"Okay. But … is it at all possible that he could've been homeless?" she offered, her green eyes taking on the serenity of a spring breeze. "Or I don't know … a junkie maybe? I mean, I didn't see him, so I couldn't say for sure, and I'm not trying to defend him for breaking in. But … when I was younger, and I …" She rolled her lips between her teeth, hesitating with a deep, hard swallow. "We used to find secluded places to do shit, you know? So, what's more secluded than a cemetery after hours?"

There was a sympathetic glint in her eye that begged to reach out and touch my heart, and I almost allowed it. I almost brushed the incident off. But her experiences must've been a lot different than mine because what I knew of breaking and entering was pain, terror, and too much fucking blood. This place was meant to be sacred; it was meant to be safe. Was I really doing my job if I allowed anybody to jump the fence and take up residence? No. And nothing was going to change my mind about that ... not even the way her tongue poked out to touch the hoop hugging the center of her bottom lip.

"I hear what you're saying," I finally replied after a few seconds went by, my tone soft but firm. "But I'm paid to care for this place, not some random guy who's probably out there, leaving his cigarette butts all over the place."

Stormy sucked in a deep breath, her gaze holding mine. An unspoken argument heated her irises, and I thought she might fire back at me. I hated confrontation. I hated fighting. And what did it say about us and whatever future we might have if we were incapable of getting through a few days without throwing verbal bombs at each other?

But then she exhaled and nodded, her anger defusing. "No, you're right," she said, no amount of reluctance or resentment in her voice, and I nodded in reply.

We exited the truck to knock on the security guard's door. I had met Max a small handful of times during my years here, but for the most part, we were ships in the night. His shift began when I was typically winding down for the day, and he kept watch as I slept. Never had I been given a reason to come to him, nor had he had one to bother me. But now, here I was, knocking on his door and anxiously awaiting his answer.

It swung open, and there he stood, a man of about my age and height but with the build of a wrestler who'd started to let himself go and a crew cut that did a sufficient job of not drawing attention to his receding hairline.

"What can I do for you, Chuck?" he greeted, all business from the start. His gaze swung to Stormy, huddled at my side, and he nodded a silent hello.

I resisted the urge to despise Ivan for doing the introductions years ago.

"Hey, Max. I was just wondering if you took care of the guy who was in here after hours."

Max narrowed one eye at me and crossed his arms over a barreled chest. "What guy?"

"I came out of my house about an hour ago and saw a man across the road from my truck," I explained. "I tried to chase after him, but he got away. I assumed you had seen him on the surveillance footage."

Max rolled his lips beneath his teeth and took a moment to think. "No, man. I've been watching the cameras all night. I haven't seen anyone."

I held my head higher and straightened my spine with an urgent need to defend myself. I knew what I had seen. I'd seen him. I'd *heard* him.

"Are you sure? He was at my house at about eight forty-five."

His deep brown eyes dipped to stare into the cold, dark night behind me and shrugged as he shook his head. "I could look at the footage, but—"

"I'd appreciate it."

He nodded slowly and swept a beefy hand inside his office. "Then, make yourselves at home."

***

Stormy and I stood behind Max's high-backed office chair, arms crossed and eyes pinned to the computer screen. Max clicked his mouse repeatedly, flipping through the two dozen cameras set up over the grounds.

"Normally, if someone trespasses, I get an alert," he explained almost absentmindedly. "But every now and then, someone comes in before the gates are closed, and I don't catch on until—" He cut himself off as a dark, moonlit image of my cottage filled the screen. "All right. Here we are. What time did you say this was at?"

I frowned. "I don't know that he was actually *at* my house," I said while thinking about the paraphernalia left on my doormat and Luke's bike.

"Hmm." Max barely nodded.

"It was at about a quarter to nine," I answered still, and he gave another little nod as he clicked a few times and began to scroll through the footage.

Trees swayed. A spider skittered backward over the lens, and I noted the way Max flinched at the close-up underside of its abdomen. Moments passed before my truck drove backward and stalled beside my gate.

"Okay." I held a hand over his shoulder. "It was around here that I came back from chasing him."

Max nodded, continuing to the point where I had come out of the house. Then, he played the footage.

The three of us watched my preoccupied walk from the house to the truck. We watched as I flipped through the keys on the ring in my pocket. And we watched as I looked up, an expression of wide-eyed alarm blanketing my face.

"See, that's where I saw him," I said, pointing at the screen.

Max nodded slowly, still watching intently, his hands folded on the desk.

But then the image scrambled, and a cloud of static covered the footage for a second before it cut to me running back to the truck.

"What the fuck?" I muttered breathlessly, my hand dropping to the back of Max's chair.

"Shit," Max grumbled, leaning forward and clicking around. "Sometimes, it does this. Hold on."

But no amount of clicking could recover the missing segment of film. There was no fall against the truck. No shouting. No break into a run. It was as if it'd all never happened, apart from the sore spot on my knee from where it had made impact.

"There's no other camera?" I asked, my blood boiling to the temperature of lava.

Max's exhalation was long as he began clicking around the screen. "I could check a few others, but this is the only one pointed directly at the house."

"Maybe he ran past another one," Stormy offered, speaking for the first time since we'd gotten out of the truck.

"Honestly, I doubt it," Max admitted with a helpless shrug. "For a property this large, you'd expect more cameras around the place, but I guess they never saw a reason for—"

"What's that?" I pointed at a blur on one of the tiled screens laid out across his monitor.

Max scratched at the scruff on his chin as he clicked, enlarging the camera feed. He scrolled through as we watched a fuzzy figure of a person dash across the screen in backward slow motion.

"That must be him," I murmured, my voice low, my anger bubbling.

Max hummed a short sound of contemplation. "Could be. This camera is right by the southern corner of the fence too. He probably ran by and hopped over. It's pretty dark and secluded back there."

"So, he's gone?" Stormy chimed in, hope lilting her tone.

"I'd say most likely," Max replied with a nod, pausing the feed to the point where the blur was in the center of the screen.

He enlarged the image, trying to get a clearer shot of the intruder's head and face. But it was too washed out from a nearby lamppost, and all any of us could see was a general silhouette.

"I'm sorry I can't do better," Max muttered, disappointed and as aggravated as I felt.

"Not your fault," I replied, blowing my anger out through my nose in a feeble attempt to slow my heart rate.

"I can try and look through—"

"No, it's all right," I muttered, straightening my back and smoothing my hands over the crown of my head.

"I'll keep a better watch on the gates." He nodded to himself, rubbing a hand over his chin. "And maybe I'll talk to the powers that be about getting some better alarms. This"—he tapped the frozen image of our intruder—"should've been enough. They're supposed to go off if someone goes over the fence—"

"So, he could still be in here?" Stormy's voice rose with worry.

Max glanced over his shoulder to offer her the first smile I'd ever seen on his face. "I highly doubt it. He was spotted, so he'd be more paranoid about hanging around. But just to be on the safe side, I'll keep watch over the house. Keep the doors locked and the alarm on. Give me a call if anything else happens."

I nodded, keeping my eyes on the floor and crossing my arms tightly over my chest, as if that alone could seal me off from the outside world and bring that ignorant sense of security back to my life.

But that ignorance had been a blindness to the truth, one that I hadn't wanted to acknowledge. It was no different than my unrequited feelings for the women of my past, just a blanket to cover my eyes from what was right in front of me.

I had never been safe here. But I saw that now, and this time, I wasn't going to be driven from my home.

***

We managed to carry everything into the house in one trip, and after crossing the threshold, I made sure the lock and dead bolt were both secured. Then, I set the alarm, and even though I knew damn well that a villain with enough motive could get past any obstacle, I felt better with these things in place than I would without.

Behind me, Stormy was assessing the pile of her belongings, her hands on her hips and her teeth gnawing at her bottom lip. Overwhelmed, she blew out a deep breath and lifted her shoulders to her ears.

"I don't even know where to begin with all of this shit," she admitted.

I walked past her toward the kitchen, my mind elsewhere. "You don't have to worry about it now."

"I know, but I don't want to feel like I'm imposing. Or taking up too much of your space. This is a lot of stuff. I—"

I turned and walked backward, lifting the side of my mouth in a strained smile. "The least of my concerns right now is your stuff taking over, believe me."

Her lips pressed tight, and she offered a soft nod before saying, "If it makes you feel any better, you have no idea that this guy will even come back. Or that he even cares about you in the first place."

I had to admit, she was right. I could've mentioned the random findings around the house, but to assume it had been him to leave them was just that—an assumption. And a completely unfounded one at that, apart from the cigarette he'd held in his hand.

The cigarette ...

Lifting my hand and rubbing at my brow, I focused every last ounce of my attention on that tiny glimpse of memory.

The way he hung his hand limply at his side as he sent a stream of smoke into the air, illuminated only by the glow of the lamppost ...

It was a trigger, one that left my stomach feeling hollow and strange. But it was one that meant nothing—I was sure of it—and I had to let it go.

"So, um ..." I wiped the back of my hand beneath my nose as I remembered I'd been on my way to the kitchen for something. "Anyway, are you hungry? I haven't eaten dinner yet."

"I could eat," Stormy said, following me into the kitchen slowly, almost cautiously.

I opened a cabinet and pulled out a box of rice. "I'm about due to run to the grocery store, so the cupboards are a little bare," I explained apologetically. "But I think I still have a bag of vegetables in the freezer, if you're okay with some stir-fry."

"That's fine with me."

I dropped the box on the counter and headed for the freezer as Stormy came to stand at the island. Her stare heated my back as I pulled out the bag of mixed vegetables, and when I turned, I found the intensity in her eyes too much to look into directly. So, I diverted my gaze to grab my wok from the pot rack hanging above the countertop and headed for the stove.

"Is this weird?" she finally asked quietly when my back was once again to her.

I poured a bit of oil into the pan and replied, "You being here?"

"Yeah."

"I don't think so. Is it weird to you?"

Her nails tapped softly against the counter. "I didn't think so, but Blake thought it was, um ... sudden."

"It is," I agreed.

"That's what I said. But Blake worries about me, so he tried to talk me out of coming."

The oil sizzled and spat as one side of my mouth lifted in a reluctant smile. "But you came anyway."

"I told you I wanted to tell you a story," she said, as if that were the only reason for her return.

Tiny bubbles scattered along the bottom of the pan, bursting before they had the chance to grow, and I kept my focus on them as I said, "Well, I'm listening."

Something told me I'd be okay to listen to her forever, if forever could ever be in the cards for me. And as she began to talk, somehow, I also began to forget all about the man across the road.

CHAPTER TWENTY-SEVEN

STORMY
MASSACHUSETTS, PRESENT DAY

It blew my mind that it'd only been a month, give or take, since I had bumped into Spider outside of Village Tavern. Only a few weeks since he'd stopped that asshole from going further in doing whatever the fuck to my body and only two since he'd threatened my life in the hallway.

The passing of time felt warped, like we'd managed to cram six months into the span of a few weeks, and I wondered if it was always like that when you met the person who somehow made your entire world make sense after a lifetime of fuckups and just ... getting by.

Charlie had never mentioned anything about fear or anxiety, and why would he? He hardly knew me. But as open as he'd been in certain regards over the past few days, he'd never once opened up about what kind of turmoil went on in his head. Maybe he thought it was too personal, or maybe he thought it made him seem weak.

But I had told him I saw him, and I had meant that in a more multifaceted way than he even understood.

He was so clearly terrified of everything. The world and the people in it. The things he saw, the things he'd seen, and the things he didn't see at all.

Shit, I think there was a good chance he was even terrified of himself, although I couldn't understand why.

Yet, for some reason, he wasn't afraid of *me*, in the same way I wasn't afraid of him. And that freaked me the fuck out and comforted me at the same time, and I could only begin to imagine the criticism I'd get from my parents for that.

But I'd deal with that another day.

What mattered right now was the stiffness of Charlie's spine as he worked on cooking us some dinner, adding rice to the vegetables in the wok. How shaken up he'd been by this douchebag who'd thought it was a good idea to trespass on a property guarded by a creepy dude who was alarmingly strong and quick with a knife.

What mattered was that I'd promised to tell him a story, and right now seemed to be as good of a time as any.

But how was I supposed to begin telling it when I wasn't sure of where it had even started?

I laughed beside myself, brushing a few strands of flyaway hair from off my forehead. Charlie didn't seem to notice as the pan sizzled and snapped with a thousand tiny bubbles, too wrapped up in his own head.

Just speak. It doesn't matter as long as I'm speaking.

"So, I don't know what kind of kid you were," I said, the words feeling weird and too big on my tongue as I tapped the countertop.

"The kind nobody wanted around," he muttered quietly, as if he hadn't intended for me to hear.

Well, fuck. I hadn't been aware that a single person could mend my heart while simultaneously breaking it. But there he was, doing just that.

"Oh. Um ... well, I wasn't the greatest kid, I guess," I said, dragging my fingers along the counter as I began walking toward the round little kitchen table. "My parents aren't assholes. I think, deep down, they always did what they thought was best for my sister and me, you know? But sometimes, I'd overhear them say shit to their friends or whoever about how, like, they had to have a second kid just to prove they could make one who wasn't destined for juvie. And looking back, I'm sure they didn't mean anything serious by it, but I think ... I think that kinda fucked with my head."

Charlie didn't turn from the stovetop, nor did he reply, but as I sat in one of the two rickety wooden chairs at the table, I did catch the tension in his jaw and the heated sidelong glance in my direction.

I reached out for one of the simple wooden black shakers in the center of the table and spun it as I continued, "So, anyway, I spent a lot of time in detention. I was suspended from school a few times. Not for anything crazy, but, like, I pulled the fire alarm a couple of times, got into a few fights that I could've avoided ... that kind of thing. And, of course, the kids I was friends with weren't exactly the type to encourage me to do better. They were the ones daring me to do it in the first place, and I had a really hard time saying no, even if I knew it was wrong."

My fingers froze around the shaker as my heart rate sped to a dangerous, concerning level. I was nearing the part I never liked to talk about, the part only two other people in the world knew about, the part that had hammered that final nail into the coffin, and I readied myself to say it and say it fast.

"So, when I was sixteen, this one friend of mine—I can't even remember her name—she had talked me into sneaking out of the house one night, which wasn't out of the norm for me or anything. But usually, we went to this clearing in the middle of the woods by the high school—The Pit, they called it." My fingers began to tremble, and I clenched my hand tighter around the shaker. "This particular night though, this girl wanted to check out a club about an hour away. So, we drove down there—my parents had no fucking clue I was even gone—and as soon as we got there, my friend found some guy to talk to and ditched me."

Charlie's back was no longer ramrod straight, but his lips curled between his teeth, and his white-knuckled fist clenched around the spatula as he moved the rice and vegetables around in the spattering wok.

"Um, so ..." A quivering breath passed through my lips as I lifted my gaze to the lamp hanging above the table. "I got to talking to this dude at the bar. He bought me a few drinks, and I got a little tipsy. He seemed so freakin' nice, you know? And I was this stupid kid who felt special because this older guy was so interested in me—"

"Stop." Charlie muttered the word, hanging his head, already seeing where this was going.

But I wouldn't. Not when I'd already started.

"He raped me," I said quickly and quietly, and with those words hanging in the air, I was sent back there in an instant. To the backseat of his car, his enormous weight pinning me down, my words and screams of protest going unheard despite the eleven people I'd watched pass by the window.

I had counted each and every one.

"Goddammit," Charlie gritted out through a clenched jaw, pinching the bridge of his nose with tattooed fingers.

"He didn't hurt me or anything," I added, as if it made anything better. "He just … didn't *stop*."

Charlie turned off the burner with a little more force than was necessary. He reached for a cabinet door and opened it, grabbing two bowls, then slammed it shut, rattling the contents inside.

"*They* didn't stop," he replied angrily, using the spatula to split the stir-fried vegetables and rice evenly between the two bowls. "That piece of shit deserves to rot in hell, yes, and I'd fucking kill him myself if I could. But all those people who were around … you can't tell me nobody had any idea, and they didn't *stop*. They heard and ignored it. Who the fuck hears a *girl* being …" His mouth twisted, but he couldn't say the word. *Raped*. "And none of them tried to do something about it. How the fuck does anybody live with that? How the fuck could they not *stop*?"

I swallowed against the knot in my throat. "I told you not everybody would."

He shook his head. "Fucking assholes. Every single one of them."

The spatula was dropped into the pan, and he opened a drawer to retrieve two forks. Then, the bowls were carried to the table, where he handed me one before sitting in the chair across from mine.

Charlie's dark brown eyes met mine, the gold flecks I'd grown accustomed to now hidden beneath a veil of anger and hatred. It was similar to the look Blake had given me when I told him and Cee about what had happened in fewer details, but this wasn't the same. Charlie didn't hold an ounce of pity for me, only anger on my behalf and hatred toward the man who'd hurt me, and an unexpected lump of emotion built in my throat.

"You didn't tell anyone," he stated.

I shook my head. "No."

He nodded like he understood while Cee had unintentionally berated me for staying silent. "I never told my parents how many times my brother's best friend hurt me."

"Physically?"

He answered with a small nod, and my heart broke a little more.

I couldn't imagine this man hurting even the smallest of creatures intentionally, not without reason. And knowing that he'd been bullied and tormented as a boy made me feel as murderous as he looked.

"I think, at the time, I was more afraid they'd be mad at me for sneaking out and having sex with this college guy," I admitted, feeling stupid. "Hell, I hadn't even had sex at all before that night, and having to say it out loud and tell them I hadn't even *wanted it* ... I just ..." My words drifted off as I cringed inwardly and shook my head.

"So, I"—my breath left my lungs as I diverted my gaze from his—"started having all these nightmares, and this other friend ... this guy, Billy ... he gave me a pill one day at The Pit, and just like that"—I snapped my fingers for effect—"the nightmares went away."

Charlie hadn't touched his food yet, but to be fair, neither had I. He wouldn't look at me though and instead stared into his full bowl of fried rice and vegetables. He shoved his fingers into his long, thick hair, plonked his elbow onto the table, and held his head in his hand. Two lines formed between his brows as his other hand fingered the tines of his fork with no intention of picking it up. It clawed at my mind to ask what he was thinking about, but I didn't think it was my place to dig deeper beneath his skin when I'd already decided this was about me spilling my truth and not begging for his.

"And I guess that was really where I started fucking up," I went on, trying to push past his obvious internal retreat from me and the conversation. "Somehow, I managed to graduate from high school, but I'm not sure it really mattered when I was surviving on pot and pills and whatever booze I could get my hands on. This one time, my little sister even followed me to The Pit—"

Charlie lifted his head abruptly, dropping his hand to the table. "Something happened to her?"

Tears pricked the backs of my eyes as my head jittered with a nod. "She, um … she met Seth, this creep who hung out with the guy I'd buy my drugs from. She liked him for some fucking reason, and … well, long story short, he forced himself on her, and she had his kid."

The words soured against my tongue, sizzling and burning like acid, as I thought about Seth and the secrets my sister, Ray—Rain—had only told me and her husband. She had sworn me to secrecy, afraid our parents would demand she get rid of the baby growing in her belly. And I had kept those secrets, never speaking of them aloud until this moment, but I still couldn't trust her with my own.

I was too ashamed. Too embarrassed of the disaster I'd allowed my life to turn into while she had still managed to thrive despite it all.

"She just wanted to be with you," Charlie quietly added.

"No," I protested, shaking my head. "I think she …" I blinked away the moisture in my eyes to stare at the ceiling. "I think she just wanted to do something other than read and—"

"Trust me," he said, pinning me with a gaze so full of pain that I thought I might crumble on the spot. "She *just* wanted to be with you."

I didn't argue his point.

Hell, for all I knew, he was right. Even if it was hard for me to envision any world in which Ray would ever want to be *with* me, let alone *like* me.

"Anyway ..." I lifted my fork to do something other than stare at the heartache reflected in his eyes and poked at the rice in my bowl. "One night, when I was twenty-one, I went down to The Pit to get high, and I watched that guy, Billy, die. Right there on the side of the road with his best friend pounding on his chest and begging him to wake up, and, um ..."

Fuck. I could still feel the bite of the February wind that night, stinging my cheeks and chapping my lips, as I'd stared over the chain-linked fence and watched in horror as Billy Porter took his last breaths.

We weren't kids, but I felt like we were, and it was surreal to say I'd known a guy who had died. A guy my age, one who I had gotten high with and fucked on more than one occasion.

"That kinda thing can really fuck you up," I muttered.

"I'm sorry," Charlie said, and I looked back at him then. Partly because I was shocked and partly because I couldn't understand.

Nobody had ever said they were sorry to me before. Not about that.

"Why?" I asked before I could stop myself.

"Because he was your friend," he replied gently.

"He wasn't a good guy," I countered while knowing I hadn't been a good person then either. "He was a drug addict whose best friend was his dealer. He cheated on his girlfriend pretty regularly, and I only know that because I was one of the girls he used to—" I bit down on my lip and shook my head, suddenly rethinking divulging that much of my strange and fickle relationship with the boy who had died.

"I don't care what he did or what you did with him," Charlie replied, his tone even and kind. "If he had meant anything to you at any point, then I'm sorry. And I'm also sorry that you had to watch him die."

I was quick to shake my head. "No. See, I won't let you be sorry for *that*. Did it fuck me up? Yes. But it also *saved* me. Because if I hadn't watched him die from taking one of those fucking pills I was popping on the regular, I would've ended up just like him. What had happened to him scared me *so* much that I didn't do it again."

Charlie hummed a small, contemplative sound as he nodded, then grabbed for his fork. "They do say everything happens for a reason. I'm glad you found reason in his death."

I cocked my head at the chill in his tone and the nonchalant way he began to eat. He was fire and ice embodied, a puzzle I was eager to figure out. But he was also predictable, and I'd quickly learned that these moments in which he'd shut down, it was directly correlated to something he didn't want to talk about.

So, I moved on.

"Yeah, so I started to take my life a little more seriously. I got a job at the front desk of a tattoo shop, and I apprenticed under their body piercer for a couple of years. Things were going okay for a while, but I was still living with my parents, and even though we kinda get along, our relationship is, um ... let's say, better at a distance. They could never accept that I'd changed or I was trying to, and I couldn't find the patience to force them to see it. Plus, they were always so much more interested in what my sister was doing, so ..."

"You left," Charlie finished for me before furrowing his brow and scrubbing the palm of his hand over his mouth.

"Yep. I came up here, bounced around between a few shops for a while until I found Salem Skin. Blake and Cee adopted me, and the rest is history."

The memory of walking into Salem Skin for the first time brought a little, nostalgic smile to my lips. The way Cee had looked up from the front desk's computer to watch me come in, forcing an air of confidence I couldn't convince myself to actually feel. I'd known of Blake Carson for a while, watched his climb to celebrity through social media, and when I'd seen the announcement on their feed that they were in need of a skilled and experienced body piercer, I had talked myself out of applying about six times before I finally worked up the courage to step into the shop.

My connection with Cee had been instantaneous, whereas the friendship I'd built with Blake took time. He wasn't an easy guy to know, and the walls he'd raised around his heart were high. Eventually though, I'd become not just a part of the shop, but a member of a family who accepted me just as I was. They never looked the other way when I broke down and admitted the gritty details of what had happened to me. They gave me shoulders to lean on while I worked on building the bridges I'd burned with my biological family. They had become my brother and sister, unbound by blood, and I loved them in ways I'd never known possible to love someone you hadn't been born to.

From the look on his face, Charlie didn't understand what that was like. And I couldn't say it surprised me, but my heart ached just the same.

I wasn't sure he'd had anyone in his life in a long, long time.

"Your friend seems nice," I carefully said, changing the subject. Afraid I'd pushed him too far by telling my story. "Ivan, right?"

He nodded without looking my way. "Yeah. And he is. Weird as hell, but aren't we all?"

"Even the Misfit Toys had each other."

That made his lips quirk in something close to a reluctant smile.

"You really should go to his wedding," I added, finally heaving a forkful of rice to my mouth before closing my eyes and nodding with instant approval.

I had to give it to the guy—he sure knew how to cook.

Charlie took a bite and, with his mouth full, said, "I'm thinking about it."

I poked at a sprig of broccoli and lifted one shoulder. "I told you I'd go. As your plus-one."

For a second, he looked like he might take me up on the idea, and I hoped he would. But then he shook his head quickly, chasing the thought away.

"It's the day after Thanksgiving. I'm sure you have stuff you have to do. Family and what—"

"Come with me," I blurted out before I knew what the hell I was saying.

Come with me? Had I really just invited this man I hardly knew to meet my family in Connecticut? And not just my sister and her family, but my *parents* too? The people who had stopped asking if I was ever going to settle down somewhere in my late twenties because I'd "clearly given up on wanting more" from my life?

Their words, not mine.

And for a second, I hoped he'd shoot me down immediately, the way he had when I initially asked him to Blake's party. I hoped he'd scoff and stare at me like a third eye had popped up in the center of my forehead.

But ...

Fuck it. No. I *wanted* him to come, and I wasn't going to pretend like I didn't. I wanted him to have a holiday surrounded by people who were at least friendly because God only knew when the last time he'd had that was. I wanted him to be there with me as my date because I *liked* him, and I wanted my parents and sister to like him too.

The invitation startled him enough to let some rice drop from his fork as he stared across the table at me. I did, in fact, feel like I'd grown a third eye, but I didn't care. All the more to look at him with.

What could I say? The dude was ridiculously hot.

"Please," I added, holding my fork tight as drunken, disoriented butterflies swarmed around my gut.

Great, I'm begging. That's a new low.

His throat bobbed with a hard swallow. "Y-you haven't asked them or—"

"I don't need to ask. I'll tell them I'm bringing my ..." My jaw flapped a few times, as I was unsure of what word to fill that blank with. "Guy ... friend."

He sputtered with a chuckle, one side of his mouth lifting in a genuine smile. "Guy friend?"

"It's much more family-friendly than *guy who makes me come harder than I ever have in my life*," I muttered with a nonchalant shrug.

He snickered. "Okay, lying isn't necessary."

"I might be a lot of things, Charlie, but a liar has never been one of them."

His rich brown eyes met mine with a curious tip of his head. I flashed him a smile and asked what that look was for, and he responded with a slow shake of his head.

"You just"—his head continued to shake—"remind me of someone."

"Someone good, I hope," I teased, scooping another forkful of rice.

He pulled in a deep breath as the corners of his mouth tugged gently downward. "The best."

Jesus fuck, he looked so *sad*. I wanted to get to the bottom of it. I wanted to dig out every one of his secrets and help him carry the load that weighed so heavily on his shoulders.

But before I could comment on the shift in his demeanor, he dropped his eyes back to his food and muttered a quick, "Okay."

"Okay what?"

"I'll go to your family's house for Thanksgiving. And we'll go to Ivan's wedding."

He filled his lungs and nodded quickly to himself, like he needed reassurance, while I sat, stunned.

"Seriously? I kinda expected you to fight a little harder at least."

He pursed his lips and shook his head. "Nope."

"Why?" I asked against a burst of incredulous laughter.

"Because you'll be there," he said with finality. "And I just decided that, for as long as we have together, I'll go where you go."

CHAPTER TWENTY-EIGHT

CHARLIE
MASSACHUSETTS, PRESENT DAY

"*The right woman won't run away.*"

Luke had said it firmly enough that I wanted to believe him, but I hadn't—I didn't.

And every day since Stormy had arrived, I awoke with the chilled fingers of dread and fear wrapped around my heart, certain I'd find myself alone in my bed. But every day, my eyes would open to find her still there. Always asleep. Always wearing a smile.

Then, just like that, the sickening feeling of being left would dissipate quickly, and we'd begin our day.

We'd take a shower together, and I'd make us breakfast before opening the gate. Then, we'd take a nice drive through the quiet, empty cemetery to the parking lot, where, together, we'd heave the two iron sides of the gate open. Afterward, we'd go our separate ways. I would begin my work for the day, and she would either head back to the cottage or get into her car to do whatever it was she had to do around the city before heading to work.

At sundown, I'd lock the gate and head back to the house to draw or read before returning to the gate, happy to see her return. I would then make dinner, and after, there was always the promise of sex and deep, wonderful sleep, void of nightmares.

Suffice it to say, I was content, and although it seemed silly and extreme to declare it the best week I'd ever had, I was also never one to use my head when it came to relationships. But Luke had said the right one wouldn't be afraid of that, nor would she run away, and as the days went on, I found myself growing less cautious and more hopeful that Stormy could, in fact, be *her*.

The right one.

I wish Luke were here, I thought as I pulled into a parking space just around the corner from Salem Skin. He would like Stormy. She had enough in common with me to make this work, but the similarities in personality she shared with him startled me.

Sometimes, she even made missing him a little more bearable.

***

I got out of the truck and walked down the street to the shop, keeping my head down to avoid eye contact with the pedestrians on the sidewalk around me. On my way, I passed the open door to a tarot reading shop, the earthy scent of nag champa drifting along the November breeze.

I didn't look inside to grab the attention of a woman standing near the doorway, her long skirt the only thing visible to my downturned gaze, but she spoke anyway.

"Your old soul has seen many things, but the other has now seen more," she said, her old voice a whimsical, singsong whisper against the cacophony of cars and chatter around me. "She was sent for a purpose. You have no reason to doubt."

Stormy was waiting for me at Salem Skin. It was her day off, but she'd gone in to set up some new supplies in her station. I had dropped her off after swinging by Jolie Tea, and she'd asked me to pick her up later in the day. She'd asked if I wanted to grab some dinner, maybe go on a real date, as she'd put it, and I'd reluctantly said yes.

She was waiting, but I stopped anyway to raise my eyes to the silver-haired woman in a gauzy-looking purple top and long, flowing black skirt.

"Were you talking to me?" I asked almost defensively and more than a little spooked.

"I was," she crooned with a flutter of her eyelids.

She wore no makeup, and her skin was heavily lined with age. But there was a soft, gentle quality in her features and a youthful sparkle in her gray eyes that told me she must've been stunning years ago.

Honestly, she still was.

I studied her suspiciously, and she huffed a short laugh.

"You believe as much as you are a skeptic," she concluded from my gaze. "But you already know. It's time to take a step forward now. The past is of no use to you, and it's all right to let go."

A muscle in my jaw jumped as I ground my teeth together, fighting against the angry words I wanted to spit into her face. But when I collected myself enough to speak, all I asked was, "Who told you that?"

She took a deep breath and dropped her chin, returning to her busy work of arranging crystals on a wire display.

"You shouldn't keep her waiting, Charlie," she said casually, palming a smoky quartz point and holding it up to the hazy light filling the shop. "You've both waited long enough."

***

In a daze, shaken and disturbed, I pushed through the shop door. Blake was sitting on the bolstered leather couch in the waiting area, his ankle crossed over his knee. He looked up from his phone to acknowledge me with a lift of his chin.

"Hey, man. How's it going?"

I tried to push down the residual effects of the tarot reader's words and act normal as I stuffed my hands into my leather jacket, taking a step toward Blake.

"All right. How are you?"

"Good," he replied, dropping the phone to the cushion beside his and standing to extend his hand by way of a friendly greeting. "Stormy said you were picking her up today."

We shook as I nodded. "She in the back?"

He told me she was, and I was about to head that way when he stopped me.

"Hey, listen. I'm getting out of here in a few minutes to pick my wife up and go to dinner with Cee and her husband, Shane. You guys are welcome to join us."

Stormy and I hadn't been on an actual date alone, never mind with *two* other couples, and instinct told me to decline the invitation without a second thought. But then Melanie came to mind, like a specter from the past passing through a vacant hallway. How she'd given herself up for my brother and his demons. How resentful she'd become and how, in the end, she'd been nothing but a shadow of what she used to be. I didn't want that to happen to Stormy, and if being together meant that sometimes, she'd want us to spend time with her found family, then I'd have to accept that for what it was and tough it out.

So, I forced my head to nod. "Sounds good. I'll run it by Stormy and see what she says."

Blake seemed happy with that answer as his lips quirked into a friendly, approving smile. "Cool. Tell her to text me if you decide to come, and I'll add you guys to the reservation."

With a smile and a, "Will do," I turned to head through the velvet curtain and down the hall to where I heard music coming from Stormy's workstation in the shop. From spending so much time in her presence, I knew the singer was Hozier and that she was a big fan. I'd started to like his work myself, and as I stepped into the doorway to listen to her sing, I realized it was the first time I'd adopted a likeness for something from a person who wasn't Luke or my parents. She'd already begun to influence me in ways that no other woman ever had, and while I knew it wasn't a negative change, the knowledge still managed to tickle my nerves with alarm.

"It's time to take a step forward now."

The tarot reader's old voice filled my head as I watched Stormy's fluffy black knot of hair bob around to the beat of the song. She knelt on the counter, one cabinet door open before her to reveal boxes of stainless steel needles and forceps. She unloaded the cardboard box beside her, stacking the equipment on the shelves as she sang along in a voice I'd found soothing in the past week. Husky, unique, and melodic.

She tried to juggle too many boxes in her hands, and one slipped from her grip. It fell to the floor with a clatter, and she cursed under her breath as she looked down beneath her perch on the counter, about to drop the others to retrieve the one from the floor.

"I got it," I said, making my presence known and stepping into the room.

As I crouched and picked the box up, handing it to her waiting hand, she smirked. "How long were you standing there?"

I stood and took the rest of the boxes from her hands, stacking them with the others in the cabinet. "Just a minute or two."

"Creep," she teased, taking the last package of forceps from the box. "Finally. God, I feel like I've been doing this for hours."

"Because you have," I reminded her with a quirk of my mouth.

She responded with a sheepish smile as she gestured to the row of hanging cabinets. "These are all jam-packed now. I might've gone a little crazy when I ordered supplies."

I shrugged and stuffed my hands back into my pockets as I turned to rest against the lip of the countertop. "Well, now, you don't have to worry about it for a while, right?"

Nodding, she hopped down from the counter. "Yeah. Like, the next five years."

There was something in the way she moved around the space, carefree and casual, that made me smirk. To think that this woman, who I'd shared my bed with for the past week, made a living from poking fresh holes into flesh sent a rush of excitement through my veins, and if I hadn't been so hyper-aware of the need for cleanliness, I might've insisted on using the convertible chair used for clients for something other than piercing. Something like laying her back, spreading her legs, and burying my face …

"What's that look for?" Stormy asked as she caught my gaze.

I shook the salacious thoughts from my head. "Nothing. Hey, uh, Blake mentioned that he and Cee were going out to dinner with their respective spouses and—"

"Are you asking if I want to go on a triple date with you?" She cut me off with a twinkle in her eye as she grabbed her coat from the hook beside the curtained door.

I crossed the room to take the heavy wool coat from her hands, holding it open so she could slide her arms through the sleeves. "I might be."

"Are you okay with going?"

I smoothed the thick, soft fabric over her shoulders and held my hands there as I took a moment to appreciate the sentiment. There was no judgment in her tone. No hidden resentment that might imply *she'd* like to go, but wouldn't for my benefit. None of the usual attitudes or annoyances of previous relationships had seeped into anything she said so far, and as I'd previously taken note of, it was *nice*.

It was nice to simply *be* without worrying about what I could be doing to unintentionally fuck it all up.

"I think so," I replied honestly, lifting my eyes to the floor-length mirror, finding hers looking back at me.

Her smile broadened, black lips framing white teeth. She lifted her chin, tipping her head back against my chest.

"We look hot," she commented, lifting a hand to lay it over mine, still resting on her shoulder.

I'd never once thought to compliment my own appearance, let alone go so far as to use the word *hot*. The grin I gave back to her was one of amusement and incredulity as I shook my head, our gazes both affixed to the mirror.

"Hot?"

"Together, I mean," she corrected, as if it made it better. "Like Morticia and Gomez."

Her smile relaxed into something a little more serene as she settled back against my chest, her hands both now touching mine. The more I looked at our reflection, the more I reluctantly agreed. We complemented each other, or maybe it was that *she* complemented *me*, making this exterior unable to shake off the gloom somewhat happier, content, and much, much less lonely.

"I think it's just you," I teased. "You make me look good."

"I"—she turned around to face me, swinging her arms up to loop lazily around my neck and tipping her head back—"don't think you give yourself enough credit."

"And I"—my mouth dropped to brush against hers—"think you should text your boss and let him know we're coming before he gets pissed off."

Stormy's eyes lit with amusement, brighter than the lights above our heads. "You're intimidated by Blake?"

She sounded doubtful, like the thought was absurd, and I scoffed.

"I'm pretty sure Blake could intimidate anyone," I countered, laughing, just as incredulous.

"Not *anyone*," she said a bit smugly as she loosened her hold on my neck to dig her phone from her pocket. Then, as she began to type, she added, "And if you think *he's* scary, just wait until you meet my brother-in-law."

***

I'd spent much of my life being afraid of something or someone. While I appreciated that Stormy might not have found much to be scared of when it came to her friends, particularly Blake, I couldn't share the sentiment. In my experience, most people deserve to be feared—or at the very least approached with caution. Blake had made it very clear that he'd taken a big-brother position in Stormy's life, and although he'd also claimed to not be the fighting type, I knew better than anyone what big brothers were capable of.

So, I muddled through dinner with simple replies and careful glances around the table. I didn't speak unless spoken to, and my attention remained more on Stormy and my plate than anything else. But my apprehensive demeanor aside, her friends were nice, and they didn't once give me reason to be nervous. It was just who I was at my core, and at thirty-eight, I wasn't sure there was much I could do to change that.

"So, are you guys going down to your parents' place for Thanksgiving?" Cee asked Stormy, flipping her purple dreads over her shoulder before digging into a pile of nachos.

The mention of Connecticut set an eclipse of moths free in my stomach, and suddenly, I had even less interest in the burrito bowl I'd ordered.

Stormy nodded as she took a bite of her hard-shell taco, sending a flurry of crumbs to the table. "Yeah. Thanksgiving at my parents' house, and then we're going to Charlie's friend's wedding the next day. I figured we'd just spend the weekend in Connecticut since we'll already be down there." She turned to address me with a wide-eyed plea. "Right?"

A dizzying rush of panic urged me to tell her every horrible thing that had ever happened to me within the Connecticut state lines. Then, she'd know why I didn't ever want to go back, why I felt I *couldn't* go back. She would understand, and she'd insist on her family coming up to Massachusetts instead. It wasn't a far drive. If we were capable of driving south, surely, they were capable of traveling north.

It was a nice thought, albeit a desperate one, but I wouldn't suggest it here in the presence of her friends.

So, I nodded and forced a smile. "Right. M-makes sense."

"If we stay overnight at my parents' house on Thanksgiving and Friday, then maybe we can stay overnight at my sister's place on Saturday. She's in River Canyon, and I've been dying to see her house since Soldier redid the kitchen."

My heart skipped a beat, though I couldn't understand why. "Soldier?"

"Oh, that's my sister's husband. I told you his name is Soldier, right? I thought I mentioned that."

Perspiration coated the palms of my hands. "O-oh, right. Yeah, you probably have."

Dread pushed the rice and beans in my gut aside, filling the space until I thought I might vomit all over the table.

What the hell is wrong with me?

It had to have been my anxiety getting the best of me. The thought of meeting Stormy's family and being back in a state that had never wanted me was slowly eating away at me, to the point of wishing I'd indulged in something harder in my glass than water.

That's all it is. That's all. I'm fine.
Soldier ...
Connecticut ...

My heart rate sped up. My mouth went dry. I ran a hand over my bearded chin, grasping at reality and this table and the people around me, seemingly oblivious to my slippery hold on the shreds of calm.

Breathe. I have to breathe.
Connecticut ... the house ... Luke ...
Soldier ...
God, why do I keep thinking about his name?! I've heard it before. I know I have, but ...

My trembling hand reached for my water glass. Twitching fingers slipped off its surface, wet with condensation, and embarrassment heated my cheeks as my eyes darted up to survey the table. Blake, Audrey, Cee, and Shane were wrapped in conversation, oblivious to my fumbling fingers. But when my gaze fell to my left, locking eyes with the watchful stare of Stormy, my heart leaped to my throat.

She cocked her head and mouthed, *What's wrong?*

I shook my head and blinked rapidly as I looked away, successfully lifting the glass to my lips this time.

But she laid her palm over my clenched knuckles, and I turned my attention back to her, my eyes meeting hers once again over the glass.

"I *see* you, Charlie," she whispered, for my ears only. Reminding me once again that she managed to see things nobody else could—or was it just that they'd never been interested? "Tell me what's going on."

It would be easy to avoid the topic. I could pretend to not have heard her, snatch a piece of the conversation between Cee and Blake and their respective significant others I wasn't currently listening to, and coolly slip myself into the mix in the way I had seen Luke do a hundred times in the past. The whole thing would be swept under the rug until we returned to the cottage, where she might or might not attempt to pick up where we'd left off. But in the cottage, there was also sex—the best distraction of all—and then there'd be sleep and the hope that she wouldn't bring it up again in the morning.

But there was a tug in my rumbling gut, pulling me in the direction of laying my secrets down. Presenting them all like a hand of cards. *Take 'em or leave 'em.* It was growing more and more exhausting to keep them locked up within my weary heart, and, oh, how equally dreadful and exhilarating it seemed to share them with someone else.

That someone could be her.

And what if she leaves?

I wasn't sure I could stomach the thought of waking up alone again after knowing what it was like to have her wild black hair splayed over my pillow.

But secrets could only remain buried for so long before they were unearthed, and the longer I kept them hidden, the angrier she'd be when they inevitably came out.

And nobody said it all had to happen at once.

Start small. If there is such a thing.

So, I trained my gaze on her hand, covering mine, and muttered, "Not now. Later." And then, suddenly, I was terrified of being alone with her, scared of reliving the memories I tried so hard to forget.

CHAPTER TWENTY-NINE

MASSACHUSETTS, PRESENT DAY

Tension fueled my goodbye to Stormy's friends, and I hoped they couldn't sense the tightness of my jaw or the ramrod stiffness of my spine as I nodded cordially in their direction. It had nothing to do with them and all to do with my anxiety about the conversation I knew would be happening the moment Stormy and I were alone.

My heart thumped an irregular beat as they walked away toward their respective cars.

My palms began to sweat when Stormy threaded her fingers through mine and turned to look up at me.

Nausea settled uncomfortably in my stomach and made my mouth water as she said, "I'm freezing. Let's go."

Go. To the truck. To the cottage. To the corners of my mind I intentionally left dusty and untouched.

"Okay," I murmured, nodding erratically. "Yeah."

She steered the way back to the truck, strolling along the sidewalk like we were taking a casual walk through a park. Her cheek pressed to my arm, one hand in mine, the other clutching the crook of my arm. If I wasn't so wrapped up in my head, I would've enjoyed it more, this closeness. The comfort of her being there. The thrill of being in a relationship—a good one, a *real* one. And I tried to be present, tried to push more affection into my fingers as they pulsed around hers, tried to not freak the fuck out as we turned into the parking lot. But that wasn't who I was, no matter how much I wished to change for her.

So, after I fumbled with the keys and unlocked the truck, I helped Stormy in, shut the door behind her, and when I was sure she couldn't see, I squeezed my eyes shut and clenched my fists. Taking one, two, three deep breaths in and out. Trying with desperation to steady my frenzied heart.

Then, I got in and said nothing. I waited for her to make the first move as I started the truck, Stone Temple Pilots' "Big Empty" filling the cab. Stormy cringed and changed the station.

"Hope you're not a big fan of that song," she said without apology. "Remember I told you about that kid Billy I used to get high with? The one I watched die?"

"Yeah."

"That song was playing when he died, and … yeah. I can't. Every time I hear it, it just sends me right back there, and …"

She gave her head a quick shake, and I know she hadn't planned it. She couldn't have. But with that single admission, that tiny anecdote that was nearly insignificant in comparison to the story she'd shared …

It was enough.

"I feel that," I whispered, my voice strained beneath an impossible weight. "I won't ever finish watching *Game of Thrones* for the rest of my life."

Stormy snorted. "You're not missing much, honestly. I could tell you how it ends if you wanted, but ..." Her amusement settled into something more somber as her gaze swept toward me. "Why?"

Here we go.

Tears were already pricking the backs of my eyes with countless threats as I swallowed and said, "Remember I told you that my brother's in prison?"

Her lips parted with a long exhale as she nodded. "Yeah," she replied quietly.

"Well, I, uh ... I was watching that show when he was a-arrested, so, um ..."

Keep it together.

She nodded slowly. "Can I ask what he did?"

Then, I took a deep breath as I pulled up to the cemetery, parallel parking outside of the locked gate. I could tell her at the cottage. I could hold off until after we at least got inside the confines of the cemetery grounds. But if I waited, if I even gave myself a few moments to think, I wasn't sure I'd be able to tell her at all.

So, with the truck running idle, I began ...

CHAPTER THIRTY

CONNECTICUT, AGE THIRTY

It was wild how quickly five years could pass when life was more or less playing out like the same old broken record.

Sleep. Work. Home. Repeat.

Sure, sometimes, I'd throw in the occasional trip to the grocery store. Every now and then, I'd set myself up on another date destined to go nowhere, just to take a break from the monotony, and once in a blue moon, Luke and I would go out to dinner or catch a movie or something. But as the years spread out before us, those dates and random outings stretched fewer and further between, and honestly, I wasn't sure I cared anymore. Maybe I'd care eventually. In a few weeks, a year, a decade ... I couldn't say. But right now, it didn't bother me.

Routine was predictable. It was comfortable. It was harder to get hurt when you knew exactly what every day would bring, and I couldn't imagine myself ever thinking differently. In fact, how had I ever been convinced that anything could possibly be better than this in the first place?

Luke, on the other hand, didn't agree.

He was worrying about me again, the way he had after our parents died. Back when Melanie had talked him into taking me to therapy.

Therapy. I scoffed, thinking about it now, as I pulled the meatloaf from the oven.

My time with Dr. Sibilia hadn't been without warrant, but she had also been wrong about so many things. Number one being that there was any benefit to baring my soul to others.

A heart could only be rejected and hurt so many times before the scars finally turned to stone.

Lately, I'd had that uncanny feeling that it was about to be hurt again. Badly. And the safest thing to do was exactly what I'd been doing—nothing.

If only I could get Luke to stop prodding at me.

"So, hey, you wanna go to the movies tomorrow?" he asked abruptly, walking into the kitchen.

I glanced over my shoulder into the dining room, looking for Luke's latest sexual conquest, only to find it empty. "Where's—"

"Sent her home. She's a vegetarian, apparently."

I looked into the pan and eyed the meatloaf he'd known I was making for three days since I'd been grocery shopping for the week. "You could've told me to make something else."

"What?" He snorted an incredulous laugh as he opened the fridge to grab a can of root beer. "I'm not sacrificing meatloaf for pussy, dude. Never gonna happen."

"And I wonder why you're single," I grumbled.

"No, you don't."

It was true; I didn't. Luke had made it very clear years ago that he was done with commitment. One serious girlfriend—one *fiancée*—had been more than enough for him, and although he'd also insisted plenty over the years that he wasn't *happy*, he also seemed to be somewhat content. And just in the way I didn't see any reason to change my own routine, far be it from me to insist he should change his.

But again, the *prodding*.

"Anyway, so you wanna go or not?"

I carried the meatloaf pan into the dining room to join the mashed potatoes and corn on the table. "Not really."

"Come on. There's probably something creepy you'd like to see."

"It's a waste of money," I muttered, sitting down and spooning some potatoes onto my plate.

"We should go out," he continued to urge, taking his chair across from mine.

There were two empty chairs beside his, another two beside mine. If it wasn't for the fact that this was the same table we'd shared with our parents, I would've had half a mind to just get rid of the damn thing and give it to someone who could use the extra seating. We certainly didn't.

"We can watch movies here. And it's Halloween anyway. We have to hand out candy."

He sighed as he sliced off a slab of meatloaf and dropped it onto his plate. "You know, you're kinda starting to freak me out again."

"So you've said."

His eyes darted toward mine. "And that doesn't matter to you?"

I took a bite of mashed potatoes and lifted my shoulders high to my ears. "Not saying it doesn't matter, Luke. I just don't know what you want me to do about it. I don't want to go out. I don't want to waste my money on movies. I just want to go to work, come home, hand out candy to trick-or-treaters, eat dinner, and draw for a while. Okay? I don't understand why this is such a problem for you."

"Because I don't think it's healthy."

"Yeah, okay. And you'd know what's healthy. Sure." I fought against rolling my eyes while I cut off a slice of meatloaf, lobbing it onto my plate. "When's the last time you got tested for STDs, huh? You know, if you're suddenly so health-conscious."

The comment was cruel and backhanded, and I knew it. Yet I felt no shame or fear in leveling him with a stony glare, only to be met with one just as angry and harsh. If he wanted to throw a punch at me, that was fine. It wouldn't be the first time, and even though I might not have gone to the gym with him in a long time, I'd stayed in shape on my own, thanks to my job at the cemetery and the weights we kept in the basement. I could take him.

Anything to keep him from going out. Anything to keep him *home*.

"You know what? Go fuck yourself." He spat the words across the table, but didn't get up from his chair.

I didn't bother responding with any of the snappy retorts that crossed my mind as we both resumed eating in tension-filled silence. And that was fine. Just so long as he dropped the subject of going out and came home after work instead.

I could remember a time years ago when I could be honest with him about the strong intuitive feelings I occasionally got. But it had been a long time since I'd had them, an even longer time since I'd felt it necessary to mention it to him, and now, I was just afraid he'd lump that in with the other reasons he thought I was going crazy—again.

Pissing him off seemed like the next best thing, and I needed him to be mad enough to come home.

***

The last bits of late October daylight left the driveway hazy as I pulled up to the garage door. Luke's bike wasn't where it belonged. The empty spot beside my car gave me a moment of gut-gurgling pause, but with a deep breath, I brushed it off. There were plenty of nights where he came home later, if he'd gotten wrapped up in a big repair job at the shop. Reason calmed me down from my panic, and I went inside to cook dinner.

Then, it was put on the table, and I began to eat, taking small, uninterested bites of a burger I had little taste for in between answering the door for the few trick-or-treaters that came by.

Luke's chair was empty. So was his spot in the driveway.

I pushed the plate away, slumped back, and scrubbed my hands over my cheeks before grabbing my phone and calling his number. It rang twice before being sent to voice mail.

"What the fuck, Luke?" I grumbled and called again. Voice mail.

"Hey, asshole," I said after the tone. "Just wondering where the hell you are. Would've been nice if you had told me not to make dinner for you. Call—"

I was interrupted by the faint vibration against my palm, and I cut off the message to find he'd sent me a text.

Calm your tits. At the movies. About to sit down.

Luke never went to the movies alone, and I couldn't chalk it up to a date. Luke didn't *date*; he was unapologetically a bang-and-run kind of guy. He was still pissed off from last night's disagreement and had gone to the movies to spite me.

My nerves sprang to life, bringing my legs to a frantic jitter beneath the table as I aggressively tapped out a reply.

Oh, nice. Thanks for letting me know. Your dinner is getting cold.

I'll heat it up when I get home.

Whatever.

You wanna come down? You could get here now and just miss the trailers.

I said I didn't want to go.

You're gonna make me sad.

That's fine.
Crying into my popcorn now.
You always liked it extra salty anyway.
I don't need my popcorn to be extra salty when I have your whiny ass to come home to later.
I'm not the one who told you to go fuck yourself. Just pointing that out.

The conversation felt like the closest thing to an apology as we were going to get, and I sighed, letting the tension leave my shoulders. But that sick forewarning never left the pit of my stomach, and I stared at my screen, waiting for those three little dots to start jumping again.

They never came.

The movie must've started, I told myself as I grabbed my plate and took my food to the living room. I set it on the coffee table and turned on the TV, hoping something would distract me until my brother once again walked through the door.

The latest episode of *Game of Thrones* was just about to come on, and I sat through fifteen minutes of previews as I choked down my burger before the announcer finally said, "And now, the HBO original series, *Game of Thrones*."

The theatrical, instrumental theme song began to flood the speakers as the image on the screen took me on a trip through the fantastical lands I'd grown attached to over the years, and I sank against the back of the worn, old couch, ready to immerse myself in the show.

That was when Luke came home.

The front door swung open with his dramatic entrance, and he slammed it shut, locking it and peeking through the big oval window.

Then, he turned around to look at me and said, "Charlie."

My mouth flooded with saliva as a wave of nausea rolled over me at the sight of his heaving chest and shaking hands. His face, drained of all color. His eyes, big and wild.

"Luke," I replied slowly, carefully. "W-what's up?"

He walked toward me, propelled by purpose. The closer he came, the louder his unsteady breathing became. "Ch-Charlie, I ..." He thrust his hands into his hair, his face crumpled, and to my horror, he began to cry. "I fucked up. Oh God, oh my *God*, I-I don't know what I'm gonna do. I-I-I don't know what I'm gonna *do*."

He came to stand before me, then dropped to his knees, grappling for my arms with shaking hands and pressing his face to my thigh.

"What did you do?" I asked, struggling to hold on to what little calm I had left, even as my heart raced to a dangerous speed quicker than it had taken for my older brother to fall apart in front of me.

Luke released his hold on my arms as he took a deep breath and sat back on the balls of his feet. He raked back his mussed-up hair and groaned as he scrubbed at his splotchy red face.

Then, he pulled in a deep, quivering breath and pinned me with his watery gaze, and just as a fresh wave of tears began to fall, he said the three words that would change both of our lives forever.

"I ... I killed Ritchie."

The words left his lips.

His breath came from his open, slack-jawed mouth in short puffs as he looked into my eyes with a wide, vacant stare. But my brow furrowed as my hammering heart banged against my eardrums. I shook my head uncontrollably, my eyes watering in response to the tears falling from Luke's.

"*What*?" There was no way I had heard him correctly. No way in fucking hell. "*Ritchie*? How did ... *what*?! Y-y-you haven't seen—"

"He was there—"

"*Where*?"

"I walked in, and he was *there*, and I tried to ignore him, Charlie. I-I tried to fucking block him out—"

"I don't fucking understand what's happening right now!" I squeezed my eyes shut and reached for my hair, stabbing my fingers between the strands and pulling tightly.

"But, *oh God*, he wouldn't shut up. He wouldn't fucking *shut up*. He never ever, *ever* knew how to shut the fuck up!"

I leaned forward, pressing my head against the palms of my hands. The adrenaline pulsed through my veins, my mind zipping in one direction to the other, unable to collect my thoughts and hold on to a single one long enough to process what was going on. Luke was here. Luke was talking. Luke was sitting before me, crying and heading seriously close to hyperventilation, and I wasn't far behind.

This is really happening.

The sobering thought cleared a path through the barrage of discombobulated nothing in my head. I dropped my hands, and despite the force behind every beat of my heart, I made my best attempt at looking my brother in the eye.

The guy who had sat right there and told me I was a lucky butthole for no longer having to go to school.

The guy who had broken his best friend's nose in the basement after he wished me dead.

Sirens joined the sound of the TV, approaching from somewhere in the distance.

He was the one who'd set me up with my first girlfriend. The one who had taken me to my first therapy session. The one who had broken it off with his fiancée to confess the truth of my girlfriend's infidelity.

The sirens were closer now.

"No," I whispered through a lump in my throat that was making it harder and harder for me to breathe. "You didn't do anything. You couldn't—"

"I did it, Charlie. I killed him," he whispered back, like the rapidly approaching police could hear his confession.

"No." I shook my head. "No, no, no. You … God, you aren't a fucking *killer*. You—"

Luke and I both turned our heads abruptly toward the cascade of red, white, and blue lights flashing against the sheer curtains covering the living room window. One, two, three cop cars pulled up to the house without a single care of where or how they'd parked.

My brother reached out and grabbed my shoulders firmly in his hands. "Look at me. Right now. Look at me."

I didn't want to look at him. I didn't want to stare into his eyes and have him tell me the things I didn't want to believe were true because how the fuck could they be? I didn't want to see him, red-eyed and tear-streaked, afraid that this might be the last time I ever saw him.

God, don't make me say goodbye.

Not again.

Bang! Bang! Bang!

The front door rattled against the force.

"Lucas Corbin!" shouted a voice I didn't know. "If you're in there, come out peacefully or—"

"Charlie!" Luke gritted from between clenched teeth. "Look at me!"

I did, and the moment my eyes met his, as terrified as my own, I was certain the world as I'd known it to be for the last fifteen years of my life had exploded and turned to dust.

"I love you, okay?"

Of all the things he could've said to me in that moment, that was what he'd chosen to say. That he loved me.

"I love you too," I said, my voice strangled. "Luke, what the fuck? I don't—"

Bang! Bang! Bang!

"Lucas Corbin!"

He looked over his shoulder and dropped his hands to his lap. "Can I tell you a secret?"

I stared at the door. "Huh?"

"I'm scared, Charlie. I'm really fuckin' scared."

He didn't give me a chance to reply. On unsteady legs, he stood. He pushed his hair back and wiped his face hastily with his palms. Then, he turned and headed toward the door, holding his head high and keeping his shoulders squared. Acting every bit of the cocky son of a bitch I'd known him to be while knowing that, deep down, he was as scared shitless as he or I had ever been in our lives.

As I watched his back, *Game of Thrones* on the TV and those goddamn lights flashing over everything in the living room, it struck like a brick to the head that I'd never see him walk through that door again.

He had killed a man. I didn't know how, and I didn't know why, but I knew it to be true.

Luke opened the door to three cops holding guns and wearing bulletproof vests. They were only doing their job, none of it was their fault, but, God, I hated them in that moment. I hated them for not giving us more time. I hated them for not letting me question my own damn brother before they could get the chance.

"Lucas Corbin?"

"Yeah," Luke replied, pushing the door open fully and raising his hands weakly. Showing them he was unarmed.

I stood slowly from the couch and took a couple of cautious steps forward.

None of this can be real.

I don't want it to be real.

God, please let me wake up. I want to fucking wake up.

The cop grabbed Luke by the arm and spun him around. He holstered his gun and patted Luke down. "Anybody in there with you?"

"Just my brother. He didn't do anything. He has nothing to do with this."

One of the other cops moved around them and stepped into the house, spotting me right away. For some reason, I held my hands up, and she offered a curt smile as she approached and quickly frisked her hands over my body.

"You can put your hands down," she said and took out a pad of paper. "What's your name?"

Somewhere within my realm of understanding, I knew Luke was being guided from the house. I knew he was cooperating, knew he was looking at me the entire time. I knew the woman beside me was asking repeatedly for my name. I knew a handful of other cops were coming into the house and searching around as if there was anything to find.

But all I could focus on, all I could process, was that I'd never see Luke in this house again. And I was alone. He had abandoned me, and as much as I'd meant it when I said I loved him, I hated him a little too.

CHAPTER THIRTY-ONE

CONNECTICUT, AGE THIRTY-ONE

When I had been thirty and Luke was thirty-three, he'd decided to go to the movies anyway, despite hating the idea of going alone. He wanted to spite me after I asked him not to go at all, as if we weren't brothers, but a bickering old couple instead.

Sometimes, it'd felt that way.

He walked into the theater with his popcorn and large soda and found himself a seat. He sat down, ready to enjoy his moment of rebellion against his overprotective, paranoid little brother, when he heard a familiar voice from the row behind him.

Luke and the various witnesses who'd stepped forward gave identical accounts of the exchange.

Like I always said, my brother had never been one to lie. An embellisher of the truth sometimes, sure, but rarely a liar.

"Hey, Zero. Finally living up to that nickname, huh?"

Luke had claimed he'd tried to ignore him, that he'd sat quietly, browsing his phone for a few minutes in an attempt to distract himself. But Ritchie had always been incapable of stopping himself from antagonizing.

"Where's your boyfriend? I mean, your brother, unless ... shit, is he your boyfriend now? You guys have always been fuckin' weird. I bet he fucks better than any woman you've been with, right?"
Luke shook his head and tried to keep his anger from spiking while the trailers began to play.

Honestly, he should've just left, and I'd told him so on more than one occasion.

Luke's phone rang. It was me. It rang twice, and he sent it to voice mail.
"God, I miss Charlie boy. Been a long time. If you tell me how he's doing, I'll tell you how Melanie's doing. How about that?"
Ritchie tossed a handful of popcorn at Luke. Instead of engaging, my brother gritted his teeth and texted me, never once mentioning to me what was happening.
"She used to talk about you, you know. Used to scream your name, too, when I was plowing into her, but I slapped her around a little. Took care of that."

Ritchie had been lying. He'd never been with Melanie. Didn't even know where she was—none of us did at the time. But Luke hadn't known that.

"Go to hell, Ritchie," Luke finally replied, stuffing his phone into the pocket of his leather jacket.
"Oh, you don't like that, do you? You don't like that I finally have that pretty little pussy all to myself, huh? Don't like that she finally came to her senses and dumped your loser ass?"

It had been sometime around this point when Luke said he'd started to struggle. Started to wonder if he should leave or if he should kick Ritchie's ass instead. If he should complain to management. If he should just fucking go home.

God, he should've just gone home.

"You know what else she said to me?"
"Will you fucking shut the hell up?" someone else in the theater shouted, finally speaking up, but Ritchie never could stop talking.

He could never stop, period, and that was what eventually killed him. Because without someone else to hold him back, Luke couldn't stop either.

Ritchie leaned forward, putting his mouth against Luke's ear. Luke tried to brush him away, but Ritchie grabbed onto his shoulders, holding him steady.

"She said she always wished Charlie boy had died in that crash too. Burned to a crisp, just like your mommy and daddy. She even said you guys would still be together if it wasn't for his psycho, whiny ass, always crying, always getting in the way. She said she would've just killed him herself if his cock wasn't bigger than y—"

He stopped talking when my brother's fist flipped up from the armrest and bashed him square in the mouth.

I hadn't noticed the blood on Luke's hand that night—I'd been too stunned—but the impact against Ritchie's front teeth had cut into Luke's knuckles.

One of Ritchie's teeth cracked, and he cried out, "Asshole! You broke my fucking tooth!"

"Asshole?!" *Luke stood up, enraged and unable to see beyond revenge.* "I'm *the asshole?!"*

He climbed over his seat and into Ritchie's row. Ritchie began to rise, ready to fight, when Luke's hands shot out, encircling his throat.

"You never left him alone. You always *made his life a living hell. And I* always *looked the other way because you were my friend. God, you were my best friend! And I let you torment my little fucking brother, and for what?! What the fuck had he* ever *done to you, huh?! He was a little fucking kid! What the fuck had he* ever *done to you?!"*

Luke's hands tightened, snapping Ritchie's bones and crushing his windpipe. Someone screamed for help; someone else screamed to stop.

That same someone screamed, "You're killing him!"

Someone else ran out of the theater, screaming for the manager or someone—anyone.

God, so much fucking *screaming*, but Luke hadn't heard any of it, and even if he had, I couldn't be sure that he'd cared in that moment.

Because then he said, "I told you once if you ever fucking said some shit about him again, I'd fucking kill you. Remember that, you piece of shit? Why can't you fucking stop?!"

But he had stopped, and Luke realized two seconds too late that his former best friend was no longer breathing, just as a security guard and a manager ran into the theater.

A few people tried to stop him on his way to the emergency exit with little success. He ran to his bike, hopped on, and sped home as quickly as he could, knowing the cops would be on his tail. Knowing there'd been witnesses. Knowing they'd heard Ritchie say his name. Knowing they'd catch him and arrest him and take him away.

All because he had to see me one more time. To warn me. To tell me he loved me.

And that had made it really, really hard to hate him, even when he pleaded guilty. Even when the judge sentenced him to twenty-five years to life in Connecticut's Wayward Correctional Facility for murder in the second degree. But especially when his eyes met mine as the guards took him away to begin the rest of his life behind bars, and I tried hard to see him the way the rest of Connecticut had seen him—a cold-blooded murderer—and I couldn't.

He was still just my brother, and it had been really, really hard to hate him then.

And it was still really, really, *really* hard to hate him now as I sat across from him at a metal table in the Wayward visitor center.

It'd been a little over a year since he'd been thrown behind bars. The first couple of months, he'd been held at a county jail before his transfer to the state prison, medium security.

Luke had once said the *real* bad guys got thrown into max, speaking like he knew what he was talking about, like he wasn't scared shitless of mingling with some of the worst people in our society, and when I'd pointed this out, he'd simply said, "I'm one of them now, Charlie. Yeah, maybe I'm fuckin' scared. I *am* fuckin' scared, but I'm no more scared of them than I am of myself."

As it turned out, he'd had a fairly good point then, I realized after I visited him at the correctional facility every other Sunday. These guys—the ones I'd seen visiting with their friends and family—weren't much different from my brother, or hell, even myself, apart from the fact that they'd committed their crimes and gotten themselves caught. Luke had even introduced me to a few of the guys he'd started to call his friends.

No, it wasn't the other guys who had scared me or left me feeling uncomfortable, unable to put a word on the strange sensation settling in the marrow of my bones.

It was Luke who had done that. Not because he'd become someone I no longer recognized. He hadn't at all, and that was the problem. He was still Luke, still my brother, still my best friend, and I couldn't bring myself to accept that this place was where he belonged, according to society.

I couldn't accept that he had used his own bare hands to rob someone else of their life. No matter how much I might've hated that particular someone else.

But that wasn't all I was having a hard time with.

I shifted my ass against the cold bench as Luke raked his hair back with one hand. He'd started to let it grow longer since he'd been locked up. I wasn't sure what had inspired the change or if he just hadn't gotten around to having it cut. If I was being honest, I didn't care enough at the time to ask. All I cared about was how angry and alone I was and how I really, really, really, *really* wished I could hate him.

"So, then Wolf just"—Luke made a flicking motion with his wrist—"chucks this fucking book at this dude's throat and told him to stop being a pussy for crying on the phone. And Soldier and I were just sitting there, like, what the fuck, man?"

He got caught up in a burst of laughter, to the point where tears squeezed out from his eyes, and all I could do was stare across the table at him, wondering if he'd always been this guy or if he'd just adapted that easily.

A sigh whooshed from him, taking the rest of his laughter with it. "Guess you had to be there."

"Yeah, guess so."

He folded his arms against the table. "So, anyway, how have things been with you? Any changes?"

I swallowed at the dryness in my throat. "Things are pretty much the same as they have been."

Luke blew out a heavy breath and rubbed a hand over his mouth. "Son of a bitch. Are you serious? *Still?*"

"It's been two weeks since I was last here, Luke. What did you think was going to happen in that time?"

"Uh, it's been over a year since I've been here. They have to get bored eventually."

I cocked my head at that, staring at my brother like he'd also lost his damn mind the moment he lost his freedom. "You think it's gonna be so easy for Tommy to get over the fact that he lost his fucking *brother?*"

"Tommy can go to hell," Luke fired back. "He doesn't need to take his shit out on you."

"His brother is *gone*," I replied harshly, enunciating every word to try and get it through his thick skull. Like he wasn't aware.

Luke flattened his hands on the tabletop and leaned over it, bringing his face closer to mine. "And so is *yours*."

"You're not fucking *dead*, Luke."

He shook his head and pushed off the table, leaning back and turning to glance out the barred window. "You know what I mean."

I didn't honor him with an answer, but I knew exactly what he meant. I was reminded of it every single day when I left for work, knowing I was going to return home to an empty house, just as I had every day since he'd lost all control and choked the life out of Ritchie Wheeler.

Of course, there was also the never-ending torment.

As it turned out, people couldn't separate a killer's family from the killer himself, and ever since that day in the movie theater, Tommy Wheeler and his poor old mother had made it their life's purpose to make mine a living hell.

It had started as shouted obscenities from open car windows or a flipped finger if we ever crossed paths in the grocery store. Then, it escalated to nasty notes left in the mailbox and garbage thrown onto the front lawn. The latest incident had been waking up to the words **LUKE CORBIN BELONGS IN HELL** written in spray paint across my car windshield.

The cops suggested getting surveillance cameras on the property to catch Tommy or his mother or both in the act to build a case against them and take them to court. But I didn't want to take them to court. I didn't want to make a big fucking thing out of it. All I wanted was to be left alone to wallow on my own shitty branch of grief, and if there was a way to establish that without having an order of protection slapped on the two of them, I'd take it.

"You know, it might sound crazy, but maybe you should talk to them," Luke suggested gently.

"Oh, right. Good idea. I'll just call them up and invite them over for dinner. I cannot foresee a single thing going wrong in that scenario," I muttered sardonically.

Luke's glare turned to stone. "Don't be a jackass. Next time you see one of them, lay it out. Tell them their beef isn't with you; it's with—"

"Do you really think they're not aware of that already? They wrote *your* name on my car, Luke, not *mine*. But you're in here, where they can't get at you. You're *protected*. Me, though?" I thrust a hand toward the window. "I'm out there, trying to live my fucking life, which has *never* been a walk in the park, in case you forgot. But then you had to go and ..."

I couldn't get the words out, no matter how badly I wanted to throw them in his face. All I could do was raise a clenched fist, then drop it to the table, shaking my head and staring out that window. Too afraid to look at him and see the guilt in his eyes. Too afraid I wouldn't see any guilt at all.

Nothing was said between us for a few minutes, and I wondered why I even bothered anymore. Every other week, I made the two-hour drive to come see him, where I'd listen to him talk about stuff that had happened since our last visit. Always with accompanying laughter. Always with a tinge of joy and excitement he'd never had before during his life on the outside, where he'd put all his focus on simply getting by and not on getting happy.

Here? He was happy. He didn't need to say it; I already knew. And I resented him for it.

"I don't know what you want from me," he finally said after minutes of silence. "How many times do I have to tell you that I'm sorry?"

"Sorry doesn't change anything," I replied, still unable to look at him. "Not for me ... or them."

I could see my car from where I sat, and I thought about leaving early. I thought about never coming back at all. I thought about what my life might be like if I ran away and never saw my brother or this place ever again. For a second, it didn't seem so bad. In fact, it was almost tempting, until I glanced back at him and realized that, despite how badly I wished I could hate him, I didn't.

"Shit's gonna get better." He said it like a promise. "It has to."

"I don't know about that."

"They're gonna move on, one way or another."

He was so certain, and I wanted to believe him, just as I'd believed him countless times before. But I never believed him about Tommy Wheeler or his mother's ability to move on. This wasn't a spat between childhood friends. This wasn't a silly rivalry over a girl. This was about death and justice, and I knew, as deep as my bones, that Tommy Wheeler was out for my brother's blood.

It was just unfortunate for me that Luke's blood was also mine.

CHAPTER THIRTY-TWO

MASSACHUSETTS, PRESENT DAY

Trauma had a way of tearing us from the present and propelling our souls back in time to relive those moments as if we'd never stopped living them. A cornucopia of smells surrounded me at once, and not a single one was the cinnamon and spice Stormy carried on her skin. The burger I'd eaten on that night eight years ago. The musty carpet of the courtroom. The sour, stale sweat and heavy, cheap perfume from the Wayward visitor center.

I could barely recall my mother's laugh or the inflections of my father's tone, but I'd never ever forget the metallic smell of fresh, hot blood, coating my hand and dripping onto the floor outside my bedroom.

My eyes were squeezed shut. I wasn't sure when I'd done it, if I'd made the conscious decision or if it had simply happened at some point in telling the first half of the horrible things I hadn't wanted her to know. But I was aware of it now, and I rubbed my fingers against my brow before prying my lids apart to stare out the windshield at the sidewalk and street signs and the shrubbery outside that hotel she'd been staying at. I didn't want to look at Stormy though. Afraid of what emotions might be reflected in her emerald eyes. Afraid she'd realize that she had bitten off more than any one person could chew by breaking into my house and forcing her way into my life.

"You okay?" she asked after I hadn't said anything for a while. Five minutes maybe, or it could've been five seconds.

"Not sure I've been okay for a long time," I replied, finding it best to be honest. Still unable to face her.

"So, that's why talking about Connecticut freaks you out."

"Yes." It wasn't the whole truth, but it was some of it, and that would have to do for now.

"Then, we won't go."

I faced her then, my forehead crumpled with surprise and disbelief. "What? I didn't say—"

She shrugged nonchalantly. "If it bothers you to be there, then I won't force you to go. And clearly, it bothers you a lot. Understandably."

My eyes danced over her face, catching glimpses of her heavily made-up eyes, the straight line of her full black lips, the firm resolve displayed in every one of her features. There wasn't a single bit of judgment or disgust found in her expression, only sincerity. She meant it. She'd give up a family Thanksgiving at home for the sake of my comfort and sanity, and she'd do it without regret … for me.

"I told you the right woman wouldn't run, dumbass."

Luke's voice struck of its own accord, and a determined rush of tears prodded angrily at the backs of my eyes.

"No," I replied, then cleared my throat to unsuccessfully push away the emotion making it hard to breathe. "The shit in my past might haunt my nightmares, but with you, I actually sleep, and that has to count for something. So, I want to meet your family, and I want to see where you grew up. I want what's important to you to be important to me, and for that, I can force the ghosts to leave me alone. At least for a while."

Even as I said the words, I wasn't sure of my ability to keep my shit together once we crossed the Connecticut state line. But if she was strong enough to stay with me—aware of my demons and all—then I could at least be strong enough to try and face them with her.

***

Stormy thrived on being in control. I was no psychologist, but I suspected that characteristic had taken root somewhere around the time of her trauma at sixteen. She needed to call the shots, to know she had the upper hand, and while I was sure a great deal of men would feel emasculated by this, it only served to make me harder. In that way—and quite a few others, I was finding—we made a good pair.

After we got back to the cottage, she revealed the lengths of rope she'd found earlier while I was out with the leaf blower.

I tipped my head with mounting curiosity and an already-raging boner and asked what she intended to do with those. She then silently replied by securing my wrists to the headboard. She stripped down to nothing at the foot of the bed, leaving me in my jeans, growing tighter by the second, and then climbed up. I watched her through hungry eyes as she crawled toward me on hands and knees while a boulder of lust sat against my chest, making it impossible to get much more than short puffs of air in and out of my lungs. So pathetically needy and eager to please and get off.

"Now," she purred, straddling my waist and continuing her slow pursuit, never taking her eyes off mine, "I'm going to let you come, but first, you'll do something for me."

She crawled up further and further until her tattooed thighs were positioned on either side of my head and her hands were holding tight to the headboard. I stared upward between the valley of her bejeweled breasts, catching her satisfied gaze and wanting nothing more than to do whatever would satisfy her needs.

She already started lowering her wet and greedy desire to my mouth when she said, "Be a good boy and eat."

And, God, I did. I licked and sucked and delved with my tongue as far as the muscle would allow, savoring every drop and pulse and moan she had to give. I worked that little barbell piercing her thin, sensitive flesh until her thighs quaked and clamped against my ears and her grip on the headboard was white-knuckled. She finished with a scream and a fresh boost to my constantly wilting ego, and then my mouth was left lonely until her painted lips came to join mine.

"I love how I taste on your tongue," she muttered in between kisses. "Like I've always belonged there."

"And what if you have?" I muttered back, my wrists straining against the ropes. Desperate to hold her more than I was to get off.

She sighed against my lips as her fingernails scraped over my chest and stomach until she reached the button at my waist. My hips jerked involuntarily, a silent plea for her to *yes, keep going* and she hummed into my mouth.

I somehow forgot about the conversation in the truck as she undid my jeans and worked her hand into my briefs. The throes of desire had the power of lulling a mind into the false sense of assuredness that nothing outside of bodily needs truly mattered. And right now, all that mattered was the way her hand fit so perfectly around the length of my erection. How soft her skin was, how good and efficient she was at jerking me off while kissing and encouraging with gentle sounds of praise. How the pleasure built higher and higher, like building blocks being stacked toward a ceiling of Technicolor static, so close now that I could almost touch it.

Then ... she stopped. Her fingertips dragged down my erection from tip to base as her entire hand slipped away. I whined pathetically, gasping as the brink of ecstasy fell out of my reach.

"Don't worry, baby," she said, peppering kisses along my jaw.

Stormy lifted away from my side and pulled my jeans and briefs down to my knees. I opened my eyes to stare into hers, pleading through labored breath, and she smiled as she straddled my waist and painstakingly lowered herself onto me, one inch at a time.

"Now, be a good boy and come for me."

And, God, I did.

***

We lay together in the darkness, but neither of us was asleep. I could hear the gears of Stormy's mind working, almost as loudly as mine, and I wondered what she was thinking. Yet I wouldn't ask. She would tell me if it was something she wanted me to know, and after a few more moments of silence, she did.

"Charlie," she said quietly, her fingers moving in gentle circles against my chest.

"Yeah?"

"Are you sure you want to come with me?"

I held back a sigh and nodded. "Yes." It was mostly the truth.

My ears were met with silence once again. The smile I'd been wearing was quick to evaporate into the night as unsettling intuition gnawed at my gut. There was more she wanted to say, probably just hanging at the tip of her tongue, but too unsure of how to say it. We hadn't talked any more about Luke or what he'd done or anything after I told my story. I'd been grateful at the time, but now, that gargantuan elephant in the corner of the blackened room wouldn't stop staring me down. Sooner or later, the fucker was going to start trumpeting, and I wasn't sure my sanity could take it.

"You can tell me what you're thinking," I said, hoping she'd take the bait.

Luckily for me, she did.

"Your brother ..." Her voice faded with hesitance as one finger traced a line down the length of my sternum and back to the base of my throat.

"Yeah?" I asked, gruff and nearly defensive.

Relax.

"You mentioned he had been engaged?"

I nodded. "Yes."

"Was this why they broke up?"

That made me smile, even if it was melancholy. Somehow, I didn't think Melanie would've left Luke for murdering Ritchie.

"No. She had left him long before that happened."

Stormy hummed a sound of contemplation, then sighed. "Does she know what happened?"

"I don't know," I answered honestly. "As far as I know, neither of us has seen Melanie since they broke up. I don't know how I would've gotten in touch with her even if I'd wanted to."

"You didn't try?"

I shook my head, frowning at the ceiling. "I didn't think it'd be a good idea to drag her back into his shit when she'd only left because she needed to get away from it. I mean, for all I know, she's already married to a great guy, living in a nice house with a couple of kids."

It was what I had always hoped for her anyway. It was what she had always deserved.

"When were you last in Connecticut?"

"Five years ago."

"Wow. That's a long time to not go home."

Yes, it was, but I didn't say so.

"Whatever happened with that guy and his mom?"

My throat seized around a deep swallow as my eyes danced across the faint beam of moonlight streaming across the ceiling. This was the part I wasn't ready to talk about. The part that I knew without a shred of doubt would make her wish she'd never known me well enough to call me anything but Spider.

My brain hopped from one flimsy answer to another, trying to settle on something acceptable that wouldn't lead to more questions, until I finally came to a brief but honest, "That's a story for another day."

God, I hated how vague it was, and she didn't seem to like it either, judging by the deep inhale she took before nodding with her exhale.

"Okay," she replied quietly. "That's fine. But you know you can tell me, if—"

"I know. I *will* tell you," I promised. "But ... another day."

"Okay."

I thought she might be done asking her questions for the night, and I hoped she was. I'd told her to ask them—hell, I'd demanded it—but even though she'd only asked a few, it was enough to send the blood rushing through my veins at a speed it shouldn't. So, when she finally settled back against my chest, her head growing heavy and her fingers falling limp, I was relieved and released the air from my lungs into the room.

Then, just as I rested my cheek against the top of her head and began to drift off, she spoke again.

"Charlie?"

"Hmm," I grunted softly.

"If you haven't been to Connecticut in five years, that means you haven't seen your brother in that long."

I swallowed, but I didn't speak, afraid of what might come next.

"Do you ... do you *talk* to him? Like, on the phone or something?"

With my eyes still closed, I could remember Luke's arms around me, his hand clapping against my back. I could picture his face as he took me in that last time, holding me by the shoulders at arm's length, before nodding and telling me to get the hell out of there.

Grief rocked me out of my almost slumber as I bit against my lower lip until the tightness in my throat subsided, only to reply with a simple word. "No."

***

A battering gale had blown its way through the cemetery, launching something heavy against the bedroom window. I jolted with a start, turning my head in the direction of the sound. Stormy didn't stir from her sleep.

With an aggravated groan, I tossed the covers off aggressively, then settled with a deep breath and reminded myself to not wake her. If I wasn't allowed a good night's rest, that didn't mean she had to suffer with me.

Taking more care now, I slipped out from beneath her arm and climbed out of bed. The floorboards groaned under my feet, adding a bit of agony to the quiet night. A gust of wind replied, and I turned to the window with a look of unease and suspicion.

It's just the wind, I reminded myself, feeling like a child. But the worrying in my gut wasn't so sure about that.

I stared at the heavy blinds covering the glass pane for a moment. Temptation to pull them aside itched at my fingers so I could see what was out there, staring in from the other side.

But do you really want to know?

No, I decided. I didn't, and I turned deliberately from the blinds until I faced the door.

I walked slowly over the floor, wincing with every step and hoping the whining planks of wood wouldn't wake Stormy. The door had been left ajar before we slept, allowing a soft light to now stream in from the hall.

My life up to this point had been a compilation of terrible memories, many that would've kept even the strongest man up at night to escape the nightmares, and I had never pretended to be a strong man. And now, standing just inside my bedroom, about to step into a dimly lit hallway, all I could think about was the night the floorboards creaked outside my bedroom door, and I had—thank Christ—grabbed the knife from inside my nightstand drawer.

I don't have a knife now.

You're fine, my mind told the rest of me, and even though I huffed a quiet laugh at the absurdity of my imagination, I wasn't sure I believed it.

The wind whistled outside. I turned back toward the window, unsure of what I expected to see. There was nothing, of course, and I shook my head, silently berating myself for being such an idiot when something passed through the light cast from the hallway. With a start, I stepped back from the doorway, nearly stumbling. Too afraid to open the door, I stared at that faint cone of light, waiting for the shadow to return. But it never did.

Holy fuck. Relax. Breathe. It's nothing. Just go piss and get back to bed.

I clenched my fists at my sides and squeezed my eyes shut as I tried to calm my rapidly beating heart. Then, with a final release of air from my tight lungs, I opened the door, ready to face whatever might be on the other side.

Nothing was there.

I took one glance over my shoulder at Stormy, half expecting her to be awake and staring at me, amusement written plainly on her face. But to my relief, she was still asleep.

"You should probably warn her that you're sometimes a neurotic lunatic," I could hear Luke saying. *"But don't worry; the right one won't run."*

I let myself smile at that as I pulled the door shut behind me, leaving it ajar, as it had been before. I went to the bathroom, did what I had to do, and left with every intention of returning straight to bed with the hope that I could find enough comfort in her arms to go back to sleep.

But as I left the bathroom, before I could turn back toward my room, a shadowy figure dashed across the living room at the end of the hall. Heart racing, I turned abruptly in that direction. My eyes hadn't played tricks on me this time—there was *something* in my house. Logic tugged at my panicked brain, reminding me sound hadn't accompanied the shadow. No footsteps or complaining floorboards to speak of. Something moving that fast couldn't have been silent. But I had seen it; I wasn't crazy, and determined to prove that to myself, I hurried the few steps from the bathroom doorway to the living room.

It was empty.

My hands lifted to grip my hair. *What the hell is wrong with me?* My heart had taken off at a full-on run now, as if it were set on running in the Boston Marathon. *I'm just tired. I'm exhausted. It was a long day. I dug up too much shit from the past. I just need to get back to sleep, and I'll feel better in—*

Another whipping gust of wind barreled against my little stone house, and although the place had been built like a fortress and could likely withstand Dorothy's tornado, the windows still rattled, and the door groaned against its hinges. I swallowed at the rising wave of nausea, threatening to spill my dinner all over the floor.

Then, from just above the stone fireplace, a framed picture of Luke and me—one of the few pictures I had in my possession—fell from the mantel. Broken glass scattered across the floor. And I swore I could smell the faint stench of cigarettes.

CHAPTER THIRTY-THREE

CONNECTICUT, AGE THIRTY-TWO

The dark circles had deepened beneath my brother's eyes over the years since he'd been locked up. Mine weren't much different. But he said nothing to me, nor did I say anything to him. Not about that anyway.

"God, I'd give anything for a fuckin' smoke," he complained, scrubbing the palms of his hands over his bristly face. "Maybe next time, you can shove some down your pants and sneak them in."

"Oh, that's a great idea," I grumbled sardonically. "Do you *want* to do more time in solitary?"

The last time my brother had been caught with a cigarette in his dorm's communal bathroom—*not* smuggled in by me—he'd been thrown into solitary confinement for a week. I hadn't been aware until I'd shown up that following Sunday to visit with him, only to find out he wasn't able to make it.

He hunkered down in his seat and rolled his eyes to the ceiling. "No," he replied with a pout. "But, man, desperate times. I haven't craved a smoke this bad in ... God, it's been years."

From the tired look in his eyes, I believed him.

I leaned back on the bench, resting my booted foot on the bar bracketed to the wall. With an inhale, my lungs filled with the stale air I had grown more and more accustomed to over the years since my brother had been at Wayward. The sour sweat and heady perfume no longer choked me the way it used to. Actually, being here, in this loud room, full of prisoners and their respective loved ones, had started to become a comfort that home no longer was.

Nobody hated me here, but outside these walls? It felt like the entire world was against me. An exaggeration, sure, but tell me if you'd feel any different when you could seldom leave your house without someone screaming obscenities in your direction ... or worse.

"You been sleeping?"

I turned from the window to look at my brother. "What do you think?"

"You should talk to someone."

"Why do I need someone else when I have you?" I lifted the corner of my mouth to offer a teasing smirk, but it was forced, and he knew it.

"Whatever happened to that doctor you used to see? What was her name?"

"Dr. Sibilia."

Luke pursed his lips and nodded. "Right, yeah, her. Why don't you talk to her?"

I cocked my head. "And what is it you think she'll do for me?"

He lifted one shoulder in a shrug. "I dunno. She could help—"

"What? Is she gonna miraculously get you out of here? Or do you think she can somehow do something to make the Wheelers stop their shit?"

"No, but maybe she can—"

"*Talking* to someone isn't going to make shit go away. It's not going to make life easier; it's not going to make me happier. So, I'm just getting by, from one week to another, and that's all there is. Isn't that what you used to do? *Get by*?"

My brother folded his arms on the table and looked off to the side. He glanced at another one of the prisoners—a guy he had once mentioned was named Wolf or Dog or something stupid like that—and lifted his chin in an acknowledging nod. Then, Luke looked away and let that friendliness drop from his face.

"That's why I mentioned talking to someone. You're keeping all this shit locked up inside, and it can't be good for you, man. You don't do anything, you don't go anywhere, you don't—"

"Where the hell am I going to go?" I laughed, incredulous. "I can barely go grocery shopping without the cashier giving me a fucking *look*. Like, *Oh, there's Charlie Corbin, whose brother is the reason why poor old Ritchie Wheeler isn't here anymore*. I don't think you completely understand what it's like—"

"Oh, right. Sure. Because you don't tell me all the time." He glowered at me.

But he was wrong. He didn't know everything. I'd made it a point to keep some of it to myself, just to keep him from feeling too bad about the situation he'd left me to deal with.

Still, I continued, "They don't *talk* to me, Luke. They don't make eye contact. They barely even look in my direction. They treat me like, like—"

"Like the brother of a murderer," he finished for me, an air of exhaustion in his tone, like he was sick of having this conversation. "I got it. I just wish you'd do something more to stand up for yourself. Even if you're not gonna throw fuckin' bricks at Tommy's car—"

"Oh, great idea. They could get me on destruction of property."

Luke groaned and went on, ignoring my sarcasm. "You need to do *something*. You need to take care of yourself. What the hell are you gonna do for the rest of your life, huh? I'm not around anymore to push you, and I'm not around to protect you. You gotta learn to stand up for yourself, even if that means ignoring their shit for the sake of living your goddamn life. Ignore them, and they'll learn to ignore you."

I pressed my lips together and dropped my gaze to the tabletop. Luke hadn't been home in two years. Twice a month for the entirety of that two years, I'd made the trek up to Wayward Correctional Facility, and nearly every time I had seen him, the conversation had steered in this direction.

He had said they'd eventually move on.

He had said they'd grow bored.

But it seemed to me that, the more I kept to myself and didn't retaliate, the worse their attacks got.

Hell, just this past week, Tommy Wheeler had stabbed a crudely made wooden cross with his brother's name painted on it into the center of my front yard. He had waited for me to step outside to shout, "You helped to kill him by fucking *existing*," before spitting on the grass and storming back down the street toward his mother's house.

I called the cops, and they came to slap Tommy on the wrist. They encouraged me once again to file for a restraining order, to which I said I'd think about it, and I'd meant it. But the truth was, I had grown to be terrified of Tommy Wheeler. Maybe even more so than I'd ever been of his cold, nasty older brother, and I was worried a restraining order would only piss him off even more and push him over the edge.

Luke didn't know any of this.

I swallowed the urge to tell him and instead asked, "So, how's your job in the laundry room treating you?"

CHAPTER THIRTY-FOUR

MASSACHUSETTS, PRESENT DAY

When Stormy woke up to find the broken picture on the kitchen island, I told her I had accidentally knocked it off the mantel while doing some middle-of-the-night dusting when I couldn't sleep.

And for the record, I hadn't lied because there was a possibility she'd think I was crazy; I'd lied because I was starting to believe it was true. That I'd officially, finally gone insane—and I was scared.

Luke had said once, sometime after he was locked up, that it took a real man to admit his fear, and this was my confession: I was horribly and truly terrified.

Stormy noticed right away.

"You okay?" She lifted her coffee mug to her lips, eyeing me over the brim with concern and confusion.

My arms folded tightly over my chest as I shrugged and nodded. "Yeah. Why?"

Her dark brows lowered over her eyes as she took a sip, then held the mug to her chest as she replied, "You seem weird. Like ... tense."

My eyes darted toward the broken picture frame. The glass had marred the photograph of Luke and me—one taken by Melanie during one of his earlier stints with sobriety—leaving half of his face untouched while the other was scraped to hell. It had broken my heart to find it'd been destroyed when it was one of the few pictures I had left, and beyond the heartbreak, there'd been the terror of how exactly I was meant to interpret this message—or if it was a message at all.

Stormy followed my gaze and let go of a forlorn sigh. "It sucks that it was ruined," she said, reading my mind. "You know, people do some crazy shit with Photoshop. Maybe we can find someone who can fix it up and print out a new one."

"Yeah. Maybe." I nodded, appreciating the thought.

"I can ask around the shop. I mean, Cee's man—you know, Shane—is a hotshot editor for *ModInk*. He probably knows someone with some serious Photoshop skills."

ModInk—as I'd learned at dinner with Stormy, her coworkers, and their significant others—was one of the top magazines in the tattoo, piercing, and body modification world. I'd never heard of it personally, but I also had no reason to. Magazines weren't my thing, and body modification wasn't either. Still, I'd found it impressive that Cee's husband was so successful, and I was grateful for Stormy's possible connections and dedication to having the photograph restored.

"I'd really appreciate that," I said, unwinding my arms to press my hand on the small of her back. I kissed her forehead and breathed in the scent of her hair, allowing the faintest touch of lavender to curl around my mind and calm my soul. "Sorry I'm off this morning. I just didn't sleep well, and …" I huffed and looked once again toward the picture. "I don't know."

It was the truth; I didn't know. Something seemed off, strange, and that sense of intuition was now heightened. The world felt like it had been set off its axis and was about to roll toward something unknown and terrifying.

"Maybe it'll actually do you some good to get out of here for a few days," she suggested, lifting her hand to press her palm to my chest.

I hoped she couldn't feel how frantic my heart was beating, out of fear and helpless panic. I hoped that, instead, she could tell that it was no longer mine, but hers and that, at some point along the way, it had ceased its normal thumping rhythm to only beat to the sound of her name.

"You kinda look like you've seen a ghost."

The statement locked every one of my vertebrae in place as I recalled the intruder I'd chased after not long ago. God, how had it not crossed my mind sooner that my run through the headstones might've been in pursuit of a ghost and not a man?

Because I've never seen one before, I told myself, remembering the blurred image of a man on Max's security camera. Remembering the hooded figure in a leather jacket, sending spirals of exhaled smoke into the air. He had run from me, yes, but maybe he'd never meant for me to see him to begin with. Maybe he was only meant to torment me from afar, to haunt me in death as he had in life because what if … God, what if …

What if the one to leave the mementos at my door was Tommy Wheeler?

***

The time passed by without any other paranormal incidents … or maybe it was that I'd been looking for them. Every day while making my rounds, every corner I turned, every bush or tree I passed by, I was looking for the scent of cigarettes and a hooded man wearing a leather jacket. Every night, I'd listen for the howling wind and the creaks, squeaks, and bumps in the walls and floorboards. And nothing happened. But I remembered all the incidents before had been accompanied by the element of surprise. Now, I was ready. Now, I was smart. But the spirit was smarter, craftier, and …

Good God, I was almost certain I had lost my mind.

Max had stopped by on a few different occasions to assure me that he hadn't seen any other trespassers on the cemetery grounds. I never had the heart to tell him what we were looking for wasn't someone of this realm but the next. He was a nice guy, and while I was sure he'd seen his fair share of questionable, possibly creepy shit while working in a graveyard, I wasn't going to be the reason he had nightmares.

It was bad enough sleep had become nearly nonexistent for me.

But at least there was Stormy, and she still hadn't run. Even as I sat, slumped with my back against the headboard, a hand over my exhausted eyes, while she stuffed an extended weekend's worth of clothes into a couple of overnight bags, she was still here.

"You're so tired," she observed sympathetically. "Why don't you take a nap before we hit the road? We're not leaving for a few hours, and honestly, it won't take us long to get there in the first place. If you want—"

"No, it's okay." I dropped my hand to my bent knee and offered her a weak smile. "I'll sleep when we get to your parents' house."

Truthfully, I wasn't so sure about that either. Being at her parents' place meant being in Connecticut, and just the thought of being within a few hours of the scene of all our crimes—Luke's and mine combined—was enough to keep me awake for days.

Trust me, I would know.

She eyed me skeptically, and I knew she didn't believe me. "You know, sometimes, when I can't sleep, I take some melatonin," she said, folding a shirt and tucking it into one bag. "I mean, back in the day, I'd suck down a bottle of tequila or pop a couple of pills, and that'd *really* do the trick. But melatonin works better than nothing."

I studied her skeptically and folded my arms over my knees. "How do you do that?"

Her lips—unpainted today, but just as beautiful and tempting—curved in a smile. "Do what?"

"Make light of your demons."

The smile faded as she hummed a gentle sound. Then, she shrugged. "I don't know. I guess because they're not really mine anymore. They're in the past. I'm more than ten years sober."

"The past can haunt us just as well as anything else, if not better," I countered, not meaning to argue, but wanting to offer another perspective. One in which the past was incapable of remaining where it belonged. "It is, after all, by nature, full of ghosts."

"That's true. But I made the conscious decision to leave my demons where they belong, and that's that."

It was my turn to grunt a sound as I nodded. "I don't think I'm that strong," I admitted in a tone flatter than the floor she stood on, challenging her as much as myself.

"I think you are," she replied without hesitation. "I think you're as strong as you allow yourself to be."

"Oh, so you think it's my fault I can't let shit go?" I tilted my head, glaring at her with a dare to continue.

She dropped her gaze to the sweater in her hands and sucked in a deep breath, thinking before continuing. Then, she carefully said, "No ... *but* I think you've spent a really long time believing you can't do anything about it."

"I *did* do something about it," I countered. "I fucking *ran*. And guess what. They're still up here." I tapped my temple with a sardonic smirk even though I knew better. My demons weren't just living in my head; they were in my fucking house.

Stormy clenched her jaw and focused on the sweater, aggressively stuffing it into the bag, unfolded. She stepped over the clothes scattered over the bedroom floor and climbed onto the bed to crawl on her hands and knees until her palms gripped my knees and her eyes bored into mine.

"Maybe instead of running, you need to look those fucking bastards in the eye and tell them to leave you the fuck alone."

She pulled my knees apart, flattening my bent legs to the mattress until she had the room to climb onto my lap. Wrapping her legs around my waist and cradling my face in her hands. My forehead fell against hers as my lids drifted shut, my lungs emptying and my hands holding tight to her crazy nest of hair.

"I'm so fucking tired," I admitted, the weary agony dragging my voice down to a whisper.

"Then, stop running away from the monsters that keep chasing you. They'll always catch up—always." Her featherlight touch soothed the lines beneath my eyes and the tension at my temples. "Don't show them your weaknesses, and they won't have anything to feed on. Stare them down and prove you're stronger than they are."

"You make that sound so easy."

"It's not. And sometimes, they'll get the better of you. But you're not alone anymore, Charlie. You realize that, right? You're not alone. And anytime you feel like running, anytime you want to hide, you tell me. I don't run, not anymore, and I won't let you either."

"The right woman won't run away."

I swallowed repeatedly at the emotion and pain clotting in my throat as I sent a thought out into the night.

"I found her, Luke. I found her, just as you always said I would."

"You just tell me what I'm fighting against, Charlie, and I'll go into battle with you."

I folded my arms around her tight and buried my face against her neck. I held on and swore to every part of my being that I'd tell her everything soon. But not yet. For now, I held her, pressing my lips to her neck over and over and over again, and with every one, I passed along the message that *I found her, I found her, I found her,* but ... no.

I hadn't found her.

She had found me.

And I was so, so tired of *running*.

CHAPTER THIRTY-FIVE

CONNECTICUT, PRESENT DAY

In the passenger seat, I kept my eyes on the painted lines zipping by, never on the passing road signs, and tried to remember the last time I'd celebrated Thanksgiving … or any holiday for that matter.

I spoke out loud, rambling needlessly to Stormy about childhood celebrations and how Melanie had tried to keep things special in the years after my parents died. It was all I could do to keep my brain from fixating on how close we were to crossing the state line.

And Stormy listened to every word, never once changing the subject. Only asking the occasional question to keep me talking, distracted and focused.

"Wasn't Melanie, like, your brother's age?"

I nodded, running my finger along the window ledge. "Three years older than me, yeah."

"And how old were you when your parents passed away?"

"Fifteen." Twenty-three years ago. God. How had I managed to survive a day without them, let alone over two fucking decades?

"So, this eighteen-year-old girl moved into your house, cooked, cleaned, cared for you guys, and made sure you continued to celebrate holidays?" Her voice hung on an astonishment I'd felt steadily ever since I'd let go of my stupid teenage angst and distaste toward my brother's former girlfriend and fiancée.

I nodded slowly, easily allowing the ache of missing Melanie to cloud my vision of the dashes painted onto the road. "Yep."

"What the hell was she trying to do, apply for sainthood?"

"Something like that," I muttered, then chuckled and lifted my hand in a flippant shrug. "I don't know. I never understood it. She always said it was because she loved Luke so damn much, but I don't know. Sometimes, I thought she just liked having a project, and with us, she had two of them—three if you count the house. But ... I don't know. Maybe she just felt bad for us."

"Or maybe she really did love you guys," Stormy offered softly, "and she knew she could care for you better than you'd manage on your own."

My gaze lifted to the blurred trees lining the side of the road, topped by a cloudy gray November sky. Melanie had passed my mind often over the years—that went without saying—but it'd been a long time since her memory had brought a twinge of a smile to my lips, a lump in my throat, and more gratitude in my heart than sadness.

"You're probably right."

"I wish I could meet her."

That brought a laugh rumbling past the rock lodged in my throat. "Yeah, well, unfortunately ..." I shook my head as the sadness overcame the gratitude.

"You think they would've gotten married if things had been different?"

My lungs filled with air and held it tight. "I do."

Stormy swallowed audibly, and I chanced a glance in her direction to find the same pain in my heart reflected in her eyes. "It's so sad that they could never work it out. I mean, I get it. I was really fucked up back in the day, and I know there was no way I could have had a decent, healthy relationship. But ... it just *sucks*. Like, you have to think, how different would everything have been if it had worked out between them?"

"I don't like to," I answered, brusque and gruff. "Not anymore."

She pressed her lips together and held the wheel tight within her grip. Her emerald eyes volleyed toward mine quickly.

"Oh, no?" she asked, her voice hovering below the nothing-but-white-noise music.

I gave my head a small shake, but unable to say that, if anything had been different, I wouldn't have run from Connecticut and my ever-persistent demons. That, if Luke and Melanie had never broken up, it was unlikely I would've found myself in Salem. That, if any of the tragedies in my life hadn't occurred, it was unlikely that Stormy ever would've been mine.

I never would've been hers.

Somehow, I managed to reach a point where that thought was more devastating than the nightmares that still haunted the otherwise wonderful and dreamless sleep I only ever achieved when I was with her. In the month that I'd known her, she had taken this shattered soul, this broken shadow of a man, and by some miracle, she'd put him back together. And, okay, maybe what was left more resembled Frankenstein's monster than what he had once been at the hour of his birth, but he was *whole*. Me! Whole. Happy.

I chuckled at the thought, but wasn't it true?

"Why are you laughing?" Stormy asked, eyeing me suspiciously from across the car.

My gaze landed on hers as my lips stretched in a smile that all at once felt awkward and weird and right and amazing. "I don't know. I'm just …" I shrugged one shoulder, tipping my head back to rest against the seat. Still staring at her. Still amazed. "I'm happy."

Her black lips lifted in an easy smile that looked so much more natural than mine felt. "Do *I* make you happy?"

"More than anything."

A small, acknowledging sound rose from her throat as she nodded, glancing at the road before looking back at me. "You make me happy too."

Then, marry me.

The thought came out of nowhere, an echo running through my head, yet it didn't freak me out the way it probably should've. No, I knew without a fraction of a doubt that I would make her my wife if I only found the courage to ask. Luke might consider that insane; others probably would too. But I never pretended to be sane, and I didn't care.

She was the one who would never run, and with a glance at the side of the road, I found she was also the one who could take me across the Connecticut state line without my body revolting with panic. I was going to do this. I was going to be okay. And I knew that was only because I was safe.

I knew it was because I was *hers*.

***

Stormy had grown up far enough away from where I had for my familiarity with the area to have blurred over time. It was my favorite thing about her childhood home.

That and the cemetery across the street.

When we pulled onto her street and my eyes landed on the hallowed ground, Stormy smiled and nudged my wrist with her knuckles.

"Makes you feel more at home, right?"

I huffed a chuckle. "A little, yeah. I'm wondering why you're so creeped out now when you grew up across the street from a graveyard."

"Are you kidding me?" She threw her arm across me and pointed out the passenger window. "This shit gave me fucking nightmares. My friends used to dare me to sneak in there at night—"

"Oh, you were one of *those*," I cut in with a snicker.

"Come on. You know I was," she tossed back. "And for the record, I only did it once and actually pissed in my pants after a rabbit scared the hell out of me. My friends never let me live that down."

I hummed a short, contemplative sound. Wondering where those friends were now. Wondering if she still knew them. But I didn't bother asking because just as I was about to open my mouth, we pulled into the driveway of a narrow, two-story farmhouse-style home with a pretty porch, painted a sunshiny yellow. Not my style, but it was welcoming, friendly, and I hoped the people inside matched their home's facade.

Stormy killed the engine and turned to face me. "You ready?"

"Nope," I answered with an incredulous huff-laugh.

"They won't bite."

But you ran, I wanted to say. *How gentle could they be if you didn't want to stay?*

But, I reminded myself, she had left home over ten years ago. Surely, things had changed, and maybe if she hadn't found a second family with Blake and Cee, she would've returned home. Maybe she still would one day, but I hoped she wouldn't.

Would I come with her if she did?

My stomach cramped at the thought.

"My sister and her kids aren't going to be here until tomorrow," Stormy reminded me. "Tonight, it's just my parents. One step at a time, okay? You let me know if it becomes too much, and we'll get some air."

I sucked in a deep breath and nodded. "Okay," I said, followed by an exhale.

We left the car together and climbed the creaking porch steps as Stormy informed me that she had lived in one of the nicer neighborhoods in town. Just a few blocks over was the high school, where she'd watched her old friend take his last breath. I had a difficult time understanding how she could so easily call that guy—Billy—her friend when he had gotten her involved in the dangerous, scary things a real friend should've protected her from. But then I remembered how important it had been for Luke to watch me to consume the vile taste of beer on my twenty-first birthday, and I kept my mouth shut.

Stormy rapped her fist loudly against the door. "I'm learning to knock louder," she said with a hint of pride.

"Smart."

"We used to have a doorbell, back when I was a kid. But then the thing kicked the bucket, and my dad never got around to fixing it for whatever reason," she explained quietly, like she didn't want to talk over the anticipated footsteps on the other side of the door.

I was reminded of the disrepair my childhood home had succumbed to in the years after my parents died.

Those footsteps came moments later. I stood up straighter, unblinking, unsure if I should put my hands in my pockets or rest one at the small of Stormy's back and did neither. They flexed at my sides instead. I clamped my bottom lip between my teeth and worried it, the patches of dry, peeling skin a futile distraction from the jittering in my veins and the inability to pull in a deep breath of air. The lock was undone, and the door swung open to unveil a man on the other side, sporting dark hair abundantly peppered with gray. Before his eyes could land on his daughter, they roved over me with a curious suspicion that teetered dangerously toward distrust. I swallowed hard, instantly sure that every one of my fears had been warranted.

Told you so, I wanted to say to Stormy, but didn't. Instead, I said nothing at all.

"Hey, Dad," Stormy said, stepping into his line of sight, her arms outstretched.

A switch was flipped, and his scowl transformed into a smile. "Ah, there's my little black rain cloud." He wrapped her in an embrace, resting his chin on her shoulder. "How was the drive down?"

"Uneventful."

"That's what I like to hear."

A hot rush of envy smacked my heart. My gaze dropped to the bleached wooden planks beneath my feet as my mind tried desperately to conjure up the memory of what it had been like to hug my dad. Tiny fragments of moments attempted to fuse together, but I was unsure if any had happened at all, and I hated that I'd allowed time to steal them away. I hadn't known it was happening, hadn't fought to keep those memories I'd thought were so important. How important could they have been if I hadn't even tried to hold on to them?

My chest puffed up with an angry breath; I was so mad that I couldn't drive down that damn highway and knock on my own father's door. So fucking mad that it'd been over two decades since I'd last hugged him. So completely and utterly mad and swept up in grief that would never fully go away that I nearly forgot where I was and barely heard Stormy making the introductions between her father and me.

"... Charlie Corbin."

I came back to the moment as she placed her hand on my arm and turned to look up at me, her smile wide and proud.

Shit. I quickly extended my hand and said, "Hello, sir. It's nice to meet you."

"Please, call me Chris." The nicety didn't quite reach his tone though, even as he clasped my hand in his.

We shook, and I looked right into his skeptical glare. *Does he know?*

A trickle of ice slithered down my spine. It was possible. Stormy might not have been around when Luke had murdered Ritchie, but her parents had. They'd never left Connecticut. They'd been here, paying attention to the news and talking to the locals. Maybe he recognized my face and knew my name, and he was now wondering how the hell to save his daughter from the Corbin curse.

He dropped my hand, then gestured into the house. "Come on in. Take your coats off, make yourselves at home. Mom's about to pull some cookies out of the oven. Miles has been going on and on and on about these peanut butter ones he had last time he was here. You should've seen him. He ..." His voice trailed off as he wandered through the door and disappeared quickly into the house, as if assuming we were on his tail.

But we stopped inside the door, shedding our jackets and hanging them on a coatrack.

"Should we ..." I waved toward the doorway he'd wandered through, and Stormy brushed me off with a flippant gesture of her hand.

"Nah, it's fine. He's just babbling about my nephew, my sister's youngest. My dad is obsessed with that kid. Like, I mean, *obsessed*."

I huffed a laugh I didn't quite feel as I stuffed my hands into my jeans pockets. "Well, I don't think he likes me very much," I commented. My voice sounded bitter. I regretted that immediately. "I mean, it's fine. I just—"

"It's nothing personal," she was quick to say, regret blanketing her features. "You gotta understand, the last guy I brought home to meet my parents was strung out on drugs. Granted, that was, like, fifteen years ago, but they know about as much about my love life as they do my career. Which is next to nothing. And, yeah, I guess that's my own fault, but …" She sucked in a deep breath and shook her head. "Anyway, don't take it personally. They're going to like you, I swear. The bar was already set pretty low. As long as you don't describe our sex life in explicit detail before passing out on the couch, you're as good as golden."

I raised one brow at her. "Sounds like a real winner."

"Yeah, well." She offered a half smile while a spark of sadness struck her gaze before spinning on her heel and leading the way through the foyer. Then, looking over her shoulder, she added, "Just remember, you're the one standing here, and he's buried across the street."

"Well, now, I feel like an asshole," I muttered regretfully, following close behind.

"I'm just saying, I chose the path that brought me to you, not him. So, as far as I'm concerned, you're the real winner here. Because I'm a fucking prize."

She grinned like it was a joke, like maybe she was poking fun at the woman she used to be. The woman who'd brought home a guy she got wasted with. But that wasn't who she was, not at her core. She'd gotten out of that life and into the one that brought her to me, as she'd said, and for that, I had to agree with her.

She *was* a prize. The greatest of them all. And somehow, for once, I could consider myself a winner because I could call her mine.

CHAPTER THIRTY-SIX

CONNECTICUT, PRESENT DAY

While Chris had been a little more on the skeptical side, Barbara—Stormy's mother—welcomed me into her home with arms wide, wide open. The moment I stepped into her kitchen, smelling cookies and fresh bread and apple pie, she wrapped me in a hug that made my heart weep and my lungs heave with an excruciatingly forlorn sigh.

God, how I missed my mother, and Barbara reminded me of her instantly. Full of love and laughter and acceptance, not at all batting a lash at my long hair or the webbed tattoos encasing my exposed hands and forearms. I supposed that probably had something to do with the type of guy she'd expect her body-piercer daughter to bring home to meet the parents. But it touched me all the same, and I knew immediately that I'd hit the jackpot when I walked through that front door.

"God, Stormy, when was the last time you brought a boy home?" Barbara asked, as if I wasn't a man staring directly toward middle age. "It's been forever."

Stormy's cheeks reddened beneath the pleasant, warm lighting as her eyes volleyed quickly toward me. "Um, I—"

"Billy, wasn't it?" Chris chimed in, a sour distaste forming the refreshed scowl on his face. He shook his head. "That guy was such a—"

"Chris." Barbara didn't look at all pleased. "We're not going to talk about that. We *don't* talk about that."

"You brought it up," he pointed out.

"It was a rhetorical question," she fired back, raising her brows and daring him with a look to continue.

He didn't.

She sucked in a breath and turned back to her daughter, satisfied. "I'm so glad that you two could make it for Thanksgiving. You must be pretty special for Stormy to want you here, Charlie," she said. "And I hope you like cookies 'cause"—she swept a gesture across the island, littered with full baking sheets—"I made a lot."

A memory came forward, one I had forgotten I'd even had until this moment. Mom baking cookies for Christmas. Rolling out the dough on the dining room table. Dumping out a big Tupperware of cookie cutters. Holding my hand as we pressed each cutter into the sticky, flattened sheet. The kitchen filling with the warm, sweet scent of sugar cookies baking, then us decorating them once they were cooled. I could remember the way they'd tasted and how much we'd enjoyed making them.

My lungs deflated, and my heart ached, but I looked up at Stormy's mother and offered a genuine smile. "I love cookies."

***

Dinner was a couple of delivered pizzas. I was surprisingly grateful for that. It had been way too long since I'd eaten Connecticut pizza, which was arguably better than that in the Salem area. Or maybe it was just that it tasted like home and things I missed, but could never have again.

"So, Stormy, how're things at the office?" Chris asked, wiping his fingers on a paper napkin after polishing off another slice. "Poke any interesting holes in anyone lately?"

The woman at my side grinned around a bite of pepperoni pizza and swallowed. "Things are good. Can't say any holes are interesting at this point, but …" Then, she sat higher in her seat, excitedly raising her brows. "Actually, there was this guy who came in, wanting a set of dermals in the shape of Cassiopeia. You know, the constellation? Apparently, that's the name of his daughter. And I thought it was really sweet."

I cocked my head, envisioning the design done in sparkling jewels against someone's skin. "That *is* ni—"

"What are dermals?" Barbara asked.

Stormy seemed eager to explain as she leaned forward in her chair, planting her elbows on the table. "I'll spare you the gory details. But basically, it's a piercing that's implanted beneath the surface of the skin. It's anchored in by a piece of metal that looks like a foot, and—"

Barbara looked absolutely disgusted, her nose scrunching and her mouth frowning. "*Anchored in?*"

"Well, what I do is punch a little hole into the skin and slip the foot under the skin. The skin then heals around it, growing through the little holes in the metal to—"

"Oh God." Barbara waved her hands frantically. "Nope. I don't want to know any more."

Stormy wilted at my side, her shoulders slumping. Her parents might not have noticed the subtle changes in her demeanor, but I did. "I mean, you asked …"

"I don't know how you can do that for a living," her mother went on, shaking her head and pushing her plate away. "I'll never understand how you can inflict pain on someone in exchange for money. I mean, it's messed up enough to want that done to yourself, but to be the one to do it? I'll never understand."

Stormy pressed her lips shut, clamming up instead of defending herself. My gaze swept from her—now picking at a slice of pepperoni, peeling its edges off the cheese with the tip of her black fingernail—to her mother, who was lifting her glass of water to her lips with a shake of her head.

I understood that it was a common thing for parents to disapprove of the choices their kids made, and I understood that Barbara's chastising had come from her heart, only wanting what was best for her daughter— even if the execution had been brash and uncalled for.

But Stormy had also told me the reasons why she'd left Connecticut. That not only had her youth been misguided, but her parents hadn't given her the acceptance she needed to thrive in their environment. It lit a match beneath my skin's surface to watch her—a strong, confident, and outspoken woman—transform into an ashamed and withered version of herself in the presence of her parents. Like she'd never stopped being that girl, wishing for their approval—and why shouldn't she have it? She'd made a name for herself. She'd crawled out of the filthy hole of addiction and God knew what else and found the light of day, and her mother had the gall to criticize?

Without another thought, I opened my mouth. "When I was eight years old, my brother's best friend cornered me in the school bathroom. He threw my backpack into the urinal and then proceeded to piss all over it. He was eleven years old, old enough to know better, and it wasn't even the first time he'd done something like that. Even though my mom never knew it was he who did all this messed-up shit to me, she knew I was horribly bullied for simply being myself. It was around that point when she pulled me out of school and taught me herself."

I took a moment to breathe, offering a pause to my story to find that every pair of eyes around the table was now on me. The realization that I was center stage and speaking my mind to an audience of people I barely knew—with the exception of Stormy—sent my heart off at a gallop. But I wasn't going to back down now, not when I was proving a point for her, so I trudged onward.

"My mom always encouraged me to be who I was, no matter what that might be. Even if it wasn't what she envisioned, which I'm sure it never was. Now, my parents have both been dead for a long time, but I'd like to think that, if they were still alive, they'd be proud of me for whatever the hell it was I was doing with my life. Because at least I'm doing *something* to make an honest living."

From the corner of my eye, I spotted Stormy's sidelong glance and the gentle lift to one side of her mouth. Her palm slid over my thigh, where she found my hand and her fingers interlocked with mine.

"And what is it that you do?" Chris asked in a monotone.

"I'm the caretaker at a cemetery just outside of Salem," I replied, holding my head high.

"Do you think that's what your parents would've wanted for you?" he asked without malice, only genuine curiosity.

I lifted and dropped one shoulder in a shrug. "Frankly, sir, I don't think it matters either way. A parent's job is only to make sure that kid becomes a good person, not to dictate every one of their life's decisions."

Chris folded his hands on the table and tipped his head with intrigue. "Do you think you're a good person?"

"Dad! Seriously?"

"What?" Her father shrugged. "It's an honest question."

Stormy's hand tightened around mine, her nails piercing my flesh. I didn't flinch at the sharp dose of pain. Her father was challenging me, sizing me up. He wanted to know if his daughter's taste in men had truly changed all that much in the past fifteen years. Could I blame him? Wouldn't I have done the same thing if I had a daughter with a history of self-destruction? It didn't matter that she was in her mid-thirties. It didn't matter that she had been on her own for over a decade. They would *always* be her parents, she would *always* be their child, and they would *always* be concerned for her well-being. I couldn't fault them for that any more than I could honestly say I was a good person.

"I don't know," I replied, holding his firm gaze.

His brow lowered with suspicion. "You don't know?"

Stormy's grip loosened. Her thumb stroked lightly over mine, and I could almost feel that featherlight touch through the barrage of reasons why I didn't think I was a truly good person at all. No, I wanted to be. I wanted to believe I was. But want wasn't the same as truly *being*.

A good man didn't abandon his older brother. A good man didn't have blood on his hands. But I did. I had walked away. I had stolen a life. I'd the choice to do things differently, but I hadn't. And knowing I'd been capable of it at all only told me I could do it again. So, how was I supposed to look into this man's eyes and tell him I was worthy of his blessing?

Fuck, why am I even here?

"No," I replied, my voice rough like sandpaper and my heart sinking like an anchor to my gut. "I don't know."

"Hmm." Chris raised his folded hands, rubbing the side of his finger against his bottom lip. "Well, would you like to know what I think?"

I wasn't sure that I did, but I lifted my chin anyway. Ready to listen to this man's assessment of my character after knowing me for a total of three hours.

"I—"

"You know what? This is stupid," Stormy interrupted in a tight, quavering voice, removing her hand from mine and pushing away from the table. "I thought it'd be a good idea to bring Charlie to meet you guys. I thought you'd like to see that I had finally, for once in my life, found a decent guy who actually likes being with me and treats me well and cooks and cleans and doesn't waste his time getting fucking high. But I guess I was wrong."

She stood and was already heading for the dining room doorway when her father spoke up. "Stormy, if you'd let me finish—"

"Dad, why did you even have to *start*?" She spun on her heel to face him. "You were already giving him the third degree before he even said anything to you. And, Mom," she went on, turning to face her stunned mother, whose eyes were misting with tears and her mouth parted with shock and despair, "all Charlie was saying was, maybe it'd be nice to support me once in a while. Like, maybe it'd be nice to just ... be happy that I'm happy. You know? Would that kill either of you?" She left the room then, her heavy platform boots clomping loudly against the floorboards as she moved through the living room and toward the front door.

God, what the hell is happening?

My gaze fell to the half-eaten slice of pizza on my plate as I remembered what Stormy had said about her parents not that long ago. About how she loved them dearly but needed the distance to keep the peace. I understood that now. How quickly it had all unfolded ...

was that my fault? Yes, maybe, but also, no. Their wounds ran deeper than my hurried attempt to defend her career.

I lifted my head to look from her mother to her father, both seeming troubled and lost. *How can they not thank God every fucking day that their daughter hadn't faced the same fate as her friend, buried across the street?*

My teeth dragged over my bottom lip as I exhaled deeply and shook my head. People never learned. They never knew what they had until it was gone—it was a common phrase for a reason—and nothing I could say was going to change that. Except ...

"I might not know if I'm a good man," I said, slowly rising from my chair. Her parents both startled at the sound of my voice and looked at me with wide-eyed acknowledgment. "But I do know that she's the greatest woman I've ever known. God smiled at me for maybe the first time in my life when He sent her my way. And I know you think it's your job to want better for her, but ..." I released my breath and pushed the chair back in, hardly able to understand how I was capable of speaking to them in this way, defending her without a hint of weakness when I'd never been capable of defending myself. "I pray every single day that she never agrees, even though she probably should. Because if anything could convince me that I'm a good man, it's knowing that she, for some reason, thinks that I am."

I didn't wait for them to speak as I turned and went in search of Stormy. Hardly able to hear my footsteps over the thundering of my heart.

***

She was on the darkened porch, leaning against a wooden post. Her breath came out in short, angry puffs of silver, fading into the cold night.

"Are you all right?" I asked, quietly closing the door behind me.

"Well, I'd fuckin' kill for a smoke, but …" She sighed and rubbed her hands vigorously over her exposed forearms. "Yeah. Well, I mean, I will be, eventually. I just …" Her sorrowful gaze swung toward mine. "I'm sorry."

Taken aback, I narrowed my gaze while I undid the buttons of my shirt. "The hell are you sorry for?"

Her weak smile didn't quite touch her eyes as she huffed a bitter laugh and thrust a hand toward the house. "For *this*. For telling you it'd be fine here. I mean, in fairness, it usually is. I don't always argue with my parents. But"—she released a long-winded sigh as I laid the shirt over her shoulders—"my sister is usually here with her kids, and the focus isn't on me, and my parents just freakin' *love* my brother-in-law. Which is a fucking joke, considering the dude has done major time and—"

"Your brother-in-law was in prison?" I hadn't expected that after the judgment her father had over me.

Stormy rolled her eyes and nodded. "Yeah. And that's …" Her eyes flitted to the cemetery across the street, now blanketed in darkness. "That's a whole other thing. But anyway, he's not a bad guy at all. I like him a lot. And it's because of him that my sister and nephew are even alive, so really, I owe him."

There was so much I didn't know about her family. In the past three minutes, she had unloaded a few facts that frayed with countless curiosities and questions. And it made me wonder. If she had told me so little about her family, just how little had they known about me? She had told me she loved her family, and I believed her. But she had also said her relationship was strained, and I was beginning to understand just how far that road traveled in both ways.

"Maybe you should talk to them," I said, standing at her back and bringing my hands to her shoulders. Absentmindedly rubbing out the tension she held there while wishing I could call my own parents and tell them everything there was to know about her.

"You saw what happens when I try to talk to them."

My mouth lifted in a smile. "I'm not sure I'd call that talking."

"Excuse me. My mom asked a question, and I tried to explain before she cut me off and disrespected me and my job. Then, you cut in, which I did appreciate, and my father proceeded to disrespect *you*. So, forgive me for not wanting to go back in there and have a fucking heart-to-heart with them but—"

She was cut off by the door opening behind us, and we turned our heads to watch as her parents came outside to join us. Her mother in a thick sweater, her father, in a coat. They'd come more prepared to weather the night's chill, and that told me they'd likely come prepared in other ways as well.

"Stormy," Chris said before clearing his throat. "We want to apologize."

My heart suddenly felt lighter at the sincerity in her father's tone. Barbara stood closer to her husband and nodded in agreement.

"We're both sorry," she said. "It's just always been like this with us. You know we love you—"

"I know," Stormy replied quietly, dipping her chin to her chest. I held her shoulders tighter.

Barbara inhaled through her nose, the sound shaky, as if she might cry. "We've just never been great at communicating, and we've never been great at accepting that you've …"

She was quiet for a moment, as though struggling to find the words she wanted, when Chris added, "Grown up."

"Yes," Barbara said, nodding. "But we want to do better. We *will* do better."

When it was clear her parents had nothing left to say, Stormy nodded and replied, "I mean, it's not like I can say I've been all that great at talking to you guys, so …"

"That's on us," Chris said.

Stormy shrugged. "Honestly, it's probably on all of us."

"Well then, let's all make a promise to try, okay?" Barbara said, her voice tight with determination and emotion.

Stormy sucked in a deep breath before nodding. "Okay."

"And we want you to know that we *are* proud of you," Chris added quickly, like he'd been waiting to say it.

"Thanks, Dad."

"Even if we don't completely understand—"

"Yeah. I know. You don't have to understand; it's fine."

Chris reached out cautiously to touch his daughter's hand with his fingertips, almost like he didn't quite know how much was too much. Then, the two of them turned, ready to head back inside. Her mother opened the door, crossed the threshold, but her father hesitated.

"Oh, and, Charlie," he said, meeting my eye. "I don't know what your story is. I hope you'll tell us one day. But for whatever it's worth, I think it takes a good man to stand up for the people he cares about. And I think your parents would've been really proud of you for that."

***

We finished getting ready for bed in the guest room that had been Stormy's childhood bedroom. For the first night in weeks, we didn't conclude our day with sex. I didn't initiate, and when she didn't either, I assumed she was just uncomfortable with the idea of her parents' room being just down the hall. When we cuddled together, her back to my chest, she confirmed as much in different words.

"The last time I had a guy in this house, my mom walked in on us fucking in the bathroom," she admitted quietly.

I didn't like the idea of her fucking someone else here. Hell, I didn't particularly like the idea of her fucking someone else at all.

"And if that wasn't bad enough, later that night, my dad walked in on us going at it again in here."

My lips pressed together as a humiliating wave of jealousy steamrolled over me. I had shared a bed with this woman every single night for weeks, and I had been at least somewhat aware of her colorful and relatively promiscuous past. But hearing about it now made me feel disgusting on various levels. I tried to remember that I was a grown man with a past of my own, and it helped to calm the envy a little, but not enough to make me feel any less ashamed.

She must've felt my arm stiffen around her middle because she turned into my embrace, pressing her hands against my chest. The room was dark, but I could just make out the outline of her eyes staring up at me.

"I was an idiot back then. I had no respect for myself or my parents, and that guy, he wasn't any better. I didn't give a shit about anything other than forgetting about life, and I did whatever I could to get there, usually with drugs, but if I didn't have drugs, sex and booze worked too."

My throat worked hard to move around the hardened lump of emotion that had appeared out of nowhere. She reminded me so much of Luke. Almost too much. And sometimes, when she spoke like this, it felt like something—maybe someone—was trying to give me a message. Like maybe, just maybe, I had been put here on this planet to be here for her, the way I couldn't be there for him.

"But I give a shit now," she continued, her tone hardened and sincere. She tapped her finger against my chest, just above my hammering heart. "I give a shit about *us*. And I give a shit about what my parents think. I want them to know we're the real thing and that I'm not just with you because ... because your friend can hook you up with some good shit or whatever. And I want them to know that I *am* capable of respecting their house rules, even if I never did in the past. I care too much about *you* and *us* to use you as a way to rebel against them. And I just ..." She released a breath, long and harsh, like she'd been holding it for a while. "I just wanted you to know that, in case you were wondering why—"

"You don't need to explain anything to me," I replied in a whisper, brushing a strand of hair behind her ear.

"I know, but at this point, you might expect that I'm just going to put out all the time." She laughed awkwardly, dipping her chin to avoid my eyes in the dark.

God, is that what she thinks? Does she believe I'm only with her because of what her body can offer?

"Stormy, I am grateful for everything, but expect nothing. If I have given you the impression that I only want you for—"

"Oh Jesus, no. I didn't mean it like that. I just ..." She huffed with amusement and embarrassment. "I just didn't want you to feel insulted that I'm just all, like, okay, kiss on the cheek, let's spoon, good night. Because I seriously love our sex life, okay, and I'd really love to go at it right now, especially with that hot way you defended me today. But ... I'm trying to do the right thing, so ..."

I rested my palm against her cheek, stroking my thumb over her cheekbone. "I'm not here to get laid in your parents' house," I said quietly. "I'm here because I want to be with you. That's all. And if you told me you never ever wanted to have sex with me again—"

"Which would never happen."

I snorted. "But if you *did*, it wouldn't matter. How I feel for you runs deeper than that. I—"

"Are you in love with me?" she asked, a touch of hope pushing her words along a breathy whisper.

The question knocked the wind from my lungs as I searched for that green gaze in the darkness. My heart was frantic, wild, unable to find a steady rhythm as it tried to burst through my bones and flesh to rest against hers. And I didn't want to lie to her despite all the fear I held in being honest, so the only word I could manage was a strained, whispered, "Yes."

She released a gust of breath that sounded almost like a laugh as she leaned into me and pressed her forehead to my shoulder.

"Wow," she muttered, so quietly that I almost didn't hear. "Nobody has ever said that to me before."

I had thought I loved Amanda, and I had been absolutely certain that I loved Jersey, and I supposed that, at the time, maybe I had. Maybe I had loved them to whatever capacity my younger self could. But I knew for a fact that I'd never felt like this—God, not even close.

I wouldn't have come back here, to Connecticut, for anyone else. I could've only done that for Stormy. Because she didn't run, and for her, I had come back.

Luke should meet her.

My cheek rested against the top of Stormy's head as I worried my bottom lip, thinking about him. Thinking about taking some time this weekend and seeing if I could drive up to Wayward Correctional Facility to visit my brother for the first time in five years.

"Charlie."

Startled from thoughts about Luke, I lifted my cheek from her head, and she looked up to find my eyes in the dark.

"Yeah?"

Her hand curled around the back of my neck, her fingertips pushing into the hair at my nape. She pulled my lips toward hers, then kissed me gently, tender and sweet. Her breath stuttered, and I realized she was crying. I smoothed those tears away and brushed the hair from her eyes as she pressed what seemed like a hundred kisses to my lips, cheek, and jaw before touching her forehead to mine.

"What's wrong?" I asked.

"I just wanted to say that I'm in love with you too."

"Wow," I whispered into the dark. "Nobody has ever said that to me before … and meant it."

Giddiness grabbed ahold of us both as we laughed, nearing hysterics, surrounded by pillows and blankets and the walls that had seen too much of her youth. But now, they'd seen something else—a rebirth. The declaration of her love for me and mine for her. And we kissed and hugged and came dangerously close to breaking her parents' house rules.

With grins on our faces, she turned in my arms and once again pressed her back to my chest. She threaded her fingers between mine and brought my hand to her mouth, where she kissed my knuckles and sighed.

"I'm happy I could be your first," she said, her elation now fogged by sleep.

I pressed a single kiss to her shoulder and whispered back, "I'm even happier to be your last."

CHAPTER THIRTY-SEVEN

CONNECTICUT, PRESENT DAY

It was Thanksgiving Day, and I awoke, more thankful than I'd been in years.

The house was flooded with a bounty of scents, the varied foods being cooked. Foods I hadn't smelled or eaten in longer than I could remember.

Stormy rolled in my arms to kiss me with her eyes still closed. "Happy Thanksgiving, Charlie," she whispered in a sleepy voice.

My lips stretched in a smile as I kissed her back. "Happy Thanksgiving, my love."

She hummed, her face painted with happiness and contentment, and opened her eyes a crack. "I like that—*my love.* It's nice."

"Well, get used to it." I kissed her again. "I'm going to—"

Below us, the front door opened, and a jubilant squeal was carried up the stairs and to my ears. Stormy hurried from my embrace to check the time on her phone.

"Oh my God, it's already eleven," she said. "We have to get up."

"*Eleven*?" I was shocked. When was the last time I'd slept that late? When the hell was the last time I'd allowed myself to?

"My sister and her family are here," she went on needlessly. I had already assumed by the excitement coming from downstairs. "I should've set the alarm. There's no time to shower. We have to get dressed and—"

"Hey." I rounded the bed to grip her shoulders in my hands. "Relax. It's okay."

"You don't get it. My sister … I love her, but she seriously has her shit together."

I furrowed my brow. "So, you feel like you need to impress her?"

"No, not …" She averted her gaze from mine and shook her head. "Not really. It-it's just … she's been through a lot of shit, right? Like, *a lot* of shit, her whole freakin' family—you don't even know the half of it. I mean, so have I, but they don't know about any of that—or not most of it anyway. And even with everything she's been through, she still manages to keep her crap together. She gets up, she gets her kids fed, she goes to work, she makes good money, and her husband … the guy is, like, a fucking saint despite … everything … and—"

"And you want to show her … what? That you're capable of getting your shit together too?" I guessed, trying to put the pieces together as they were laid before me in a jumbled mess.

Stormy sighed and lifted her shoulders in a weak shrug. "I guess. Kind of. I think I just want her to feel for me the way I feel about her, you know? Like …" She gnawed at her bottom lip, the silver hoops clicking against her teeth before saying, "*Proud*."

There was such an endearing innocence reflected in her eyes, one I could empathize with. This woman before me had walked through her own version of hell and made her way out of it, only to try and pick up whatever was left of her life and make something out of it. She'd done well for herself, and now, she only wanted her family—all of them—to see that, hey, despite it all, she'd officially made it.

Hell, with all these recent thoughts of seeing Luke, wasn't I desperate for the same approval and confirmation that I'd turned out okay?

Stormy laughed beside herself and closed her eyes, hiding the tears that had begun to well. "I know that sounds so fucking stupid. Like, why do I even care? I'm thirty-five fucking years old. What does it matter what my little sister thinks of me or you or whatever?"

She went to move away from my touch, but I stopped her, gripping her shoulders just a little tighter.

"It's not stupid," I assured her. "I can't even begin to tell you how badly I want Luke to meet you. And not even because I think he'd like you—which I do—but because I want him to really see that, by some fucking miracle, I actually managed to get this lucky."

Stormy stared into my eyes and nodded. "You want him to see that it was all worth it."

I didn't know entirely what she'd meant by that. The years he'd taken care of me? All the times he'd driven me to therapy? Ritchie's murder? All of it? I didn't know, yet I seemed to understand.

"Exactly."

"I would love to meet him one day." She smiled, and I smiled back.

"Okay. But first, I want to meet your sister." I caught a heady whiff of roasting turkey, and I groaned. "And I want to eat that dinner because, fuck, it's been a long, long time since I've had turkey."

***

Stormy led the way down the stairs while I followed a few steps behind, like a shy, nervous little kid. The living room was filled with the ruckus made by a very young boy and the enthusiastic yammering of an older boy, both holding on to the attention of Stormy's parents. A younger woman with light-brown hair pulled into some sort of complicated-looking braid, stood near the couch, shaking her head and laughing at the boys. From the emerald hue of her eyes, I knew she had to be Stormy's sister, Rain.

"Hey! Did we wake you up?" Rain asked, hurrying across the living room to pull Stormy into a hug.

"Nah, we were already awake," Stormy replied, squeezing her sister tight.

Rain's eyes lifted to mine before I could divert my gaze. Old habits died too hard, and my social ineptitude had grabbed hold of me in the presence of her sister's teasing smirk.

The two separated as Rain said to me, "Hi, I'm not sure we've met."

"Oh!" Stormy looked over her shoulder, momentarily flustered, and extended her hand to me. I took it and allowed her to pull me forward to stand by her side. "Ray, this is Charlie. Charlie, my sister, Ray—or Rain—"

"But I prefer Ray." Ray was a little younger than Stormy, but her eyes twinkled with the wisdom of someone who'd seen more than even I could imagine. "It's nice to meet you, Charlie. I think …" She gave Stormy a questioning sidelong glance. "I feel like I've seen you before … like … I don't know … I can't—"

"When you guys came up last month, we bumped into him outside the restaurant," Stormy cut in, her cheeks reddening with embarrassment. "But I didn't know his name then. I had called him—"

"The Spider," Ray finished, her face lighting up with instant recollection as she nodded. "That's right. The tattoos." Her eyes dropped to my forearms and hands. "Well, it's nice to officially meet you, Charlie."

"You too," I replied while trying to place her in my memory.

She had remembered me, but could I remember her? It felt shameful that she hadn't made as much of an impact on me as I apparently had on her.

She gestured toward the two boys, engaging Chris in separate but equally enthusiastic conversations. "Those are my kids. The tall one is Noah, and the short one is

Miles. I'd introduce you, but obviously, I'd be interrupting something very important."

I lifted one side of my mouth. "Yeah, don't worry about it. I'll say hi later."

"Where's Soldier?" Stormy asked, looking around the living room.

Soldier ...

My gut churned with the panic I'd felt weeks ago at the sound of his name.

Ray sighed with agitation, and I looked back at her in time to watch her eyes roll. "Miles is on an apple-juice kick. It's literally all the kid will drink, and Mom forgot to grab some at the store. So, Soldier ran out to find an open store."

She laughed beside herself and lifted her eyes to mine, obviously attempting to pull me into the conversation. "You know, kids."

Actually, I didn't. It might've been silly and sheltered of me, but I couldn't say I honestly knew much about kids at all. I'd been one at some point, and I'd had brief interactions with them throughout my life—mostly while working or running into a grocery store. But apart from that, I couldn't say I knew anything at all about what they were like.

But still, I pushed my lips to smile and forced a laugh. "Yeah."

Chris stood up from where he'd been sitting on the couch with the boys on either side of him. He announced to them that Grandma had been up all night, baking cookies for them, and he led the way into the kitchen. Only the younger boy—Miles—followed while Noah made his way over to where I stood with his mother and aunt. He eyed me warily, eyes narrowed. There was distrust written in the premature lines forming between his brows. Stormy had mentioned her sister had been through some things, never divulging what those things might've been, but now, I wondered. Had her son been through those same things? What had happened to make him eye a stranger that way? Like he had every reason to believe I was up to no good.

He reminded me of … well, me.

"Hey, kid," Stormy greeted him.

She reached up to wrap her arms around his neck. He hugged her back, but his eyes never left me. So much suspicion was held in that darkened gaze, too old to belong to a kid this young. How old was he anyway? Sixteen? A little older maybe?

"God, you're getting too tall," she complained, her tone teasing.

He ignored the jab though and instead asked, "Who's this?"

Ray bumped her hip against her son's and said, "Your aunt Stormy has a *boyfriend*."

I didn't have to know much about kids and teenagers to understand a post-traumatic response when I saw one. So, I held my hand out to him, treating him with respect—like a man—so as not to give him the impression that he had reason to worry about his aunt.

"Charlie Corbin," I introduced myself. "You must be Noah."

"Uh-huh," he grumbled, nodding. He was slow to take my hand, but he did. "You bumped into us, right?"

I chuckled awkwardly. God, did they *all* remember me? "Apparently."

He was a few inches shorter than me, putting him at maybe six foot even. Good-looking kid with the same eye color as his aunt and mother—a startling shade of green, the color of springtime and new beginnings. But he had the haunted look of dead autumn and deader winter buried beneath that bright green, where he likely dwelled in a past darker than I wanted to acknowledge. A cold trickle of ice carried down my spine as I gripped his hand in mine. Fuck, I hadn't expected to feel like this, so much empathy and compassion for this kid, but I did. I wanted to know what had happened to him, and I wondered how I could find out without overstepping boundaries I had no business wandering beyond.

He dropped my hand and cleared his throat, crossing his arms over his chest. "I like your tattoos. They're cool."

"Thanks."

"Do they mean anything, or do you just like spiders?"

I huffed a soft chuckle, glancing down at the webs covering the backs of my hands and fingers, traveling up my forearms and disappearing beneath the sleeves rolled up to my elbows. "Uh ... both."

His eyes widened at that. "You like spiders?"

"Love them actually."

"Seriously?" He was amused, incredulous.

Ray took Stormy by the arm, whispering something about letting us bond, and dragged her toward the kitchen, leaving me alone with the scrutinizing teenager.

I wasn't sure I could call it bonding, but it was certainly something.

"My mom hates spiders," Noah said, turning to watch his mom and aunt walk away. Then, he looked back at me as he continued, "My dad hates them, too, but Mom hates them more. So, she has him kill them. Or me, if he isn't around."

To be honest, I wasn't sure we were talking about spiders at all. Not entirely anyway.

"I don't kill them, if I can avoid it," I said.

Noah nodded, keeping those arms tightly folded against his chest. Guarded. "That's cool, I guess."

"Yeah, they're not so—"

The front door opened, not far from where we stood, and in walked a tall, burly man whose bicep muscles could be made out through the fabric of his sweatshirt. He stood easily four or five inches taller than me with a shoulder span that could overtake a bull, let alone someone like me, nearly frail in comparison. *Weak.*

"Hey, Dad," Noah said. "You find the apple juice?"

This was Soldier, and he looked every bit of one despite the longer hair, uncharacteristic of anybody in the military. But maybe he'd been enlisted at one point. A Marine perhaps. I hated to admit it, but my anxiety peaked at the sight of him, reminding me of every moment I'd been tormented by Ritchie.

Or his brother. I cringed, hoping it was inward, but knowing it wasn't.

Soldier lifted the bottle in his hand. "Found it. Thank God. I wasn't prepared to listen to that tantrum."

"Same though," Noah muttered, laughing.

The giant of a man put the bottle down on an end table and pulled his sweatshirt off, revealing arms of steel blanketed in a patchwork quilt of tattoos. When I really took notice, I saw that every visible area of skin—apart from his face—was covered in ink. And while I couldn't say I found tattoos intimidating themselves, they certainly completed a picture when they were on a guy like this.

A guy like this. Shit. I was stereotyping, and I hated stereotypes. *Shame on me.*

Then, his eyes landed on me, and I swallowed. He cocked his head, curious recognition igniting in his golden eyes. That look only meant one thing. He'd seen me before, and the oddest part of it was that, in that moment, I realized I'd seen him too.

Probably from outside the restaurant. He must've stood out enough for me to remember him.

"Dad, this is Aunt Stormy's boyfriend," Noah said, taking the reins in making the introductions since neither of us was clearly taking the first step. "Charlie, this is my dad."

"Charlie," Soldier repeated, taking a slow step toward me and extending his hand. "Soldier."

"I know," I replied stupidly, then quickly added, "Uh, Stormy told me. Your name, I mean. Or … nickname?"

I took his hand, and we shook slowly. Both of us taking the moment to assess the other.

"Nah, not a nickname."

"Oh. Sorry." I wanted to tuck my tail between my legs and find a hole to die in.

But Soldier didn't seem to mind the way I would've initially expected him to. "It's all good."

He stared at me for a few silent moments before his eyes narrowed, like he was trying to place me somewhere, retracing the steps in his mind. "Man, this is gonna drive me crazy. I feel like I know you from somewhere. Where have I seen you before?"

Noah looked up at his father, who, now that I really thought about it, didn't look like him at all. It could've been nothing, but for some reason, it felt like *something*.

"We bumped into him outside that restaurant Aunt Stormy took us to last month. Remember?"

An awkward laugh pushed past my lips. "Apparently, everyone remembers this but me." But that wasn't true either, was it? Because while I definitely didn't remember Noah or Ray, I *did* remember seeing this man. Yet my attempts to place him at the scene itself were feeble. *Why is that?*

"Huh." That clueless look on Soldier's face remained, even as he nodded slowly. "Yeah. That might be it. I kinda remember something like that."

"He's the guy with the spiderweb tattoos," Noah pointed out, gesturing toward my hands.

Soldier looked down to assess them himself, and then his brows lifted with the sudden hit of memory. "That's right. She called you The Spider. God, that was, like, the beginning of last month, and here you are now, about to have dinner with us. That's crazy."

It really was wild. How quickly things could change. Of course, I'd been no stranger to that life truth; I'd been aware of how suddenly the entire world could be flipped upside down from a very young age. But never had things changed so quickly for the better. That part was new, and I wasn't so sure I'd ever get used to it. Somewhere in my mind, I was still navigating this chapter of life with caution, not wanting to be too surprised when the next dose of trauma came to bite me in the ass.

"Things moved pretty quickly," I replied for the sake of saying something and offered a sheepish smile while my brain raced through every possible scenario in which everything could blow up in my face.

"So it would seem." Soldier smiled, but it seemed forced, as if, like me, he still couldn't make sense of it. Like somewhere, a piece of the puzzle was still floating around, left unchecked, and nothing would feel right until it was put in its place.

***

The feeling lingered into the evening. Even as we all sat around the table, eating one of the best Thanksgiving feasts I'd ever had, I would glance across the table to watch Stormy's brother-in-law. His mannerisms. How he talked to Stormy's parents. What he looked like when he smiled or frowned or was deep in conversation. I hadn't intended to stare so intently at times, but there was a voice inside my head, screaming at me to *remember, remember, remember*, and what the fuck I was supposed to be remembering, I didn't know. But I hoped that, if I just watched him enough, if I listened enough, it would eventually come to me.

"So, Charlie," Chris said, deciding to drag me into a conversation for the first time all night. His attention had been fixated so much on his youngest grandson, and I couldn't say I blamed him. Miles adored him, and from the looks of it, the feeling was mutual. "Stormy told us earlier that you *live* in the cemetery?"

He asked the question as if it were the most asinine thing he'd ever heard.

I couldn't help but chuckle.

"Yeah, I do. I've lived there for the past five years."

Noah gave me a genuine smile for the first time. "Awesome."

"What's that like?" Chris buttered a biscuit as he shrugged. "Do you ... do you have a house there? Or do you—"

"Do you sleep in one of those houses they bury bodies in?" Noah blurted out, his face beaming with boyish intrigue.

I chuckled again. "A mausoleum, and, no, they don't usually let us camp out in those."

Noah's grin broadened, his eyes gleaming with devilish delight. "*Usually* is the key word there, right?"

It felt good to joke with him. It felt good to make him smile. But I turned to Chris and informed him that, yes, I had a house, not wanting him to believe his daughter was shacking up with some weirdo who pitched tents between the headstones.

"You're not scared?" Chris asked.

I shook my head. "There's nothing to be scared of." Which was only half of the truth. I'd believed for a long time that there was nothing to fear, but that was *before*.

Before the trinkets were left. Before the intruder. Before the scent of cigarettes lingered where there'd been none. Before I was haunted by the man who hunted me.

"What about ghosts?" Barbara asked, her face contorting like she'd just seen one.

"They're there," I answered casually, truthfully. "But they don't bother me." *Well, not until recently anyway.*

"It's not so bad," Stormy jumped in, hooking her hand around the inside of my elbow. Coming to my defense, as I'd come to hers. "You get used to it. And actually, it's really nice. Like being so close to the city but also being far away from the noise and the people. Plus, the neighbors are *super* quiet."

Her hand tightened on my arm, and I couldn't contain my smile.

Barbara shivered, and I half expected her to say something, the way she'd made a snide remark about Stormy's job last night. But she kept it to herself and instead asked the last thing I could've possibly wanted to talk about.

"I know your parents are no longer with us, but do you have any other family? Any siblings?"

Soldier's eyes diverted from the food on his plate to look at me, and I thought I might've seen something shift in his gaze.

I pulled in an unsteady breath. Stormy squeezed my arm tighter now, keeping me grounded in the moment. This wasn't a topic I wanted to discuss despite how innocent of a question it was. Most people might say that, yes, they had a brother, but I could guarantee very few of them would then follow it up by saying said brother was spending his Thanksgiving in prison because he'd murdered his childhood best friend. And I could lie, but a quick Google search would prove that to be bullshit, and then what? Sure, I could easily explain that my reason for lying was to save me from judgment and humiliation, but to what end?

So, I kept my eyes on my plate and replied, "I have a brother, yeah." My voice sounded like it'd been raked across a cheese grater.

"Oh, what is he doing today?" Barbara asked.

"Older or younger?" Chris asked.

"Where does he live?" Barbara again. "Is he married?"

Why couldn't I have just taken my chances and lied?

I shook my head, unable to address any one person at the table, not even Stormy. "He, um ... he's older, and n-not married, no. He, uh ..."

"Charlie's brother is actually in prison right now, and he doesn't like talking about it," Stormy interjected.

Dammit, I knew she had meant well. I knew she was trying to help. But all I could do was hold my breath, waiting to hear what they had to say. Waiting for another slew of unwanted questions about why and how long and whatever the fuck else.

Thankfully, they didn't come.

"Oh," Barbara replied, clearly taken aback. "I'm sorry. I didn't mean—"

"It's okay," I quickly said, lifting my eyes enough to meet her gaze. "It's just a touchy subject."

"Of course," Chris said, then cleared his throat awkwardly.

Then, Noah startled us all by saying, "Hey, Dad was in prison too. It's okay. None of us care about that kinda crap."

It was a sweet sentiment and one I probably should've appreciated more. But at the mention of his father, I looked up at Soldier, and I found him staring right back at me. One brow lifted, hand gripping his fork, but not moving. I thought he might scold his son for saying something, for divulging a part of his past that maybe he hadn't wanted mentioned in a stranger's company.

Instead, he asked, "What prison is your brother in?"

I swallowed around a ball of lead and said, "Wayward."

He released the fork in his hand and sat back in his chair. "What did you say your last name was?"

Soldier, Soldier, Soldier ...

We stared each other down as I repeated his name in my head. Who the fuck named their kid Soldier? And why the hell did I feel like I knew it from somewhere? Why the hell did I feel like I'd *heard* it before? Not from Stormy, but ... on the news? He'd been in prison, I knew that, so ... whatever his crime, wasn't it possible I had ...

Soldier, Soldier ...

"... Soldier and I ..."

My lips parted at the sound of Luke's voice ringing through my head. Remembering a time, a Sunday years ago, when I'd gone to the visitor center to bitch and moan about what a shit show life had turned into while my brother was living it up behind bars. Remembering a brief mention that had been so inconsequential at the time, so stupid and pointless, only for it to now feel so damning.

And Soldier remembered too.

The table went silent as he lifted his finger and wagged it at me. "Your brother ... oh my God, your *brother* ... we called him Zero."

A torrent of emotions raced through my mind and heart at the sound of that nickname, at the realization that not only did he know my brother, but they were *friends*. At the knowledge that I had somehow—by some stroke of misfortune or luck or fate or whatever the fuck you wanted to call it—managed to fall in love with a woman whose brother-in-law just so happened to have shared a prison dorm with my brother.

I simultaneously wanted to scream, cry, run away, and wrap this guy in a big fucking hug.

But because I couldn't manage any of those things, I huffed a laugh that was tight and constricted by the sadness and disbelief wedged inside my throat. "I always thought that was the stupidest nickname."

"Holy shit," he said, bewildered.

Ray looked from her husband to me to Stormy. "This is absolutely insane."

"It's certainly a small world," Barbara seemed to agree.

That it is, Barbara, I thought, unable to take my eyes from a man who'd spent more time with my brother in recent years than I'd been allowed. A man who, I realized, might know far more than I was willing to admit. One who could potentially have the power to ruin everything. *It is a small, small, small fucking world.*

CHAPTER THIRTY-EIGHT

CONNECTICUT, PRESENT DAY

The moment that puzzle piece had slid into place, Soldier's cautious demeanor toward me had disappeared altogether. So had Noah's, and I suspected that had everything to do with his father and nothing to do with me. Now, the two of them chatted with me like we'd been best friends forever, and on one hand, I enjoyed it. Soldier knew things about my brother that I didn't. He had stories that I couldn't tell, and the moment dinner was finished, and we retired to the living room to give our bellies a rest before dessert, he dived headfirst into one like he'd been waiting to share it forever.

"God, your brother, man ..." Soldier leaned back against the couch cushions, crossing his ankle over his knee and stretching his arm across the back.

His eyes twinkled with mirth, and his grin made my own cheeks hurt. Luke always had that effect on people. He was likable, even at his worst, and at his best ...

The guy could've gone places if he hadn't messed things up so damn badly.

But we'd already established that.

"I gotta tell you about this one time. So, there was this lady officer at Wayward—I think her name was Shawna, but I could be wrong. Anyway, she came to work there sometime around the time Zero—uh, Luke," he corrected for my benefit, probably, "was brought in. We called him Pretty Boy for a while, for obvious reasons, and Shawna, or whatever the hell her name was, agreed, I guess. 'Cause it didn't take that guy long to, uh"—he raised a brow and shifted his gaze toward the toddler playing with a set of blocks on the floor—"*get friendly*, if you catch my drift."

Noah rolled his eyes in Soldier's direction. "You act like I'm a little kid. I know what sex is, Dad."

Soldier pulled in a deep breath and met the teenager's glare. "Yeah, I'm well aware. The censoring was for your little brother, wiseass."

"Oh." Noah's cheeks pinked as he sank deeper into the cushions.

"Anyway," Soldier continued, the blended look of amusement and nostalgia returning to his face, "the way it was there, you could get away with some stuff, if you knew your way around. But if you weren't careful, it was easy to get caught. So, one night ..." He stopped for a laugh to bubble past his lips, and I missed my brother so much that my heart throbbed angrily in my chest. "Luke and Shawna met up in the dorm bathroom. Now, I don't know if you know what that looks like."

I shook my head.

Soldier sat up straighter and began to gesture with his hands, like he was painting a picture. "So, you have a row of urinals, a few stalls, and then a row of showerheads. That's it. Not many places in there to hide, is what I'm saying, okay?"

I nodded.

"So, Luke was in there with Shawna, who wasn't, uh, exactly discreet. I was awake, reading in my bunk, and I heard footsteps coming down the hall. I thought to myself, *Oh shit. This lady's about to lose her job, and Zero's about to get a crapload of solitary*. So, I jumped out of bed, got to the bathroom, and there was your brother with this chick up against the wall. She saw me in there, asked if I wanna get in on the action, and I was like, 'No, lady, and honestly, you probably wanna stop unless you wanna be out of a job in the morning.'"

He paused again to laugh, and I smiled, excited to know what came next.

"Luke never told me about this," I said as I waited.

Soldier wiped the moisture from his eyes and said, "Oh, man, just wait. It gets better."

He cleared his throat to continue, and now, he had the attention of Chris, Barbara, Ray, and Stormy, who had all come in from the kitchen after clearing the dinner table. Stormy came to sit by my side on the love seat, automatically taking my hand in hers as her head rested comfortably against my shoulder. All our eyes were aimed at Soldier, with the exception of Miles, who was more interested in building towers.

I imagined myself looking in on this sight, like a fly on the wall. All of us sitting around, sharing stories about a man not with us, the way you did when remembering fond moments with the dead.

The thought struck hard and morose. *Sad.* I didn't like it. It didn't sit well. I couldn't decide if I wanted Soldier to go on or just shut up altogether. But because he couldn't read my mind, he began to speak again.

"So, there was this other guard—"

"Harry?" Ray asked.

Soldier shook his head. "Not Harry. He was usually there during the days. No, this dude was, uh ... not the nicest guy in the world. They scheduled him at night 'cause a lot of guys liked to pull shit when it was lights out, like good ol' Zero. Anyway, we heard footsteps coming toward the bathroom, and Zero shoved Shawna toward one of the stalls. Then, before I knew what this freakin' guy was doing, he grabbed me, yanked my pants down, and shoved me up against the wall where he'd just had Shawna. The guard walked in, saw us there, naked from the waist down, and he said, 'Huh. It's about time someone made Mason their bitch. I always knew he'd sound like a woman.' Then, he turned around and left, having no idea whatsoever that Shawna was hiding in the stall, standing on the toilet seat."

Ray waited for him to stop speaking before asking, "Oh my God, that's so funny. What did you do?"

He looked at his wife, taken aback. "Are you kidding me? I turned around, punched him in the fuckin' face, and told him to buy me dinner first the next time he decided to rub his junk all over my ass."

I couldn't help it; I laughed. We all did—hard. I laughed until my stomach ached and my face hurt, and when I was done, I realized I was also crying. Not from the laughter either—well, not entirely anyway. No, I was just *sad*, and I knew I'd said it before, so many times, but fucking hell, I missed my brother so damn much. I wished he'd been the one to tell me that story. I wished he'd known he could tell me about it. But ... well, actually, I wouldn't have let him, would I? I never did. I had hated him so much for sharing any of the goodness he'd found behind bars, hated him so much for leaving me to fend for myself in a world that had never wanted me, and I'd spent every minute of my limited time with him making him feel bad for me.

Now, I just wished I'd had allowed him to make me laugh instead.

I quickly dried my eyes and played it cool, like it was only the amusement from Soldier's story that had forced the tears to stream down my face. Nobody seemed to pay any attention to my emotional slip or hasty recovery, not even Stormy. But when my eyes landed on Soldier, I knew he knew, and I didn't like it.

"I saw him not too long ago when I was visiting my uncle Levi," he said, suddenly somber and more serious than I preferred. "He said he hadn't seen you in a long time."

Barbara glanced at me, suspicion in her eyes—or maybe I had imagined it.

"I moved," I replied sheepishly.

"Yeah, I know. He said you had to leave."

Oh God, oh God, oh God, oh God, help me.

My eyes dodged toward Stormy, then to her mom, dad, sister, nephew, then back to Stormy. They had all stilled, all keeping their gazes on the floor or their hands or the chocolate-colored couch cushions, like they could sense the tension filling the air and didn't want to let a sliver of breath loose, so as not to upset the balance.

"I relocated," I answered stupidly, like rewording the same response would end the conversation.

"From what he said, you had no reason to run away like that. You hadn't done anything *wrong*, Charlie," Soldier said, laying it out and confirming that he did know. God, maybe he knew everything. "You know that, right?"

Stormy turned then, her gaze drilling a hole into the side of my face. "What is he talking about?"

Soldier tipped his head back, his lips parting. Realizing in an instant that he was the only other person in this room who had any idea about what had happened outside my bedroom door.

My throat struggled to swallow the fear down as I tried to speak. "I—"

"Nobody in town would leave him alone after his brother was thrown in prison," Soldier cut in, surprising me with grace. "He had to get away to live his life."

"Oh," Stormy whispered, nodding. "Right, you told me about that."

"Y-yeah." That damn lump in my throat wouldn't budge.

Soldier caught my attention as he stood up, groaning, as if standing were the most taxing job on the planet. He walked toward the coatrack, and it was then that I noticed the slight limp to his gait.

"Ray, you okay with me heading across the street for a few minutes?" he asked, already pulling his jacket from its hook.

"Yeah, I'm good here," she replied softly, a slight smile touching her lips.

Soldier slid his arms into the leather sleeves as he turned to face me. "Charlie, you wanna take a walk with me?"

Fuck, fuck, fuck. "Uh, sure."

Memories of Ritchie bending my finger back, close to the point of breaking, rushed at me like a speeding freight train as I stood on legs of rubber.

"I meant it, you know. You should have been in that car."

"Aw, how sweet," Stormy cooed, clueless. "They're bonding."

If by bonding she meant she was likely to find my lifeless body in a patch of dirt at the side of the road somewhere, then I was willing to bet money on her being right.

***

Soldier was more intimidating now than he had been inside Stormy's parents' house. The two of us walked side by side through the open cemetery gate. We were alone, far enough away for my screams to be muffled to any listening ears, if I could scream at all with his gigantic hands encircling my neck. And it struck me as fitting, as I surveyed the neatly kept grounds, that I might find my end in the very place I found the most peace.

A consolation prize, if you will.

"You know, I really don't see anything wrong with having secrets," Soldier said, abruptly disturbing the silence. He held his head low, watching the ground as he walked. Leading us along a dirt path, deeper into the graveyard. "I think it can be kind of a selfish thing—to keep something to yourself. Not, like, in a damning way, but just ..."

He sighed and tipped his head back, eyes holding on to the setting sun and a painted sky. "Well, like, for example, sometimes, when I'm heading back home from Wayward, I like to stop by this place. It's not really on the way or anything, but I like to come by and pay my respects and, I dunno, just hang out with an old friend of mine. Ray doesn't know. I've never told her, and she's never asked me why some days I'm home later than others. And maybe that makes me an asshole. Some people would probably have me crucified for keeping something so seemingly innocent from my wife. But ..." He lifted his shoulders and dropped them heavily. "It just feels personal, you know. Not so personal that I wouldn't tell her if she asked, but ..."

"I think I get it," I replied, almost as quiet as the breeze that blew between us.

"Yeah, but I don't think you do. Because the thing is, some secrets ... they gotta come out, man. You can't keep them inside, or they're gonna drive you insane. And if they don't manage to do that, they're definitely gonna drive her away when she eventually finds out."

So, we were talking about me. I should've picked up on that, but hadn't. But at least he wasn't threatening me. That was something.

Soldier turned down one row of markers, and I followed.

"We're a lot alike, I think," he said. "I'm an orphan too. My dad was killed in a car accident before I knew who he was, and my mom was murdered by the piece of shit who tried really fuckin' hard to kill me."

My head whipped to the side to stare at him. "Holy shit."

One side of his mouth tipped upward in a smile that didn't touch his eyes. He patted his thigh. "Shot me here and"—he laid his hand over his stomach—"here."

"Damn." My mouth went dry as I thought about the scar near my groin. "I'm sorry."

"Yeah, well, it's fine. I'm still here, and he never got his hands on Noah or Ray. That's all that matters. *They* are all that matters. And that's why, when they asked me why I'd been in prison, I told them. They wanted to know my story, and I didn't hide it. I was scared shitless of what they'd think of me, yeah, but I wanted them to know. It wasn't a secret to be kept because, when I really think about it, it's not a secret at all. A quick Google search of my name will tell you everything that happened. But I told them anyway because they mattered to me and I wanted them to know."

We came to a stop, and Soldier gestured toward a bench, wordlessly telling me to take a seat. I listened, and he sat beside me.

"I can't tell you what to do, Charlie. But if I'm guessing correctly, Stormy matters a lot to you, like Ray matters to me. And I think she deserves to hear it from you before she Googles your name 'cause I'm willing to bet it's all there, if she digs deep enough."

Actually, she wouldn't have to dig very deep at all, but I didn't say that. He was too busy making a point, a good one, and I was going to let him finish.

"We're a lot alike," he said again. "I blamed myself for a long time for what had happened. But it took telling my friend Harry and Ray and accepting their acceptance to make me realize that it *wasn't* entirely my fault. I did my time for the part of it that was, but I hadn't made Billy take that fucking pill. That was all on him. That was *his* fault, and he's been paying the ultimate price for that for almost twenty years."

Billy.

I followed Soldier's gaze to the gravestone across the way to see *WILLIAM "BILLY" PORTER* carved into the granite. The year he was born would've made him the same age as Stormy. He had died of a drug overdose, from what Soldier was saying, and so had Stormy's Billy, her old friend who'd gotten her into drugs. The old friend who had fucked her and gotten himself killed by taking drugs given to him by his drug-dealer friend.

Holy shit. Soldier was that drug dealer.

"I did some shit I'm not proud of," he said quietly, as if reading my mind. "I had my reasons, and they made sense at the time, but I was a stupid, desperate kid. I know better now, and I wouldn't make the same decisions if I could do it all over again. That's where we're different, Charlie. Everything that happened to you ... *none of it* was your fault. You have blood on your hands, just like me, but there isn't even a shred of blame on you for what happened. She isn't going to judge you for that."

"*I* judge me for it!" I exclaimed, my voice ringing out to disturb the peace. "I wasn't supposed to meet someone. I wasn't supposed to grow attached. I wasn't supposed to be *happy*. I wasn't supposed to do anything but live my miserable life and feel sorry for what I had done. This"—I thrust my hand in what I thought was the direction of Chris and Barbara's house—"was never *ever* supposed to happen."

Soldier hadn't so much as flinched in reaction to my abrupt outburst. But he turned then and leveled me with a gaze full of empathy and understanding. "Yet here you are."

I slammed my back against the bench, the cool stone bleeding through my jacket to my spine. "I don't want to tell her," I confessed aloud for the first time.

"I know. But if I can be honest with you, I think you're more afraid of reliving it than you are of her reaction. I think that's really what you're running from, Charlie. Not what she might think, but what you *already* think. And let me tell you something—you're never going to heal until you face this shit head-on. You're never going to find peace—nobody will. Luke will never find peace, the dude who attacked you won't either, and if you can't move forward for yourself, then do it for them. Tell her that part of your story because whether you like it or not, it *is* a part of who you are. You can't take it back, you can't erase it, but you can learn to accept it, and I'm telling you this from experience—she can help you do that, if you just give her the chance to try."

***

What kept me awake that night wasn't the conversation in the graveyard or the unsettling truth that Stormy's sister's husband was the same man to end the life of her friend, Billy—

Thank God, I thought, then quickly scolded myself for even allowing such a horrible thing to pass through my mind.

It was a dirty little silver lining, wasn't it? Had he not swallowed that poisoned pill, Stormy might've met the same fate with him later—or instead of. It was unlikely I'd have ever met her, and that deserved its own *thank God*.

But, no, what kept me from finding enough peace to sleep beside her was the awful betrayal of my damn brother spilling my darkest secret to men I didn't know. How many of them had there been? Soldier alone was one too many. And never mind that anyone could pull up an internet search on Connecticut's Corbin brothers and find anything they wanted to know. Soldier hadn't learned of either incident from a fucking Google search; he'd heard from my brother. My *brother*!

"Some secrets ... they gotta come out, man," I could still hear Soldier saying.

And, sure, I saw his point in regard to spilling the ugly details to Stormy—I had never *not* planned to tell her, for the record, but that didn't mean I wanted to, and it didn't make it easy.

But what the hell business had my brother had to talk about me to his prison buddies without my consent, like some gossiping girl in the retail break room?

Maybe he was looking for advice or ... or ... or ... help.

Stop making excuses for him.

They're not excuses though. Right? They're valid reasons. Maybe he just didn't want to carry the weight of it alone. Maybe ... maybe ...

Unwanted tears sprang to my eyes as I thought, *Maybe he just felt helpless, knowing there was nothing he could do. Maybe he knew I was going to leave. Maybe he knew I couldn't take it anymore. Maybe he knew the years of us being an ironclad duo were coming to an end, and he needed to air his heartbreak to the only friends he had left in this cruel, fucked-up world that had never ever, ever been kind to either of us.*

Wasn't he allowed that?

Wasn't he allowed to feel sad in the way I had so many times before?

I rubbed my hand over my face, smearing the tears down my cheeks. I was getting ahead of myself. I knew nothing. But I could find out. I could see him.

Am I ready for that?

No. No, I'm not, but I want *to be, and that has to count for something.*

Stormy rolled over and laid her arm over my chest. I wanted to sleep. We were having lunch with Stormy's parents. We had Ivan's wedding later that evening. But, God, insomnia was an unforgiving bastard that would never give me grace, not even when I needed it most.

"Hey. Why are you awake?" Her whispered voice was half slurred with sleep, but I understood.

"Soldier scares the shit out of me," I half joked, hoping she couldn't tell that I'd been crying. "I'm terrified he's gonna come get me in my sleep."

I felt her smile against my chest. "Soldier is one of the good guys. Don't let him freak you out."

"He wasn't always a good guy," I pointed out, almost bitterly. Alluding to knowing more than she knew I knew.

I hadn't told her what we'd said in the graveyard. That would've led to more of an explanation than I was ready for.

But when will you be ready, huh?
Some secrets are meant to be told.

"He told you?"

"He told me he was the one who had killed Billy. Unintentionally, but ... still."

Her hand fell from my face and returned to its spot on my chest. She nodded. "Soldier's situation was a bad one," she quietly explained, the sleep fading from her voice. "Lots of us make bad choices—*hard* choices—out of desperation. It doesn't make him a bad person; it never did. It took me a long time to understand that, but I get it now. Billy just got caught up in it. Honestly, if Soldier's mom's pills hadn't killed him, someone else's would've.

He was never getting out of that shit, and he was going to drag everyone else down with him. I'm not glad he's dead, but I'm glad he's out of my life. Does that sound terrible? I feel like it makes me terrible."

For the first time maybe ever, I willingly allowed Tommy and Ritchie to enter my mind. "I understand. And if that makes you terrible, then so am I." Except I knew I was—terrible, I mean.

I just didn't want to face that she could've been too. But she wasn't, of course, despite what she'd said. She was only human, and humans were never perfect—even the ones who seemed to be.

"Yeah." She sighed a slightly mournful sound, and I imagined she was thinking about her old friend. "But anyway, you can stop BSing me now. I know you're not afraid of Soldier slitting your throat. So, what's really going on?"

I huffed a humorless laugh. "How do you know I'm bullshitting you?"

"Because I see you, Charlie. So, what's up?"

It was funny how that happened, wasn't it? Someone could know you your entire life and never truly see who you were. But then you could only know someone else for a month, and they could know you better than you knew yourself.

"*If you don't marry that woman, you're a fuckin' asshole,*" I imagined Luke saying, and I couldn't have agreed more.

But I had to tell her a story first, and even though it was late at night and we had a lunch and wedding to attend, there was no time like the present.

CHAPTER THIRTY-NINE

CONNECTICUT, AGE THIRTY-THREE

After a catastrophe, time passed in a way that felt like walking through sand. The ground beneath you had too much give. You sank and tripped and kicked up the dust over and over again, just trying to reach the solidity of the boardwalk. It wasn't far—you could see it. You watched as others walked the planks easily, coasting through life with their heads held high without a single care. You could practically feel those hot boards beneath your feet, could feel the memory of those sun-bleached knots and grooves from a time when you'd walked them too. But with every sure step closer to sturdy ground, you stumbled backward into the abyss of your grief and trouble.

I wasn't sure anybody I'd ever known could understand this more than me. Or maybe I was just being self-centered.

The death of my parents had fucked everything up, and that was the harshest truth of them all, I thought. It wasn't their fault; I couldn't blame them for dying. As a child, I'd catch myself thinking that way without the rationale of a levelheaded adult, but I knew better now. Still, it didn't stop it from being the truth.

Their demise had, in turn, in a way, been mine as well ... and Luke's.

He'd been too young to take care of me. It wasn't my fault for not understanding this and wanting to stay with my big brother, to hold on to some normalcy—I'd only been a kid myself. But Luke never should've insisted on it. He should've sent me to live with our grandmother. He should've ignored my demands, ignored my constant tears, and forced me to go. And I would've felt unwanted for a while. I would've hated him; I would've hated life. But I would've grown up to understand why he'd done what he did, and maybe he wouldn't have lost himself to booze. He wouldn't have lost Melanie. Maybe, just fucking maybe, he wouldn't be sitting in a prison hours away, and I wouldn't be lying here, wondering what the fuck I should do about the terrorist down the street.

Tommy Wheeler.

I believed it might've been his mother who'd instigated Project Make Charlie Corbin's Life a Living Hell. But somewhere around the two-year mark after Ritchie's death and Luke's incarceration, she'd given up, leaving poor Tommy to carry the torch on his own.

I hated him, but I didn't want to because I also understood. I could put myself in his shoes and empathize with why he felt this need to torment his brother's killer's only living relative into permanent hibernation. He was pissed off and resentful and missing his own big brother—God only knew why, but who the fuck was I to talk? In his mind, the imprisonment of the man who'd stolen his brother's last breath wasn't enough. The punishment didn't fit the crime, and it wouldn't until Luke's corpse was covered in dirt, and, dammit, *I got it.* But I couldn't do a fucking thing about any of it, and I still had to somehow live my life, and why the fuck should I have to spend the rest of it paying for something I'd had no part in?

Doesn't he understand that? I did nothing.

Tommy had never been an idiot. Sure, he'd always been a dick. Not as much of one as his brother, but a dick nonetheless. But he'd never been *stupid.*

"He's not stupid," I muttered to the dark abyss. "He's crazy and desperate."

That was what it was. His desperation to avenge his brother had cost him his sanity, and he had lost it. It was the only explanation for why I'd caught him on camera, his pants around his ankles, taking a shit on the front lawn. And how else was I supposed to explain his complete disregard for a court-ordered restraining order and regular visits from the cops?

"Yet the fucker still walks," Luke had muttered just a few days ago, the last time I'd seen him. He didn't bother to mask the bitter disgust in his tone. "The guy's been torturing you for three fuckin' years, and the worst that's ever happened to him is, what? A night in a fuckin' holding cell? It's horseshit!"

He wasn't wrong; the whole situation was horseshit. And it wasn't that the local cops didn't feel for me or anything. Actually, my relationship with them had become a decent one. I was now on a first-name basis with a few of them, and they were all aware of Tommy Wheeler's reputation. But the problem was simply that Tommy hadn't done anything bad *enough* to warrant more than a few slaps on the wrist, a handful of overnights at the station, and a couple of hefty bills after violating the restraining order.

Yet.

He hadn't done anything bad enough *yet*. And that was what Luke was worried about. He was worried about me. So was I. I lived in a constant state of paranoia, terrified of what or who might be lurking just around the corner. It was no way to live, Luke always said, and I agreed. But what the fuck choice did I have?

"I could leave. That's always an option." I shook my head and pinched the bridge of my nose, squeezing my eyes shut. "Yeah. And go *where*?"

He'd probably just follow me anyway.
Not if he didn't know where I went.
Tommy's not an idiot. He'd find me.

I rolled my head against the pillow to glare at the damn alarm clock. Fuck, I had to be up for work in just a few hours. But it was now Halloween, the three-year anniversary of Ritchie's murder and my brother's arrest, and Halloween meant no sleep was going to be given to me. Not tonight.

Three years. A whoosh of breath squeezed itself from my constricting lungs as a torrent of grief barreled over me. *How the fuck has it already been three years?*

That was something Tommy didn't get—I was grieving too. I didn't expect him to care, but it would be nice if he at least *tried.* He never would though because nobody gave a fuck about the family of a killer. Nobody ever did.

I rolled over in my bed, determined to sleep even if it was only from lulling myself with a handful of shed tears for the hopes and dreams I'd once had for the life Luke would never lead. The altar he'd never stand at with Melanie. The kids they'd never have. The uncle I'd never be allowed to be.

Happiness. I cried for the happiness we were never permitted to have.

***

The room was still dark when my eyes snapped open. The glowing red numbers on the alarm clock said I'd only been in a dreamless sleep for about forty minutes.

"Fuck," I groaned, rolling over in an angry, frustrated heap of blankets and sheets.

My resolve to sleep was firm, but I expected it to take a while to come along again. Yet heaviness rolled along my limbs and up my body to settle in my head. I sighed, satisfied, hunkering deeper into my cozy cocoon.

Creak.

I bolted up, eyes open. Asking myself what that was but knowing exactly what *it* was—the floorboard just down the hall at the top of the stairs. The one that'd been squeaking my entire life. But *why*? Older houses were prone to unusual sounds. They were full of the moans and groans and sighs of the people who'd lived before, but that floorboard never made a peep unless—

Creak.

Closer.

My intuition had been strong for as long as I could remember, and it'd never been stronger than it was then. Someone was in the house, and I knew who it was.

The light from the hallway shone brightly from beneath my closed bedroom door, streaming across the floor and stopping just before my bed. But now, with one more creak of the floorboard, it was blacked out by his form.

Fear was my closest friend. Had been since I'd been a child. But in this moment, adrenaline overpowered my desire to cower and cry beneath my blanket, like a little boy wanting nothing more than to crawl between his parents in their bed, where it was always safe.

As fast and as silently as possible, I grabbed my phone from the nightstand, keeping my eyes on those shadowy feet beneath the door, and swiped the screen to call for emergency services. The call connected immediately, the operator's voice muffled beneath the blood whooshing past my ears. As if happening in slow motion, the doorknob turned slightly in the sheer blanket of light cast from the night-light beneath my desk, and there was no time to provide the details of my emergency to the operator.

But I kept her on the line.

There was a hunting knife in my bedside table drawer. Luke had given it to me for Christmas years ago, and I'd laughed at him when I opened it, even after seeing the spiderweb design etched into the serrated blade.

"What use do I have for a fucking knife?" I'd asked.

"It looked cool," Luke had said, red-cheeked and embarrassed as I laughed. Then, he added, "And, hey, you never fuckin' know, man. You might need to go hunting at some point."

I'd tucked it into my drawer in the far back, never wanting to look at it again. It'd been a waste of money then, money we could've used for food or something equally practical.

But now, as I carefully, quickly, quietly opened the drawer and reached back for its carved handle, I thought, *Maybe his intuition was just as good as mine.*

But I'm not the one hunting. I'm the fucking prey.

The 911 operator kept mumbling into the blanket as I climbed out of the bed and crouched to the floor, knife in hand. The door pushed open, just a crack at first and then all the way. His tall, shadowy figure stretched across the floor, falling over my head.

Get past him. Run. Down the stairs. Out of the house. Run. Down the stairs. Out of the house. Run, run, RUN.

I forced my lungs to steady as I repeated the self-given instructions over and over. He took one, two slow, cautious steps into the room, eyes likely on my bed. But when he realized it was empty, his steps grew more urgent, more impatient, loud as he approached the bed.

Then, he spoke. "Where are you, Charlie boy?"

My throat was dry, and I resisted the urge to swallow. My hiding spot wasn't great by a long shot, but I didn't want to chance giving myself away. Not just yet.

Tommy Wheeler must not have noticed the phone on the blanket, and the operator—bless her soul—stopped her relentless chattering. But she was there. And hopefully, she was doing whatever she did to track my location to send someone over.

I just hoped she wasn't too late.

"Are we playing hide-and-seek?" Tommy asked.

I shifted my gaze to his shadow, dangerously close to where I crouched on the floor. He held something. A gun? His figure was so distorted by the lack of light that I couldn't be sure.

"I'm gonna find you—you know that, right? And when I do, it's game over. Lights out. Bye-bye, Charlie boy."

Was he drunk? His movements were sure and steady, but the way he was speaking, a little sloppy and slurred, said otherwise.

He's going to kill me.

Of course he was. What other reason did he have to break into my house in the middle of the night? But hearing him say it, *knowing* it, changed things somehow. It forced a fear greater than any I'd ever felt, but it also filled me with a willingness to live. To prove him wrong.

I'm getting out of here, Tommy boy.

"Where are you, huh?" He threw the blanket back, as if my six-foot-three frame might be hiding in there somewhere. The phone was sent flying, crashing to the floor. "Where the fuck are you, you little pussy bitch?!"

I'm not in here. Turn around. Look somewhere else.

He turned around to face the door, tapping whatever it was against his thigh. I glanced up from my hiding spot, looking over the pile of disheveled sheets to peek at him. The blade of a knife gleamed in the hallway light, and my stifled sigh of relief surprised me.

It's a fair fight, I thought, gripping the handle of my own. *But, God, please, don't let me have to use it. I don't want to. Don't make me. Please.*

Tommy, turn around. Get out of here. Before you do something stupid.

He glanced over his shoulder, and I ducked back down, praying he couldn't hear my thundering heartbeat.

"Charlie!" he shouted, his anger rising.

He spun on his heel and barreled toward the closet. He threw the door open, swept my clothes to the side, and roared through his mounting rage. He kicked the pile of sketchbooks stacked on the closet floor, sending them scattering.

Then, he did something unexpected. He bent down, picked one up, and studied whatever had been scribbled onto the page.

This is it. Run.

I moved carefully, readying my limbs to take off. Then, as he turned the page and cocked his head, I stole the opportunity and ran.

Yes! Yes, yes, yes, I chanted, bolting past Tommy and making it out the door as he screamed a curse and threw the sketchbook at my floorlength mirror, shattering it into a thousand pieces.

The stairs weren't far from my door, just a few paces.

I can make it. I'm gonna make it. I have to fucking make it.

Then, as I was about to descend the first step, a sharp pain shot through my scalp as Tommy's hand wrapped around my hair and pulled me back. I reached around me, digging my nails into his flesh as I yelled incoherent obscenities.

"Shit! Fuck! Tommy!" I squeezed my eyes shut, keeping my knife-wielding hand at my side, praying I wouldn't have to use it. "Please. Stop. God, just fucking *stop*!"

"You know I can't do that," he said, releasing my hair for a moment of relief before hooking his arm around my neck.

His forearm pressed against my Adam's apple, crushing. I gasped and wrapped my hand around his wrist, pulling on him enough to lessen the pressure on my throat.

"Goddammit, Tommy," I gasped, struggling to maintain my grip. "W-we can talk, okay? We can fucking *talk* about this shit. Just stop. Y-y-you don't want to kill me."

"Don't you fucking tell me what I want to do!"

My mind raced, desperate. "No, no, listen to me, Tommy. You don't want to kill me. You want to kill Luke, right? *He* killed Ritchie. *He* killed your brother. What the fuck did *I* do? God, what the fuck did I ever—"

He raised the hand holding his blade and pressed the point beneath my jaw.

I squeezed my lids shut, silently cursing the tears that had already begun to stream from between my lashes as a torrent of, "Oh God, oh God, oh God," passed through my lips. Wishing I were dreaming. Praying that I was and that I'd wake up to a pool of sweat and a heart on the brink of bursting through my chest.

"Don't you fucking *dare* tell me what I want." He emphasized every word, hot breath and spittle raining against my ear. "Luke took my brother from me. So, I'm going to take his. That's fair, right? Eye for an eye and all that shit."

The tip of his knife pressed firmly to my flesh and hot, hot, hot heat trickled down the side of my neck.

I'm bleeding. He's going to slit my throat. This is how I'll die.

The blade moved, traveling slowly along my jawline. Acceptance had barely begun to creep in, an odd sense of serenity and a sensation close to relief, when a scream tore through my throat, and I raised my other hand and sliced Tommy's arm. It was enough to make him lower his weapon and loosen his hold on my neck.

"Fucking asshole," he gritted out from between clenched teeth.

He dropped his injured arm from my neck long enough to give me another dash of false hope. I attempted the stairs again, but Tommy recovered quickly. His hand gripped my bare arm and yanked me toward him. I stumbled on the step as he dragged me, thrusting me against the wall opposite my bedroom door. My eyes met his, and diluted black pupils stared back. Sweat dripped from his brow. He blinked rapidly, looked away, then looked back to at wide-eyed gaze. The function of his hands and body were somehow controlled, but the movement of his eyes were erratic. Crazed.

"God, Tommy, what the fuck are you on?" I found myself asking, as if it mattered. "Stop, okay? Just stop, *please*. I'll do whatever you want me to do, okay? I-I'll leave—is that what you want me to do? You'll never have to see my face again, okay? I'll—"

"You know what I was thinking on the way over here?" Tommy asked, his voice low as he brought his nose to mine.

I shook my head. God, his breath stank, like booze and shit.

"I was thinking …" He huffed a laugh, blasting my face with rancid heat. "I was thinking about what Ritchie"—his voice cracked, and damn me and my fucking heart because I actually, almost, felt bad for him—"said that one time. Remember?"

"No," I answered while wondering where the fuck the cops were.

How long had it been now? It'd felt like hours, but … no, it was probably only a few minutes, maybe three, four.

"Oh, come on, Charlie boy. Yes, you do. That day we dumped your folks in the ground. He said you should've been in the car with them. You remember that?"

A fresh wave of tears wet my face as I nodded. "Y-yeah. I remember that."

"Yeah," he said, hoarse and whispered. "And I was thinking, he was right." I saw his eyes shift to mine, but what I didn't see was his hand readying the knife low, near my hip. "None of this shit would've happened if they had just let you die with them."

Then, his knife plunged into my lower belly, just barely above my groin, slicing through flesh and muscle. I gasped, my mouth gaping as I stared into his cold, crazed stare. I saw nothing there, and I felt nothing, although I knew my blood was pattering against my feet and my mother's worn, matted carpet.

"Better late than never though, right?" Tommy asked, shrugging nonchalantly.

"You never fuckin' know. You might go hunting one day." Luke's voice. The knife. The one in my hand.

"You need it today. You need it now." Luke's voice again. *"Use it. Now, Charlie."*

So, I did.

I raised the serrated hunting knife, painted black and etched in silver spiderwebs, and thrust it into Tommy's lower back. His eyes bulged, staring into mine, but he held me to the wall. His strength was waning, but he wouldn't let go. I pulled it out, desperation and determination helping to deafen my ears to the revolting squelching of blood and guts and flesh, and jabbed again. This time, he stumbled away, hitting his back against my bedroom doorframe.

His hands fumbled, touching his chest, stomach, then rounding to find the blood pooling at his back. His widened eyes held mine. "W-what did you do?"

He knew what I'd done, and so did I.

"I'm sorry," I breathed, my blood-soaked hands wrapping around the knife in my belly. Wanting it gone, but too afraid to pull it out. "I'm sorry, Tommy. I-I'm sorry."

Then, before he could reach out for me, I ran, not risking the stairs this time, terrified Tommy would regain the strength to come after me again. Instead, I ran past the open bathroom and to the door that had remained sealed for nearly two decades. I entered my parents' bedroom and slammed the door behind me, making sure to lock it. Aged dust and stilled time enveloped me in a cocooning embrace as I stumbled to their bed, made and untouched. Waiting an eternity for their return. I collapsed onto the flowered comforter Mom had loved and Dad had hated, laid my head on her pillow, and inhaled the final shreds of her scent as I bled into their sheets.

I listened to Tommy shout in the hallway. Listened to him stumble closer and closer. Listened as his hand landed weakly against the door once, twice, three times until he no longer could.

Then, as my breath slowed and my eyes shut to the closest I'd ever come again to being under my parents' protection, I listened as the sirens approached.

And all I could think, all I could hope for was, *Please, please, please, please,* please *don't let him die* ...

CHAPTER FORTY

CONNECTICUT, PRESENT DAY

"I killed him."

The truth exhaled out of my lungs with the most surprising sense of relief I'd ever felt. I was grateful for the darkness shrouding Stormy's childhood bedroom. Grateful I couldn't see the look of shock and horror on her face. She would be right in feeling both, now knowing that the man she loved had stolen the life of another, but I didn't want to *see* it. I saw it enough when I looked in the mirror.

She was so quiet, barely breathing beside me. I licked my lips, suddenly dry and desperate for moisture, and I filled the dead air with more stupid, terrible words.

"He died at the hospital. I found out while they were stitching me up." I touched the one-inch jagged line at my jaw and then the place where Tommy's knife had protruded from my lower abdomen, just above my groin. "They told me I was insane for caring, but I just kept asking, 'Is Tommy dead? Is he all right? I didn't *want* him to die. I-I didn't *mean* to kill him. I just ... I just wanted him to stop. I ..."'

"You did what you had to do," Stormy croaked, her voice sounding like it was full of splinters. Like it hurt her to speak.

Hanging my head, I tried to decipher the inflections in her tone. How she was feeling. What she was thinking.

"But I could've stayed with him," I replied quietly. "He was defenseless at that point. But I ran. That's all I fucking do. I run. I'm a fucking coward. I'm—"

She grabbed my arm and gave it a harsh jerk. "Will you *stop*?"

I finally turned to face her, and although the room had been swallowed in midnight darkness, I could make out the affection and heart-shaking sympathy in the tip of her eyebrows and the tears glistening on her cheeks.

"Jesus, Charlie! He wanted to murder you for something you hadn't even done. Do you not understand that?"

"Of course I do."

"Then, why the hell are you acting like you murdered him in cold blood?"

"I *killed* him, Stormy." I enunciated every word, every painful syllable. "Do *you* not understand *that*? His blood was literally on my hands. His mother's last son was ripped from this world because of—"

"Don't you dare say because of you," she muttered through gritted teeth. "Don't you fucking *dare* say that."

"Haven't you been listening to me?" I asked, exasperated.

"Yes! And we must've been hearing two different versions of this story because what I heard was, this fucking psycho came to murder you. And you"—her hand slid down my arm to grab mine so, so, so tightly—"were the fucking unbelievably brave badass who fought back. You're not a *coward*, Charlie. *You fought back.*"

I wasn't hearing her. I couldn't. "No. I—"

"And I'm so glad that you did because if you hadn't, I wouldn't have met you. Nobody would've stopped that piece of shit outside of the hotel. Maybe *he* would've murdered *me*, but he didn't. Because you were there, and you were there because you hadn't died. Think about that for a second, okay? Think about that before you say anything else."

I looked away and breathed out a quivering breath, raking a hand over my face and beard. She was right—but I was right too. Mrs. Wheeler had buried both of her sons because my brother and I had killed them. I hadn't killed Tommy intentionally, but it didn't erase the fact that it'd happened.

"Whatever happened with their mom?" she asked in a whisper.

I shrugged helplessly. "There wasn't any question about whether it'd been in self-defense or not. The 911 call had been recorded, of course, so there wasn't any kind of investigation. Very cut and dry, the cops said, so …" I shrugged again. "Anyway, I never heard from Mrs. Wheeler again. Honestly, she'd moved on a couple of years after Ritchie died, but Tommy didn't. He just … couldn't let it go."

"It's sad," Stormy said, her hand pulsing around mine.

"Yes, it is."

"But I mean it, Charlie. Stop blaming yourself."

I returned my gaze to hers, this time without the need to defend myself. A rock formed in my throat, and emotion pricked the backs of my eyes. "He didn't deserve it, Stormy. He just missed his brother."

"I know."

"I tried to talk sense into him."

"I believe you."

"He wouldn't *listen*."

She brought my hand to her lips, kissing my knuckles. "His mind was already made up."

An unexpected sob forced itself past the lump in my throat. "I see him when I sleep. I-I think … I think he's haunting me. I can't get him out of my head. I hate myself. Goddammit, I hate myself so fucking much."

Stormy dropped my hand and knelt before me. She cradled my sodden face in her hands and found my eyes in the darkness.

"Let it go, Charlie," she whispered, touching her forehead to mine. "And until you do, I'll love you enough for both of us."

***

When I woke to sunlight and a new day, I could hardly believe I'd fallen asleep at all after emptying my soul and crying until my eyes were swollen and my face was sticky. But by some miracle, I climbed out of bed with a lighter heart, and for just a few minutes, I thought I could look at my hands without seeing Tommy's blood all over them.

I knew trauma took longer than an overnight to scab over. But Stormy's acceptance and affection had proven to be a pretty decent Band-Aid, and I imagined that I might see a day where I hardly thought about that night at all. Maybe I could even learn to forgive myself.

I hoped so.

***

We had a nice, light lunch at a local restaurant with Stormy's family. Soldier sat beside me and asked if I felt better after telling her my deepest, darkest secret, and I turned to him, taken aback because how could he tell?

But he only smiled, nudged his inked knuckles to mine, and said, "I know relief when I see it. Lean into it, man. You're gonna be okay."

For once, I actually allowed myself to believe it.

After we ate, Soldier and Ray took their boys back home, two hours away in a town called River Canyon. And at the point where we watched them drive away, I found I was looking forward to seeing them again later in the weekend. Soldier no longer freaked me out, no longer reminded me of the bullies of my past, and I hoped he had another story or two about Luke to tell. I wanted to hear them. I wanted to hear everything.

Stormy and I headed back to her parents' house for a brief respite before we were due at Ivan's wedding. He had claimed we could wear what we wanted, likely as another incentive to get me to show up. But Stormy had twisted my arm and convinced me to wear a suit, insisting that the best man was strictly prohibited from wearing beat-up jeans and scuffed combat boots. So, for her, I listened, and while she was getting ready in the bathroom, I dressed in the bedroom where we'd slept the last two nights.

I was just buttoning my sleeve cuffs when she opened the door. She walked inside with a downcast gaze, shyly unable to meet my eye as I took in the swing of her long-sleeved, floor-length dress, as black as her raven-colored hair. It was modest and simple, the squared neck hardly revealing, save for the smallest glimpse of cleavage, nearly hidden behind an oval onyx pendant. Her fingers smoothed down the delicate lace overlay, fussing with the material before her hands flew to her hair, piled high in her trademark knot of chaos. Random strands had been left out haphazardly, as per usual, to frame her face, and she always—at least as long as I'd known her—wore the look with confidence. Today though, she seemed unsure and self-conscious as she turned from my wandering eyes to hurry for the mirror above the dresser.

"My mom's hair straightener isn't working, so I had to just wing it, but, fuck, man, I look like I stuck my tongue in a freakin' outlet. I can't go to a wedding, looking like this. Maybe I should braid—"

I stepped behind her and took her hands in mine, putting a stop to her fussing. Then, my eyes met hers in the mirror's reflection and said, "Did you know that spiders make different webs depending on their species?

A lot of people don't realize this. They're taught that all webs look uniform, often symmetrical. You know, like paper Halloween decorations or cartoons."

I lowered one of her hands to hang at her side, then held the other up, palm facing us. With the tip of my finger, I drew a circle in the center. "Orb weavers make webs like that, and they're beautiful, damn near perfect. They're the type of webs many people would use in art. I guess because they find them more visually appealing, the way some people might find someone conventionally beautiful to be more suitable for modeling.

"But the webs I like—the ones in my drawings and the ones on my body—are made by the black widow. Less uniform, uncontrolled, and untamed."

Now, I drew haphazard lines against her soft flesh. She flinched at the featherlight touch and laughed airily as I intertwined our fingers and held her hand tight.

"To me, I see them as a more accurate depiction of life. Messy. Unpredictable. Yet, somehow, it all makes sense. Every strand is put there for a reason, and as wild as it might be, it's still just as beautiful."

I lifted my other hand to touch the ends of her hair. "The black widow changes for nobody, and neither should you."

Stormy swallowed, her face flushed and heated. "When you talk like that, I have a hard time believing I deserve someone like you."

A brusque, humorless chuckle made its way up my throat as I diverted my reflected gaze from hers. "You act like I'm perfect, and I'm far from it."

"No, and neither am I. But I think, together, we make something that's pretty fucking close."

***

We showed up at the wedding venue ten minutes before the ceremony. Traffic hadn't been on our side, and I had spent the last twenty minutes of the drive stressed that we would be the reason for things not going according to plan. But as it turned out, there hadn't been much of a plan to begin with. No instructions, no rehearsal.

"Life isn't orchestrated, Chuck, and that's not how I want to start my marriage to the love of my life," Ivan said, leading the way to the head of the aisle after I questioned what I was expected to do. "Just hand me the rings when the judge asks for them."

"Wait, what rings?" I asked, already panicking. "You didn't give me—"

"Oh, I knew I was forgetting something!" He dug his hand into his breast pocket and dug out two matching gold bands. They were dropped into my open palm as he said, "The judge will ask to have the rings, and you just hand 'em over, Chuck. Easy-peasy."

"Sure. Got it."

I glanced into the small crowd of seated guests and searched for Stormy. She was easy to spot, sitting toward the back at the end of a row of chairs. My little black cloud in a flood of spirited color. She lifted her hand in a slight wave, the corner of her lips curving into a smile. I waved back, glad I wasn't there alone with too many strangers. I was also glad she had talked me into coming because from the looks of it, Ivan didn't have a whole lot of people there on his side.

That's how your wedding will be.

My eyes held Stormy's as I thought about the wedding day I knew we'd eventually have. How empty my side of the guest list would look. Did it matter? Her friends could become mine. Her family would become mine. They would all be *ours*. But the thought that I had nobody to offer to the mix—apart from Ivan and his newfound lady love, of course—hurt in a way I'd never expected.

Maybe Luke could get a pass. Maybe he could come. He could be your best man, and then at least, you'd have one member of your family there. The only one left.

Tears pricked at my eyes as a violinist began to play an instrumental rendition of a song I vaguely recognized, but couldn't name. I sucked in a deep breath and ignored the constricting of my chest and the tightness in my throat. My attention reluctantly turned from Stormy to watch the end of the aisle, where a woman I didn't know by looks but by name emerged in a white gown that dusted the ground she walked upon.

"That's my Lyla," Ivan said, sounding more thrilled than I'd ever heard him. "Isn't she the most beautiful thing you've ever seen?"

I couldn't say that she was when the most beautiful thing I'd ever seen was sitting at the end of a row, green eyes aimed at the bride while fussing hands brushed away strands of her wild hair. But Lyla was indeed beautiful, emanating a love for my friend, even from where she stood feet away. Proving there truly was someone for everyone.

"I'm happy for you, Ivan," I said, laying my hand over his shoulder. "I really am."

He tore his eyes from his bride long enough to look up at me for the briefest moment, surprise written plainly in his stare. "Thank you, Chuck," he said with awe and sincerity. "But I'd argue that I am far, far happier for you. That Stormy has breathed a life into what was once an empty, hollow husk of a man, and I'm honored to have witnessed your rebirth. The kids would say to wife her up, and I sincerely hope that you do."

I startled even myself by laughing, about to reply to my friend who was quite possibly even stranger than me. But Lyla arrived at the altar, and whatever I thought of saying left my mind as I listened intently to the vows and the official words, passing the rings to the judge when he asked and watching as Ivan and Lyla kissed for their first time as husband and wife.

They walked down the aisle in a hurry, holding hands and laughing in a way I could only describe as giddy. I strolled languorously behind, deep in thought with my hands buried in my pants pockets. When I came to stand beside Stormy moments later, she looped her arm through mine and reached up to pinch my chin between her thumb and forefinger.

"Whatcha thinkin' about, Spider?" she asked, using a name she hadn't referred to me as in what felt like an eternity, but ... had it only been weeks?

It seemed impossible, yet I knew it was true, and why had time been passing so oddly since I'd met her?

"I've never been to a wedding before," I confessed, sweeping my gaze around the emptying ceremony room.

"This was my second."

"Which was the first?"

My gaze landed on the open doorway to watch as Ivan and Lyla greeted their small group of guests, stopping frequently to stare into each other's eyes with gleeful disbelief and elation.

I want that.

"My sister's," Stormy replied, tightening her hold on my arm with hers. "Theirs was a lot like this. Soldier doesn't really have any family. Just us and his friend Harry. So, it was really small and informal, but it was nice."

"I'd always assumed my first and last would be Luke's."

I looked down at her in time to watch her head tilt and her brow furrow.

"Why your last?"

"Because"—I shrugged—"I didn't have friends and I wasn't sure I'd ever actually get married myself. I had a hard time imagining life progressing much outside of Luke and Melanie."

. A coalescence of affection, pity, and sympathy pooled in her eyes. "And you were content to be their third wheel?"

"Honestly?" I huffed a chuckle, seeing entirely why she'd feel sorry for that younger version than me. "Yeah, I was. They were home; they made me feel safe. At the time, that was all that really mattered."

She nodded. "And now?"

Luke and Melanie and the dysfunctional, imperfect, but loving home that they had forged for us to live ... it had been everything to me for what seemed like the longest part of my life even though I'd been without it now for longer than I'd had it. Yet losing it, losing *her*, had obliterated everything. The pieces of who we—Luke and I—were had scattered in a thousand directions. And although I couldn't say he'd ever found his happiness—I wasn't sure he'd even bothered to look—I knew, in the most bittersweet of ways, that I had found mine.

I'd just had to run away to do it.

"You," I said, my voice splintered with a rush of emotion. "You're all that matters."

CHAPTER FORTY-ONE

CONNECTICUT, PRESENT DAY

Black velvet night shrouds the cemetery as bare feet slap furiously against sodden ground. There isn't enough air in the world to fill my lungs. My arms pump, my heart pounds, my legs protest with each step taken. Every part of my body begs to stop running, even if to take a short break, but there isn't time for that.

The scent of cigarettes permeates the moist air. He is close.

"Leave me alone!" I cry, breaking free of the trees and finally stepping onto the blacktop.

The cottage on the hill is within view, illuminated now by a crack of lightning slashing across the angry sky. Home is right there, so close that I can taste it, taste her. Behind that door, I'll be safe—she'll make sure of it.

I take another step across the rough road before gnarled, shadowed hands reach out from the asphalt. Gripping my ankles, feet, legs. Holding me still, holding me down.

"No!" I cry, tears streaming down my face, arms reaching out toward the house. "No, please! Let me go!"

"Charlie."

That old, familiar voice from my nightmares breaks through the trees at my back. Icy tendrils slither down my spine as I squeeze my eyes shut, shaking my head.

"Go away, go away, go away ..." Like Dorothy and her red slippers, I chant the wish over and over and over until the rain ceases in its onslaught.

A cool, calming breeze blows the wet strands of my hair from off my shoulders, and as if by the wind's command, the grasping, clawing hands retreat back into the surface of the road, once again solid beneath my feet.

A breath of relief escapes my lungs, and I think of her. Stormy.

"I'm coming home, my love," I whisper, then open my eyes to the hooded figure of a faceless man, standing mere inches from where I stand.

"Don't forget what's important, Charlie. Don't forget me."

His hands reach out to grab me. I step backward and trip over something hard and solid, falling to my hands and knees. Turning, I see the grave and the name etched into the headstone.

Then, I scream.

"Charlie! Wake up!"

With a desperate gulp of air, I snapped my eyes open to find Stormy's wide, terrified gaze staring down at me, her hands gripping my shoulders.

"Oh my God," I gasped, clapping a shaking hand over my sweat-drenched forehead.

I wasn't in the cemetery. I was in her parents' house, in her old room. We had come back after the wedding to sleep. I was safe, I was okay, and I reminded myself of all these things, yet I couldn't calm my heart or steady my lungs.

"Here." She left me momentarily to grab a bottle of water from the nightstand. She uncapped it and handed it to me. "Drink this."

I did as she'd said, swallowing what was left of the bottle in two hearty gulps. It helped, and as I pulled myself into a seated position, I focused on forcing steady breaths in and out, in and out, in and out, until I was sure I wasn't going to hyperventilate.

"Holy shit," Stormy said on a breathless whisper, pushing the loose, frazzled strands of hair off her forehead. "You scared the hell out of me."

"I'm sorry." Despite the water, my throat felt dry and sore.

"You just started yelling and yelling, and it took a good ... I don't know ... thirty seconds to wake you up."

I furrowed my brow, turning to look at her with a sinking feeling in the pit of my gut. "Really?"

She nodded. "That must've been one hell of a nightmare."

With my arms folded over bent knees, I told her what I could remember. Running through the storm, weaving through the headstones, trying to get back to the cottage. The hands reaching out from the road, holding me in place. The faceless, hooded man. What he had said.

"Then, I saw this grave and ... couldn't stop screaming," I mumbled, feeling simultaneously spooked and foolish.

"What did it say?" Stormy asked, clearly invested.

I shook my head, trying to envision the dirt-encrusted stone. "I can't remember. You know, like ... when you try to read something in your dreams and you can't process what it says, but dream you knows?"

She bit down on her lip. "Damn. I wanna know what it said."

"It was probably Tommy's," I grumbled, now rolling my eyes and flopping back against the headboard.

The early morning light streamed in from between the curtains. I didn't know what time it was, but I knew it had to be too soon to be awake. We'd come in close to midnight, and I'd made it a point to not set my alarm, granting myself the permission to sleep until my body was ready to wake.

I guessed my mind had other plans.

***

Exhausted and buzzing with a fresh bout of paranoia, I sat in the passenger seat of Stormy's car, allowing the music from the radio to entertain us in an otherwise comfortable silence. She'd insisted on me trying to rest on the drive to her sister's house in River Canyon, which was roughly two hours from her parents' house. But every time I closed my eyes, there was that faceless, hooded man again and his words ...

"Don't forget what's important, Charlie. Don't forget about me."

I wasn't a stupid man, but it didn't take a genius to decipher what this nightmare symbolized. Tommy—or my subconscious, whatever—didn't want me moving forward from that Halloween night years ago. His ghost wanted me to dwell in a mundane purgatory of reliving that nightmare, repenting my sins for the rest of my days in this life. I'd been so agreeable a few months ago. I hadn't fought against the torment his spirit continuously dealt upon mine. But that was before I'd found happiness. It was before I'd found *her*. Now, I was fighting it. I was battling against him, struggling to escape the hold he still had on me.

It explained so much, now that I thought about it, and maybe the secret was to simply ignore it. Maybe, eventually, he'd just ... fade into the background, the way things often did after enough time passed.

But he was there every time I closed my damn eyes, his face shadowed by that hood.

Fuck.

The chiming of my phone startled me. Stormy jolted, turning her head toward the center console, where it sat beside hers. A surprising name flashed across the screen, and I furrowed my brow.

"It's Max."

I answered. "Hello?"

"Chuck, man, sorry to bother you during your time off."

My back straightened against the car seat as my eyes met Stormy's. "It's fine. Is everything okay?"

"Oh, yeah, everything's good. Or, you know, I think so. I don't wanna worry you or anything. But I did wanna mention that last night, while I was watching the security cameras, I thought I saw something—"

"What?" Dread rolled over my gut as every ounce of oxygen was sucked from the car.

"Well ..." He laughed abruptly, a sound of hesitation and disbelief. "You know, maybe it's better that I ask you this first. Chuck ... do you believe in ghosts?"

"Kinda hard to work where we work without believing in them."

"Right. Yeah." He cleared his throat. "So, um ... I was watching the cameras, and the one facing your place flashed. Like, the screen flickered, and at first, I thought maybe it was a bug crawling over the camera lens. But this went on for a solid two, three minutes, man, so then I started wondering if the connection was bad. 'Cause that's what it was like, like the signal was off or something, you know? And then, boom, it just stopped, like nothing had happened."

Stormy glanced at me from across the car and mouthed, *What's up?*

"And all the other cameras were fine?" I asked, my mouth dry, my hands trembling.

"Totally fine, man. It was just that one."

"Huh," I grunted, sucking in a tremulous breath. "That's—"

"But, listen, that's not the end of it."

I swallowed against my parched, constricted throat. "Okay."

"I kept thinking about it for the rest of my shift. I just had this feeling about it, you know? Couldn't shake it off. So, before I went to head home, I drove down to your place to check things out."

Oh God, my heart couldn't have pounded any harder. "And? Did you find anything?"

Max built the anticipation by feeding a few moments of silence through the line before saying, "Yeah, um … it was a letter."

That thundering organ in my chest stopped beating altogether. "A *letter*?"

"Yeah, hold on. I have it … in my …" Max grunted, and then there was the crinkling of paper. "Okay. It says, *There can be no tie more strong than that of brother for brother*. What the hell, man, right? It was just … lying there on your doormat."

"Poe," I whispered, wiping my hand over my mouth.

"What?"

"It's, um … it's a quote from Edgar Allan Poe," I said, coaxing my voice to hold steady despite the tremors coursing through my nerves. "Th-thanks, Max. I, uh … I appreciate you letting me know."

"Yeah, no problem, Chuck. Just gave me the fucking creeps, you know? Figured you at least deserved to know what you were coming back to. Someone's out there, leaving you quotes about brothers." He huffed another chuckle, just as humorless as before. "And whoever it is, man … they must've fuckin' *reeked* of cigarettes when they were alive."

***

The dead can't hurt the living, I kept telling myself on the duration of the ride to Soldier and Ray's place. The last thing I'd wanted to do was allow my anxieties and fears to blacken the nice reprieve from real life Stormy and I had been having over the last several days. But Max's findings sat at the forefront of my mind.

What time did it happen? I wondered. *Could it have been around the time I woke up from that nightmare?* It was eerie, disturbing, and ...

Borderline insane, I silently reprimanded, thrusting my hand through the tangled lengths of my hair.

God, it was so unfair that, just when it seemed I was gaining everything, I also seemed to be completely and utterly losing my damn mind.

"Are you ready to tell me what Max said?" Stormy asked, parking the car outside a bright and cheery colonial-style house in an equally bright and cheery suburb.

There was the faintest tinge of impatience in her tone, nearly undetectable but there all the same. And who could blame her? She had suggested I rest on the two-hour drive, but she hadn't mentioned anything about uncomfortable silence and nervous knee-jittering while my eyes remained fixed on the trees and buildings that passed. A healthy relationship wasn't healthy at all without honesty and unhindered communication, yet there I was, brushing her off once again because I was terrified of what she'd think of my supernatural suspicions.

Christ, hadn't she proven herself to me already? If she hadn't run for the hills after learning I'd unintentionally killed a man, why the hell would I think for a second that she'd be at all bothered by my fear of the potentially undead?

She turned to me, a helpless plea in her eyes, and the guilt of having clammed up again wrapped its tendrils around my unnerved body.

"I'm sorry," I said, speaking for the first time since ending the call with Max. "I should've just said something before. I'm just … trying to wrap my head around it, I guess." I huffed out a humorless chuckle and rolled my gaze toward the window. "Honestly, I've been trying to do that for the past couple of months, but …"

"What? What's going on?"

"Tommy is haunting me," I said point-blank, and the moment the words were out of my mouth, I wanted to find a deep, dark hole to crawl into. "I-I know I've said it before, but I mean it. And honestly, it's probably nothing …"

I was downplaying when I knew I shouldn't. It wasn't *nothing*. It hadn't been nothing since the first time I'd found the cigarette butt on the back of Luke's bike. But those other incidents, I could brush them off as bullshit pranks committed by local teenagers—maybe even those kids who'd tried to start shit with me a while back. I could loosely explain the hooded man—*apparition?*—I'd seen across the road from the house, the one Max had caught on camera.

But I couldn't explain this.

It was easy to brush things away when you were the only one to see them happen, but it was harder when there were witnesses.

So, before we climbed the steps to her sister's house, I told Stormy everything. Every moment I'd found something, every time I'd been struck with the scent of cigarette smoke. And she listened intently, not once flinching or snickering.

I didn't deserve her.

"And you think it's Tommy?" she asked after I laid it all out.

"Who else would it be?" I challenged.

"No, I know. I'm just failing to understand why he'd pick now to torment you when you said it's been, what, five years?"

"The only thing I can think is, I've spent those five years damning myself to a life of solitude. But I have you now. I'm *happy*. But maybe he doesn't like that. Maybe …" I squeezed my eyes shut and pinched the bridge of my nose, painfully aware of how this all sounded. "Maybe my self-torture was enough before, but it wasn't *long* enough. So, now, he's taking matters into his own hands."

It was ridiculous. Even as I said the words, I couldn't believe they were leaving my mouth to hang in the air around us. The absurdity of it all echoed with irritating flicks against my brain, and my cheeks heated more and more from the embarrassment with every passing second.

"I mean, I guess," Stormy finally replied, sounding unconvinced. "It kinda feels like a stretch to me though. I think, if I were a pissed-off ghost, I wouldn't have waited five freakin' years to make you lose your mind. I'd have been right there the whole time, making your life a total living hell."

"Thanks," I grumbled while chuckling at the sincerity in her tone.

She reached out and laid her hand on my thigh. I took it, sliding my fingers between hers until our palms touched.

"We'll figure it out," she declared softly, determined.

We. I sighed into the security of that little word and nodded. "Yeah," I agreed. "We will."

And just like that, I swept another incident under the rug and allowed myself, once again, to believe that everything would be fine.

If only I'd known how terribly, terribly wrong I was, if only I'd listened to the intuition that had never stopped talking since I was a boy …

If only …

CHAPTER FORTY-TWO

CONNECTICUT, PRESENT DAY

Salem's history had always called to my dark and macabre heart, a place where the misunderstood had once been exiled and punished, only to now be accepted and celebrated. And I couldn't say for sure that there'd ever been magic in this world, but Salem had certainly felt magical to me then. It still did, and it was the only place I could ever envision myself calling home.

But there was a special kind of magic in the air that lay over River Canyon, Connecticut, too. I'd felt it the moment I stepped out of Stormy's car to look up at a cloudless, bright blue sky, the sun warm against my face. I sucked in a deep breath, cool and crisp, and was surprised to feel the expansion of my heart, thumping steadily with a peculiar sense of new life and contentedness.

I could learn to love this, I'd thought then, and I was still thinking it as we walked down the small town's quaint Main Street.

Strangers to me were all friends with Soldier and Ray, greeting them with warm smiles and friendly waves. They all knew the kids by name, all offering the sense that they looked out for one another like true neighbors should. It was something out of a movie, something I'd once believed to be impossible, but there it was, acted out before me with every shake of the hand and genuine grin.

They were all glad to meet me, and I believed them.

"Any friend of Soldier and Ray is a friend of mine," many of them had said, and how nice was that?

They didn't treat me with anything but acceptance when I hadn't even found that type of welcome in Witch City, where the misfits and misunderstood were taken in with open arms.

You were different then, I reminded myself. *You didn't want to be welcomed. You didn't want to be accepted. You wanted the exile, and they gave it to you. How could you have expected anything more?*

I followed our group past picturesque shops and restaurants as my brain worked its way through the past several years while appreciating the life Stormy's sister and brother-in-law had found for themselves in this coastal small town. It was truly amazing when I considered where Soldier had come from. A drug dealer who'd done time after a manslaughter charge? God, the fact that he wasn't living in a run-down shack somewhere, sliding his way back into old habits, was nothing short of a miracle, and I started to think …

Maybe there was room in the universe to grant me one too.

***

"This is where I work," Soldier announced as we walked into the town's grocery store.

The Fisch Market was larger inside than it appeared to be from its storefront. Light-colored hardwood floors with tall, wooden shelves to match and bright fluorescent lights filled the space. We walked past the line of carts by the door, through an impressive produce section, and toward the back of the store.

Soldier wanted to pick up his paycheck before we headed down to Dick's Diner for dinner. We reached a plain wooden door, and Soldier knocked, only to be answered immediately by a cheerful voice.

"Come in, come in!"

Soldier opened the door to reveal a small office space and greeted the rotund older man behind the desk with a smile. "Hey, Howard. Sorry to bother you."

"Oh, stop it. You're never a bother to me, and you know it. Here for your check?"

"Yeah."

"All righty, just give me a second here." The man stood, and it was then that he seemed to notice that Soldier wasn't alone. His smile broadened at the sight of our small group, kids included. "Well, this is a surprise! Ray, Noah, Miles! It's nice to see you guys. And it looks like you have company?"

Ray returned the grin. "You remember my sister, Stormy, right? She stayed with us when—"

"Yes, yes, of course," Howard said, hurrying around the desk as fast as he could to take Stormy's hands in both of his. "It's nice to see you again, Stormy."

"You too," she replied, placing her other hand on my arm. "This is my boyfriend, Charlie."

It was absurd of me to expect that this introduction would go similarly to the way it had with her father. This man wasn't her father. For all I knew, this man meant next to nothing to any of them, outside of him being Soldier's boss. Yet it filled my heart with an unexpected warmth when both of his hands moved from hers to take mine, his grin never faltering.

"Charlie, lovely to meet you. How long are the two of you in town?"

"Until tomorrow night," I answered, even as my head filled with an abrupt whisper. *But you never know, do you?*

"Wonderful! I hope you enjoy your stay here. My wife is the mayor, in case these two kids haven't told you yet." He addressed Soldier and Ray with a wink. "If you need anything at all, just give us a holler."

I couldn't begin to imagine what we'd need in less than twenty-four hours, but I thanked him graciously anyway.

Then, he turned and hurried to the desk drawer, insisting that he didn't want to keep us longer than necessary. He produced a check and handed it Soldier's way, and the two men briefly talked about the job. Something about a shipment that would need to be accepted and unpacked.

"I'm visiting Uncle Levi tomorrow," Soldier told Howard. "But I'll be around after, if it can wait."

Howard nodded. "Oh, that's fine. I can be here to accept the delivery if you don't mind—"

"Do I *ever* mind?" Soldier asked in a teasing tone.

Howard chuckled and glanced my way. "I have to practically *beg* this guy to take a day off work." Then, he clapped his hand against Soldier's arm. "I won't keep you guys. Have a great night, and, Soldier, I'll see you tomorrow."

We left the store, falling in line once more as we walked to the diner. Stormy chatted with her sister while holding Miles's hand. Noah talked endlessly to Soldier about one thing or another, and if my mind hadn't been so focused on something else, I might've taken note of how wonderful their relationship seemed to be for a teenage boy and his close-to-middle-aged father.

But instead, I mulled over something Soldier had said back at The Fisch Market.

"I'm visiting Uncle Levi tomorrow."

His uncle Levi was at Wayward Correctional Facility. If Soldier was going up to see him, that likely meant the visitor center was open, and if it was ...

***

That night, after we ate dinner and got back to the house, after we played a board game with Soldier and Ray and retired to their guest room, Stormy and I lay in bed, naked and tangled up in the bliss of having made love for the first time in days. She peppered my throat with a thousand kisses before landing number one thousand and one at the corner of my mouth, her lips spreading in a wide, sated grin.

"God, I will never get tired of fucking you," she muttered in a dreamlike daze as she lowered her head to my shoulder. "I love that you take my weirdness and just accept it."

I released a breathless huff. "You're not weird."

"Okay, well, most men don't always like to be dominated. They think it's emasculating or something."

"Nah. I like giving you the reins to do whatever you want to me," I said, one side of my mouth curling upward in a grin, remembering the filthy words she'd said to me. The way I'd become malleable in her hands—as always.

"Don't you dare come until I tell you to. Do you understand? Say you understand."

"I understand."

"Do you feel how wet I am around your cock? Do you feel how tight my pussy is, just for you?"

"Yes."

"You want to come, don't you? Is my good boy ready to come?"

"Oh fuck. Oh God, yes."

"Then, come for me, baby. Come inside me. Feel my pussy milking your cock. Yes, that's it, good boy. Ahh ..."

Stormy huffed a husky laugh that held just the slightest touch of embarrassment, her fingertips tracing a line down my sternum to my navel, then back again. "That's why I love you. You don't just humor me; you *like* it."

"It's just one reason why we're perfect for each other," I muttered, pressing a kiss to the top of her head. "I just hope your sister didn't hear."

"Oh, trust me, I've had to listen to her and Soldier enough for one lifetime. Payback is a bitch."

I snorted and tightened my arm around her shoulders, the ghost of insecurity snaking through my nerves. "Okay, but what about the kids? I think I've finally won them over. The last thing I want is—"

Stormy propped herself up on an elbow, her eyes meeting mine in the soft glow cast from an outside lamppost. "Everybody loves you. Don't worry about that."

My jaw clenched, and the muscle pulsed. "It doesn't take much to turn that around."

"You would have to do something ridiculously fucked up for my family to not like you. Break my heart, and I can't guarantee I won't send Soldier after you." She smirked, her eyes twinkling with jest. "Do you plan on breaking my heart, Charlie?"

"I already told Blake I'd hurt myself before I ever hurt you, and I only intend on protecting your heart, not breaking it."

"Then, I guess my family will love you forever," she said, her voice quivering with hushed excitement.

"Yeah?" I lifted my hand, brushing a strand of her hair off her forehead. I traced a line through the collection of silver hoops lining the outer edge of her ear. "And what about you? Will *you* love me forever?"

"Spider," she scoffed, rolling her eyes. "My soul doesn't know how to not love yours. All I had to do was meet you to know that I had been put into this universe to hold you and protect you and shelter you from every terrible thing that had ever come your way until you were strong enough to face it on your own. And whenever that happens, if ever it does, my soul will stand beside yours, even while the rest of the world has been conditioned to run from us both."

Spiders and storms. Two of the most common fears, and separately, we were the embodiment of them both. But we'd saved each other, hadn't we? We'd given each other shelter, a place for our hearts to heal and love.

"Fuck," I uttered breathlessly, staring up into her glittering eyes. "You can't say shit like that without expecting me to propose."

Stormy's smile wilted from her face to make way for an expression of surprise, as if she hadn't seen that coming. "What?"

"You have no idea how much I cannot wait until the day I make you my wife," I said, holding her gaze.

"I want that more than anything," she replied on a held breath, swallowing. "Oh God, is that insane?"

"Maybe, but maybe that's how you know it's real."

Her laugh was abrupt and nearly maniacal as she thrust her mouth against mine. She pressed her hands to either side of my face as the kiss immediately deepened, tongues gliding and twisting and feeding on the taste of each other. My fingers slid along her jaw, plunging into her hairline and tangling that wild mane of black around my hand, and I forgot all about my concerns of corrupting the kids sleeping on the floor above our heads, only needing her naked body once again over mine.

She straddled my waist, and my hardened length was sheathed in her wet heat in one fluid motion. I swallowed her moan as I fed her mine, never breaking that fevered kiss for a second as she rode me with slow, patient thrusts. God, how I loved her and how our sex could be a frantic, passionate coupling of power and submission in one moment and a lazy display of closeness with no need for anything but skin against skin in the next. How lucky I was to have this, how blessed I'd been in my middle age to have met her.

"I want you to meet my family," I blurted out, my lips moving against her open mouth.

"Oh, yeah?" she asked breathlessly before sliding her pierced tongue against my throat.

I wasn't sure she'd heard me correctly, so I clarified, "I want you to meet Luke. Tomorrow."

Her attention was captured as she sat up abruptly, her hands held to my heaving chest. "What?"

I nodded, hardly able to believe it myself as I verbalized what I'd been considering for days. "I want to see him tomorrow, and I want you to come with me."

Her eyes flooded, and mine followed suit, both from the anticipation of seeing my brother for the first time in five years and the sheer fact that this incredible, amazing woman could care so much about me to know how large of a step this was for me to take.

She clapped her hand over her mouth, stifling a sob. Then, she bobbed her head in a frantic nod and whispered from behind her palm, "Okay."

"Yeah? You'll go?" My heart soared with hope and an uncontainable amount of happiness, so much that I thought it'd explode.

"God, Charlie." She held my cheeks in her hands, bent over, and kissed me with the gentleness of a spider's legs walking along its intricately spun web. "You didn't need to ask. You already know I will."

***

Just outside the window, birds chirped from an overhanging tree in the bright November sunshine.

Just outside the bedroom door, young laughter filled the hall, followed by scampering footsteps.

Inside the room, Stormy had woken before me, standing beside the bed and pulling her knit black sweater over her head. She glanced over her shoulder to find my eyes open, watching her, and she smiled.

Yes, everything seemed good, even normal, but the tumultuous feeling that spread from my gut to my lungs to my heart … it was old and familiar, but not something I'd felt quite this strongly in a long, long time.

Eight years. It's been eight years since Luke was arrested.

"Soldier's already up and ready to go," Stormy said, sitting on the edge of the bed beside me.

She was beaming with happiness and excitement, and somewhere beneath this feeling, I was too. But …

something wasn't right. *I* didn't feel right, and I couldn't help but think I needed to be cautious, wary.

"Okay," I said, sucking in a deep breath and allowing my lips to curl into a broad grin. "I can't believe we're going to do this."

"You wanna change your mind?"

No. Yes. I shook my head. "No, I need to do this. I just feel kinda ... I don't know ... nervous maybe?" *Was* it nerves though? God, I couldn't tell, and I hated that I couldn't read my own damn mind.

She nodded, a glint of sympathy touching her eyes. "Of course you're nervous. You haven't seen your brother in years, and from what you said, the last time you saw him wasn't a happy memory."

"No," I said, fiddling with the blanket's stitched seam while remembering the hurt and heartbreak in Luke's eyes before I'd turned to walk away.

"But you're taking a step toward making it right, and that's so freakin' brave of you. I hope you realize that."

I guessed I did. It took a coward to run away, but it took a great dose of courage to turn around, and I was trying. I *wanted* to try. So, despite the unease settling deep in my bones, I got up and got ready to go. And by the time I was dressed, boots on and hair brushed and pulled back in a low ponytail, I had successfully allowed my excitement to overtake that disgusting urge to change my mind.

I was going to see Luke. I was going to see him and hug him and touch his face and probably cry when I did ... and I couldn't fucking wait.

Stormy and I burst out of the guest room door, hoping we hadn't missed Soldier. As luck would have it, he was just getting ready to head out the door when he spotted us, dressed and eager to leave.

He lifted his brows curiously. "You guys leaving already?"

Stormy wrapped her arms around one of mine. "Actually, we were hoping—"

"We wanted to get a ride with you to Wayward," I cut her off, feeling I should be the one to say it, the one to ask. "If you don't mind."

Soldier tipped his head, slowly sliding his arms through his jacket sleeves. "Wayward," he repeated, not quite a question, but not quite understanding.

"Yeah," I said, already heading to the hooks hanging beside the door, reaching out to grab Stormy's and my jackets. "I wanna see Luke before we head back to Salem. I'm ready. I can't let—"

It was then that I realized Soldier hadn't replied, hadn't acknowledged what I was saying at all. I looked over my shoulder to witness that unease I'd woken with reflected now on Soldier's face. That same discomfort, that look of foreboding and pain, and, God, why the fuck did he have to look at me like that?

And it was the oddest thing because somehow, I knew *why* he was giving me that look. I just knew with every bit of intuition I'd ever been cursed with. But I didn't want to verbalize it. Didn't want to accept what I now felt deep in my bones, what was now festering with disease in my churning gut, what was now making every bit of sense. Didn't want to speak it aloud, as if that alone would make what was already true the truth.

Soldier opened his mouth, then closed it again, turning his head to fix his gaze on something else. Something other than me. "Charlie," he said, his voice gruff. "*Fuck*, I don't know—"

"You don't know *what*?" Stormy snapped, her voice tight and angry. "You're not going to take us? Seriously? After *everything*?"

But it wasn't rejection on his face. It was pain, regret, and a tremendous sadness I had no choice but to feel. He reached up to touch his brow, rubbed his fingers against his forehead, and released a forlorn breath.

My parents' passing. Melanie's departure. Breakup after breakup. Ritchie's murder. Tommy's death.

None of it would hold a candle to the fragile truth making Soldier look like that. Like the weight of a thousand unhappy endings was just sitting precariously on his shoulders, waiting to fall, to crash and burn.

"Charlie," he whispered, my name passing his lips for the second time. "They didn't tell you. God—"

"They didn't tell him *what*?" Stormy shouted, rushing to my defense as I shook my head.

"No," I commanded, praying that if he never spoke the words, they'd cease to be true. "Please. No."

Soldier's brows tipped angrily as he ignored my protests, my *pleas* for him to stop. "Dammit, they didn't *tell you*," he repeated through gritted teeth. He pushed his hair back with a hand. "Fucking hell, Charlie. God …" He released another breath that left his shoulders slumped. "I don't know how to say—"

"Then, don't," I whispered, but the damage had already been done, hadn't it?

He'd already breathed a life into the queasiness in my gut, put a name to the terrible feeling I'd had for months. But I could've lived with that, could've found a way to tamp it down and carry on the way I'd been for the past five years. Just as long as he kept the words to himself.

But Soldier wouldn't listen. He wouldn't leave it alone. He wouldn't just back down and continue on with his damn day with the same ignorance I needed to keep myself from losing it in his living room.

"He died, Charlie."

I squeezed my eyes shut and turned away from Soldier, the angel of death, the worst one to ever touch my shitty life. My hands rose to my hair; my head shook. Trying to chase those words away before they could take root in my brain and infect every last breathing part of my body.

Stormy gasped. "What do you mean, he *died*?" Her voice rose in pitch, full of desperation and despair.

But I couldn't look at her, couldn't face the pain she had no business feeling. Her sister was alive. She was somewhere in this house, playing with her kids.

Luke never had kids.

Luke will never *have kids.*

My chest constricted, and I fought against the wave of grief trying to barrel me over. No. No, I wouldn't let myself do this. Wouldn't let myself drown in the reality. I could ignore it, and I would've, wouldn't I? If I had never met Stormy, if I had never met *him*—Soldier—I never would've known.

I never would've known.
Luke is dead.
No. No, you don't know that.

But ... I *did*. I'd known for a while, hadn't I? I hadn't needed Soldier to verbalize it. I'd *known*.

Soldier began to speak, his voice laced with torment and the stress of having to bear such horrible news. I guessed nobody wanted to be the guy to tell someone his brother had taken his last breath. But I didn't give a fuck about that. Didn't give a fuck how he felt or what he had to say or how Stormy's soft footsteps had begun to approach or that her fingertips barely grazed my arm.

"No," I said in a harsh rasp, holding my hands out and stepping out of her reach, bumping into the coats. "Don't—"

"Charlie," she whispered, pleading, "I'm—"

"N-no. I need ... I need to get out of here. I-I need ..." The words rushed from my lips as my eyes snapped open, putting an end to what Soldier had tried to say and the comfort Stormy was trying to provide. Trying to put a stop to the tendrils of grief, but they had already begun to wrap themselves around my heart. There wasn't much I could do about that. I knew better.

I hurried toward the door, engulfed by a flood of sunshine shining through the windowpane. My hand touched the doorknob, and I was ready to barrel through and into a world where maybe, maybe, *maybe* my brother was still alive. But before I could turn the knob and leave, I glanced over my shoulder to find Soldier wearing an expression of sympathy and regret and Stormy wearing one of shock and disbelief and so, so much heartbreak that I couldn't fucking stand to look at her.

Luke is dead. I turned from their eyes and stared at the row of hanging coats, not quite seeing their textures and colors, but instead seeing a discombobulated montage of moments. My hand gripped tightly to the smooth metal doorknob, growing warmer beneath my touch.

How can he be dead?

"But what if we can't stay together?"

"That's not going to happen. That won't ever happen."

Dead? How the hell can he be dead*?*

I shook my head in disbelief, acutely aware of the pain stabbing at the backs of my eyes. The desperation to cry, but the tears wouldn't come. Not yet. I knew they would eventually, but … not yet.

"I don't understand," I whispered to the coats, then the door, sliding a hand over my face.

No. It had to be a joke. There was no way, no way at all that my resilient older brother was *gone*. No way at all that I could still remain in this world without him in it. He wasn't allowed to die. He wasn't allowed to leave me without anybody else in this fucking world. He wasn't allowed to disappear before I had the chance to see him again, before I had the chance to apologize for running away and being too much of a coward to fucking *talk* to him.

"Charlie," Stormy whispered, but I ignored her as I spun on my heel to face Soldier and moved quickly to stand toe to toe with him.

"Are you *sure* he's dead?" I demanded to know, looking up into his eyes. And, fuck, there was the tiniest bit of hope alive in my battered heart, holding on to the possibility that he was wrong.

But just like that, Soldier extinguished that tiny flame with a slight nod of his head. "I'm so sorry, man."

A solid, painful lump rose in my throat as I stared at his face. "You'd better not be fucking with me right now." The words rushed out of my lips as my finger stabbed at his chest, my voice crackling and breaking beneath the burden of a sorrow so tremendous that I should've shattered. "I swear to God, Soldier, you'd better not be—"

"I'm not fucking with you, Charlie," he said gently, wrapping his hand around mine, lowering my finger from his chest. "I thought you knew. I'm so fucking sorry. I should've said something. I just ... I—"

"He's *dead*," I said as an acute awareness of my chest collapsing under that horrific grief overcame me.

My knees shook, but somehow, I remained standing as I squeezed my eyes shut, hearing my brother assure me that nothing, nothing, *nothing* would tear us apart. *Fucking lies*.

"I can't breathe," I uttered, my voice choked as my hand grasped at my chest. "God ... *Luke*. I can't fucking breathe."

Life as I knew it blackened around the edges as a hazy scrapbook of old, worn-out memories played before my eyes. Luke's voice, his stupid smile, his insistence on getting me Amanda's number, his obnoxious wink, his relentless teasing, his fist connecting with my jaw, his arms wrapped around me, his begging to give him the damn phone as our parents died, his threats that he'd kill Ritchie if he ever said another thing about me, about *me*, *about me* ...

He had kept his promise. He had kept his fucking promise. God, why hadn't I remembered that? Why had I spent so many years angry with him when he'd only kept his goddamn promise? Or was it that he'd kept it that made me so mad? Some promises were meant to be broken, so why couldn't that have been one of them?

He'd be alive.

No, I didn't know that. Nobody could know that. But ... I *felt* it. He'd be alive today had he not defended me, had he not killed Ritchie, had he not been in prison. If he had been with me all this fucking time—where he was meant to be—he would be *here*.

God, why can't you be here?

Somewhere outside of myself, Soldier grabbed my arms before I could fall. His warbled voice called to Stormy in a commanding tone, saying something about helping him.

God, you were so fucking stupid, I sent out to the universe. *You were so fucking stupid—you always were—and now, you're dead. Now, you're dead—you're fucking dead—and where does that leave me, huh? Where does that fucking leave me? I wasn't supposed to be left alone here. You always knew I hated being alone. You were supposed to take care of me. You were always supposed to be here. You were supposed to be the one watching out for me, the one guiding me through this shitty fucking life, and you went and ... what? What the fuck did you do this time, Luke? What the fuck did you do? And why couldn't you have waited to see me before you did it? Why couldn't you have let me say goodbye?*

"Hey, Charlie," Soldier said, his voice breaking through the noise. Soothing yet demanding. "Focus on me, okay? Take a deep breath."

He ordered Stormy to get a bottle of water from the kitchen as Ray entered the living room, instantly startled and concerned about the scene playing out before her as her husband laid me back on the couch while I struggled to control my seizing lungs.

"What's going on?" she asked before ordering Noah to keep Miles away for a bit. She hurried over to the couch and knelt beside Soldier.

You fucking asshole, Luke. You fucking asshole. You weren't supposed to do this to me. You weren't supposed to do any of this to me.

"He's hyperventilating," Soldier said. "Charlie, man, come on. Breathe with me, okay? Inhale ... exhale ..."

I squeezed my eyes shut, seeing Luke's cocky grin and quickly shaking it away. *No.* I focused on pulling a shaky breath in, another shaky breath out. Slowly, I calmed my lungs, focused on Soldier, and then ...

"I will see you again."

"No, you won't, Charlie."

"Oh God." My eyes squeezed shut to the abrupt downpour, a deluge of tears, spilling messily into my hair and ears. "*God.*"

I balled up my fists, pressed them to my eyes, and replayed that last day. Over and over and over, if only to ingrain the sound of his voice into my head, knowing that one day, I wouldn't remember it at all.

CHAPTER FORTY-THREE

CONNECTICUT, AGE THIRTY-THREE

Somewhere in this room, a kid was crying for their daddy. Couldn't tell if they were a boy or girl—it didn't really matter either way. That kid's dad was a prisoner, and why he was a prisoner also didn't matter, not in this circumstance. Because what mattered to that kid—a toddler, from the sounds of it—was that he or she would have to walk out of here and go home to live life without their father. That kid didn't care about why their dad was locked up, didn't care what he had done. All they cared about—all they'd probably *ever* care about for the foreseeable future—was that they couldn't be *together*.

To that kid, there was nothing more unjust than that.

Fuck, every single guy in this place was a husband, son, father, friend ... a *brother* ... *something* to *someone*. Something *important*. But the people out there, beyond the concrete and bars and barbed wire ...

They didn't give a fuck about that. There was no compassion to be found within their so-called *good* and *forgiving* hearts, none at all. To them, these guys were no better than rabid animals that deserved nothing more than to be put down. *Monsters.*

Like me.

God, I'm no fucking better than these guys.

"Charlie!"

The crack of Luke's voice pulled me back down from the black cloud that had taken up permanent residence over my head. I snapped my gaze away from the dirty window to stare at my brother, and the deep concern reflected in his eyes.

"W-what?" I stammered, blinking the image of Tommy's blood mixed with mine away from view.

He studied me for a moment, tipping his head as his worried gaze bounced around my face. I couldn't tell what he was focused on more—the deepened circles carrying the weight of my tired eyes, the length of my ratty beard, or the unkempt tangle of hair touching my shoulders—but I guessed it didn't matter. I knew he looked cleaner, *better*, than me, and so did he. But could anyone blame me? Kinda hard to sleep in the same house where you'd almost lost your own life—and where you had taken someone else's.

It was even harder to sleep when, in your heart, you felt you deserved to be *here*. Locked behind bars with the other monsters.

"You're really freaking me out, man," Luke said quietly, as if he didn't want anyone else to hear his concerns. "Tell me what I can do."

I couldn't help laughing, shaking my head and looking away. There wasn't a shred of humor in that laugh. "You can't do shit, and you know it."

"I can try—"

"Oh, fucking hell, Luke. Stop trying to be the goddamn hero, all right?" My eyes dragged their way back to him. "You're not a fucking hero. You're *here*."

The worry on his face wasn't wiped away by my brashness. "Yeah, and?"

"You're a *murderer*," I spat, so bitter.

"I'm aware," he said, still quiet, still gentle, still *worried*.

"You fucking *fuck*." I laughed again, rolling my eyes to the water-damaged ceiling tiles. "You know, Luke, if you had been as worried about yourself as you are about me, then maybe you wouldn't be here. And I wouldn't be here. And I wouldn't …" I ground my teeth hard into my bottom lip, hating myself immediately for the crack in my voice and the flood in my eyes.

"What?"

I lifted my hands from the table, only to drop them again. "I wouldn't …" I tried to blink the tears away, but they began to fall despite my efforts, and I didn't care. "I wouldn't have killed Tommy."

Luke was already beginning to shake his head as understanding fell over his face. "Charlie, we've talked about this. He *attacked* you, and you *defended* yourself. You did nothing—"

"I should be *here*," I whispered, sweeping my tearful gaze around the visitor center. "I'm a murderer, too, and I should be here, with you."

"Stop it. You're not a murderer."

"That's probably not what Mrs. Wheeler thinks."

"Yeah, well, fuck what she thinks. She raised two pieces of shit who—"

"Who were killed by two other pieces of shit," I interrupted loudly, bringing a few of the other inmates and their families to look in our direction. "One of whom is out in the world, capable of … of …"

"Of *what*, Charlie?" It was Luke's turn to look utterly exhausted. "What the fuck is it that you think you're capable of?"

I kept my mouth shut, unable to say it.

He shook his head, disbelief on his face and something like amusement in his eyes. "You think you're gonna snap and kill someone else, huh? You think you're just gonna"—he shrugged nonchalantly—"walk into a Walmart and decide, *You know what? I hate that lady's ugly pants, and I'm gonna bash her head in with the nearest meat tenderizer*?"

I scrunched my nose and dismissed him with a wave of my hand. "Oh, shut the hell up. You know what I mean—"

"No, Charlie, I don't." He huffed, incredulous. "I mean, by your logic, that's how it is. You're a cold-blooded killer. You could snap at any moment. You could—"

"Do you think you'd choke the fucking life out of some random asshole if you weren't in here?" I leaned further across the table, anger fueling my every move.

Luke slumped into his seat and gripped the back of his neck, dropping his eyes to the table. "Our situations aren't the same, Charlie. I made a *choice*. I—"

"And I *chose* to grab that knife out of my fucking drawer. I saw my options and *chose* to stab Tommy in the back instead of letting him murder *me*. I *chose* to live, no matter what that meant for him."

"Okay, and I *could've* chosen to walk away when Ritchie wouldn't shut the hell up, but I *chose* to wring my hands around his goddamn neck instead. I *snapped*, Charlie. I lost control over myself, and *that's* why I'm here. You didn't *snap*. You didn't lose control—"

"Oh, but I'm totally fine right now, right?" I gestured to my face. "I mean, I don't know if you've noticed, but I'm not fucking sleeping. I'm hardly fucking eating. Shit, I can't remember the last time I took a shower."

He nodded. "I know. I understand. And that's why I'm gonna tell you to get help. Talk to the doctor. Check yourself into—"

"I'm leaving."

Shit. I hadn't meant to spring the news on him like that, but I couldn't keep it in any longer. And now, Luke stared at me, surprised and unblinking.

"You're *leaving*? What do you mean?"

"I mean, I'm leaving," I said, a little calmer than before. A little sadder. I swallowed down the familiar feeling of grief and continued, "I didn't want to, but ... I can't stay in that house, Luke. I can't fucking do it anymore. I haven't been okay in, in years, but after what happened with Tommy, I just can't do it."

He slowly began to nod and sucked in a deep breath. "Okay. Okay, yeah. I understand that. I've been telling you for years to get out of there, to get the hell out of town and start over. I just …" He cocked his head and shrugged, as if to say, *I just never expected you to do it.*

I just never expected you to leave.

"I still don't want to," I whispered. "But I don't think I have a choice."

"You don't need to make excuses to me," Luke replied, too cool to let his feelings show. "You gotta live your life, man, and it's about damn time you did. Honestly, I'm …" He shrugged again, slouching back against his seat. "I'm proud of you."

"Oh God, shut up, Luke." I shook my head, dragging my hand over my face and letting it drop once again to the table. "Don't be fucking *proud* of me. I'm not *living my life*, you asshole. I'm *running* from it."

"Or, you know …" He paused for effect, pinning me with a meaningful glare. "Maybe you're finally running toward it."

I stared back at him for several long, thundering beats of my heart, studying every weathered line etched into his skin and the healthy color in his cheeks and the neat trim of his hair and beard. He held a new spark in his eyes, beneath the fresh layer of sadness and concern I'd put there, and the knowledge that he was truly *content* struck me square in the gut. Sober and good. God, he was *good*—still! After three years in this place, he was still good and thriving, as much as he had been in that first year, if not more. But the anger I'd felt then was no longer evident. What I felt now was … envy, yes, but also comfort. Comfort that I was leaving him in a good place.

I let that settle in now as my shoulders sagged under the weight of a despair I couldn't do anything about. I was leaving him. He knew. It was out in the open. I'd known about it longer, of course, but I hadn't said it aloud to anyone—who would I have said it to? I hadn't even given my notice at the cemetery yet, too afraid to speak the words before I had told Luke. There had still been a possibility of changing my mind then, but now, seeing how okay Luke was, knowing how much I wasn't … I knew it was right, as wrong as it still seemed and how much it hurt in a way nothing ever had.

Luke lifted one side of his mouth in a smile. "Where are you going?"

I cleared my throat and lowered my gaze to the table. "Salem."

"You've always wanted to go up there."

"Yeah."

"You already got a job?"

I hesitated before jerking my head in a half-assed nod.

"Still burying bodies?"

A laugh huffed past my lips. "What else would I do?"

The choked chuckle that scraped its way up his throat gave away his own sadness. "You're such a freak."

"Yeah. It's a, uh … a pretty good deal. There's this little house in the cemetery."

That seemed to startle him, and I almost found it in me to laugh. "You're going to *live* there? Are you insane?"

"Seemed pretty perfect to me—"

An alarm grabbed our attention. We knew what that meant, yet we both turned our eyes toward the old guard manning the door to the prison.

"Fifteen minutes until visits are over. Wrap it up, folks," he said in a tired voice, pushing his silver-framed glasses onto his nose.

The brick tied around my heart seemed to double in weight as I thrust my hand through my hair. Fifteen minutes, and I'd walk away from my brother for the last time until … when? When would I see him again?

"Maybe I shouldn't go," I blurted out, desperate and scared and unsure I was making the right decision at all.

"Ah, come on. Don't do this. You made up your mind already, man, and that's good. You need this."

My eyes welled up with tears, but I kept my stare on the table, unable to look at him.

"What are you gonna do with the house?"

"I, um … I'm not gonna sell it," I croaked. "Not yet anyway. I guess I wanna keep my options open for now."

"Okay," Luke replied, seemingly satisfied with that answer. "I mean, you could get all the way up there and find you fuckin' hate the place."

I tried to laugh, but the effort alone brought a horrible ache to settle in my chest.

"You won't though," he added gently, and I finally looked up to find his lips had curled into the saddest, most heartbreaking smile I'd ever seen him wear. "You're gonna be fine."

"I *will* come back," I felt the uncontrollable urge to say. "I *will* see you again. I will talk to you again. I just … I need time, but I *will*." I said it as a promise, as much for me as it was for him. And for the briefest glint of a moment, there was satisfaction in it, and I thought, *Yes, this is good. This will be okay.*

But then Luke's lips spread wider, but they didn't reach his eyes as he shook his head. "No, you won't, Charlie."

That brick tethered to my heart sank deeper into a bottomless abyss as my lips fell open, and a harrowing sound of despair left my throat in protest, but he held up his hand before I could speak.

"And that's okay. *I'm* okay, and I mean that." He held my eyes with a sincerity that startled me despite the assessment I'd been making for years. "I'm *happy*, man. Truly. I am so seriously happy with my life, as fucking crazy as that might seem to you right now, but I mean it. I want you to trust that, and I want you to go. It's about fucking time you were happy too."

"All right, folks," that old guard spoke. "Five more minutes. Say your goodbyes."

Goodbye.

God, no. *No!* This wasn't a goodbye. This wasn't anything but an extended *see you next time*. I couldn't say when I'd be back, I couldn't say when I'd feel ready to come back or talk to him, but I *would*. Luke had to know that. He *had* to.

He stood first. "Come on, man. You're not leaving without giving me a hug."

I blew out a trembling breath before slowly rising to my feet. I stood to the side of our usual booth against the wall and was struck with the realization that I didn't know when I'd sit here again. Luke lifted his eyes to stare into mine, making up for those three inches I had on him, and he laughed.

"I remember when you were just a scrawny little shit," he said, poking me in the chest. "Tommy Wheeler picked the wrong guy to fuck with."

I rolled my eyes toward the window, shaking my head while imagining Tommy's blood still staining the matted hallway carpet. "Shut up, Luke."

"Come here." He wrapped his arms around me, and I let him. One of his hands cupped the back of my head while his other gripped my sweatshirt, and with a heaving sigh, I lowered my forehead to his shoulder and clung to him with every last ounce of strength I had left in me. "You're gonna be okay, Charlie. You will. I know you don't think so now, but I swear, you'll be okay."

"You don't know that."

"Yes, I do. If I can be okay in this fucking place, you can be okay in the city of your dreams."

I didn't care that I was crying. Didn't care that Luke wasn't. I held on to him, digging my fingers into his back and repeating over and over and over to myself that this wasn't the last time I'd see him, this couldn't be the last time I'd see him; I wouldn't let this be the last time I'd see him. But the lack of confidence and certainty in every one of those insistent thoughts dragged me further and further into the depths of sorrow until I could barely breathe.

"Come on," he said with finality. He clapped my back and unraveled his arms, still gripping the back of my head as he took a step back. Then, he pressed my forehead to his. "Listen to me. I have zero regrets. None. I would do every single fucking thing again, Charlie—"

"If you're trying to comfort me, it's not working," I murmured, my eyes still watering and my hands still gripping his white T-shirt.

"I'd do it *all* again, Charlie, if it meant you finally, *finally* finding the strength to get out on your own," he said, ignoring me. "That's all I ever tried to do. To protect you and to make you strong, and I guess, in my own fucked-up way, that's what I did."

The alarm rang again. Visiting time was over. Always a rule follower, I reluctantly dropped my hands from Luke's shirt to hang, trembling at my sides. Luke held on a second longer, then took a step back toward the door.

"Take the bike," he said, pointing at me and taking another step. "I want you to keep it."

I had no use for a motorcycle, but still, I nodded.

"And take Mom's clock. You always liked that ugly piece of shit."

"Okay."

Another step. "And if you ever find the balls to do it, go to Salem Skin and get some ink from that dude for me. The one on Instagram."

I scoffed and rolled my eyes.

He took another step backward, disappearing a bit into the crowd of visitors and inmates. My heart lurched forward, begging me to say fuck the rules and hug him again, but I didn't. I stayed put, my fingers twitching and my lungs heaving.

"Find some creepy-ass woman who'll protect you from that little black rain cloud over your head," he said, a teasing gleam in his eye. "And let her, okay? Don't be a fuckin' pussy about it. If you have to, just think, *What would Luke do?*"

He took another step, and my chest cracked open.

You'll see him again, I reminded myself, but, Christ, why didn't I believe it? It was him—I knew it. It was his insistence that I wouldn't. But he was wrong, dammit. He was *wrong*, and still, it killed me to watch him leave.

Imagine how he feels.

Luke lifted his hand in a wave before turning toward the door, his back to me. He took that hand and wiped his eyes.

I shook my head, cursing under my breath before saying, "Fuck the rules," and called his name as I closed the gap between us.

He turned, his eyes glistening with tears and curiosity. "You're not changing your mind—"

"Thank you," I said, pulling him into another hug.

The guard at the door took a step toward us and said, "Guys, time to break it up."

"What the hell are you thanking me for?" Luke asked.

"Everything, just … everything," I replied hurriedly, swallowing the sorrow and stepping back. "I'll come back, okay? I promise. I'll come back. When my head is on straight, when I can think clearly, when I can do *this* without losing my shit, when—"

"Corbin," the guard warned, but Luke ignored him.

"Sure," he said to me, nodding and reaching out to grip my shoulder. "I love you, Charlie."

I looked into his eyes, desperate to memorize every glint, every twinkle, every crease. "I love you too."

He nodded, satisfied, and turned to acknowledge the guard wearing the silver-framed glasses. He lifted his chin in a nod and said, "Sorry, Harry."

I watched as he passed through the door and turned down a hallway I'd never see. He walked by a window looking into the visitor center, where I still stood, and caught my eye. Then, he winked and disappeared, leaving me there with my empty promise and broken heart.

CHAPTER FORTY-FOUR

CONNECTICUT, PRESENT DAY

"*I will see you again.*"

"*No, you won't, Charlie.*"

My head was held in my hands as I replayed those words on repeat, words I'd kept at bay for all these years.

Stormy held her arm around my shoulders, one hand clasped to my knee, while Ray brewed coffee and tea in the kitchen.

Noah had been ordered to take Miles out of the house, to find something to do with him around town and give the rest of us the quiet and space to handle things ... as if there was something any of us could do about any of it. Still, I appreciated Ray's urgent order to her oldest son, and I appreciated Noah's lack of protest in spending the day with his much younger brother. Because it had been done out of respect for me, and that was something I could never take for granted.

And then there was Soldier. Sitting across from me on the coffee table, his elbows on his knees and his hands clasped against his forehead. Telling me what he knew of my brother's last moments on earth instead of visiting his uncle in prison.

I didn't want to know what had happened while wanting to memorize every word until I felt like I'd been there myself.

"This is just what Levi told me," he reminded me for the second time, making sure I understood this wasn't his firsthand account. "But they had brought in this new kid. Young guy, not even twenty yet. He was there on a few robbery charges after he failed to appear in court—or at least that's what Levi told me.

"Anyway, apparently, this kid has a freakin' mouth on him. Like he doesn't know when to shut up, can't take a hint ... that kind of thing. Levi said he'd already gotten thrown into solitary a few times for mouthing off too much to the officers. But ..." Soldier pulled in a deep breath. "Levi said that, overall, he's an okay guy. Just young and stupid, you know, and Zero ... Luke ... he liked him. They became buddies."

I couldn't help but laugh as I dropped my hands from my head and let them rest on my thighs. I leaned back against the couch, keeping my eyes on the ceiling. "Yeah, he would. Probably saw himself in the kid," I muttered more to myself than anyone, thinking about my brother as a teenager and the shit he'd say.

Soldier nodded before releasing a heavy sigh into the room. "Well, one day, this kid said some shit to the wrong guy. Big, mean fuckin' dude named Spike. I didn't know him well, but that's why. You didn't wanna get mixed up with him, and this idiot kid went and spewed some bullshit at him in the cafeteria. Levi didn't hear what it was or anything, and honestly, I guess it doesn't really matter. This fucker pulled a shiv on the kid, went straight for the jugular, but Luke got in the way."

I lifted my head abruptly to pin my eyes on Soldier and the somber expression on his face. "He was *killed*?"

"God, Charlie, I'm so sorry," Stormy whispered from beside me, resting her cheek against my shoulder and squeezing my knee.

As he pulled in a deep breath, Soldier closed his eyes and nodded. "Levi said Zero was always defending this little shit. The kid has a mouth on him, yeah, but from what Levi told me, it's like he's overcompensating, you know? He's picked on a lot by the other guys. They tease him about everything, and … I dunno … Luke took him under his wing or whatever and made it his mission to protect him."

A pained groan ripped through my throat as I dragged my palm over my face, turning my gaze toward the window and the bright sun streaming through it.

He had lost me and found some other pathetic loser to fill the void. Someone else to defend and protect.

The kid might've reminded him of himself to a point, but at the heart of it, the kid had reminded him of *me*. But this time, he'd been the one to lose his life.

"You fucking idiot," I sent off to the universe, hoping it'd reach his ears.

"Levi said that big, nasty fucker actually apologized to Luke while he was lying there," Soldier added in a gruff tone, and I closed my eyes, trying to imagine my brother on the floor of some cold, dirty cafeteria, a pool of blood spreading beneath him.

"Was he alone?" I asked.

"No," Soldier replied. "That kid—Jimmy's his name—and Levi were there when he died."

I tried to be grateful. I tried to cling to that tiny shred of comfort, knowing that Luke hadn't taken his last breaths alone, but what the hell did it matter if I hadn't been there? God, what if he'd been scared? What if he had been thinking about me? What if, instead of holding the hand of some fucking prison buddy, he had wished I'd been there instead? What if, at the very end of it all, he'd cursed me for not keeping my goddamn promise?

I shook my head in some pathetic attempt to shake every one of my thoughts and questions away because not a single one of them mattered. Nothing in life slammed a door shut quite like death did, and regardless of what I might or might not believe about an afterlife or whatever came next, there was nothing I could do about it *now*. Questioning and regretting changed nothing, and whether I liked it or not, it was something I'd just have to force myself to accept. I knew this. I was smart enough—mature enough—to acknowledge it, but, holy fuck, that didn't mean I didn't hate it.

Slowly, I began to nod as a weak, trembling sigh whispered past my lips. "Okay," I said quietly. "Thanks. For telling me."

"I'm sorry it had to be me," Soldier said, that hint of anger returning to his voice. "Those fuckers over there ... I don't know why they wouldn't have called you. I just—"

"They wouldn't have known where to find me," I cut him off, shame dripping from every word. "I changed my number, my address. All they had was my name, and they probably didn't care enough to look it up."

Stormy looked at Soldier then, and through the corner of my eye, I could see the curiosity creasing her brow. "What about his body?" she asked him. "What do they do when a prisoner dies?"

"They send them to the police coroner, and they contact their family, but ..." His eyes met mine, and he grimaced apologetically. "If they don't have someone to call, I guess they just ..." He shrugged in lieu of an answer, one I would've preferred not to hear.

Still, I wondered.

"How long ago did this happen?"

"Um ... end of September," Soldier said quickly, as if pulling from a recent memory, and that startled me. "Yeah, it wasn't long ago. It was literally right before we went up to Salem to visit you," he added, looking to Stormy.

"Huh," I muttered, nodding as a thought crossed my mind.

Then, I grabbed my phone.

***

"Sir, all inmate deaths are handled by the local police department," the woman on the phone told me.

I paced from one end of the guest room to the other as I nodded. "I see. And, um ... can you tell me how, uh, long ago he was killed?"

"Are you the inmate's next of kin?"

"I'm his brother."

"You should have received notification—"

"I-I didn't ... I wasn't ..." I pinched the bridge of my nose and released a breath through puffed cheeks, trying to gather what was left of my patience and sanity. "I've been away for a-a while, and I didn't, um ... hear about what had happened until just now, so—"

"I see. What did you say the inmate's name was?"

Was. My stomach churned sickeningly. "L-Lucas Corbin."

The clacking of keys filled the silence as I waited for her to give me the official date of death. I braced myself, aware that Luke's demise was about to become real, final. The other side of the dash on an epitaph.

"September 29."

The air left my lungs as my eyes filled with a fresh, hot batch of tears. "His birthday had just passed," I whispered into the phone, as if this lady, this cold stranger, truly cared.

"I see that," she replied, implying with her tone that maybe she actually did hold some genuine sympathy.

"He was forty-two," I muttered, quickly doing the math.

Forever forty-two.

"I'm very sorry for your loss."

I swallowed and nodded as I sat on the edge of the bed. "Yeah," I whispered, barely audible. "Thanks."

"I can give you the local police department's number if you want to try giving them a call."

"That'd be great. Let me just grab a pen."

I grabbed my sketch pad and Sharpie out of my backpack, and as I uncapped the marker and told her to go ahead, I thought about the irony of this moment. Luke had been the one to get me my first drawing pad and pack of markers, and there I was, using those very implements to jot down the next step in hopefully laying his body to rest.

Life is so fucking weird, I thought to myself, popping the cap back into place and thanking the woman for helping in whatever way she could.

"Did Luke, uh … did he have any personal belongings or anything?" I took a chance asking, and she sighed into the phone.

"Honestly, if their things aren't collected pretty quickly after the family is notified, all the stuff is usually trashed or pilfered by the other inmates," she said matter-of-factly. "I'm sorry."

My heart sank even as I said, "Yeah, it's okay. Just figured I'd ask."

I hung up and dropped the phone to the bed, giving myself a moment to sigh before making the next call. My eyes glanced at the time glowing on my cell phone's screen, and I huffed a bitter laugh. Two hours ago, I had thought my brother was still alive. I'd been on my way to introduce him to the woman I knew so deeply in my bones that I would one day marry, and now, I was just trying to bury him. Or whatever was left of him anyway.

"Fuck," I muttered, scrubbing my hands over my face.

I didn't want to handle this shit. Luke had handled things last time, when Mom and Dad had died. Well, him and Nana. Now, they were dead ... they all were. I was it, all that was left.

The door creaked open, and Stormy poked her head in.

"Hey." She entered tentatively, cautiously. She closed the door behind her, letting it click shut slowly, while keeping her eyes on me. "How are you doing? No, wait, that's a stupid question. I'm sorry. I'm just—"

"No, it's okay," I said, outstretching my hand to welcome her in.

"God, Charlie." She accepted the warmth of my palm encasing hers and sat beside me on the bed. "I know I've said it a million times already, but I am so, so, so fucking sorry. I can't even imagine how you're feeling."

"Not great," I answered with a humorless laugh. "But ... I think I'm glad I know."

That was when I noticed the stiffness of her limbs and the thrumming of her pulse. Her phone was clutched in her hand, the screen glowing bright. I asked her if there was something she wanted to say, and she stammered with nervous intent.

"Um ... I-I didn't know if now would be the right time to bring it up, but ..."

"Tell me anything to get my mind off this shit."

"Well ..." She blew out a deep breath and lifted her phone, her eyes meeting mine. "While you were on the phone, I googled Luke's name."

After all this time, she only decided now to utilize the search engine at her fingertips. After there was nothing more for me to tell, no more secrets between us, and I loved her for it.

She turned the phone's screen toward me, and a picture of Ritchie looked back. I knew it well. It was the friendliest, least menacing picture the media could find of him. One from his days of coaching the high school football team. His smile was nice enough, but his eyes were as cold as a shark's.

"W-why are you showing me this?" I asked, fighting the nausea that rolled through my gut at the sight of his face.

"This is him, Charlie," Stormy whispered, her eyes glistening with tears. "This ... this is the guy who ... h-he was at that bar. W-when I was sixteen. He ... he—"

"He's not a good guy, Charlie. You have no idea. He's bad."

"Are you serious?" I asked, but of course she was. Why would she lie? "Are you *sure*?"

She nodded slowly, one tear slowly trickling down her cheek. "Believe me, I'm sure."

My heart lurched into my throat as I looked between the picture of Ritchie and her face, and all at once, a new, special kind of hatred toward him began to grow, along with a brand-new sense of gratitude toward my brother. Who had unwittingly murdered the man who had raped the love of my life long before I knew her name ... and only God knew how many others.

God, what were the chances? How the hell was it even possible that I would meet her so many years later and—

"So, um …" She pulled in a deep, quivering breath and removed Ritchie's face from her phone screen. "Did the, um … prison give you anything useful?"

I cleared my throat and held up the sketch pad resting on my thigh. "Yeah, uh … the number for the police department that conducted the investigation and autopsy. The woman on the phone said they might still have his body, but … I don't know. I kinda think it's a long shot, but I should probably take it."

She nodded. "Might as well. Just in case."

I filled my lungs in preparation and snatched my phone from the bed, ready to dial. Stormy asked if I'd prefer she leave, and I told her to stay, needing her to hold my hand and keep me warm when the cruel touch of heartbreak threatened to encase my spirit in ice yet again.

The phone was answered almost immediately by a gruff, impersonal tone. I explained the situation all over again, and the cop on the line listened intently before sighing. He asked for my brother's name and did a little digging on his end, typing on a keyboard and grumbling incoherently to himself.

Then, he finally said, "Ah, yeah. We picked him up back in September, on the twenty-ninth."

"Right. Um … you wouldn't happen to still have his body there, would you?" It felt ridiculous to ask, like they just kept dead bodies lying around.

The man was silent for a moment, then said hesitantly, "No, we, uh … we released the body to the next of kin."

What the fuck?

My brow creased immediately. "But *I'm* the next of kin," I replied. "He was my brother. We're the only two left in our whole freakin' family. So, if you didn't release his body to me, then—"

"Sir, if you want to come down and bring the proper identification with you, we can talk about this further."

I shook my head as my heart took off at a pace I knew couldn't be healthy. Stormy sat beside me, her hand clenched around mine, as her eyes watched my reactions, concerned and worried.

"My brother didn't *have* anybody else," I pressed further, panicking and growing exceedingly angry. "Who the hell did you give his body to?"

Bizarre scenarios filled my head as I imagined Ritchie and Tommy's mother, Mrs. Wheeler, going down to the police department, claiming to be my brother's next of kin. Scenarios in which she gleefully celebrated her unexpected, unplanned vengeance for her oldest son's untimely death. Scenarios where she praised the big, mean man who'd inadvertently done her dirty work for her.

"Listen, I shouldn't be giving you this information without seeing some ID," the cop said, dropping his voice close to a whisper. "But I don't know where you're located, and I'd hate for you to drive all the way here just to show me your license. But if you're saying *you're* your brother's next of kin, then there's either something really weird going on here or your brother was keeping some pretty big secrets from you."

I didn't want to mention that it'd been five years since I'd seen or last spoken to Luke. I was sure there was plenty that'd happened within that time that I had no clue about. But then again, my life had been at a standstill throughout most of that time, and I hadn't been the one in prison. What reason would I have to believe Luke had done more with that time than me?

"Why do you say that?" I asked, my gut rolling around an angry bundle of nerves.

"Because the person who came in here, claiming to be his next of kin, was his wife."

CHAPTER FORTY-FIVE

CONNECTICUT, PRESENT DAY

A *wife. Luke has a* wife.
Had, I reminded myself amid the shock.
The initial emotion that bowled over me was anger. He had been married—in prison, no less—and I'd had no clue. I felt betrayed, lied to. But that anger was quick to dissolve as I almost immediately reminded myself that he'd done nothing wrong by living what little life he had left. It was *my* fault for forcing a divide between us with all of that time and distance. It was *my* fault for not coming back, the way I'd said I would. The way I'd *promised*.

So, after hanging up with the police officer, I allowed myself a few minutes to lean against Stormy and cry—again—through every bit of regret and sorrow I held in my beaten heart. I cried harder than I'd ever cried before in my life, until my throat was raw, my head ached, and there was nothing left to cry. And after, when I knew there wasn't anything else I could do, I asked Stormy to give me a ride.

Initially, it was a long shot—I knew that when I'd suggested it—but now, as I stared out the window of her car, I realized that my uncanny intuition had been right yet again. But that didn't mean it wasn't fucking with my head to stare out at the house I'd grown up in—the house Luke and I had unwillingly allowed to fall apart and then abandoned—and see this clean, painted, well-manicured home with a car in the driveway and a toddler's tricycle on the lawn.

And I thought, *No way. There's no fucking way*, because denial was somehow an easier pill to swallow than the truth. That my brother had married someone with a kid—or was the kid *his*?—and that wife and kid were now living their lives in this house I still paid the taxes on. Cleaning it up, fixing it up, making it a home.

Respectful squatters.

"This was your house?" Stormy asked, following my line of sight.

I cleared my throat past an uncomfortable swelling of emotional distress and said, "Yep."

"What are you going to do?" Stormy asked in a hushed tone, looking out at the house with wonder and disbelief.

"I don't know."

"You can't just kick your brother's wife out."

I glanced over my shoulder at her, sitting behind the wheel. "Did I say I was going to kick her out?"

"No, but you look like you want to."

I huffed an irritated sound. I wasn't lying; I didn't know what I wanted to do. I didn't even know who this woman was—*if* that was who was living here in the first place. The cop hadn't provided that much information—just in case I wasn't who I had claimed to be, he'd said, to protect the privacy of a seemingly innocent woman.

Would she feel so protected if I just rang the doorbell right now?

I didn't want to scare her. I just wanted to ask a few questions. I wanted to know who she was, if the kid was my brother's, if … if …

If he forgot about me.

"I'll be right back," I said abruptly, opening the car door.

"You want me to come with you?" Stormy asked, already opening the driver's side, but I shook my head.

"No, not yet. Stay here. I'll come back if I need you." *I always need you.* But I needed to do this alone.

She hesitated for a moment but eventually replied, "Okay. I'm not going anywhere."

I hardly acknowledged her as I shut the door behind me. I couldn't help it as I slowly made my way from the curb to the driveway, eyeing the freshly painted mailbox, where Tommy had once left a pile of dog shit. The place at the end of the asphalt, where he'd spray-painted a death threat, now gone, like it'd never happened. I foolishly wondered if the bloodstain was still in the hallway, if the crimson handprints had been wiped away from the walls and my parents' bedroom door, knowing damn well that they were long gone, just like the peeling paint on the siding and doorframe.

God, even the door itself is different, I thought as I carefully climbed the steps to the front stoop. Feeling an awful lot like a stranger to a place I'd known since birth.

I didn't belong here anymore. And I didn't know why that hurt the way it did, but ... God, it really, *really* did. It had been my choice to walk away, to abandon this place until I was ready to return, but somewhere along the line, it had stopped being *mine* despite my name on the deed, alongside Luke's.

Standing in front of the door, I tried to peer through the frosted glass windowpane, but the image was too distorted to make out anything but a couch and a TV in places they'd never been before. I reached out to the doorbell and hesitated, wondering if I should just leave and continue to live my life in ignorant bliss, the way I'd been for the past five years. But ... how blissful had it been when I couldn't stop thinking about my brother and what he was doing? This was my chance to get answers. This was my chance to know how he'd spent his last years alive, and didn't I deserve that? I mean, I might not have deserved much, after all of my wrongdoings and broken promises, but I deserved *this*. I deserved closure.

Without another thought of doubt, I rang the doorbell. And I waited.

Footsteps approached from where I knew the staircase to be. A muffled voice called out, saying something I couldn't hear, but it wasn't meant for me, I realized, as another voice answered. The footsteps came closer, and with every single one, my heart rate escalated. This was it. This was the moment when I'd meet the woman who'd married my brother while he was incarcerated.

God, who the hell marries someone while they're in prison with little chance of getting out? I pulled in a quivering breath, waiting for the door to pull open. *Who the hell marries a* murderer?

The distorted figure of a woman came into view, and the locks were undone. I clenched my fists at my sides, urging my feet not to run back to Stormy's car. The front door was pulled open, and my heart stopped all function as a head of strawberry-blonde hair and a pair of sparkling blue eyes were revealed to me. She startled at the sight of me, as I did at the sight of her. Her gaze roaming over my tall frame before landing on my face, hands clinging to the doorknob and doorframe, staring at me and blinking away the paled-face impression that she'd somehow seen a ghost.

Then, as if happening in slow motion, the air was forced from my lungs as she launched her body against mine, her arms wrapping around my neck and mine around her waist.

She trembled as she held on tight. Her tears wetting my neck, down to the collar of my sweater, her gentle sobs filling my ear.

"Charlie," she whispered, digging her fingertips into my shoulders.

I exhaled and finally gave myself permission to cry with her as I whispered, "Melanie."

"You came back."

I couldn't help but laugh, waterlogged and warbled. "So did you."

She didn't laugh with me. She only cried harder, louder, burying her face into my shoulder. I breathed her in, filling my senses with the memories of my youth and the one thing—the one *person*—who had always made things good at a time when nothing was good at all. And I couldn't believe she was *here*, couldn't believe she was in this house, couldn't believe she and Luke had ...

God, what *had* happened?

"*Why* are you back?" I asked gently, my cheek moving against hers.

Reluctantly, she let go, stepping back and away, but not before pressing her palms to my cheeks and smiling despite the tears still cascading over her face.

"God, *look* at you," she whispered, shaking her head, bewildered. "Luke would be so happy. He'd ..." She pulled her lips between her teeth, her face crumpling all over again. "God, I'm so sorry, Charlie. I'm so, *so* sorry. I thought about you all the time. I wanted to find you. I just ... I didn't know how, and—"

"It's okay," I said, taking her face between my hands and brushing her tears away with my thumbs.

"No, it's not." She held my wrists and forced a smile. "But I guess it has to be, right? You're here now. You're *back*."

"Yeah." I nodded and pulled in a deep breath. "I'm here now."

***

Melanie welcomed me into the place where my parents had brought me home from the hospital nearly thirty-nine years ago.

"There's so much I have to tell you," she said, and I agreed.

There was so much I needed to hear—and so much I had to tell her too.

But first, I returned to the car to retrieve someone she needed to meet.

"What's going on?" Stormy asked, her eyes trained still on the house and the open front door.

"I want you to meet someone," I said eagerly, grabbing her hand and pulling her from the car.

Stormy eyed me suspiciously as she climbed out. "You know who she is? Is she your brother's wife?"

I wiped my hand against my forehead and looked over the car at the house, reality resting against my shoulders with a strange but comfortable weight. As if an old puzzle piece had been found and put back into place. As if everything—well, almost everything—was once again *right*.

"It's Melanie," I said, shaking my head with disbelief.

"Melanie? Your brother's ex-fiancée?" Stormy sounded as shocked as I felt. "They got back together?"

"I … I have no idea. I mean, obviously, but … I don't … she was going to tell me everything, but I came to get you first."

I held her hand as I began to walk back to the house, but she stayed put. I turned to find an unsure expression on her face, her brows pinched and her teeth digging into her bottom lip.

I tipped my head and asked, "What's wrong?"

She shrugged before replying, "Are you sure you want me here? It's … so personal, and …"

"What do you mean?" If I wasn't mistaken, she seemed uncomfortable. "Why wouldn't I want you here?"

"Because this is between the two of you. You're *family*, and she's so ... she's so *special* to you—"

"There is *nobody* on the planet more special to me than you," I assured her, squeezing her hand. "And after I just spent the past few days with your family, I want nothing more than to welcome you into what's left of mine. Please. I don't want to go in there alone."

Her chest dropped with her exhale as she looked up to my eyes and nodded. "Okay, Spider. Let's do this. Introduce me to your family."

***

The living room had been rearranged, the carpet had been ripped up to reveal the hardwood floor hidden beneath, and the walls had been dressed up with a fresh coat of paint. But otherwise, the ground floor of my childhood home had remained the same, and that was both a comfort and a curse.

Everywhere I looked, I saw Luke. I saw myself. I saw our childhood, and I saw the years alone. I saw the blood I'd dripped to the floor that Halloween night five years ago, and I saw Tommy's unconscious body being removed on a gurney. Melanie and Stormy could sense it, too, as I eyed every corner with apprehension and cautious nostalgia. The two women hadn't even shared formal introductions yet, but as if by an unspoken agreement, they said nothing while I slowly walked through the living room, sweeping my gaze overhead as I approached the dining room.

"I tried to keep things as much the same as I could," Melanie finally said as I ran my hand over the stone mantel above the fireplace, where I wasn't sure my parents had ever burned a fire.

I knew I hadn't.

"It looks good," I said and meant it, even if the melancholy in my tone made it seem like a lie.

"Are you sure? Because I didn't know if I—"

I glanced over my shoulder to see her standing by the couch, timid and eyeing me warily. "Melanie, this is *your* house. You don't need my approval."

She dropped her gaze to the area rug beneath the coffee table and shook her head. "No. It's not. I ... well, Luke and I ... we always assumed I'd live here for a while, but we didn't know for how long. And if you ... *when* you came back, you'd want to move back in, and we'd find a new place to live, so ..."

There were so many questions to ask, and I didn't know where to start. So, as I stuffed my hands into my pockets and turned to face her, I asked the first one that came to mind. "Who's *we*?"

Melanie swallowed, her gaze volleying between Stormy and me. It dawned on me then that she was a stranger to me now, and I, to her. We shared a history, we shared an old, mutual love, and those memories and emotions would outlast both of us. But I didn't know who she was now, and she couldn't predict how I'd react to ... well, anything.

She's scared of you. You're a killer now.

Yeah, well, she married one too.

I shook my head, unable to stop my incredulous chuckle at the thought. God, I couldn't believe she and Luke had been married. After all this time, after everything ...

"What?" Stormy asked softly, taking a step toward me.

"I just can't believe any of this is happening," I said, unsure I ever would.

Melanie nodded. "You know, why don't we sit down, and I'll just ... start from the beginning?"

"Yeah," I agreed. "That's a good idea."

I turned first and headed toward the dining room because as much of a stranger as I might've been to this house, it had been mine once. The table—the exact one—stood exactly where it always had, and from behind me, I heard Melanie and Stormy quietly introducing themselves to each other as I envisioned countless dinners, countless birthdays, countless hours of homework and conversation and arguments. I envisioned Luke and me, alone. Envisioned that last time he'd asked me to do something with him, to go to the movies, and I swallowed down the pain of wishing I had just gone. It wouldn't have killed me to just go, so why hadn't I? I couldn't remember, and that was the worst part of all.

I took a seat in the chair Luke had always sat in, somehow feeling closer to him by doing so. Stormy sat beside me, where Melanie always had, and Melanie sat across from us, in the exact chair I'd always chosen as mine. Our roles had been oddly reversed; Melanie was suddenly the third wheel, and it seemed both right and unnatural at the same time.

"So, did you meet each other in Salem?" Melanie asked, pouring three glasses of iced tea from the pitcher in the middle of the table.

I realized that the only way Melanie would've known where I'd been was if Luke had told her, and I wondered how often he'd talked about me. Had he thought of me as often as I'd thought of him? Had he missed me?

"Yeah," Stormy replied, accepting one of the full glasses. "He had saved me, so I repaid him by giving him no choice but to go out with me."

Melanie flashed me a pair of teasing eyes as she passed a glass to me. "So, still as antisocial as always, I take it?"

"Honestly, worse," I said with a gruff, self-deprecating chuckle. "But I'm getting a little better with it, I think."

Stormy bumped her arm against mine. "You are."

Melanie lifted her chin as she watched us, took in the way Stormy looked at me and the way I looked at her, and said, "This is all he ever wanted, you know."

I turned to her and furrowed my brow. "What?"

She shrugged as her eyes flooded. "Luke. All he ever wanted was for you to find someone. That's all. He never cared about himself. He figured he'd get out in a couple of decades or so, and he knew we'd be okay one day … or, you know, as okay as we could be. But you …" She bit her lip to stop it from trembling as she wiped at a tear before it could slide down her cheek. "He was so afraid of you being left alone, Charlie. He didn't want you to be alone. He'd talk about it all the time, about how he hoped you had finally found someone up there and that you weren't just ... holing up wherever you were."

My lungs fought for air as Melanie spoke, and my gaze dropped to the table, to where Stormy's hand was holding mine. Quietly, gently, like a hushed winter's snowfall, pieces fell into place, ones I dared not speak out loud. Ones I dared not acknowledge to anyone. But my heart thudded, and my leg jounced beneath the table, and I wondered ... I couldn't stop myself from wondering ...

I cleared my throat and blinked the thoughts away as I said, "So, um ... what happened? How did you and Luke get back together? I'm guessing it was after—"

"Actually," Melanie interjected with a nervous laugh, "we had started writing letters shortly after he was convicted."

And just like that, I was angry. "Are you serious? And he didn't tell me?"

Her eyes reflected her apology as she said, "I guess he didn't think he could. You were so ..." She sighed and looked away. "You were having such a hard time, and Luke never wanted to rub it in your face that, despite everything, things weren't so bad for him. He didn't blame you for it or anything, and he wasn't really intentionally hiding things from you. In both of our defense, we didn't know what was going to come from being pen pals."

I wanted to find it in me to stay mad, but she was right. I'd been focused on nothing but myself and the circumstances of my everyday life. There were times I hardly allowed Luke to get in a word during our brief visits, and when he did speak, I barely listened. I guessed I'd just assumed nothing of note would be happening to him. After all, he was the one behind bars. But little had I known, it was when he'd been made a prisoner that he was finally set free.

"So, then ..." I wiped my hand over my mouth, working the timeline out. "When did you get back together?"

"Right before you left," she replied without a second thought. There was a hint of regret in her tone. "We had arranged a private visit. I didn't want the first time I saw him after all those years to be in the visitor center, surrounded by so many people. I needed time to get used to things, you know, seeing him like that. But then ... the rest was history."

From the corner of my eye, I watched Stormy's lips spread into a smile. "And just like that, you took him back."

Melanie laughed and rolled her eyes. "I guess Charlie's told you about us."

Stormy nodded regretfully, and Melanie dismissed the apology.

"We were so messed up back then. *He* was so messed up."

"Yeah, he was," I agreed as a barrage of drunken nights came back to me. The fights. The hangovers. The countless fuckups.

"But, honestly, as insane as it sounds, he was the best version of himself when he was at Wayward. Sober, attentive, honest, healthy ..."

It was all true. I had seen it myself, and I nodded along with every word.

"I had never stopped loving him," she admitted, addressing me fully. "And I tried moving on. I really did. I had a couple of boyfriends I kept around for a year or two, but ... it wasn't the same."

My heart ached, and my shoulders dropped as I nodded. "He never stopped loving you either, Mel."

"I know." A rueful expression fell upon her face as she fiddled with the rings on her finger. "That first time I visited him, he asked me if I still had my engagement ring." She laughed incredulously, like she could hardly believe it all herself. "I told him I did, and he said, 'Then, what the fuck are we doing, Mel? I love you; you love me. Let's just cut the shit and get fucking married.'"

I fell back against my chair, my chest heaving. "Wait. You were engaged before I *left*?"

Melanie nodded, the regret heavy in her gaze. "I'm sorry, Charlie. I asked him why he didn't tell you that day, when you told him you were leaving, but he just ... he didn't want to stop you. He didn't want to give you any other reason to change your mind. If you had stayed, we would've told you, of course. But then you left, and we just ..." She pulled in a deep breath and met my eyes. "I want to tell you that we were miserable. I want to tell you that we only ever spent what time we had missing you and—"

I surprised her with my abrupt laugh. "*Why?!*"

"Because I don't want to make it sound like we *never* missed you!" She was laughing with me despite the tears that flowed freely down her cheeks. "We did, Charlie.

God, we did, so much. We talked about you all the time. We wondered where you were and what you were doing … but we were so *happy*. Those years …" She pulled in a deep breath and lifted her gaze to the ceiling. "They were short, and there weren't enough—oh my God, it wasn't *enough*—and they were *so* fucking hard, but they were *ours*. We—"

Just then, the sound of footsteps descended upon us from the stairs. Melanie turned her head suddenly, a look of surprise on her face, as if she'd forgotten momentarily where she was. She stood from the table, wiping her hands over her face and smoothing her shirt down. I looked at Stormy, who glanced curiously at me, and I wondered what other surprises were in store.

"Mommy?" a little voice asked, accompanied by the sound of small, pounding feet against the hardwood floor. "I want snack."

Melanie's gaze met mine for a brief moment as she asked, "Um, sure, yeah. What—"

"Oh! I didn't realize you had company."

The startled sound of an older woman's voice drew my attention, and I turned to look into the weathered eyes of Melanie's mother. I hadn't seen her in years, but I'd recognize her anywhere. Her hand was flattened to her chest as her eyes squinted, studying me as she approached with uncertainty.

"Mom, you remember Charlie, right? Luke's younger brother?"

And then her mouth fell open as recognition settled upon her. "Wait, Charlie? Is that really you?"

I nodded, swallowing against the need to break down yet again. "Yeah, it's me."

"Oh my word." That hand remained against her chest as she shook her head, taking a few steps closer. "Stand up so I can take a good look at you."

I did as she'd asked. She was standing a foot from me, her eyes still squinting as she studied my frame. It occurred to me then that her mother's eyesight had begun to fail her in her older age.

"You certainly grew up, didn't you?" She laughed, smiling with affection.

"People do that," I said, chuckling.

"And who's this?" She peered around me to eye Stormy with curiosity.

"This is my girlfriend," I said, then made the introductions just as not one, but two little boys entered the dining room.

It struck my heart with joy and a desperate, horrible ache to see how much they both looked like Luke ... and *me*.

They looked like *us*. Like they'd been plucked out of a picture from the past and were dropped in my present to stare at me with wide, uncertain eyes.

The smaller of the two came to stand beside Melanie and wrapped his little hands in her sweatshirt. "Mommy," he said in a quiet voice. "Who dat?"

Melanie looked down at him with an affection I remembered only from my own mother as she smoothed his floppy, dark hair away from his forehead, leaving her hand there against his crown. "This right here is your uncle Charlie," she said in a soothing tone, looking back at me, her eyes glistening with tears and a happiness I hadn't expected.

Uncle Charlie. Uncle. Charlie.

The moment seemed too surreal to be happening. But it was, in fact, happening. I was an uncle, a title I never in a million years thought I'd hold, but there it was.

"Uncle Charlie?" the older boy asked, wandering in to stand beside his grandmother. "But Uncle Charlie is a little kid."

Melanie's laugh blended seamlessly with a sob, and she held a hand over her mouth as she contained her emotions. "That was in the pictures I showed you, from when Daddy was a little boy too. But Daddy got bigger, right?"

Daddy. The word pierced my heart with a flaming hot arrow, and I struggled to take a breath.

God, Luke ... you're a daddy. *A father. And I'm only now finding out about it, and you're not here.*

The little boy nodded slowly, working things out in his mind. "Yeah ..."

"Well," Melanie said, ruffling the hair of the boy at her side, "so did Uncle Charlie."

I lifted my hand to wave at the two little boys, acting every bit as awkward as I'd thought I would be as an uncle. "Hi," I said. "It's nice to meet you."

"This is Danny," Melanie said, looking down at the smallest boy. Then, referring to the one who couldn't quite keep his skeptical gaze off of me, she said, "And that's Lucas. LJ."

I pushed my mouth to smile as I nodded. "How old are you guys?"

"LJ is four," Melanie's mom said, "and Danny is three. Little Man is upstairs, asleep."

I looked at Melanie, surprised. "There's three?"

She sucked in a deep breath before jittering her head in a nod. "The baby ... he's just a little over twelve weeks old." Her bottom lip protruded for a moment before she pulled it back in and forced a deep, controlled breath. "His name is Charlie too."

Twelve weeks. Just a little over three months. He was a baby, an *infant*, and he would never know his father outside of whatever pictures there were of Luke. And it hit me then how much loss had brought us all here, to this moment. My parents. Stormy's friend, Billy. Ritchie. Tommy. Luke. God, if any of them had lived to this day, what would have changed? Hell, would any of this have happened at all?

Was it possible that, in some alternate universe, my parents were still alive, and we—all of us—were gathered here, in this dining room, having a casual family dinner, unaware that somewhere out there, I was forever mourning the family I'd spend the rest of my life without?

But I have them, I thought, sweeping my gaze around the room. My eyes met Stormy's, and she wrapped her arms around one of mine. *I have her.*

And that was *something*, wasn't it? I wasn't alone. I was so far from alone, and beneath the cover of grief that I knew I'd carry for the rest of my life, I knew I was happy. Truly, *truly* happy.

CHAPTER FORTY-SIX

CONNECTICUT, PRESENT DAY

"Charlie! Wait!"

It was deep into the night by the time we were leaving Melanie's house. A frosty chill sliced through the sweater I wore, and Stormy shivered as she ran toward the car to get it warmed up. I turned on my heel to watch Melanie run down the steps in a pair of flip-flops, trying to keep her cardigan wrapped tightly around her while clutching a piece of paper in her hand.

"Mel, you're going to freeze out here," I scolded.

"I know." She was breathless by the time she reached me, short, silvery puffs leaving her mouth and dissipating into the air. "But I remembered this, and I didn't want you to leave without it."

She held the paper out to me. I took it from her and realized it was an envelope. My hand trembled as I looked down at my name scrawled in Luke's shitty handwriting.

"What is this?" I asked stupidly.

It was obvious what it was.

My brother had written me a letter.

"I don't know," Melanie replied. "I never opened it. Luke had given it to me over the summer and said, 'When you see Charlie again, give him this.' I told him I didn't know if I'd *ever* see you again, and even if I did, he could give it to you himself, but ..." She sucked in a deep breath and shuddered as she hugged herself tighter. "He insisted I hold on to it, so ..."

I nodded as a sickening ball of dread burned a hole through my gut.

"I-I think ..." She squeezed her eyes shut and shook her head.

"What?" I asked softly.

Her shoulders dropped with an exhale, and she opened her eyes to pin me with her gaze. "I think he *knew*. Like, I-I think he knew he was going to die. Not necessarily when or how or-or-or anything like that, but ... he *knew*. And I didn't realize it at the time, you know? Because your mind doesn't want to go there, but looking back, I see it. All these ... little things he was doing, things he'd say ... giving me that letter for you ... God, do I sound crazy?"

"I will see you again."

"No, you won't, Charlie."

I dropped my gaze from hers and eyed the letter in my hand. "Not crazy," I muttered.

She blew out another silvery breath and waved her hand in the air, as if dismissing the idea. Like it was too insane to believe. Or maybe she just didn't want to think about it anymore.

"Anyway, I'll let you go," she said before wrapping me up in what had to have been the two hundredth hug she'd given me since Stormy and I had reluctantly decided it was time to head home. "I love you, Charlie. And please, *please* come back soon. Come back whenever you want. It would be good for the boys. And it'd be good for me too. We can go to the cemetery if you want, to visit your parents and Luke and—"

"I love you too," I cut her off, unsure I could hear any more without breaking down again. "And I will. I'll come back soon."

She smiled against my chest. "You know, Christmas *is* coming."

I sighed and nodded. "I'll be here."

"Good." She patted my back and stepped away, glancing toward the car. "Both of you, okay?"

"Okay."

An overhead lamppost caught the teasing glint in her eye. "Seriously though, Charlie, you'd better marry that woman."

I rolled my eyes and felt my cheeks heat despite the late November chill. "Oh God …"

"No, come on! You obviously love her, she loves you, and you are absolutely perfect for each other. You might think you have plenty of time to spare for stuff like that, but believe me, you don't. There's never enough. *Never*."

The moment was sobering, and I could only nod as I said, "I know."

She offered one last smile before taking a step back and turning around, heading toward the house that was no longer mine.

"I mean it, Charlie!" she called, glancing over her shoulder. "Stop wasting time! And if you don't, I wouldn't put it past your brother to come haunt you until you do!"

I laughed in reply and nothing more. Because what Melanie didn't know—what *nobody* knew—was that I now believed he already was.

***

It was after midnight by the time we returned to the cemetery, and what a long day it had been. A long, exhausting, emotionally taxing day.

The moment I locked the gate behind us and returned to the car, Max called to say hi and ask how my little getaway had been. I started to say it was okay, good, or some other basic, blanket answer that would barely touch the surface, but then I thought better of it and considered that, you know, maybe I *wanted* to talk to Max. Maybe I wanted to be his friend the way Ivan was my friend.

Without allowing myself the time to reconsider, I replied, "It's a long story, and I'd tell you if we weren't exhausted."

"Ah, I get it, man."

I swallowed and blew out a deep breath as we turned to drive up the hill toward our little stone cottage. "Maybe I'll stop by tomorrow night, if you aren't—"

"Sounds good, man. I'll have the coffee ready," he replied, and I swore I could hear the smile in his voice.

It was one I returned. "Make mine decaf."

"You got it, brother."

Brother. Fuck.

Stormy parked the car as I dropped my eyes to the sealed envelope in my lap. In the darkness, I couldn't quite make out my name scrawled in Luke's shitty handwriting, but I knew it was there. I could sense it, the bold black pen taunting me with a plea to read the words inside. I would, but not yet. Whenever I was ready … or gave myself no choice but to be ready.

I wished Max a good night and hung up. Stormy glanced at me, and though it was dark, I could see the details of her soft smile.

"You ready?"

I blinked my tired eyes toward the house. The small iron sconce hanging beside the heavy wooden door, casting a halo of misty light within the layer of fog. What a dreary, rainy night it was. How fitting.

"No." The word was released with a sigh. "I feel like, the second I walk through that door, life will resume the way it was before, and everything will be the same. But it's *not* the same. Nothing will ever be the same again."

It probably sounded like nonsense, but not for me. The last time I'd suffered tremendous loss, my life had perfectly reflected the way I felt inside. After our parents died, everything Luke and I had known was turned onto its bloody, misshapen head. It had been chaotic and messy. But now, my brother was dead. He'd been dead for two months, but for me, the wound was fresh and oozing. It hadn't been given the chance yet to scab over and likely wouldn't for quite some time. Yet I still had a job to do, a girlfriend to love, and a cemetery and all its inhabitants to care for. I had a life to live, and it couldn't come to a screeching halt despite the piercing ache throbbing, dull and deep, in my chest. I couldn't let that happen, but how the hell was I supposed to push forward in a world my brother no longer called home?

"I don't think it's supposed to be the same," Stormy replied, her voice gentle. "Honestly, I think, sometimes, we're supposed to experience pain in order to make us change."

I gnawed on my lip, keeping my eyes fixated on that ring of light, blurred at the edges. "I just wish it didn't hurt so fucking bad."

Her palm covered mine. I didn't take her hand or wrap my fingers around hers, but feeling her touch was enough to help me breathe.

"I know. But if it *didn't* hurt, could you say you ever loved him at all?"

As if the question were a bullet, piercing my brain and soul, I threw my head back against the seat and exhaled through the crushing pain against my heart. "What the hell is the point of loving anything then if the road always ends like this? Why would anyone *choose* this?"

It wasn't meant for her, nor was it meant to hurt her. But the moment the words left my mouth, I felt the guilt from saying them at all. I pressed my eyes shut and shook my head, muttering a stupid apology, but her fingers lay over my lips, halting my voice from saying anything else.

"You know, I thought the same thing for a long time," she said. "Why give myself to another man if the possibility of being hurt again was there? Why give myself permission to love if it eventually, in one way or another, leads to pain? And, yeah, it is a choice we make to open ourselves up like that, but I think we make it because, ultimately, that's what living is all about."

I snorted at the irony of these words being spoken by a woman in black, shrouded in shadows and adorned in more silver than a werewolf hunter. "What? Love?" I asked, sounding a little more condescending than I'd intended.

"*Everything* is better with love, Charlie," she replied, curling her fingers around mine. "It can survive anything, and where there is love, nothing is empty ... not even death." She sniffed a gentle, quiet, humorless laugh and turned her head, and while I couldn't make out her eyes well in the darkness, I knew she was surveying the hallowed ground surrounding us. "When you really think about it, places like this wouldn't even exist without it. What would be the point?"

"For *history*," I forced from my lips and tightening throat.

She turned back to me and tipped her head. "But who gives a fuck about history without the *love* to keep it alive?"

The light from the sconce flickered, tugging my attention toward it once again. A plummeting sense of grief and sorrow collided with the tiniest bit of hope and desperation as I waited for it to flicker again, but moments passed and nothing. I was being stupid, looking to a light bulb for signs and reassurance, but there was a pull there. *Something.*

"I love you," Stormy said despite all my naysaying, her fingers pulsing around mine before letting go.

Those words touched my heart with the promise of the worst heartbreak of my life if she were to die before me, yet I found every bit of salvation within them, and my soul longed to curl up beneath the shelter that only she could provide.

But I had something to do first.

"I love you too," I replied with resignation.

"Even if it might kill you one day?" she asked teasingly, lifting her hand to cup my cheek.

"Well, by your logic, that's the best kind of love there is," I said, my tone matching hers.

She hummed a small, contemplative sound as her thumb stroked my flesh. Then, she yawned and pulled away to unbuckle her seat belt.

"I'm gonna lie down," she told me, opening the car door. "You coming with me?"

"I will," I promised. "But I think I'm going to sit out here for a few more minutes first."

She paused in climbing out of the car to glance at me, as if she might protest my need to be alone. But then she whispered, "Okay. Whatever you need to do. But I'll be there when you're ready."

I nodded my appreciation, but said nothing else as she climbed out of the car and closed the door behind her. I watched as she walked up to the house, keys hanging from her hand. She unlocked the door and glanced over her shoulder at the car for only a brief second before disappearing inside. A light in the living room illuminated the lattice-framed window, a call beckoning me to come home, and I would. But there was a letter in my lap, and though I wouldn't read it yet, I knew the author was somewhere out there, and he'd been trying to grab my attention for a while now.

It hadn't occurred to me initially. At first, I thought those little signs and mementos had been left by a stalker, and then, when it was apparent that I was being watched by a more supernatural entity, I assumed it was Tommy coming to torment me in his afterlife. But the only thing that hadn't made sense in that was, why now? Why had he suddenly, after five years, decided now would be a good time to start haunting me?

The answer was, he hadn't, and I'd put that together nearly immediately after learning when exactly Luke had died.

I opened the car door and stepped outside, letter in hand. I held it up to the night sky before clutching it to my chest and looked from one side to the other, half expecting to see that cigarette-smoking, hooded man who'd been bold enough to visit me weeks ago.

God, how had I not recognized him?

Because I didn't want to.

"Got your letter," I said, only feeling a little foolish for talking aloud to seemingly nobody. "I, uh … I don't know when I'll be able to read it. I don't know if I'll *ever* be able to read it, to be honest with you. A-and it's not that I don't want to, you know. It's just that I, um …"

I hung my head and gripped the back of my neck, squeezing my eyes shut and pulling in a deep breath. "This is such bullshit, Luke," I struggled to say against the tidal wave of emotion that wanted to sweep me away. "It's such fucking bullshit, and I'm not ready to say goodbye to you, okay? I feel like-like-like if I read this fucking letter"—I held it up again, shaking it for the stars to see—"then I'm saying goodbye to the last piece of you that I have, and I won't do it. I *can't*. Okay? Maybe I will one day, maybe I'll be ready, but it's not today. I don't give a fuck if that's what you'd do because now, I have to do what *I* would do, and that is to run as far away from this as I can. Not forever. Just … for now. Okay? Can you be good with that?"

With tears streaming unabashedly down my face, I lifted my head and surveyed the hill my house stood upon. Nothing had changed. Everything was as it had been moments before, and the sconce beside the door remained still and shining.

"I'm so stupid," I muttered to nobody, shaking my head. "God, I'm so fucking stupid."

There was nothing left to say. There was no point. Nobody was here, lingering between the veil separating the living from the dead. Nobody was listening. Nobody had ever listened.

I deflated with a forlorn sigh, clutched the letter in my shaking hand, and dragged my feet toward the door. Knowing that life would continue as it always had, knowing it would never feel the same again, and knowing my only choice was to accept it or die.

And I had to choose to live.

It was what Luke would've done.

CHAPTER FORTY-SEVEN

CONNECTICUT, PRESENT DAY

Where's Stormy?
 Not wanting to open my eyes yet, I reached my hand across the bed to blindly pat the empty mattress. It was unexpected. Stormy wasn't one to wake up early without me, and suspecting something might be wrong, I opened my eyes to climb out of bed.

"What the hell?" I bolted upright, immediately awake as my breath caught in my lungs, and I swept my bewildered gaze around a room I hadn't slept in for over five years.

This isn't my room, I thought, remembering the tour Melanie had given us just the day before. *This is Danny's room.*

But it wasn't the room of a toddler; it was *mine*. Everything was as it had been years ago. The back of the door, defaced with my scribbled art. The dresser, piled high with black sweatshirts and black jeans. The closet, opened and showcasing a pile of sketchbooks. The floor, not cluttered by toys, but with a pile of laundry I hadn't yet washed and a box of Sharpies I must've knocked over at some point.

I'm dreaming. Of course I was dreaming, and of course I'd dream about this place. I often did. *But why does it feel so real?*

I swung my legs out of bed and slowly walked over the worn carpet to the mirror beside the door. It was intact, not shattered the way I'd left it, but my bare chest and arms were etched with the asymmetrical lines of the black widow spiderweb I'd gained from my life in Salem. And why this struck me as odd in a dreamworld, I didn't know, but I tipped my head with curiosity and confusion when the scent of cooking eggs wafted up to my nose.

Stormy? But Stormy didn't cook, and I laughed. *I guess that's how I know it's a dream.*

I studied the back of the door for a moment, allowing myself the time to appreciate the rough drawing. It was good though, for a sixteen-year-old with zero artistic experience. That kid had been in so much pain and anguish; he was so lost, weathering a storm he didn't know how to survive. Yet he did, and somehow, he found shelter. In a town he identified with. In the heart of a woman who hadn't given him a choice but to love her back. That kid back then, he'd had no idea what to do but suffer the abuse of the pelting rain, dodging bolts of lightning and quivering from the thunder's monstrous boom. But …

"We turned out okay," I muttered to the door, to that scared little spider beneath the angry clouds and lightning and torrential downpour. "Not everything is okay, but *we* are."

Then, following the scent of eggs, I opened the door, half expecting to see Tommy's blood still staining the hallway carpet. But it wasn't, and I was glad, knowing this would be one of those *good* dreams. They didn't happen often, but I was grateful when they did.

I ran down the stairs, feeling lighter and happier than I had in months, wondering if it was, in fact, Stormy in the kitchen. Or maybe it was Mom—God, it'd been a long time since I'd dreamed about her, and I wished that I would. Maybe it was even Dad or Melanie, two people who hardly made appearances in my sleep, and I let the excitement bubble up to an uncontained boil as I bounded through the dining room to the kitchen doorway.

But there was nobody there, nobody manning the stove as the eggs sizzled in a frying pan. I was in an abandoned house; it was only me, and the happiness I'd felt was quick to vanish, leaving only panic in its place.

Turning on my heel to survey the rest of the kitchen, the hallway leading to the basement, and the dining room entrance, I began to mutter, "What the—"

"Shit, shit, shit."

I spun quickly to face the hallway, where the bathroom door was thrown open and the last person I'd expected to see ran out to hurry back to the stove. Luke caught my eye and lifted one side of his mouth in a casual, lopsided smile.

"Hey, Charlie. You wanna grab me a spatula?"

"Uh …" I stammered as a hard, tremendous lump formed in my throat. "Y-yeah, sure."

I wasn't ready to face him, even if only in my dreams, yet I couldn't take my eyes off him as I reached out to grab our mom's favorite spatula from the kitchen utensil holder. I handed it back to him, noting the way my hand shook. Why was I scared of him? Why did I wish it'd been someone else? Did I think he was *mad* at me?

"Thanks, man." He looked at the pan before quickly swinging his gaze back up to my widened eyes. "Can you stop looking at me like that? Jesus. You're giving me the fuckin' creeps."

I blinked rapidly and diverted my gaze to nothing in particular. "S-sorry. I just, um …"

"Didn't expect to see me cooking? Yeah, well, believe it or not, prison has a way of building skills you didn't have before. So, basically, what I'm saying is"—he spread his arms out and gestured toward his chest—"I'm a domestic god now."

I leaned against the counter, gripping the ledge tightly to keep myself steady, and fixed my eyes on the sizzling pan as he continued scrambling the eggs. "Um, w-well—"

"Charlie, listen." Luke turned the burner off and pulled a plate from the cabinet above the stove. The eggs were dumped unceremoniously onto the dish, and the pan was dropped back onto the stovetop with a clatter. Then, he grabbed a fork from beside me on the counter and pointed it in my direction. "Neither of us knows how much time you have here, so we can't waste it with you tripping over your freakin' tongue, okay?"

"H-here?" I shook my head, furrowing my brow. "The hell are you talking about? I'm dreaming. This is a dream, and—"

"Sure, sure, right. Whatever you gotta tell yourself. Come on." He gestured for me to follow him. "Walk with me."

Luke hurried past me with his eggs and into the dining room, where he pulled out his usual chair and plopped down. I slowly rounded the table to my place across from his as he shook the salt and pepper shakers vigorously over his eggs, and just as I was about to sit, he cursed angrily and dropped his fork to the table.

With a jolt, I asked, "W-what?"

"Forgot the fuckin' ketchup." He glanced over his shoulder into the kitchen, then back at me. "Hey, you're still up. You wanna grab it for me?"

"Uh, yeah. Sure."

There was something off about this dream. Something strange about this interaction. It was so real, so *normal*. The floor was solid beneath my feet, and the ketchup bottle was cool in my hand as I pulled it from the fridge. The eggs on Luke's plate smelled as real as those I cooked for Stormy and myself on a nearly daily basis, and he was everything I remembered him to be. If I hadn't known better, I would've thought I wasn't dreaming at all. Like I'd jumped into a time machine somewhere and taken a trip back to eight years ago, before Luke was arrested and changed our lives forever—again.

As I stared at him, taking a heaping bite of his eggs, now covered in ketchup, I wished so badly I weren't dreaming.

With his mouth full, he looked up at me and pinched his thick brows. "What?"

I swallowed the need to cry before saying, "I'm just really glad to see you."

"Yeah." He nodded, jabbing his fork into the eggs. "I'm glad to see you too. I've missed you."

"I've missed you too."

He shook his head as he took another bite. "But listen, I don't want you to blame yourself for not coming back, okay? You didn't break any promises to me. You had said, when you got your head on straight, you'd come back, and you did. You just didn't know I was already gone." He snorted as he chewed before breaking out into a bubbling chuckle. "Okay, let's be real here. That chick … Stormy? *She* put your head on straight. But …" He pointed at me, wagging his finger. "You *let* her. That's the important thing. You didn't run away."

"She didn't either," I replied quietly.

"Yeah, I knew she wouldn't," he muttered beneath his breath, smirking to himself as he shoveled another forkful into his mouth.

I reared my head back. "What?"

"Oh, come on, Charlie," he said, laughing. "After everything you know now, you really think that was all you and her?"

I slumped against the back of my chair. "I don't—"

"You're killing me here." He wiped his hands against his pants as he sat back and pinned me with an amused glare. "The *wind*, man. Anytime you were, like, second-guessing shit or ready to turn her down, there was the wind, blowing and nudging you toward her. And the fuckin' *birds*. I know you noticed the fucking—"

"I have no—"

"Oh, bullshit." He laughed boisterously, crossing his arms and grinning like he'd never been happier. Fuck, it made me feel happy too. "You *knew*, Charlie. Don't tell me you didn't. You knew all along something was up. You knew I was gone, and you knew I was there"—he cast his arm out, gesturing the entire room—"*everywhere*. You didn't want to admit it; you didn't want to *say* it, not even to yourself, but ..." He leaned toward the table, folding his arms against its surface. His eyes met mine with more sympathy than I thought I could bear. "You knew. You always knew."

There wasn't a question anywhere in his voice, nothing but facts, and I was drowning, fighting the urge to gasp for air as I stared into his eyes. Too afraid to look away. Too afraid he'd disappear. Too afraid of being without him in this godforsaken house for another second.

"Remember, I know you, Charlie," he said quietly. "I don't lie to you, and you don't lie to me. Right?"

I was aware of every muscle in my throat shifting as I swallowed before croaking, "Right."

"And I know you knew."

One single rogue tear slipped down my cheek as my lips fell open with the two most poisonous words I'd ever spoken. "I knew."

"And yet you *still* insisted that Tommy was haunting you." Luke rolled his eyes, shaking his head and chuckling loudly. Funny how I couldn't find it in me to join him.

"I didn't *want* it to be you," I admitted angrily, the edge in my voice sharp enough to slice through his laughter and leave his face somber.

"No," he said, pulling in a deep breath as he nodded. "I get that. But …" He cleared his throat and smiled, a little smug and a lot pleased. "It's fine. You're not alone anymore. You're okay."

I huffed an incredulous laugh, finally pulling my gaze from his to lift my eyes to the ceiling and shake my head. "I'm never going to be *okay*, Luke. I can't go through the shit we've been through and end up *okay*. I can't …" A knot formed in my throat, and I struggled to swallow it down as my chin quivered and my eyes swelled with tears. "I-I can't lose you and be *okay*."

"Maybe not right now. But you will be. She'll make sure of it."

She. Stormy. Even as I sat across from my brother in some weird half dream, half reality, the tug of longing settled against my heart. I knew I'd wake and be with her. Hell, I knew that, right now, she was lying beside me in sleep. But I missed her.

"I like her a lot, Charlie. She was made for you, man. God, I wish I could've met her."

"Well, you would've if you hadn't gone and gotten yourself killed."

He grinned. "Yeah, I know. But, hey, it's all good. *I'm* good. You're good despite what you wanna believe.

Everything's *good*. And, I mean, considering everything that has happened to us, that's pretty fuckin' amazing."

I wasn't sure everything was good. How could it be? He was gone. He'd left behind a wife and three kids—all of whom were unlikely to remember him. He'd left me before I had the chance to uphold my promise of returning. All this shit, all this pain and heartbreak, yet he claimed to be good. It pissed me off. It pissed me off so much that he could be *good* with being dead. It pissed me off more than when he'd stolen a life and gotten thrown behind bars. Because it was selfish. It was so fucking selfish … but that was Luke, wasn't it? He'd always been a selfish fucking asshole. Only caring about his own demons, his vices, his anger and incapability to keep it under control, his—

"You're wasting time, Charlie. Focus."

Through the red-tinted rage I'd been consumed by, I locked eyes with my dead brother. Mine, I was sure, reflected every bit of my volatile ferocity, but his was soft and understanding, albeit stern. It did nothing to quell my anger. In fact, it only served to push me even further.

"God, fuck you, Luke."

He nodded, allowing me to shove him around with infuriating patience, like some born-again evangelical saint who'd made his peace and was unmoved by the blasphemy of others. "You can feel how you want, but—"

"No, seriously, fuck you." I shook my head, dropping my gaze to the plate in front of him and the remnants of scrambled eggs. "Fuck you for drinking.

Fuck you for pushing Melanie away. Fuck you for simply *existing* instead of fighting to get her back. Fuck you for killing Ritchie. Fuck you for-for-for …" I reached up, gripped my hair, and tugged as a low, primal groan rasped through my constricted throat. My hands dropped back to the table with a resounding *thunk*, rattling his plate and fork. "Fuck you for *leaving*. Fuck you for that most of all. All these people … your wife, your kids—your fucking kids, Luke! You have fucking *kids*, and you *left* them! You left them without a dad, just like you and I were left without *both* of our parents, but at least we *remember* them. At least we had something to miss, something to be sad about, something to hold on to, but them? *Your* kids? Goddammit, Luke, they're never going to know you. They won't remember you the way I do. The way Melanie does, and—"

"And did you ever think that, maybe, *that* might be a good thing?"

My brows pinched as I tipped my head and stared across the table at him. "What?"

He clasped his hands on the table and shrugged nonchalantly. So much for *running out of time*. "You ever think it might be a good thing that they won't have to remember their dad, the murderer, rotting away in prison? You ever think it might be a good thing that I can live through stories, told by you and their mother, and not just through monitored phone calls and arranged visits?"

I swallowed and slowly shook my head. "I think stories are better than nothing, sure. But I don't think they hold a candle to the real deal. Stories can't hug you. They don't have a voice or touch or *warmth*. So, again, fuck you for leaving. I'll never be *good* with that, just so we're clear. There's nothing *good* in that, no matter what you might think."

He pressed his lips in a tight line, and a morose, sad expression blanketed his face. The wrinkles etched into his forehead and at the corners of his eyes deepened, aging him just a little in the heavenly light filling the dining room. And it dawned on me then that maybe it was possible that this whole *we're good, everything is good* act was simply that—an *act*. Maybe it was what he'd had to tell himself to make his own peace with the way life—his, mine, all of ours—had turned out. Maybe it was what he felt he needed to tell me to move on. Hell, maybe it was what I should start telling myself to make it through the next day and the next, until this brand-new, searing, *horrendous* pain blended seamlessly with the old ones.

Maybe I should just wake up and be done with this.
Maybe I need to run away again.

"I'll never not be sorry, Charlie," he replied, low and gruff. "I won't say I'd do it differently because it doesn't matter now. I won't say I regret anything because it doesn't matter now. But I do want you to know that I'm sorry. For whatever it's worth, I'm sorry."

I shrugged, my shoulders feeling fifty pounds heavier than ever before. "It doesn't matter now," I said, parroting his words.

"No, it doesn't." He tugged at the back of his neck and deflated with a sigh. "But listen, okay? I want you to read that letter."

I squeezed my eyes shut and laid a hand against my brow, shielding him from the tears I was struggling against. "I really don't think—"

"Read the letter, Charlie. As soon as you wake up. Read the letter. Promise me you'll read it."

The edges of this vivid dreamworld were growing hazy. I could feel it slipping through the cracks between the realms of sleep and awake. Any moment now, I'd wake up, and Luke would be gone again. I didn't want to lose him. I didn't want to say goodbye, and somehow, for some reason, this felt like one. The hardest, most permanent goodbye.

I stood up from my chair and hurried around the table to where Luke was already standing. We collided in a hug so full of warmth, his body firm against mine, and if I hadn't known better, I would've said it was real. I wanted it so badly to be real.

"I'm going to miss you so much," I said.

"I know." He held the back of my head the way he had that last day I saw him at the prison. "Promise you'll read that letter."

My fingertips dug into his T-shirt, my mind aware of how soft the material was beneath my touch. "Only if you promise I'll see you again."

I felt him smile as he nodded. "Yeah, Charlie. You will. Now, wake up. Live your life. Marry that woman, for fuck's sake. Tell her to look up Ritchie's picture. And read that letter."

***

Charlie,

This is weird.

Honestly, there are a few things that are weird about this, but I think the one that takes the cake is knowing that, if you're reading this, I'm probably dead. Like, I'm alive right now while writing it, but ... fuck, man, remember how you used to get those feelings about shit? Like, you knew something was going to happen, something bad? That's how I feel. I've felt it for a while. I've felt it ever since this new kid rode in. I took one look at his face, and I don't know how else to explain it other than to say it was like seeing the Grim Reaper in the flesh. This fucking chill went straight down my spine, man. Gave me the fucking creeps from the get-go, and you know what's even crazier than that? I like him. I like being around him. Actually, he reminds me of you, which probably sounds like a big slap in the face to you right now since I just described him as the Grim Reaper. But you know what I mean. He's got this lost thing about him, like he needs a friend, someone to take him under their wing. Nobody else would, and I just kept thinking, what if that was Charlie? So, he's my friend, and I like him. But I also think he's gonna be the end of me, too, which is why I'm writing this now.

First of all, chances are, if you're reading this, you probably already know that Mel and I got back together. Surprise! Actually, we officially got back together a little before you hit the road. I wanted to tell you the last time I saw you. I had planned on it, and I thought it'd make you happy. But then I saw this look in your eyes, like you were finally done with this place, and it hit me like a ton of fucking bricks that, in that moment, my happiness couldn't trump your chance at finding your own. You needed to leave. I needed to make sure you left. I had a feeling about that too. I knew you'd find a life—more of one—up in Salem.

You wanna know something absolutely insane? I actually had a dream recently that you were gonna meet a chick with a shitload of piercings and tattoos. I saw you guys riding around on the bike, and I was just watching you like some weirdo, smoking a cigarette between the trees in a fucking graveyard. Like, I couldn't say anything to you, but I could watch, and I could see that you were happy. Actually, I think I was dead in the dream, but anyway, I woke up, just knowing I had done the right thing by letting you go without telling you about me and Mel. And I'm not sorry for it, for the record, in case you're pissed about it.

We have three kids. Can you believe that shit? If you had told me ten years ago that, one day, I'd not only be in prison, but also married to my dream girl and a father to three boys, I would've said you were fucking insane. But that's how it is. And I'm not gonna lie to you ... it fucking sucks. No, not that I have her back or that we have the boys, but most days, I don't feel like I have them at all. I feel like I'm wasting her life. I feel like the biggest piece of shit on the planet that I not only convinced her to marry me again, but that she just kept getting pregnant. And, yeah, sure, she had a say in the matter. She could've said no. She could've not sent me that first letter altogether—I'm assuming you already know that we were pen pals for a while. She could've insisted on birth control instead of insisting we didn't use anything at all. I mean, fuck, Charlie, you know what she said? She said she had always wanted babies with me. She said she had never stopped wanting them. She said she wanted her house—our house—full of pieces of the two of us, and I wanted to say no, but I couldn't because I wanted that too. I didn't want her to be alone, and I guess I thought that, if she had our kids, she wouldn't be. And she's not. She's the best mother on the fucking planet, and I love my family more than I've ever loved anything. Hell, I didn't know I was this capable of loving anything so much. But, holy shit, I miss them. I miss them all the fucking time, and I wish I hadn't killed Ritchie.

I wish I had listened to you, Charlie.

I wish I had never gone to that fucking movie. I wish, more than anything in the world, that I had gone to see Mel instead because she was single then. She was out there, missing me and wishing I would call or show up or whatever the hell, and instead of cleaning up my shit and doing the right thing, I had to go ahead and kill someone. Jesus fucking Christ, I killed someone. I took Ritchie's life, and, yeah, he was an asshole. He had always been an asshole, and the world is better without him. But I wish I could find a reason why it happened because right now, I feel like ... he didn't deserve to <u>die</u>. He didn't deserve that. Tommy didn't deserve it. Their mom didn't deserve it. God, Charlie, you didn't deserve it either. You more than anyone. You were always this innocent bystander to all of this shit, caught in a crossfire of my stupid fucking mistakes, and you have no idea how much

I regret that. You have no idea how much I wish I could take it all back. But we make our beds, don't we?

Anyway, since I'm dead, I need you to do a few things for me.

First and foremost, sign the house over to Mel. Let it be hers. She doesn't need money, and she doesn't want it. But she needs the house. She and her parents have already done a shitload of work on it—I'm assuming you've already been back, if you have this letter—and she's already made it hers. I want my kids to have my roof over their heads—that's all. I want them to at least feel connected to me in that way.

Second, I want you to be in their lives, and I don't mean as that uncle who sends a card every once in a while when you remember a birthday. I want them to know you. Be weird, creepy Uncle Charlie. I want them to know me through you. They're gonna need it because if this feeling I have is right, they're not gonna have me for much longer, and our youngest ... he's only a couple of days old, man. He doesn't even know me now. How the hell is he going to know me ten years down the road if it isn't through you? And, sure, he'll have Mel, of course, but ... the thing is—and I've told her this—I don't want her to be married to my memory forever. If something happens to me, I want her to move on. I want her to find someone who will actually be there for my kids. I want her to finally find the man she's always deserved, and you and I both know that's not me. I fucking love her, and for some reason, she loves me, but I am not in a million years who she deserves. He's out there somewhere, and I want her to find him once I'm gone. But that only makes your presence more important in their lives because you'll be the only connection between my kids and me. They'll know me through you, and you'll see me in them, and I don't know if I'm just losing my mind or what, but I feel like, one day, you're both gonna need that. So, just be there, okay? Please. Whenever you can, be there.

Third, if that dream was a premonition and you happen to find a woman as creepy as you with a shitload of piercings and tattoos, don't let her go and don't run away. Happiness looks good on you, man. I always knew it would.

I'll be smoking a cigarette and watching from between the trees.

Love you, bro.

—*Luke*

EPILOGUE

MASSACHUSETTS, THREE YEARS LATER

A blanket of white held the cemetery in a state of hibernation. Tangles of black sprigs reached out from the snow, buried and suffocated and longing for the breath only spring would provide. We were months out still, and I couldn't say I was looking forward to it much myself, apart from the distraction.

There was no need for landscaping in the winter. Only shovels and snowblowers. The mower was as asleep as the greenery outside, and I missed its rumbling reprieve.

The winter left too much time to think, too much time to dwell and reminisce. Christmastime especially.

I hated Christmastime and the sadness it brought. Before everything had changed again, I'd face the holidays with feigned disinterest. I had forced a blissful ignorance toward those days of celebration and continued with life as if it were any other day of the year.

But like I said, that was before.

Now, there was a Christmas tree in the corner and stockings hanging from the mantel. There were strings of garland tacked around the doorframes and twinkling lights strung along the roof and the rafters. There were in-laws and nephews on the road and a turkey in the oven.

And the kicker? It was my idea.

Stormy would've been fine with heading down to Connecticut to spend Christmas Eve with Melanie and the boys and Christmas Day with her family. Stormy would've been happy just to see them and celebrate the holiday surrounded by the people who loved us and accepted us for who we were.

But it was me who had stared at the guest room ceiling in her sister's house in River Canyon and said, "Why don't we do Christmas at our house?"

Stormy had hesitated despite the reluctant excitement glimmering in her eyes. "Wait," she had said, sitting up naked to look down at me. "Are you serious? You want to host a holiday?"

I'd shrugged then and replied, "Yeah. Why not? We used to have holidays at my parents' house all the time when I was a kid. I kinda miss it, I think."

But what I hadn't taken into consideration then was that Luke had been there, helping to hang the ornaments and drink the hot chocolate. His stocking had hung beside mine, and his presents had been stacked beneath the tree. There were no presents for Luke now. He lived in the sky, in a little box on the mantel beside our picture, and in the occasional scent of cigarettes, carried along a breeze while I rode his bike around the cemetery. There was no need for hot chocolate where he was, and suddenly, I had little desire to celebrate.

Whatever they told you about grief dulling with time was bullshit. You just got better at hiding it while its deep cuts opened over and over and over again, bleeding all over your broken heart.

Slender, tattooed arms snaked around my waist, hands clasping and hugging. "You okay?"

No matter how well I could hide the pain from everyone else, Stormy could sense it from a mile away. She saw me, and her blinders had yet to go up, even years later.

I sucked in a deep breath, pulling in the scent of cinnamon, black pepper, lavender, and burning wood as I lifted my eyes to the sky. "I think so. Trying to be."

Her lips touched my back as her arms squeezed around my middle. "Ray called. She says they should be at the gate in a few minutes."

I nodded and urged my strength to build back up, like steel-plated building blocks. "Okay. Did you hear from Mel?"

"Yep. They're not far behind."

"Good. You wanna take a ride with me?"

Stormy's arms left my waist as she came to stand before me. One hand reached out to take mine while her eyes searched my gaze with an expectancy that left me turning away and laughing uncomfortably.

"What?" I asked, staring at the glittering lights peeking through the branches of our tree.

Her hand pulsed, tightening around mine. "Are you sure you're okay?"

"Yes." I swung my eyes back to hers before I could get lost in the shine of the tinsel. "Once they're all here, I'll be fine. I'm just …" I lifted my hand and gestured to the window and the falling snow. "You know."

"I do, and that's why I'm asking. Because if you're not—"

An impatient groan scraped through my throat as I wrenched my hand from her grasp to wrap my arm around her shoulders and pull her body against mine. My lips pressed to the top of her head, and my nose was buried in her pile of thick black hair. As I breathed in her scent, with her hands lying flat against my chest, an aromatic salve was slathered over the oozing cracks in my heart, and just like that … I was whole.

Thus was life.

Over and over again, I was shattered by the force of memories both bittersweet and terrible, only to be put back together and healed by this one evergreen woman.

I hated to imagine what would've become of me had she not come into my life.

"I'd tell you if I wasn't," I said gently, my voice muffled by all that hair.

She deflated with a long exhale, then nodded. "Okay."

She didn't ever say it, but she worried about me from time to time, especially around the holidays. I never complained about her pressing, and I didn't complain when she suggested I see Blake's psychologist, Dr. Travetti. It was just nice to be worried about and cared for.

"Anyway," she said, stepping back and patting my chest, "I'll hang back here and keep an eye on dinner. The last thing we need is for the house to go up in flames."

I huffed a laugh and reached for my coat. "I guess that'd be my luck. Okay. I'll be back."

Stormy pressed her palms to my cheeks and stood on her toes to touch her mouth to mine. "I love you," she said, her breath warming my lips.

Then, I found myself smiling, although it was a bit reluctant at first as my brain left the dreary cellar of memories and the people I missed. I kissed her again while sliding my arms into the sleeves of my coat.

"I love you too, my love. So much."

***

"Uncle Charlie, what's that?"

We had barely gotten out of the truck when Miles pointed toward one of the mausoleums in the distance.

Ray and Noah were busy unloading their car of presents while Soldier helped Melanie unpack hers, leaving me to wrangle three rambunctious boys who'd spent too long on the road on Christmas Eve.

"It's a house for dead bodies," LJ quipped, running over from his mother's car.

"No, it's not!" Danny fired back, angry and insistent.

"Tell him!" LJ shouted, looking up at me. "That's where you keep the corpses."

"What's corpses?" Miles asked as Noah trudged past the younger boys, a bulging bag of presents in his arms.

He glanced at me with that old, tired look I'd learned to expect from him in the years since I'd met him.

"You wanna help me out here?" I asked, nudging my head toward the gaggle of little kids crowding at my feet.

He smirked and kept walking as he said, "Nah. You're on your own, bro."

Warmth flooded my chest, even as the mounting panic of having to explain what a corpse was to a five-year-old rattled my nerves. I couldn't say when I'd gone from being simply Charlie to bro, and I wasn't sure he would ever be comfortable calling me Uncle despite my two-year-old marriage to his aunt. But I had learned to take whatever I could get from Noah, and I was happy.

"Hey, hey, hey." Mel grabbed the attention of the three young boys as she hurried from her car, a bundled-up Little Charlie in her arms. "You guys leave Uncle Charlie alone. Don't be asking him questions you don't want the answers to."

I snorted. "Oh, I think they very much want the answers to them. I just don't wanna give them."

Her nose was already reddened from the cold, her cheeks a pinched pink. She smiled and bumped her hip against mine. "Thanks for having us up here."

Little Charlie—or LC, as we'd started calling him—reached his mittened hands out toward me, and without hesitation, I gathered him in my arms. "Come on, guys," I said to Danny and LJ. Miles had already begun running toward the open door, where his aunt Stormy was waiting. "Let's get inside before I have to stuff you in that mausoleum over there with the other corpses."

LJ and Danny gasped while Melanie gawked.

"Charlie!" She swatted at my arm. "Oh my God, you can't say that! They don't even know what a corpse is!"

"You might wanna ask them about that," I said, leading the way up the hill to the open door, where the scent of dinner and home carried through the wind.

Somewhere in the mix, I thought I might've caught the faintest hint of cigarettes, or maybe I just wished I had.

***

Ivan and his lady love, Lyla, showed up a little while later, just in time for dinner. I greeted my best friend with a hug before giving one to his better half. They quickly joined the others at the table and made themselves at home with the people they'd grown to know and love over the years since Stormy's and my families came together.

My side at our wedding hadn't been all that much smaller than hers, as it turned out. In fact, it'd been nearly even.

Stormy hurried out of the kitchen, carrying the last tray of food, and laid it down before taking her spot at one of the two remaining empty seats. I stood back for a moment and took in the sight of the living room, unable to believe that, not too long ago, this room only held two wingback armchairs and a little table for my sketchbook and marker. Now, those wingback chairs were shoved against the wall beside the couch, blocking the view of the TV, to make room for the two folding tables positioned end to end to accommodate all our guests. All our friends. All our family.

Blake, Cee, and their respective partners and kids—along with Blake's twin brother, Jake, of course.

Ivan and Lyla.

Chris and Barbara.

Ray, Soldier, Noah, and Miles.

Melanie and the three boys who all bore an uncanny resemblance to my brother and me.

It was a full table, a full house. One I'd never envisioned having for myself again after I lost everything repeatedly without fail, but here I was. The spider who hadn't just weathered the storm, but watched it pass to make way for a sunny day and a brighter future. One where loneliness wasn't an option … and I was good with that.

"Hey."

I had been staring at my mom's wall clock when Stormy's voice penetrated the barrier of my thoughts. The spell was broken, and the chatter of voices and clatter of utensils met my ears.

I looked at her and her uncertain smile as she asked, "You okay?"

Was I okay? I wasn't sure I wanted to be. It didn't seem right to be okay in a world full of holes, spaces that the people I'd loved and lost left behind. But how could I not be okay when those spaces no longer felt so vast in a life now full of people who wanted me in it?

I walked around to sit beside my wife at my place at the table. I put my arm around her shoulders, kissed her temple, and inhaled her particular scent of cinnamon, lavender, and spice.

Then, I said, "Yeah, I'm okay."

And you know what?

I actually meant it.

If you or someone you know is suffering from substance abuse, there are people out there who want to help.

Don't wait until rock bottom.

Don't wait until it's too late.

SAMHSA

(Substance Abuse and Mental Health Services Administration)

1-800-662-HELP (4357)

ACKNOWLEDGEMENTS

Now comes the part where my anxiety goes nuts because I don't want to forget anyone.

Thank you to my husband, Danny, for being the Stormy to my Charlie. A wise man once said the right one won't run, and you never have, no matter how dark things get.

Thank you to my son, Jude, for sleeping through the night. Without that, this book never would've been written. I love you more than life.

Thank you to my sister, Karen, for all the time we've spent brainstorming. One day, when the bills are all paid, you'll get a cut of the royalties for your services. Just … you know … don't hold your breath.

Thank you to the rest of my family—my parents and my sister, Kelly. Your belief in me, your support, and all the help you give me in various areas of life … I don't know what I would do without you all.

Thank you to Jess for being the most unexpected friend I ever could've asked for. You have brought so much to my life, and I could never repay you for it all. I love you forever, and I will leave you thirty-minute voice messages until the end of time.

Thank you to Tori for coming into my life at the right time. You have no idea what you've done to my career, and I could never thank you enough. You are a gift—one I will be grateful for for the rest of my life.

Thank you to Jovana for turning my art into a freakin' masterpiece. You are an absolute treasure to work with, and I wouldn't trust anyone else to do the immaculate job you do. Plus, the "OMG TEARS" commentary is entertaining AF. But same, girl. All the tears.

Thank you to Murphy Rae for yet another INCREDIBLE cover. I mean, dude, you and I should get married at this point. The wavelength we are riding is more in sync than the one I'm riding with my husband. There's something to be said for that.

Thank you to every reader and every influencer who has ever bought one of my books, reviewed one of my books, made a post, message, video, ANYTHING. You keep me going. You make me believe. You are the most valuable part of this book life I'm living, and I could never repay you for that. I mean it. You are the backbone of everything I do, dear reader, and don't ever forget it. Thank you.

ABOUT THE AUTHOR

Kelsey Kingsley is a legally blind gal, living in New York with her husband, her son, and a black-and-white cat named Ethel. She really loves Halloween, tattoos, and Edgar Allan Poe.

She believes there is a song for every situation.

She has a potty mouth and doesn't eat cheese.

Holly Freakin' Hughes

Daisies and Devin

The Life We Wanted

Tell Me Goodnight

Forget the Stars

Warrior Blue

The Life We Have

Scars & Silver Linings

A Circle of Crows

Where We Went Wrong

Hoping for Hemingway

32 Rowan Blvd

The Girl in the Front Row

The Hero in Her Story

Saving Rain

The Spider & the Storm

The Kinney Brothers

One Night to Fall
To Fall for Winter
Last Chance to Fall
Hope to Fall

Made in the USA
Columbia, SC
22 July 2024